"McKenzie endows what could have been a formulaic, tired plot with finely drawn characters, broad humor, and a sweet and satisfying romance between equals. Her descriptions of rehab are as candid as they are sympathetic. She laughs with her characters at the pain, frustration, and, at times, absurdity of the recovery process, which here includes a stint on a trapeze, without laughing at the misery and destructive behavior that bring people to treatment. Her relentless positivity is contagious. She is a writer to watch." —*Booklist*

"Catherine McKenzie, in her debut novel, ably invites the reader into the story. . . . For readers who enjoy a light, breezy love story, this book clips along well and satisfies. Many will likely find this book enjoyable and a worthy debut effort by Catherine McKenzie."
—*New York Journal of Books*

"If *Bridget Jones's Diary* and *High Fidelity* had a literary baby, the result would be *Spin*. A funny heroine and plentiful music references make this book a standout. McKenzie's tale of girls gone wild and gone to rehab is ripped straight from the latest tabloid headlines and will keep readers intrigued to the very last page." —*RT Book Reviews* (top pick)

"The characters are easily imagined and well thought out. . . . Making her U.S. debut, Canadian author McKenzie introduces a modern literary heroine who will remind readers of Sophie Kinsella's 'Shopaholic' protagonist: flawed but compelling . . . compulsively readable."
—*Library Journal*

"McKenzie's deliciously tart sense of humor and her tough yet tender heroine are as refreshing as a perfectly mixed mimosa."
—*Chicago Tribune*

Praise for

ARRANGED

"Who says chicklit has to end with a wedding? Canadian author Catherine McKenzie's new book, *Arranged*, marries off her heroine, the relationship-challenged magazine editor, Anne Blythe, by the midpoint, after a mysterious marriage broker hooks her up. The perfect strangers become estranged, but getting to happily-ever-after has rarely been so entertaining." —*Chatelaine*, January 2011

"Catherine McKenzie brings a smart twist to marriage and relationships in her second novel, the story of unlucky-in-love Anne Blythe. *Arranged* is crafted with pathos and subtle humor, and through it McKenzie's heroine learns—the hard way—that the happiest endings are often the ones least expected."

—Shawn Klomparens, author of *Jessica Z.* and *Two Years, No Rain*

"Catherine McKenzie's *Arranged* is a satisfying and entertaining romance that puts a very contemporary twist on old-fashioned ideas about marriage. I inhaled it in an afternoon, rooting for its heroine to find the love she longs for."

—Leah Stewart, author of *Husband and Wife*

"A novel that explores what happens when what you think you want collides with what you really need. Catherine McKenzie's *Arranged* is a rare book: smart, funny, honest, and absorbing."

—Therese Walsh, author of *The Last Will of Moira Leahy*

"Just when you think you've got *Arranged* figured out, time and again, Catherine McKenzie delivers the flawless, unexpected twist that keeps you glued to the book."

—Cathy Marie Buchanan, author of *The Day the Falls Stood Still*

Forgotten

FORGOTTEN

Catherine McKenzie

WILLIAM MORROW
An Imprint of HarperCollins*Publishers*

FORGOTTEN. Copyright © 2012 by Catherine McKenzie. Excerpt from SPIN copyright © 2012 by Catherine McKenzie. All rights reserved. Printed in the United States of America. No part of this book may be used or reproduced in any manner whatsoever without written permission except in the case of brief quotations embodied in critical articles and reviews. For information address HarperCollins Publishers, 10 East 53rd Street, New York, NY 10022.

HarperCollins books may be purchased for educational, business, or sales promotional use. For information please write: Special Markets Department, HarperCollins Publishers, 10 East 53rd Street, New York, NY 10022.

FIRST PUBLISHED IN CANADA IN 2012 BY HARPERCOLLINS PUBLISHERS.

FIRST U.S. EDITION

Library of Congress Cataloging-in-Publication Data has been applied for.

ISBN 978-0-06-211541-6

12 13 14 15 16 OV/RRD 10 9 8 7 6 5 4 3 2

For Tasha

For always being there.
May you always be.

Prologue

My mother's funeral was a small affair on a hot Tuesday. Her best friend, Sunshine, spoke about their girlhood together like it was more real to her than the airless, flower-filled room we sat in. A few of her colleagues from the university wore black and looked sad. My boyfriend, Craig, pulled at the collar of his shirt and held my hand awkwardly. Only my best friend, Stephanie, had any clue what to say, how to comfort me.

Afterward, I walked around half-awake for days, but at night half-awake was too awake to sleep. I knew I should take the pills my mother's doctor slipped into my hand shortly after he pronounced her dead, but I didn't want to lose control of my thoughts of her. I wanted to remember her as she'd been while I grew up, not what she'd become as she lay dying. And I didn't trust my sleeping brain not to betray me.

A week later, I sat stiffly in front of the lawyer from my firm who was handling her affairs.

"You know that your mother's estate is small. All those medical bills—"

"Yes, I know." My mother wanted to die at home. So we both paid to make that happen.

He peered at me over his bifocals. "In fact, your mother liquidated most of her assets a few months ago. She used the proceeds to pay for her funeral and to buy this."

He handed me a manila envelope. Inside was a first-class ticket with an open return to Tswanaland, an African country I knew almost nothing about, and a thick brochure.

I flipped through the glossy pages. It was full of lions and zebras and elephants. Oh my.

"She booked the trip in your name."

I thought back to those last few days at my mother's bedside. How her bedroom, once cozy and comfortable, and my favorite room in my childhood house, had turned antiseptic, medicinal. How the only remnants of its past were my mother's favorite photographs, scattered among the pill bottles on the nightstand. And how she told me not to make the same mistakes she had. Not to postpone the things I was passionate about, even if they seemed out of reach.

"I always wanted to go to Africa, you know," my mother whispered, her voice a raspy echo of the lilt I knew and loved.

"I know."

It was the one thing everyone knew about her. Easy to please at Christmas, or on her birthday—just give her anything that might've come from that mysterious continent and she was thrilled, transported. Our bookshelves were full of such gifts, mostly bought with my allowance, or by my father before he left us.

"I want you to go instead," she said.

"Mom . . ."

"Please, Emma."

I wanted to ask her why, but her soft brown eyes implored me not to question, to simply accept. I laid my weary head on her fragile shoulder. She patted my hand gently, and I felt ashamed. How could I be anything but strong for her in this moment, maybe her last? How could I require comfort? But I did. My mother was dying, and I needed my mommy.

"I will, Mom. I promise."

"Thank you."

She closed her eyes, a smile on her worn face.

She held on for two more days but never regained consciousness. Her death was a fractional thing. One moment, she was still and pale, but alive. The next, she was gone. It seemed like almost nothing had happened, but that almost nothing changed everything for me.

"You're up for partnership this year, aren't you?" the estate lawyer asked, his hands laced across the crisp white shirt that contained his belly.

"Yes."

"This might be problematic, then."

"What do you mean?"

"I've taken the liberty of speaking to the Management Committee, and they've agreed to reimburse you for the purchase."

My head snapped up. "You what? Why?"

"We expect you to need a little time off, but . . . take my advice, dear, this trip wouldn't be well received."

Anger flooded through me, and some of the fog lifted from my brain. "Are you saying that if I go, I'm putting my career in jeopardy?"

"I wouldn't put it quite so bluntly." He smiled condescendingly. "You litigators, you're all the same."

I stood angrily, the brochure clutched in my hand. "Who do I have to talk to about this?"

"I don't think that's a good idea."

"I'll bet."

I left his office and marched up the two flights of internal stairs to the litigation floor. Matt Stuart, the head of my department, was sitting at his big oak desk, visible through the glass wall that separates him from the hoi polloi. He was on the phone.

"Can I see him?" I asked his assistant, a matronly woman in her midfifties.

"What's the urgency level?"

"Off the charts."

"I'll see what I can do."

I went to wait for him in my smaller office down the hall.

My desk was full of sympathy cards and large, colorful bouquets. Their scent was almost overwhelming. I stared at my email in-box full of I'm-so-sorry messages until Matt rapped on my door. As usual, the sleeves of his pin-striped shirt were rolled up to his elbows. I could see the marks of his fingers in his thick silver hair.

The deep bass of his voice radiated concern. "Emma, I'm very sorry for your loss."

He'd said the same thing at the funeral. It was all anyone was saying to me since my mother died. What else was there to say?

"Thank you."

"Nathalie said you wanted to see me?"

I laid it out for him. My mother's gift. What I wanted to do. What Mr. Patronizing Estate Lawyer had implied. I spoke with a certainty I didn't know I had. With a resolve that surprised me.

"I want to go to Africa," I told him. "Will you help me?"

Three anxious days later, the Management Committee relented. I could have a month off, but it came with a catch: I wouldn't be put up for partnership this year. My uncharacteristic desire to do something other than work eighty hours a week had given rise to "certain concerns about my long-term commitment to the firm." When I got back, I'd have to wait an extra year before being considered.

As I listened to Matt, I was too relieved to experience the right amount of anger. I'd been worried that if I complied with my mother's dying wish, I'd be throwing away everything I'd worked for. So the choice Matt presented me with might've been harsh and unreasonable, but I welcomed it. Another year of semi-slavery in return for a month for my mother.

It seemed like a fair exchange.

Sunshine drove me to the airport a few days later. She was leaving shortly herself, returning to her faraway life in Costa Rica. Craig and I had said our goodbyes the night before, the air full of the tension created because I wouldn't let him come with me, even for a little bit. If my mother hadn't just died, we would've had an argument, maybe a fatal one, but she had, so we tried to ignore my clipped "no" in response to his offer, and his begrudging acceptance of my explanation that I needed some time to myself. We tried, but we didn't quite manage it.

I stood with Sunshine at the Security entrance, as far as she could take me. We hugged, holding on a little longer than usual, as if, when we let go, the tie that bound us together would be severed, irreparable. When we finally broke apart, Sunshine stroked the side of my face with her rough fingers and turned to go.

"Sunshine?"

"Yes?"

"Why do you think Mom wanted me to take this trip?"

She smiled. "I can't tell you that, Emmaline. It's yours to discover. And you will."

Her certainty was so total that I almost felt reassured. But then she walked away, and the weight of my life settled on my shoulders. I shuffled through Security and waited at my gate. Ensconced in my first-class seat, I finally took the pills the doctor gave me the day my mother died. I slept dreamlessly as the ocean danced below.

And when I awoke, I was in Africa.

Chapter 1
Out of Africa

Six months later . . .

I'm sitting on my suitcase beside the muddy road that leads through the village, waiting for the signs that indicate the arrival of transport—birds taking flight, a tremor along the ground, and, since the rains started, the sound of mud slipping through off-track wheels.

Birds wheel overhead, their cries a constant background music. The air is thick and damp, a physical thing that's been getting heavier by the month.

I remember the first time I saw this place: the ragged row of shacks with their corrugated iron roofs; the gathering circle made of big, round boulders; and the frame of a half-built schoolhouse, its wood a bright, freshly sawn yellow. The rough structure reminded me of the buildings I always imagined Laura Ingalls Wilder living in as I read her books over and over again as a child.

The safari guides left me here, sick, sick, sick, promising to come back as soon as they could with a doctor, but it hadn't worked out that way. Instead it was Karen and Peter—the NGO workers who were building the schoolhouse—who nursed me back to health, using up their small store of medical supplies.

Karen is waiting with me now. Peter's in the village behind us. The confident blows of his hammer ring out, a practiced rhythm. A few children sit watching him, hunched on their heels, eager for him to be finished. When he's done, classes will begin, and they're keen to start learning.

After all these months of working on the building alongside him, I can't imagine not being here when it's finished.

"Maybe I should stay a few more days," I say.

Karen shakes her head, her brown face and matching eyes calm and certain. "We need to get you home, Emma. It's almost Christmas."

I shudder. I'd almost forgotten. It's so hard to keep track of the days here. Christmas without my mother. This seems like a pretty good reason to stay exactly where I am. But I've used that excuse for too long now. It's time to get back to my life.

"You'll be home soon, though, right?" I ask, because my home is also Karen and Peter's. I don't know why we had to come all this way to meet. Life works like that sometimes, I guess.

"A few weeks after Christmas, if everything goes as planned."

"I'm glad."

In the distance I hear the low rumble of an engine, and I know it can't be long now. I stand and face Karen. She's ten years older than me and a head taller—stronger, broader, more substantial somehow.

She puts her hand in the pocket of her loose work pants and pulls out a small Mason jar full of dirt. Reddish like the ground. Like the mud slipping through the tires under the thrum of the approaching engine.

"I thought you might like this to add to your collection."

I take it from her. Some of the dirt clings to the outside, sticking to my fingers. "Thank you."

A Land Rover is visible now, only seconds away. I slip the jar into my pocket and embrace Karen. Her arms are steely around me. She smells like the humid air and the tall, bleached grass, like I must too.

"You'll say goodbye to Peter?"

"You said goodbye to him yourself ten minutes ago."

"I know. But you'll tell him?"

She holds me away from her. "I will."

The Land Rover shudders to a stop, spraying mud in our direction. A large piece lands with a *splat* on my pant leg. I wipe it off as a short, stocky man in a sweat-stained shirt gets out.

"You are ready to go, miss?"

"Yes," I say. "Yes."

I'm mostly happy for the mud on the long drive back to the capital. It clings like a film to the windows, obscuring the worst of the view. But after a while it's impossible not to wipe it away and stare at the changed countryside. The odd jumble of images. A too-white running shoe lying at an odd angle on the side of the road. Things on the ground that shouldn't be— trees and twisted metal. The ground seems rippled, folded, like a mirage over a hot highway. And as we get closer to the epicenter, there's a smell that must've been much worse before the rains came. That might never be washed away.

The level of devastation, even after all these months, is shocking and saddening. And as the Land Rover bumps slowly along, my mind slips back to the long days listening to the one radio in the village—its voice so faint sometimes it felt like messages from the moon—trying to imagine what was happening. But no amount of listening, no amount of imagination, was enough to conjure up the destruction outside my window.

I feel helpless, and now I want to go home very much indeed.

The airport is chaotic. Though it's been a week since a few airlines resumed service, the staff working the counters in the half-rebuilt building don't have reliable electricity or working phones. When I find the end of the line I almost weep at the length of it, but there's nothing to be done. It moves at the speed it moves—glacial—and crying or yelling won't change anything, though I observe several people trying both tactics over the next four hours.

When I finally reach the counter, the thin, dark-skinned woman behind it is much politer than I would've been. She takes my open-ended ticket and passport and finds me a place on a plane to London leaving in two hours. Security consists only of two impossibly tall men giving passengers the evil eye as they pass through a metal detector that's seen better days. I file through quickly and have time to locate some food at a small kiosk that's selling, of all things, Chicago-style hot dogs. I wolf down two of them gratefully, and when my plane is finally ready to depart, I shuffle onto it feeling like I'm running away.

The plane rattles across the roughly patched runway, which is full of cracks and tufts of grass, and leaves the ground. The turmoil below is momentarily toy-village small, and then invisible below the clouds. I rest my head against the hard molded plastic and am asleep in minutes.

At Heathrow, a rainy sleet almost keeps us from landing. It's midday—early morning back home—and the sun's nowhere to be seen.

I make my way slowly through the massive structure. The airport bears the markings of the season. Extra lights and Christmas trees try to give the place a festive air. Compared with where I've been, it's so clean and bright it feels like it was built yesterday, like the last lick of paint is still drying. The cooled and filtered air scratches the back of my throat, and I feel dusty and dingy as I pass the clean, clean faces around me.

I find the counter for my airline and use my open-ended ticket to book myself a flight home. As I search for my gate, I keep an eye out for somewhere to send a message to Stephanie and Craig, something I haven't had the chance to do in a long time. Too long. But I don't want to think about why I let that happen, and I wouldn't have any answers, for that matter, if I did.

I pass a few public computer kiosks full of people who look like they've settled in for more than the time I have before my flight. I queue up behind one anyway, until I notice its user pushing unfamiliar coins into a slot, buying ten more minutes. The only change I have would barely buy me a Coke in a vending machine back home.

I give up and reach my gate with thirty-five minutes to spare. I take a seat next to a man in his midthirties typing aggressively on his laptop. A glance at his screen shows an email full of caps and exclamation marks. I feel a flash of sympathy for s.cathay@mail.com.

He looks at me with an unfriendly expression on his face. "Can I help you?"

"Oh, sorry . . . it's just . . . do you think I could borrow your computer for a minute? I really need to send a couple of emails, and all the kiosks are full, and I don't have any coins, and . . ." I pause to catch the breath that has turned borderline hysterical, a good imitation of those people at the airport I was happy to leave behind.

The angry man's eyes widen in dismay, his expression softened by my tone. "Hey, don't freak out on me, okay?" He shoves his laptop into my lap. "Send all the emails you want, all right?"

I thank him and open a new web browser, leaving the angry email in place. My fingers feel clumsy on the keys, and I have to erase my first few attempts to enter my account information. When I finally get the combination of letters and numbers right, I'm informed in angry, flashing red type that it's been shut down for sending too much junk mail. I curse silently under my breath at the spammer who hijacked my account.

"Is something wrong?" the less angry man asks.

"My account is blocked."

"Why not just open a new one?"

Why not, indeed? I tap on the keys, and in a few moments emma.tupper23@mail.com is up and running.

I hit the Compose Mail button and pause. What the hell am I going to say after all this time? How do I even begin? Are they even going to *want* to hear from me?

I can feel the minutes slipping away. I brush those thoughts aside and type Stephanie's and Craig's email addresses in as quickly as I can.

From: Emma Tupper
To: stephanie_granger@oal.com; craig.talbot@tpc.com
Re: Coming home!

Hey guys,

This is such an odd email to write! I'm so, so sorry I haven't written till now. I'll explain everything when I get home, I promise. Anyway, I'm in London. My flight is leaving soon and should be arriving around 4 p.m. I'm on BA flight 3478. I can't wait to see you both. I've missed you so much.

Love, Em

I read it over quickly. It'll have to do. I hit Send and hand the computer back to my neighbor, thanking him as a chime sounds. A polite, clipped voice announces that preboarding is about to begin. Anyone with small children or needing assistance should come to the gate. General boarding will begin momentarily. I stand and stretch, taking a last opportunity to look around. So this is London. All I've ever seen of it is the airport. I'll have to remedy that someday.

The polite voice calls the first-class passengers. I line up briefly and walk down the gangway. The plane is brand spanking new. Each passenger gets a capsule, a private space to eat, sleep, and watch six months of movies. Maybe it's the flashy technology or the warmed-up, lemon-scented towels the flight attendant brings, but a beat of hope starts in my heart. I'll be back where I should be soon, and then, like the song says, everything will be all right.

But everything is not all right, which I should know when there's no one at the airport to meet me. Or when the ATM spits out my card like it's contaminated, and my car isn't where I left it in the long-term parking lot.

I should know, but I'm too distracted. Despite everything that's happened, I feel too happy.

I'm home.

Finally, the air smells familiar. I understand the curses hurled at me as I cross the road without looking properly. Even the cold bite of winter and the annoying loop of jangly carols escaping from the outdoor speakers seem perfect, as they should be the week before Christmas.

So, when I give up looking for my car and sink into the back of a cab, I don't have a clue. In fact, it's only after I hand over my last forty dollars to the ungrateful driver and try to put my key into the lock of my apartment that I begin to panic.

Because the key doesn't fit. The lock doesn't turn.

And it has begun to snow.

Chapter 2
The Old Apartment

Perfect, just perfect.

I put down my bag and climb the steep, exterior iron staircase to the apartment above mine. Six months ago, it was occupied by Tara, an out-of-work actress who practiced her lines loudly at three in the morning. We have a tenuously friendly relationship, but she has my spare key, which will hopefully work better than the rusty version hanging from my key chain.

It's after sundown, and the darkness feels close, oppressive. The snow falls down around me in broad flakes, illuminated by the porch light. I ring the bell. The *ding-dong* echoes loudly. I push the button again with a sinking heart, certain she isn't home. It's been that kind of day. That kind of year, come to think of it.

I hug my yellow rain slicker close over my summer clothes as I climb back down the slippery steps. The soles of my canvas shoes aren't meant for winter. I lose my footing on the second-to-last step and land hard on my ass.

"Shit!"

"Are you okay?" a man asks, his voice deep and concerned.

I look up at him as I try not to whimper from the pain. He's wearing a black peacoat and a gray ski cap over his dark hair. Midthirties, maybe a little older. Well-spaced eyes, a regular nose. A five o'clock shadow is spreading along his jaw. A stranger, and yet somehow familiar.

He smiles sympathetically. A flash of white in the dark. "That looked like it hurt."

It feels like it's going to hurt forever, but I try to be stoic. "Some."

He extends his hand. "Need a boost?"

I place my cold hand in his gloved one, and he eases me to my feet. He's about six inches taller than my five feet, five inches.

"Thanks."

"No problem." His slate-green eyes glance up the stairs I tumbled down. "Were you looking for Tara?"

"I was. Do you know her?"

"She's an old friend."

Something niggles at the back of my brain, but I can't quite get there. "You wouldn't happen to know when she'll be back, would you?"

"She's shooting a pilot out west. She won't be back until the new year."

"Damn." I shove my freezing hands into my pockets, hoping to find a cell phone I know isn't there. I meet his eyes and something clicks into place. "Have we met before?"

He starts to shake his head no, then stops himself. "Mmm. Maybe—"

"Tara's birthday party," I say, connecting it. "Two years ago?"

A warm summer night. Tara's apartment was full of new faces as she shepherded Craig and me around, introducing as she went, waving a glass full of red wine.

"You were there, right?" I ask.

"Yes, but—"

"Do you think I could borrow your phone for a second?"

He hesitates. "All right." He digs into his jeans and pulls out an iPhone. He presses the Power button to bring it to life. The screen stays blank. "Sorry, the battery must be dead."

"Crap," I say, feeling a spark of panic.

His face is a mixture of pity and reluctance. "You could use my landline, if you like."

I scan his features. His eyes seem kind, and the end of his nose is red from the cold. Spidery flakes are collecting rapidly on his hat. My gut is telling me this is the way women end up as headlines on CNN, but what choice do I have? Besides, he knows Tara. We've met, even.

"That'd be great. I'm Emma, by the way."

"Dominic."

Dominic. Yes, that's right. And he was standing next to a

striking woman with a name like mine. Emmy, maybe. Or Emily. Understated elegance. Long red hair. A well-matched couple, looks-wise.

"Nice to meet you. Again. You live close to here?"

"Sure do."

He turns and walks toward my front door, puts a key into the lock, and pushes it open.

I suck in a great lungful of cold, snowy air as my blood pounds in my ears.

No, no, no. This *cannot* be happening.

But it is.

What feels like years later, I'm sitting in my living room on the chocolate-brown leather couch it took me months to find, shivering.

"It's in the kitchen," Dominic says as he shrugs off his coat and hangs it on one of the brushed-nickel hooks I installed in the entranceway. He sounds like he's a million miles away, speaking across a bad phone connection.

"I know," I whisper, the words sticking in my throat.

Dominic walks into the room. He's wearing faded dark jeans and a gray, zipped-neck sweatshirt, both of which hang loosely on his slim frame, like he's recently lost weight. There are flecks of gray in his thick, closely cropped hair.

"What's that?"

I take and release a ragged breath. "I said, I know where the phone is."

"I seem to be missing something."

Buddy, you have no idea.

"This is my apartment."

"Excuse me?"

"This is my apartment. This is my couch. And you've just invited me to use my phone."

Confusion floods his face. "What the hell are you talking about?"

"You think I'm crazy, right?"

"I don't know what to think."

"I'm not crazy." I sound unconvincing, even to my own ears. "This is my apartment."

"Why do you keep saying that?"

The doorbell emits a loud burst of sound, startling us both.

"That'll be the movers," Dominic says.

"The *what*?"

The doorbell rings again. Dominic walks to the front door and opens it, revealing a squat man in a pair of coveralls holding a rolled-up piece of dark blue fabric.

"You ready for us, man?"

"Yeah, come on in."

Dominic steps out of his way. The moving man puts the fabric on the ground and rolls it down the hardwood floor that leads toward my bedroom.

I stand up and my legs almost give way. Blood is rushing from my head like I've taken a stopper out of a drain. I steady myself on the slippery arm of the couch. "What are you doing?"

He glances at me. "I'm moving in."

"But—"

"Look, I know you keep saying this is your apartment, but I have a lease that says otherwise. Here, I'll show you." He picks up a backpack that's propped against the wall and unzips it. He pulls out a sheaf of loose papers and flips through them. The squat moving man returns and heads outside. His boots leave a wet imprint on the fabric.

Dominic locates a typed, legal-size document. He hands it to me. "You see?"

I read through it twice, though I understood it perfectly the first time. It's a lease between Dominic Mahoney and Pedro Alvarez for 23A Chesterfield—this very apartment—dated last week.

"There must be some mistake."

"I don't think so."

Blackness swirls around me. I feel like I've just been woken up from my pod in the Matrix, covered in primordial goo and struggling for breath. But if this is some alternative reality, where's the wise mentor who's going to explain what the hell is going on?

"The faucet in the bathroom sticks when you turn on the hot water. The radiator in the bedroom clangs at exactly 11:12 every night. The—"

"What are you doing?"

"I'm proving to you that this is my apartment."

"I believe you used to live here, okay, but—"

"No, I didn't *used* to live here. I live here, end of story."

The moving man returns, his arms full of cardboard boxes. "Where should I put these?"

"In the larger bedroom," Dominic says, waving down the hall. He walks past me and sits on the couch, resting his hands on his knees. "All right . . . Emma, did you say your name was?"

"Yes."

"Let's get to the bottom of this."

He motions for me to sit next to him. I don't want to, but I'm not sure my legs will hold me much longer. I sit on the far end of the familiar couch. There's a thin film of dust on the coffee table. The air smells faintly of decay.

"Okay," he says. "Say this is your apartment—"

"It is."

"Then why would Pedro rent it to me?"

"I've been away for a while."

"Did he know you were going to be away?"

I think back to the hazy days before I left, full of packing and shots and the trippy antimalarial pills that gave me the worst dreams. "No, I didn't tell him."

"Why not?"

"Because my rent gets paid automatically, and I was only supposed to be gone for a month."

He cocks an eyebrow. "How long have you been gone for?"

"Six months."

"How did that happen?"

"I don't really feel like being cross-examined right now."

"I'm just trying to figure out what's going on."

I stand up.

"Where are you going?"

"To use the phone."

I follow the blue carpet down the hall, glancing at my bedroom as I pass by. My cream bed and dresser are right where I left them, but there's nothing personal about the room anymore. No pictures of my mother, no collection of jars full of dirt from the places I've been, no detritus scattered across the surfaces, only dust. It's like I've been erased. Turned to ash.

I feel sick to my stomach, but I press on to the kitchen and the phone. And there it is, sitting on the counter, a fancy touchscreen one that rings like the ones on *24*. My fingers are slippery on the keys. I dial Craig's home number. The tones beep in my ear, but instead of ringing, all I get is that loud, rude *dah, dah, dah*, followed by a mechanical voice telling me the number's no longer in service. I hang up and dial again, with the same result. Then I dial Stephanie's number, but there's no answer; it just rings and rings and rings. When I finally give up on her answering, I force my shaking hand to dial Craig's office number. It's after six on a Saturday, and I'm not surprised I get his voice mail. His familiar voice tells me he'll be out of the office for a week and to dial zero in an emergency. My hand hovers above the button—if this isn't an emergency, I don't know what it is—but I know all I'll get is the night service. An endless loop of voice mail.

I slam the receiver hard against the counter. The report sets my ears ringing and joins the buzzing sound in my head. My brain cells feel ready to explode. Breathing seems optional.

"Hey, be careful," Dominic says from the doorway. "You're going to break that."

I drop the receiver and push past him, heading toward the front door.

"Emma. Hey, Emma, wait . . ."

Dominic's calls follow me down the hall, but they don't stop me. I need to get outside, away from this place where everything looks like it did six months ago, only it's a showroom version of my life.

I yank open the front door. I nearly bump into the moving

man and his tower of boxes, but I weave at the last moment, and I'm outside in the blustery night. It's snowing in earnest now, a blizzardy snow that blots out the tall buildings and shrinks the world down to the few feet in front of me. The air is thick with the smell of burnt rubber from the spinning wheels of the passing cars.

I slip and slide the six blocks to Stephanie's. When I get there, half-frozen, fully desperate, all the lights in her ground-floor apartment are off. I peer through the glass front door into her lobby; there's mail peeking out of the metal mailbox next to her door. Despite the signs of absence, I push and push the buzzer anyway, hoping, praying, she'll somehow be there. Because if she isn't, I don't know what I'm going to do. I have no idea where Craig is or how to reach him. And Sunshine doesn't even live in the country.

When I've lost the feeling in my index finger, I sit down on the snowy stoop. A jolt of pain shoots down my leg from where I smacked against Tara's step earlier, and I cry out.

The door creaks open behind me. A wiry man in his mid-forties pops his head out.

"You the one ringing the bell?"

I brush the snow off my lap and stand up. "Yes, I'm sorry. I was trying to reach Stephanie Granger. She lives in 1B. Do you know her?"

"Uh-huh."

"Do you know where she is?"

"She's away, I think. I heard her telling the super."

"Did she say when she'd be back?"

"I didn't hear that."

His eyes shift furtively. I take a step back.

"Okay. Thanks."

"Uh-huh."

He shuts the door. It closes with a loud click, the lock another thing that's turned against me today.

I push my hair back from my face and take stock of my situation: I have no money, I can't reach my friends, and a stranger is moving into my home.

A pod in the Matrix is looking pretty good right now.

When I get back to my apartment, the moving man is closing up the back of his truck. He flips his hand at me in acknowledgment as he climbs into the cab, then puts the truck in gear. I watch his red running lights fade as he drives into the storm. When all I can see is white, I turn and trudge up the snow-filled walkway. I hesitate at the front door, not sure this is where I want to be. But I'm soaked through and my teeth are chattering like a wind-up toy and my suitcase is still inside. So . . .

I ring the bell. Dominic opens the door moments later.

"I wondered when you were coming back," he says, his eyes dark with concern. Whether it's for his safety or mine, I'm not quite sure.

"Here I am."

"You want to come in?"

I nod and cross the threshold into the warm entranceway. The hallway beyond is full of boxes held together by wide, clear tape. BOOKS, reads the label on one. KITCHEN, says another.

Dominic walks down the hall and returns with a light-blue towel in his hand.

"I thought you could use this."

"Thanks."

I wipe the moisture off my face and neck. As I defrost, some of the feeling starts to return to my hands, but I'm not sure that's a good thing. Comfortably numb seems like a better option right now.

"Why don't you take off your coat?"

I shrug it off and hang it next to his.

"I made some coffee. Would you like some?"

"All right."

I follow him into the kitchen. The smell of a dark roast permeates the air. The walls are still the bright yellow I painted them when I moved in, and my blue flowered curtains are hanging in the window.

I sit down at the old pine farmer's table Stephanie gave me

for my thirtieth birthday, resting my hands on the smooth surface.

Emma Tupper, this is your life. On drugs.

Dominic pours some coffee into a matte black mug that's the first thing I don't recognize. I wrap my hands against its hot warmth, breathing in the tart fumes.

"I found something that might interest you," he says, sitting across from me.

He pushes an envelope across the table. It's a credit card bill by the looks of it, and it's addressed to me.

I feel an odd sense of Cartesian relief. I receive mail, therefore I am.

"So you believe me now?"

"Yeah, well, when I found this, I called Tara in L.A."

"And she confirmed that I live here?"

"She did. But she also said you disappeared."

"I didn't disappear. I was just away for longer than I was supposed to be."

He bites his lower lip, trying to decide something. "I guess this is your apartment."

"That's what I've been saying."

"Maybe I should've believed you, but—"

I soften my tone. "I know this must all seem crazy."

He gives me a tentative smile. "I'm sure it'll make sense eventually."

I take a sip of my coffee. It's strong, but I doubt even a triple cap would make an impression today.

"I guess we'll straighten it out with Pedro tomorrow," I say.

"Right. Can I call you a cab or something?"

Oh my God. He expects me to leave. But I can't. I can't.

My mind whirs, trying to come up with a solution that doesn't involve asking a stranger if I can stay in my own apartment, but I come up with nothing.

"Do you have Tara's number?" I ask eventually.

"Why?"

"I need to ask her something."

He nods toward his iPhone, sitting charging on the counter. "Her number's the last one I dialed."

I walk to the counter and hold the sleek device in my hand. "Do you think you could give me some privacy?"

He mutters something unintelligible under his breath, but he leaves the room. I hit Redial with my index finger, and in moments I'm talking to Tara. She wants to hear all about my trip and where the hell I've been all this time, but I get right to my point.

"This guy, Dominic. Is he all right?"

"What do you mean?"

"I mean, can I trust him?"

"What kind of question is that? Of *course* you can. Especially after what he's—"

"Okay, thanks. That's all I wanted to know."

"No problem, but, Emma—"

I end the call, basically hanging up on her, but I'm so worn down I can't muster the energy to care. I'll apologize later.

I find Dominic in the hall, sorting through the boxes. I watch him for a moment, staring at the sharp line of his hair where it meets his neck.

"Dominic?"

"Yeah."

"Do you think . . . I could stay here tonight?"

He turns around slowly. "Don't you have somewhere else you can go?"

"No."

I get the impression he doesn't really believe me, and as the silence grows I'm sure he's going to refuse, but instead he says, "All right. You can stay. Temporarily."

"Gee, thanks."

"What did you expect me to say?"

"What's with the hostility?"

"Sorry. I'm having a bad day."

And I'm not?

"Right." A wave of tiredness passes through me, and my teeth start chattering again. "Do you mind if I take a bath?"

"Sure, whatever."

I walk to the linen cupboard that's nestled into the hallway outside the bathroom. The shelves are bare, like I knew they would be somehow.

I feel sheepish about asking, but: "Dominic, do you have any more towels?"

Looking resigned, he roots through a box on the floor outside my bedroom. He pulls out two more light-blue towels and a bar of soap.

"This do you?"

"Thanks. And"—I take a deep breath—"truce?"

He mulls it over. "Yeah, all right."

"You wouldn't have any idea where the rest of my stuff is, would you?"

"Is something missing?"

"My pictures, my books, my winter clothes . . ." My memories, my life. "None of it seems to be here."

"I rented the place furnished, but I never saw anything like that."

Feeling defeated, I hug the towels to my chest and head toward the bathroom. The best thing about this apartment, it has cream marble floors, white subway tile in a brick pattern halfway up the walls, and a separate tub and shower. The walls are a soothing blue-gray color. If I breathe deeply enough, I can still smell my favorite shampoo.

I lock the door behind me and strip down, letting my wet

clothes scatter on the floor. I inspect my backside in the full-length mirror. There's a large red circle where I hit the step. It stands out angrily against the white of my skin. This bruise is going to be lasting and painful. Kind of like the effects of today, I expect.

I run a steaming hot bath and slide into the tub, sinking up to my ears. I stay like that until the water cools, letting the heat penetrate down to my bones. Then I scrub every part of me with the bar of soap until I feel like I'm down to the next layer of skin.

When I've finally had enough, I drain the tub and wrap myself in one of Dominic's towels. I twist my hair into another, then recover my suitcase from the hall. I head toward my bedroom out of habit. Without my things, the room feels like it's moved on, like my bedroom in my mother's house after I came home from college. I unzip my suitcase and survey the contents, hoping to find something I know isn't there: warmer clothes. All I have are shorts and tank tops and the linen pants I wore home. I feel cold just looking at them.

I sit on the edge of the bed, overwhelmed again. New skin isn't a buffer against the reality I'm facing. I should've left the old skin on.

There's a soft knock on the door. "Emma, is it okay if I come in?"

I wrap the towel tighter across my breasts. "Sure."

Dominic opens the door. "I was thinking . . . you've been gone since summer, right?"

I nod.

"Do you have anything to wear in this weather?"

"No."

He walks to the boxes lined up against the wall and opens one of them. He takes out a pair of gray jogging pants and a black T-shirt.

"Take these."

"What? No, I can't."

"Don't be ridiculous." He puts them on the bed.

"Thanks."

"There's some sheets and blankets in that big box in the corner."

"Do you mind if I sleep in here?"

"I figured you'd want to. I'll take the other room."

"Listen, about before—"

"We'll figure it out tomorrow."

"Right. Well, good night."

He gives me a half smile. "Pretty fucked-up day, huh?"

"That sounds about right."

He leaves, and I change into his clothes. They're too big, but they're clean, cozy, and smell like fabric softener. I make up the bed with the sheets and blankets I find in the box

Dominic mentioned, then search my suitcase until my hand comes against a hard surface. I pull out the jar Karen gave me and place it on the nightstand; at least there's something that's mine here now.

Beyond exhausted, I climb in between the sheets feeling small and alone and lost.

Even in my own bed, I am lost.

Chapter 3
Missing, Presumed Dead

When I arrived in Tswanaland—a small country tucked between Zimbabwe, Zambia, and Botswana—worn out and groggy from the sleeping pills and the long, long flight, I felt immediately like the whole trip was one big mistake. Maybe it was the alien landscape, or the way the airport was thick with people. But as I collected my luggage and searched for the tour-company sign among a sea of unfamiliar faces, it occurred to me that I hadn't really thought the whole thing through. I'd never traveled alone before, for one thing, and hadn't taken more than a week off in years. And though I loved my mother very, very much, Africa was never on the list of places I wanted to visit; it was always the place she wanted to go but never did.

But what I really wasn't counting on was how actually being there brought her death home to me in a way the previous few weeks hadn't. I'd gone there to finish mourning her, and instead, the wound her death caused suddenly felt fresh and like someone was digging a knife into it.

After what seemed like too long, when I was about to give

up and catch the first flight home, I found a group of people circled around a tall, thin man dressed in jeans and a Counting Crows T-shirt. He had a white sticky label on his chest, like the ones you get at conferences. MY NAME IS BANGA, it read, but he said to just call him Bob. He'd be guiding us for the next month, he told the excited-looking group around me. He couldn't wait to show us his country.

My fellow travelers were buzzing with the adventure of it all. But me?

I hated the place on the spot.

In the morning, the sunlight seeps through the cream muslin curtains I always meant to replace with darker ones and pries me from sleep too soon. It feels like it's early, though there's no longer any clock on the bedside table to confirm it. A small crash, a muttered oath, and the faint whiff of coffee tell me Dominic must be up too.

I want to pull the covers over my head and sleep until I can sleep no more, but I have places to go and people to kill, specifically Pedro, so I rise and help myself to a pair of Dominic's jeans and a wool fisherman's sweater from a box marked OLD CLOTHES. The jeans and the sleeves of the sweater are much too long for me, but I roll them up and French-braid my hair. Then I pick up the cordless phone from the bedside table and dial Stephanie's and Craig's numbers again, with the same result as yesterday. I rack my brain, but for the life of me I can't remember their cell numbers. Because they were in my BlackBerry, of course, that constant buzzing companion, which I left behind in a fit of pique at the powers that be at work.

After I wash my face and use the bathroom, I follow the smell of coffee to the kitchen. Dominic's sitting at the table reading the newspaper, sipping from a mug. His hair is mussed, and he's wearing a pair of striped pajama bottoms and a white T-shirt.

"Morning."

He lifts his head. His eyes are red-rimmed. "Morning."

I pour myself some coffee and sit across from him. His eyes flit from my face to my sweater.

"You know the stuff in the boxes is mine, right?"

"I'm sorry. I didn't think you'd mind."

"I guess I don't, but maybe you could ask me next time?"

"I'm hoping there isn't a next time."

He rattles the pages in front of him. "Right."

I pick up the front section of the paper. It's been a while, but nothing seems to have changed. The headlines are the usual mix of sordid local news and impending world doom. There's a serial rapist on the loose. A Manet was stolen from the Concord Museum. There might be massive solar flares hurtling toward us, or then again, maybe not. NASA is "studying" the situation. They'll get back to us as soon as they have more information.

I toss it aside and consider the man across the table. "Dominic, who are you?"

His mouth twists. "Oh, right, we never had that who-are-you-and-what-do-you-do-besides-steal-women's-apartments conversation."

"I think it might be a good idea given our present circumstance, don't you?"

"That's where we're different. I prefer to remain anonymous."

"Are you making fun of me?"

"I might be."

"Are you going to answer my question?"

He pauses for a beat, then puts down the paper slowly. "I'm a landscape photographer. Raised Catholic by way of fourth-generation Irish parents who wish their ancestors never left County Cork. I have, of course, sloughed off their foolish notions and fully embraced the Church of Scientology. What about you?"

My lips twitch. "I'm a lawyer. Raised some kind of Protestant, I never got the details straight. Have up to now resisted recruitment by Scientologists or any other cult."

We smile at each other, and then something about the normalcy of our banter reminds me that my life isn't at all normal right now, and I'm fighting back tears.

"What is it?" Dominic asks.

"It's just . . . this conversation is way too casual for today."

"I'm sorry, Emma. I don't mean to take your situation lightly."

"It's fine." I take a slow sip of my coffee, trying to focus on the type in front of me, but the words won't stay still.

"You want to talk about it?"

"Not really."

"A woman who doesn't want to talk about things. Interesting."

I almost laugh again, despite myself. I feel like I'm standing in the middle of a sun shower. How can you cry and laugh at the same time?

"So," I say, "I thought I'd go kick some scuzzy landlord butt. You want to join?"

"It'd be my pleasure."

Half an hour later, we open the front door on a changed world. The sky is that clear, crystal blue you only see in winter, and the sun shines down on fluffy white banks of snow. The air smells cold and stings my nostrils. It's beautiful but daunting.

I pull the hat Dominic loaned me down over my ears, zip up his ski jacket so it's covering my face, and trudge through the knee-high snow to the street. The traffic is light and the mostly plowed street seems safer than the uncleared sidewalks.

Dominic's wearing the same coat and hat as last night and

has a professional camera slung around his neck. He raises it quickly and takes a shot of a half-buried car parked across the street. A gust of wind blows a trail of snow off its roof, like the plume of snow at the top of Everest. His shutter clicks, clicks, clicks.

"You coming or what?" I call.

"Coming, coming." He follows my footsteps out to the street. "How were you planning on getting to Pedro's?"

"I thought we'd walk."

"Twenty blocks?"

"It's not that far."

"If you say so."

We walk abreast, next to the tall snowbanks the plows created. Dominic's boots crunch the snow beneath us; my canvas shoes merely sop up the cold. As we walk, my mind starts to throw out thoughts I'd rather not think. Like how none of this would be happening if my mother were still alive. Like how if I ever find Craig and Stephanie, they might never want to speak to me again. And where am I going to sleep *tonight*?

"How come you moved so close to Christmas?" I ask Dominic to distract myself.

"What kind of question is that?"

"I'm just making conversation."

He looks away. "Something . . . came up, and I had to move suddenly."

"Sorry I asked."

"Forget it. This is it, right?"

We stop in front of the large three-story brownstone Pedro runs his real estate empire out of. A string of multicolored lights blinks on and off around the doorway. There's a boy of about twelve in an unzipped, oversized ski parka shoveling snow. I ask him if his father's home and he gives me a non-committal nod. We climb the steps and I ring the bell.

I'm about to ring again when Pedro opens the door in his shirtsleeves and a pair of black slacks. A two-day beard grows across his prominent chin.

"What do you want?" he asks without any trace of recognition.

"I want to know why the hell you did what you did," I say through clenched teeth.

His body tenses. "What's your problem, *chica*? What did I . . ." He stops as he catches sight of Dominic behind me. I can see the dots connecting behind his eyes. "*Madre de Dios.*"

"That's the understatement of the year, man," Dominic says.

"My *problemo,* Pedro, is that you rented *my* apartment to Dominic here, and half of my stuff is missing."

"You didn't pay your rent."

"Of course I did. I had an automatic payment set up. Like always."

He shakes his head. "The payments stopped in the fall. I got a judgment."

"Bullshit," I say, but as the words leave my mouth, I remember how my ATM card wouldn't work at the airport.

"No bullshit. *Espère.* Wait." He turns and walks toward a room off the right side of the hall. Inside, there are papers strewn across a desk and several black filing cabinets. He opens one of the drawers and pulls out a yellow hanging folder. He extracts a stapled document and walks it back to me.

I take it from him with a sense of foreboding. It's a judgment from the Rental Board giving Pedro the right to expulse one defaulting tenant (me) and to remove all her effects from the premises. I scan through it. The familiar words—*nonpayment of rent, notice, service*—swim in front of me, beating into my brain. Though I was waiting for something like this, it feels worse seeing it typed, sealed, official.

And then one phrase stops me cold.

It's this: *Furthermore, the Tenant is missing, presumed dead.*

I run down the street, tripping over the end of Dominic's jeans, heavy and wet from the snow. The air sears my lungs.

Missing, presumed dead. How is that possible? Why would anyone think I was dead? I called . . . I spoke . . . I . . .

"Emma, wait up," Dominic calls from behind me.

My legs buckle. I fall to my knees into a snowbank. The cold seeps through the fabric.

"Are you all right?"

I have no idea how to answer that question. Instead, I drive my hands into the snow, the crystals hard and bitter against my skin.

"Emma, you're scaring me." He touches my elbow. "Come on, you can't stay like this."

"Leave me alone."

"No, I don't think so."

He tucks his hands under my elbows and lifts me to my feet. He turns me around and takes my hands in his, brushing away the snow. They tingle and sting, but I don't care.

I'm dead. I'm dead.

"Emma, your lips are turning blue. You need to get inside."

I stare at him. I can't think, can't speak, can't move. I'm dead.

A cab lumbers down the street and Dominic flags it. He bundles me into the back and gives the driver the address. I curl myself into a ball, resting my head against the worn seat leather. It smells like car polish. The sky out the window looks impossibly far away.

When we get to the apartment, I open the cab door mechanically and follow Dominic up the walk. We go inside, and I take off my coat and shoes and drop to the couch robotically. I sit with my hands between my knees while Dominic turns on the gas fire and brings the blankets from my bed. I huddle under them, feeling numb.

Dominic sits on the coffee table facing me, waiting, worried, his palms flat on his thighs.

"Thanks for bringing me here," I say eventually.

"Of course. Are you feeling better?"

"I guess."

"You want to tell me what's going on?"

"That judgment . . . it said that I was . . . missing . . . that I was maybe . . . dead."

"Jesus. Why would anyone think that?"

I hold my knees to my chest. "I wish I knew."

"Well, why were you gone so long in . . . where were you, anyway?"

"Africa."

"What were you doing there?"

I hug my knees tighter, willing myself to stick in the present. "My mother passed away and she left me a trip."

"What about your father?"

"I don't have a father. I mean, I don't know him. He left when I was three."

"I'm sorry."

I shake my head. "It doesn't matter."

Dominic flexes his hands on his knees. "So you went to Africa, but you were only supposed to be there a month?"

"Yes."

"What happened?"

"I got sick early on, but also . . . I was in Tswanaland."

"You mean you were there when the earthquake—"

"Yes."

He stands abruptly.

"Where are you going?"

"Hold on a sec, I've got an idea."

He leaves the room, returning in a moment with a thin silver laptop.

"I was thinking. How would Pedro know to tell the court you were missing?"

"Good point."

I take the laptop and open a web browser. I google *Emma Tupper Attorney*. The first hit is a link to the *Post*'s webpage. I click on it and an article loads.

The title says it all: "Rising Star at TPC Goes Missing." I race through the article. I'd been in Tswanaland on safari. I'd gotten sick and been left in a village near the game reserve so the guides could get a doctor. I'd called a few friends and told them I'd be back in the capital on the twentieth. The earthquake struck on the twenty-first, 8.9 on the Richter scale, twenty miles from the capital. Much of it had been razed to the ground, wiping out the country's infrastructure and killing thousands. All foreign nationals were strongly encouraged to register with their embassies (built to First World standards, they were some of the only buildings left standing) and take home the rescue flights that were sent in the following weeks. But I never turned up, and no one could find any trace of me. Officials assumed the worst and placed me on a list, a bad list. The conclusion was sad but obvious. "She'll be greatly missed," Matt was quoted as saying. "She had a bright future ahead of her."

"What did you find?" Dominic asks.

My eyes dart to his, then back to the computer screen that says I'm probably dead. Which would explain a few things. Like the dead feeling in my heart, for one.

Dominic takes the computer from me, his eyes scanning the screen. He emits a low whistle. "Fuck."

"I don't think that even comes close to covering it."

"You're right. I'm sorry."

"For what? This isn't your fault."

"Just the same." Dominic puts down the computer and walks toward a box in the corner. He pulls out a bottle of Scotch and a glass and pours several generous fingers. He hands it to me. "Here, drink this."

I stare into the glass. The amber liquid glows. "This isn't going to solve anything."

"You never know."

I toss the whole thing back in two long gulps. It burns

like fire and tastes like the bottom of a peat bog. I look up at Dominic. He's watching me like I'm made of glass and he's a ball-peen hammer. One sharp blow and I might shatter into a million little pieces.

I could use something to blunt the blow.

"Hand me that bottle."

Chapter 4
Some Samuel Clemens

I've had this recurring dream for months.

It's day three of my trip. We've spent two days tracking elephants and giraffes under a sky so wide and flat it feels like being lost in a watercolor painting. The air smells like dust and sunbaked hay. My ears are full of the whir and peal of birds. As the bleached-out sun moves toward the horizon, a lioness charges out of the tall grass and leaps at the throat of a zebra that's lazily strayed away from the herd. With her victim dying at her feet, she emits a series of low roars, calling her pride to the feast.

I roll down my dusty window to get a better look. I can smell the blood and hear flesh being ripped apart. I'm repelled, yet I can't look away. My fellow travelers snap pictures and shoot video until the zebra is carrion.

When we get back to camp, we're excited and chatty in a way we haven't been till now. Roy and Dorothy, a white-haired retired couple, sit at the rough picnic table scrolling through the pictures they took on their camera.

"Look, Do, he took that leg right off."

"*She* took that leg off, dear. It's the females that do the killing."

Bill the ex-army guy is telling Max the still-hippie about the wildebeest he killed on his last trip to Africa. Laurie, Max's girlfriend, tells me she thinks Max brought her on the trip to propose, and she's feeling nervous, wondering when he'll do it.

The guides make us dinner. Banga-just-Bob complains that he has a headache. I see him pop a couple of aspirin while he stirs the meat stew. When it's ready, I tuck into a large serving. It tastes good but foreign.

I feel a hand on my shoulder. My mother is standing next to me. She looks like she did before her illness, only less substantial somehow. Diaphanous.

"Don't eat that," she says. "He's sick."

Before I can say anything, she turns and walks away. I drop my bowl. It lands with a thud in the dirt, shattering. The dusty ground sops up the gravy thirstily. I call out to her, but she doesn't react; she just keeps slowly walking away, wearing something white and floaty.

I try to run after her, but I can't make my legs work. The sun disappears below the horizon. I can't see her anymore; there's just a white spot where she was a minute ago—the trace of her like a bright light leaves on the cornea. I feel as I did when she died, like I've lost her all over again.

Banga-just-Bob strikes a match and tosses it into the waiting fire ring. The flames leap up as a troupe of performers circle the fire, their red robes the only flash of color in a suddenly black-and-white world.

The stars dance above them in the massive sky. I watch their ceremony like I watched the lions earlier that day, barely breathing. The fire dies down. One of the performers locks his eyes onto mine and beckons me with a flick of his wrist. I walk toward him slowly, still searching for my mother out there in the blackness. He places his long, cool fingers on my forehead, pressing gently.

"You're sick," he says. "You're sick."

I awake with a start. My head is throbbing and my stomach feels empty. Yesterday, after several belts of liquor, all I wanted to do was crawl back into bed and disappear. So I did. I slept and dreamt, and slept and dreamt, and now it's Monday morning.

I push off the covers and cross the cold floor. I climb back into Dominic's clothes and go to the kitchen for something to eat. The sight of the phone on the counter sends a pang through my gut. I really, really need to speak to someone in my life. I carry the phone to the table and dial the never-forgotten number for Stephanie's parents. It's early—just after seven—but they'll be up. I can imagine them even:

Lucy in her workout clothes drinking orange juice before she meets her "girls" for a morning walk, Brian reading the newspaper in a starched shirt and tie even though he retired five years ago.

"Good morning!" Lucy chirps into the phone.

"Hi, Lucy. It's Emma. Emma Tupper."

I hear the sucking in of breath and a loud *smack!* "Brian, Brian!"

"Lucy? Hello, Lucy?"

There's a scuffling noise and then a deep male voice. "Who is this?"

"It's me, Brian. It's Emma."

"If this is some kind of sick joke—"

"No. It's really me. I'm okay. I'm home. I'm . . ." My voice trails off. I'm at a loss for what to say, how to explain something I don't even understand myself.

"It's really you?"

"Yes."

"Oh, thank God. We've been so worried. And Stephanie . . ." He stops. I listen while he struggles for control.

"That's partly why I'm calling. Where *is* she?"

"Oh, Emma. She went looking for you."

Now it's my turn to struggle for control. "What? But how could she? How could you let her?"

"We couldn't stop her. Not once the travel embargo was lifted."

"Have you heard from her since she left?"

"She called us from London, but we haven't heard anything since. It says on the Internet that the phone systems there still aren't working reliably."

I close my eyes, thinking of all that twisted metal I saw on the road. "When was she supposed to arrive?"

"Three days ago."

I nearly throw the phone across the room in frustration. Three days ago! Six months apart and a day separated us. That's not right, Universe. Not right at all.

"Do you have her cell number?"

"Yes, of course." He rattles off the numbers. I write them down mechanically on a square of newspaper. "We're very glad you're all right, Emma."

"Thank you."

"I think Lucy's a little too emotional to talk right now, but I'm sure she'd love it if you could call later. Right, darling? Yes. Later would be good."

"I'll try."

"Thank you, my dear."

I hang up and rest my head on my arms. Stephanie's parents thought I was dead. I can't imagine what that must've been like. Stephanie and I spent so much time together grow-ing up that I had honorary daughter status. And Stephanie, stubborn, loyal Stephanie, is off looking for me. Is that where Craig is too? Are they both searching for me while I'm right where I'm supposed to be?

"Morning," Dominic says, shuffling into the room in a pair of khakis and a blue fleece pullover. I raise my head. He looks, if anything, more tired than he did yesterday. Darker circles, wan skin.

"Hey."

"You okay? You look pale."

I let the phone drop to the table. "You ever have to call someone to let them know you're not in fact dead?"

"God, no."

"Yeah, well, I don't recommend it."

He sits across from me. "You have many calls like that to make?"

"Probably." I slouch in my chair, the potential of the calls pushing me down.

"What if you went to see the police? Maybe they could help you get the word out?"

"The police?"

"Yeah, you know, maybe that detective who was quoted in the article, the one in charge of your case?"

I mull it over. "I probably *should* check in with them. If they really thought I was . . . missing."

"Right."

I put my hands on the table and push myself up. "I guess I should get on that."

He stands and shuffles to the fridge. I watch as he opens the door and reaches for a bottle of orange juice like he belongs here, like this is his home. Which I guess it is now. Which probably means that I need to get out of here. But where am I supposed to go? The only place left is my mother's house, a place I can't face yet.

"Dominic?"

"Yeah?"

"Do you think you could lend me some cab fare?"

He puts the juice container on the counter and pulls out his wallet, looking bemused. He extracts two large bills. "This do you?"

"More than, and thanks. I owe you one."

"I'll remember that."

I wait for the detective assigned to my case for forty-five minutes in a dingy lobby painted public-building green. My nose prickles with the smell of too many bodies and disinfectant. There's a sad-looking tree in the corner decorated with a silver garland. The piped-in Christmas Muzak must be a deliberate tactic to loosen up suspects' tongues. I don't care what I have to confess to, just make "The Little Drummer Boy" stop! *Pa rum pa pum pum.*

"Ms. Tupper? I'm Detective Nield."

I stand and shake his hand. Midfifties, tall, well built. He has a round face and steely blue eyes that remind me of Paul Newman in *The Color of Money.*

I follow him through a large open space filled with men, women, desks, and ringing phones to his personal cubicle. The taupe fabric dividers are decorated with a collage of mismatched faces. It takes me a moment to realize that they belong to the people he's looking for. I find my own picture in between those of a small child with a gap in her front teeth and a white-haired man squinting at the sun from the deck of his boat. It's a close-up of my face smiling crookedly at the camera. The last time I saw this picture, it was attached to Stephanie's fridge. Now it's dangling from a red pushpin in a police station. Not good.

I sit in Detective Nield's brown vinyl visitor's chair. He reaches into a pile of papers and pulls out a blue lined form. He squares it on the blotter in front of him and clicks the end of a ballpoint pen.

"Now, Ms. Tupper," he says, his voice gravelly from cigarettes, or maybe whiskey. "Why don't we start at the beginning? What were you doing in Tswanaland?"

I wipe my sweaty palms on Dominic's jeans. "My mother died. She left me the trip in her will. She always . . . it was important to her that I take the trip. So I did."

"And you were with Turnkey Tours?"

"Yes. But if you know that, why do I—"

He smiles sympathetically. "Standard procedure. We like to verify the information we've gathered with the MP if we can."

"MP?"

"Missing person."

"Oh. Yes. All right. Ask away."

"You arrived on June fifth?"

"That sounds right."

"And then you traveled to the game reserve?"

"Yes. It's about two hundred fifty miles from the capital."

"What happened when you got there?"

"The usual safari stuff, I guess. Looking at giraffes and elephants."

He nods. "When did you get sick?"

"The fourth day. I picked something up from one of the guides."

"Do you know what?"

I think back to the fever and chills. One minute I was fine. The next I couldn't sit up. I could barely swallow. Breathing felt like a chore.

"I'm not entirely sure. I was too sick to be moved very far, so they brought me to a village where some NGO workers were building a school."

"What are their names?"

"Karen and Peter Alberts."

"What NGO were they working for?"

"Education Now, but they're from here, actually. They should be back in a few weeks, if you need to speak to them."

"I doubt that will be necessary." His pen scratches along the page. "How long were you sick for?"

"About a week."

"And you called Ms. Granger and Mr. Talbot?"

"Yes. A few days before the earthquake."

"You told them that you were heading back to the capital? That you were coming home?"

"I was supposed to take the next transport back, but it never arrived."

"You were in the village when the earthquake struck?"

I nod, though I wasn't technically in the village. Instead, I was on the first of the many walks I'd end up taking in the coming months. Walks I took when I couldn't stand to be around anyone anymore. When I needed to cry, to shake, to fall to the ground and huddle there until the tears dried up.

On that day, I sat on the hard ground with my back resting against a rough tree, thinking about going home. The river trickled behind me, and I watched a snake slither through the edge of the dead grass at my feet. I remember almost wishing it would bite me, inflict a wound that would distract me from my broken heart, my painful brain.

Then the air was full of the *thwap, thwap* of birds and the squeals of animals I couldn't identify. I looked around in confusion, and before I could rise to my feet the air started vibrating, shaking, cracking.

Earthquake, I thought, having been through a few small tremors in my lifetime. But nothing like this. The sound was so loud, the shaking so violent, I felt like I was inside it, like the heaving ground might open up and swallow me, gulping me down whole.

I clung to the tree out of instinct, nature's door frame. Its unfamiliar fruit fell like bombs around me, exploding in all directions. And when the ground finally stopped shaking and the roar subsided, I stood unsteadily and felt glad to be alive.

"Yes," I say to Detective Nield, "that's right."

"You were lucky."

"Yes."

"Yet . . . you never managed to call home again?"

I feel a twinge of guilt. "No. The earthquake knocked out the power supply, took down cell towers . . . we couldn't make calls. We were stranded."

"And the airport was closed until a few weeks ago?"

"Yes, when we heard that international flight services had

started up again, I took the first transport back to the capital."

"You didn't have any problem going through Immigration? Your passport should have been flagged."

"No. Nothing."

He frowns. "That doesn't speak much for our security systems."

I think back to the bored customs official who didn't scan my passport. "I guess I don't look like a terrorist."

"Mmm."

"Can I ask you a question?"

"Of course."

"How come you thought I was . . . dead?"

His eyes turn serious. "Mr. Talbot and Ms. Granger filed a missing-person report when you didn't evacuate with the rest of the tourists. With all that was going on over there, it was impossible to get anyone on the phone, and extremely difficult to obtain the names and addresses of the others who were on the tour with you. When I finally was able to track them down, all they could tell me was what we already knew. We all thought you were in the capital—"

"Like I said I would be."

He nods. "That's when you were placed on the list."

"I see."

"I'm sorry we didn't do better."

"I'm sure you did all you could."

"That's very generous of you, Ms. Tupper."

"I'm alive, right?"

He smiles. "You are."

"What do I do now?"

"I'll give you some forms so you can reactivate your bank accounts and the like."

That's not quite what I was getting at, but it'll do for now.

"Thank you. Why were they frozen?"

"Standard procedure."

"Right. Well, do you need anything else from me?"

"No, I don't think so. We'll take care of issuing the press release."

" 'The report of my death has been greatly exaggerated,' or some other such Samuel Clemens?"

His top lip curls. "Something like that."

"All right. Thank you." I stand to leave.

"Can I make a suggestion before you go?"

"Of course."

"I've dealt with many people in your situation—not the exact same, mind, but people who've gone missing—and they mostly found it a struggle to reintegrate into their lives. It's not just a question of picking up where you left off."

"What are you saying?"

"Only that I can recommend someone to talk to, if you'd like. A psychologist who runs a victims' group."

I've never liked the word *victim,* and I certainly never thought I'd be one.

"But the people you're talking about, they were abducted, right?"

"Generally, yes."

"It's not the same for me. I wasn't really missing; everyone just thought I was."

"Nevertheless, your friends and coworkers thought you were dead. That will have ramifications—"

I cut him off, switching into Emma Tupper–superachiever mode. "Thanks for your suggestion, but I'm going to have all this sorted out in a couple of days. Once people know I'm alive, everything will fall back into place."

"I admire your courage, Ms. Tupper. And I hope you're right."

"I'm not courageous. I'm just a sidebar in tomorrow's newspaper." I extend my hand. "Thank you for trying to find me."

He grips my hand firmly. "I'm glad everything turned out the way it did."

"Me too."

I turn and walk through the maze of police officers and clerks toward the exit. Along the way, I pass a large whiteboard full of columns of names written in red and black marker. My last name is there too, in red block letters, like I'm this week's victim in an episode of *The Wire.*

I know what happens next; I've seen it on TV countless times. In a few moments someone, Detective Nield maybe, will erase my name and rewrite it in black. When the year's over, I'll be erased forever. And the space I took up, small as it was, will be available for someone else.

Red to black. Case solved. I once was lost, and now I'm found.

Easy.

Chapter 5
All Work and No Play

Worn out from my conversation with Detective Nield, I don't feel up to tackling Thompson, Price & Clearwater just yet. Given how they reacted when I wanted a month off, I can only imagine the Management Committee's selfish indignation when I got myself killed. *Just who was going to handle the Samson trial, and the rest of her caseload?* Ugh.

Instead, I take refuge in the food court that sprawls through the basement of the office tower where TPC is located. I sit hidden behind a pillar in what used to be the smoking section (if you breathe deeply enough, I swear you feel like you're smoking), taking in the familiar smell of Thai, Lebanese, and Burger King. This has been my dining room away from home ever since I started working here. It makes me feel nostalgic, though I'm not quite sure for what.

One of the questions on law school applications should be: *Can you survive solely on fast food?* Instead, every school I applied to asked why I wanted to be a lawyer. I think we were supposed to write about all the good we wanted to do, but I wanted to be honest. (If I was going to uphold the law, I figured I should at least *start out* being honest.) Unfortunately, I was pretty sure telling the truth wasn't going to get me in. Because the truth was, I wanted to be a lawyer because I liked arguing. I liked it so much I'd argue either side of anything just for the hell of it, whether someone asked me to or not. Anytime, anywhere.

And that's not an appealing characteristic, right? Being argumentative? *I want to go to law school so I can learn to argue so well no one will ever dare disagree with me again . . .* Won't I be popular then? Won't I be happy? Oh well, at least I'll be right.

But it worked. I wrote five hundred words about how much I liked to get inside the tiny little facts of every public issue so I could trounce anyone who dared take me on, and I was accepted to every school I applied to. Shit. I probably even took the place of a few people who truly *wanted* to better the world. A couple of schools offered me the scholarship I needed, and one, a big fancy one that makes people "ooh" and "aah" when you tell them you went there (yup, that one), gave me a full ride.

I took that ride, of course I did. Even though my mother didn't want me to. It's funny, because the *last* thing she wanted me to be was a lawyer. She wouldn't tell me what the first thing was—that would be too easy, too controlling, too direct—but

I still remember clearly how her face fell when I announced, some time around the tenth grade, what I wanted to be when I grew up. "Why would you want to do that?" she said before she could help herself. Was she the only parent in history who was dismayed when her child made this kind of announcement? Maybe not, but her reaction surprised me.

Anyway, off I went to law school, my mother wishing me luck and providing unending support. And when I finished within sight of the top of my class, I had my pick of jobs. TPC had the best reputation in litigation and promised I'd be allowed to speak in a courtroom before I turned forty.

I signed on. The hours were brutal and the work was sometimes mind-numbing. But they held up their end of the bargain; I got to speak in court. And that's when I realized I didn't like making an argument. I *loved* it. Especially if there was something on the line (millions of dollars, say, or the survival of a company), and I won. Of course, everyone likes to win. Winning is better than losing, after all. But I *loved* it.

So for the years between twenty-seven and thirty-four, I worked hard to make sure that if I argued, I won. And the work meant there wasn't time for much else. Something had to give, and it was my friends I gave. I stopped returning calls, and one by one, they stopped making them, until it felt like all that was left were Stephanie, Craig, Sunshine (when she was around), and my mom.

I don't know if it's sad or just life that I didn't think about it much. I didn't have that many friends. So what?

But now I'm regretting some of the choices I made. I'm feeling it.

Boy, am I ever.

I smooth out the piece of newspaper with Stephanie's cell-phone number on it and punch it into the dirt-cheap phone I bought at a kiosk in the mall with some of Dominic's money.

Stephanie's phone rings, rings, rings, then clicks to voice mail.

"This is Steph. Please leave a message."

"Steph, whatever you're doing, sit down. It's me. Emma. I'm okay. I'm back, and most importantly, I'm alive. I'm so, so sorry I wasn't able to call sooner. Please don't hate me, okay? Call me as soon as you get this message, whatever the time. My new number is 555-7982. Okay now, breathe. I love you."

I hang up and hold the phone in my hand for a minute, willing it to ring, though I know I might not hear from her for days. God, maybe even weeks. Why, why, why did she have to go looking for me?

"Ohmygod."

I look up into the stunned face of Jenny Macintosh, my twenty-two-year-old assistant. She's fond of tanning and is wearing a black shift dress whose skirt is way too short, but that's the thing about Jenny. She looks and talks like she should have a camera crew following her around while she parties till 3 A.M., but she's smart as a whip and, in the year we worked together, saved my ass more than once.

"Hi, Jenny."

She hugs me tightly. "You're alive."

"Yeah."

"But they told us that you were dead, and we had this service and everything."

Jesus. They had a *service*. I'd been memorialized, summed up, dispatched into the past tense. I wonder if anyone cried.

She flops into the chair across from me. Her latte sloshes over the side of her cup. "This is just too freakin' weird."

You're telling me.

"Careful, you're going to spill your drink."

She blinks slowly. Her eyes start to fill with tears. "Where were you all this time?"

I fill her in, touched by her concern. She listens quietly, her baby-blue eyes round saucers of bewilderment.

"That's like something out of a movie."

Yeah, one of those depressing ones where the main character's life starts out badly and just gets worse and worse. Those movies all have a turning point in them, though, when something happens to tip the balance back toward goodness.

I'm going to get one of those soon, right?

"I guess."

"Does anyone else know?"

"At the office? No, not yet. I'll be heading up there in a minute."

"Oh," she says, sipping her drink. "I work for Mr. Wilson now."

"That's great, Jenny."

"And Sophie took your office."

That figures. If there's such a thing as a nemesis in real life, then Sophie Vaughn is it. I'm not exactly sure why she has it in for me, but it seems like she has ever since I started working at TPC. Okay, that's not entirely true. I'm pretty sure hooking up with her ex at my first office Christmas party had something to do with it. (Not my proudest moment, but I didn't even know they'd been dating till afterward.) But still, tangling with her always reminds me of the fights I had with the popular girls in high school. I guess you can take the popular girl out of high school, but that doesn't mean she'll stop acting like it's high school. Or maybe life after high school isn't any different from life *in* high school? What an awful thought.

"I'm not surprised."

"Yeah, she must really hate you. I mean, why else would she . . ."

"Why else would she what?"

She fidgets with the chunky ring on her index finger. "We should go upstairs and tell everyone the good news, don'tcha think?"

"I guess so."

As I walk with Jenny through the mall, a knot forms in the pit of my stomach. Everyone at the office thinks I'm dead. They wore black, listened to someone (Matt, probably) talk about how dedicated I was, ate some finger sandwiches, and went back to work. I doubt many of them have given me much thought since. Judging by Jenny's reaction, my showing up out of the blue is going to be a shock. I probably should've called ahead.

Too late now.

The elevator opens onto the cherry-wood-paneled lobby. Light floods through the floor-to-ceiling windows behind the large receptionist station, where two nearly indistinguishable women with slicked-back black hair answer the constant flow of calls in their public-radio voices. "Thompson, Price and Clearwater, how can I help you?" There's a string of white mini lights running along the edge of their shared desk. A massive Christmas tree sits in the left corner, its pine smell permeating the air. A menorah glows gently on a coffee table next to it.

TPC covers all its bases.

I spend the next twenty minutes watching the shock of my return spread through the office like a wave. As I walk down the long carpeted corridor of the litigation floor, everything becomes eerily quiet, amplifying the sound of the ringing phones. Lawyers stick their heads out of their offices with their mouths hanging open. I get some high fives, a few slaps on the back, and the ubiquitous thumbs-up.

It's kind of fun, in the way it must be in those first few heady weeks of celebrity. Until I get to my old office, a place that feels more like home than my apartment.

Only now it's Sophie's office, and it's full of her furniture, which has been reconfigured so her back's to the hall. Her long, ash-blond hair is perfectly straight above the thin shoulders of her signature black Armani suit. She's talking on the phone, the handle tucked against her cheek.

Feeling disoriented, I turn away. Matt comes striding down the hall with the same look everyone else is wearing. He pulls me into a great bear hug, lifting me off my feet. And it's this uncharacteristic display of emotion from a man who's challenged me, and nurtured me, and made me work so hard I developed a twitch in my right eye, that breaks the fragile veneer that's been checking my tears.

"I'm sorry, Matt," I say a few minutes later in his office after I've used his handkerchief to dry my face.

He sits next to me on the ultramodern couch in the corner of his cavernous office. His silver hair glints in the bright halogen lights that shine down from the ceiling. The smell of his expensive aftershave is strangely comforting.

"What are you apologizing for?"

"I don't know. Disappearing, I guess. I must've left you with an awful mess. The Samson trial, for one."

"Don't worry about that, Emma."

"Was it postponed?"

"No, Sophie did the trial," he says gently.

"Oh, right. Sure."

"What happened to you?"

I take a sip of the water his secretary, Nathalie, brought me and tell him my story. He listens with the total attention that makes him a great trial attorney.

"You didn't know we thought you were . . . missing?"

"No. Didn't Craig tell you we spoke?"

A jolt hits me as my mouth forms his name. *Craig.* I'd forgotten all about him and come instinctively to Matt's office instead.

"You spoke to Craig today?" Matt asks.

"No, I meant when I was in Africa, before the . . . I've tried calling him since I got back, but his home number's been disconnected, and I don't have my BlackBerry, and his voice mail said something about being out of the office . . ." I stop myself, feeling the heat rise up my cheeks.

"He's on the west coast working on a deal. I'm sure his assistant will have his coordinates."

"Right. I should've thought of that."

"Nathalie," he calls out the door, "please find out when

Craig Talbot will be back, and get his numbers from his assistant."

"Will do," she answers.

"Thanks, Matt."

"Of course. Have you given any thought to what you're going to do now?"

"What do you mean? Can't I . . . I mean, I thought I'd come back to work."

Matt's eyes slide away from mine. My stomach re-forms into a hard knot of nervousness. In my experience, nothing good ever comes from a man who can't look you in the eye.

"Matt, what is it?"

"I'm just a bit surprised you want to come back, after everything that's happened."

"What do you mean? What else would I do?"

His eyes return to mine. I can't read their expression. "Have you given any thought to going back to school?"

"Why would I want to do that?"

"Perhaps a change might do you some good."

"Why would I need a change?"

"No reason. Forget I said anything."

I put my hand on his arm. "Matt, come on. What's going on?"

He clears his throat. "Nothing, only . . . you might find it hard rebuilding your practice after being gone for so long, that's all."

"Susan was gone longer when she had her baby."

A muscle twitches in Matt's jaw. Bringing that up was a mistake. Susan's yearlong maternity leave was extremely controversial. Rumor had it that she had to promise she wouldn't have another kid to get it.

Why do I like working here again?

"That's true. But, Emma, her clients knew she was coming back."

I put two and two together. "And mine thought I wasn't."

"Yes."

"You mean . . . my clients have all been reassigned?"

Matt looks sad. Sad for me. "I'm sorry, Emma, but yes."

This is *not* good. Partnership in TPC is based on a complicated formula of billable hours and number of clients. You have to have a certain client base that generates a certain number of billable hours to even be considered. So what Matt just said means I'm not a year away from partnership; I'm going to have to start back at the beginning, as if I'd just graduated. As if the last seven years had never happened.

No wonder he thinks I should go back to school.

"But I can still come back if I want to?"

"I'll have to check with the Management Committee, but if that's what you really want, I'll back you."

"It's what I want," I say with more certainty than I feel.

"Well, well, well, what do we have here?"

Sophie's standing in the doorway with her arms crossed across her chest. Her perfect veneer of makeup emphasizes her high cheekbones and gives definition to an otherwise weak chin. Her apple-green blouse matches her cat eyes.

"It's true," she says in her precise diction. I catch a whiff of Chanel No. 5, a scent I used to like before I met her.

"Looks like it."

"Well, that's just grand. Everyone was *so* concerned."

"I'll bet."

She looks me up and down. "You're looking well."

I push up the sleeves of Dominic's sweater, feeling dowdy.

I will not let her goad me into saying something bitchy in front of Matt. I will not let her goad me . . .

"How are you enjoying my office?"

Damn. And I was trying so hard too.

"Have you finished the opinion for Mutual Assurance yet, Sophie?" Matt says with a disappointed tone in his voice.

Mutual Assurance is one of the firm's biggest clients. Aspiring litigators cut their teeth on the hundreds of cases it throws TPC's way every year. In my first year at the firm, I wrote *The Defendant denies the allegations in paragraph x, y, z* so many times it felt like I was doing lines for punishment.

"You'll have it by three."

"Good."

"What are you working on?" I ask Matt, trying to seem interested.

"Someone stole a Manet from Victor Bushnell's collection. Mutual is on the hook for millions if we can't find a contractual exclusion that applies."

"Right, I saw that in the paper this morning. I'm sure there must be something."

Sophie gives me a Cheshire smile. "Of course there is. Why don't you stop by my office later and we'll catch up?"

"Will do," I say brightly, both of us knowing it will never happen.

She leaves, and I lean back on the couch, feeling worn out by our exchange. Six months away has left me too weak for a catfight.

"I wish you girls would get along better."

"I know, Matt. I'll try."

"Good."

"So, when do you think I can start?"

Chapter 6
Far and Away

Six months is a long time to spend in the company of strangers. Not that Karen and Peter aren't great people. People who I now love dearly. But in those first few days and weeks, when I was weak and missing my mother in a way I hadn't since I was eight and had to be fetched home from Girl Guide camp, I felt cautious around them. Unsure of my place.

This feeling was compounded by the obvious connection between them. And while I'm sure—I know—they had squabbles and different points of view, their relationship seemed easy and seamless.

I was jealous, I admit. I wanted that closeness, that connection. Something I thought I had until I saw the real thing, up close. Something I thought I knew until it came time to explain myself.

It was a few weeks after the earthquake when Karen asked me about Craig for the first time. We knew by then that we'd be cut off from the world for a while, that we weren't going anywhere. That the power and cell service weren't coming back on anytime soon. The quake had knocked out the hydroelectric dam that supplied power to Tswanaland and the surrounding countries, and had felled cell towers like trees in a clear-cutting operation. We were safe, better off than most, but alone.

Karen found me on my daily walk, the Daily Weep as I'd started to call it, poking fun at my own behavior to try to break the spell I seemed to have placed myself under. It wasn't working yet, but I had hopes.

"Is this about the boy?" Karen asked as I brushed my tears away and wiped the dust from my shorts.

"No, it's about . . . I don't know what it's about, really."

She raised her eyebrows in a way that said—to me—that maybe it should be.

I stood and followed her through the grove of jackalberry trees. There was a circle of flies hovering around my ears. I stifled the useless desire to swat them away. Wasted energy that only seemed to bring on more flies, not fewer.

"What is this boy like?" she asked in a tone that reminded me of my mom. My mom always wanted to know about the boys I was dating and never showed her disapproval, even when I was sometimes trying mightily to attract it.

I searched for a description. "Tall. Cute. A lawyer."

"You have a lot in common?"

"Oh, sure."

"How come he didn't come with you on the trip?"

I ran my hand over the back of my neck, wiping away an accumulation of dust and sweat. "He wanted to."

"But?"

"I don't know. The trip didn't seem to be about him, us. I thought . . ."

"That if you had some space, you could figure things out?"

"Yeah, maybe."

She shook her head and took a left along the path, a direction I hadn't been in before.

"What?" I asked.

"Well . . . we don't know each other very well, Emma, but it seems to me that if you have something to figure out about a person, it's better to do it with him than without him."

"You're probably right. Where are we going, anyway?"

"We'll be there in a minute."

A breeze blew. The leaves rustled overhead, mixing with the buzzing insects, creating a din I hadn't grown used to yet, especially at night.

We walked in silence through the last stand of trees before coming to a large grass field. Karen came to rest in front of a dirt mound that I realized after a moment was a rounded piece of corrugated iron painted to fade into the landscape.

"Here, help me open the door," Karen said.

"What is this thing, the Hatch?"

"Huh?"

"Nothing."

"It's where we keep our food supplies. I want to take stock to figure out if we need to start rationing."

"Do you really think that's necessary?"

Karen glanced at me over her shoulder. "We're going to be out here for a while, Emma. I thought you understood that."

"No, I know, it's just . . . rationing."

She nodded. "More serious than boyfriend troubles?"

"Something like that."

I stood next to Karen and put my hands on the rough edge of a round piece of metal, thick like a manhole cover. We pushed against it, the arms in our muscles taut, and I thought at first that it wouldn't budge. But then the seal gave, emitting a sound like a door into a clean room, and it rolled across the ground to reveal a relatively large bunker lined with cheap metal shelving. Karen picked a flashlight up off the nearest shelf and clicked it on. She snapped it into my hand.

"You take the right side and I'll take the left, all right?"

It was hot and stuffy inside; a patch of sunlight followed us through the door. I looked down the long, dark row of jars and cans, half expecting to see the Dharma Initiative's logo somewhere. It looked like there was enough food for months, but I guess that was the point. I watched as Karen took a clipboard off the wall and affixed a sheet of paper to it, then I did the same, adjusting the flashlight to illuminate a tub of peanut butter.

Another day in paradise.

When I get home from TPC, it's after dark, and the apartment is cold and empty. I turn up the heat and walk toward my bedroom. On the way, I glance into the room where Dominic's been sleeping. It's full of boxes, and there are a couple of blown-up black-and-white photographs in large black frames propped against one of the walls. I'd always meant to turn this room into a proper study. Maybe Dominic is going to make it a darkroom. Either way, I really shouldn't stay here for much longer.

Feeling exhausted, I decide to take a shower. I peel off Dominic's clothes and step under the hot spray. Maybe if I scrub hard enough, I can erase this day along with another layer of skin?

Not bloody likely.

If only my mother could see me now. I know she thought I needed to change some things in my life—why else would she have sent me so far away from it—but she couldn't have meant for me to have to go through this. And why did she think that, anyway? I was on the brink of partnership at a prestigious law firm. I had a handsome boyfriend. I was, to be honest, the daughter to boast about, the one other parents used with their own disappointing children, saying, "Why can't you be more like Emma?"

Craig, Craig, *Craig*. His numbers are still sitting in my coat pocket, uncalled. What the hell is wrong with me? Why isn't he the first thing on my mind? Why hasn't he been for months? Craig, the perfect guy on paper, who loves me and wants to be with me and understands me, but who didn't feel like enough a continent away.

When my hands turn to prunes, I turn off the shower and wrap myself in a towel. I hear my cell phone ringing in the distance.

Steph!

I run from the bathroom and skid across the floor toward my coat.

"Hello?"

"Em?"

"Craig?"

"Jesus Christ, Em." He sounds upset, really upset. "When I didn't hear from you again, I thought . . . I mean, they said . . ."

"I know."

"Where've you been? Why didn't you call me?"

"Didn't you get my email?"

"What? No. When did you send it?"

"Four days ago. Five, maybe. From London."

"The first time you tried to email me was five days ago?"

"No. I mean, yes, but I couldn't before. There wasn't any way—"

"Do you really expect me to believe that?"

I sink to the floor, resting my back against the textured wall. "But it's true! If you only knew what it was like there. I tried to contact you, more than once, but there just wasn't any way."

"But even if that *is* true, it doesn't explain why you haven't called me since you've been back."

"I know, Craig. But I did try. Your home number is disconnected. And your voice mail at work said you were away. I didn't know how to reach you."

"Why didn't you try emailing me again? Or calling someone else at work?"

Yeah, why didn't I?

"I don't know. Everything has been kind of overwhelming since I got back. My landlord rented my apartment to someone else and threw out all my things. Matt thinks I should go back to school, and Stephanie's missing—"

He sighs loudly. "Okay, Em, please. Stop."

I can imagine him, wherever he is, running his hand over his face, his fingers squeezing his temples. Craig's never liked confrontation. He doesn't have the stamina for it. It's why he left litigation for the corporate department. It occurs to me that I'm using my knowledge of him to get myself out of trouble that I should be in. My chest feels tight, like someone's squeezing, squeezing, and I'm glad I'm already on the floor.

"I'm sorry, Craig. I'm just trying to tell you what happened."

His tone softens. "Tell me."

I give him the synopsis.

I leave out the thoughts in my head.

He listens the way he always has, with sympathy and interest and intelligence. When I tell him, briefly, about Dominic, he even offers to let me stay at his place, if I need to, though he seems tentative in his offer, like he hasn't quite forgiven me. But the longer we talk, the further I feel from the distance I felt in Africa.

"I'll be home in three days," he says when I'm done.

"Not any sooner?"

"No, I'm sorry. I can't."

And what's wrong with being with Craig, anyway? What's wrong with having a perfect-on-paper life?

"It's okay. I understand."

"We'll talk when I get back, all right?"

Nothing. That's what. And only someone who doesn't know how good she has it would think there is.

"Yes."

He pauses. "I missed you, Em."

Maybe this is my turning point?

"I missed you too," I reply. And in this moment, it's the truth. "Let's talk tomorrow."

"I'd like that." He pauses again. "Good night, Em."

I take a deep breath. This is our code for "I love you." No matter what the time of day, he always says, "Good night, Em," and I always answer with "Sleep tight, Craig."

So he still loves me. And don't I love him too? Haven't I always? If he were standing before me now, wouldn't I walk into his arms, breathe in the familiar spicy scent of his skin, and feel safe?

"Sleep tight, Craig."

I can almost hear his smile down the line, and as I stand and close the phone, there's an answering smile on my face. Right at this moment, it feels good to hear Craig's coded "I love you."

"Who were you talking to?" Dominic asks.

I squeal in fright, jumping a foot in the air and spinning around to face him. He's standing in the entranceway, unbuttoning his coat. His camera bag rests at his feet.

"You shouldn't sneak up on a girl like that."

"Apparently not."

I feel a cold draft and realize I've let the towel slip, partially exposing one of my breasts. I pull it up hastily, hoping Dominic didn't notice. One glance at his face tells me he did.

"Um, I think I'm going to get changed."

"Right. You hungry?"

"Very."

I close the door to the bedroom and lean against it. My head feels like a buzz saw has been let loose inside it. I lie on the bed for a while, trying to collect my thoughts. When that proves impossible, I change into another set of Dominic's old clothes (cords and a sweater with holes in the elbows) and pull my damp hair into a ponytail. In the kitchen, Dominic's standing over a large orange stew pot, a wooden spoon in his hand. The cutting board on the counter is full of meat and vegetable scraps.

"Whatever that is, it smells amazing."

"It's Irish stew."

"An old family recipe?"

"But of course."

I sit down. The table holds two wineglasses and an open bottle of red wine. I pour a large glass and swallow a mouthful. It tastes delicious and familiar. Too familiar.

I look at the label. It just happens to be my favorite wine, several cases of which were in my storage locker (along with my road bike, my skis, and any number of things I shudder to think about) the last time I checked.

"Where did this wine come from?"

"I found it in the storage locker."

My heart gives a hopeful beat. "You didn't happen to find anything else down there, did you?"

"Just some questionable framed movie posters."

"*The Breakfast Club* is not a questionable movie."

"True, but have you watched *Pretty in Pink* lately?"

"John Hughes was a formative influence."

"I can tell."

I take a few sips from my glass, thinking over the conversation with Craig, wondering if I should take up his offer to stay in his apartment. Whether the solitude of the familiar or the company of a stranger is the better choice. Assuming, that is, that I have a choice.

"Um, Dominic, I know I only asked to stay the one night, but—"

"You need some more time to find a place?" he says with a resigned tone.

I nod, feeling guilty about keeping Craig's offer a secret. But I feel reluctant about staying there without him. I can't quite locate why, but it's enough for me to press my luck. "Is it okay if I stay a bit longer? I can pay you rent if you like."

"Sure, why the hell not?"

I take a seat at the table, trying to decide whether his flat tone implies acceptance or sarcasm. I don't know him well enough to tell. I decide to take it as acceptance, thank him, and change the subject.

"You never said—how come you were looking for an apartment at Christmas?"

His hand clenches the knife he's holding, his knuckles turning white.

"Dominic, I'm sorry, I didn't mean—"

"No, I know."

"It's just, you know all these details of my life, and you're—"

He puts the knife down. "Still anonymous?"

"Yeah."

He picks up the bottle and pours some wine into his glass. He takes a large swallow. "This is really good."

"I can't believe Pedro missed it."

His lips smile, but it doesn't travel to his eyes. He takes a deep breath. "A couple of weeks ago, I came home early from a business trip and found my fiancée in bed with my best friend."

"I'm sorry, Dominic. I had no idea."

"Me neither." A cruel look crosses his face. "And you know what's funny? Getting married was *her* idea. 'People get married,' she said. So I spent more money than I could afford on a ring, and I took her to this little inn up north. I even got down on one knee next to a lake at sunset, for Chrissakes."

"That sounds really nice, sweet even."

"That's what she said. But she was already sleeping with Chris when she said yes. Turns out it's been going on for months. Maybe longer." He drains his glass in one long swallow, then refills it nearly to the rim. "And that's what I don't get. Why get me to propose to her if she didn't really want to be with me?"

"Maybe you're the guy she thinks she should be with."

"Yeah, maybe. Anyway, most of my friends, they're 'our' friends, and while I'm pretty sure they're taking my side, I just can't face the whole pity party. When I remembered Tara saying something about the apartment downstairs being for rent, it seemed like the perfect solution. And that's how I ended up here."

"I'm sorry."

"Yeah, well, fuck it, you know? Fuck *her*." He half empties his glass. "Fuck the both of them, come to think of it."

"Thank you for telling me."

"Sure. You want to eat?"

"Absolutely."

He fills two soup bowls with large helpings of stew. It tastes as good as it smells.

"You know, this is far and away the best Irish stew I've ever had."

"Thanks, but I'm guessing your taste buds have been good-taste-deprived recently."

"You may have a point, but it's still really good."

"How was the police station?" he asks.

"Only slightly less painful than work."

"Maybe tomorrow will be better?"

I raise my glass in a mock toast. "Here's hoping."

Chapter 7
Imagine the Possibilities

Africa again. Same dream, same smells, same wide-open sky.

Only this time? When my mother appears? She doesn't warn me that the coughing, flushed guide who's serving dinner is sick. Instead, she tells me to eat everything on my plate like a good little girl. There are starving kids in Africa.

And in that moment I know. My mother knows I'm going to get sick.

My mother *wants* me to get sick.

"Emma? You awake?"

My eyes fly open. I expect to see Karen's face poking through the tent flap, but it's only Dominic, standing in the doorway in his striped pajamas holding a cell phone in the palm of his right hand.

"I think so."

"Your phone keeps ringing."

I sit up. My throat feels dusty, and my skin feels like it's spent too much time in the sun. "Sorry, did it wake you?"

"I needed to get up anyway. Here, catch." He tosses me the phone. It flies through the air in a perfect arc, landing in the blankets in my lap.

I look at the blinking message light and my heart starts to race. Please, please, please let it be Stephanie. I flip it open and look at the number. It's local and familiar. A little too familiar. I dial into my voice mail, ready to be disappointed.

"Hi, Emma, it's Matt. I've spoken to the Management Committee, and it's looking good, but there are a few things I wanted to discuss with you. Call me at the office when you get this message."

I close the phone and slump down.

"Bad news?" Dominic says.

"Good news, I think. About work."

"Are you sure that's good news?"

"I like my job."

He gives me a skeptical look.

"What?"

"Nothing. I've just never met a lawyer who actually liked what she did."

I throw back the covers and stand up. The cold seeps through my naked feet. "Well, now you have."

"Who'd you want the call to be from?"

"My best friend, Stephanie. She's gone looking for me."

"Ah."

I nod. "That about sums it up."

"Coffee?"

"That'd be great."

I stare at the phone in my hand. I never called Stephanie's mother back like I promised I would. And maybe, just maybe, they've heard from her. I punch the buttons and get Lucy on the first ring. I'm not the only one anxious for news. She's glad to hear from me, but she doesn't know any more than I do. Of course they'll call me the minute they know anything. I hang up with a hollow feeling in my heart. When I thought of coming home, all those months, I never thought I'd feel more alone here than when I was halfway around the world.

"Do you want eggs?" Dominic asks from the kitchen.

"Yes, please," I yell back. "I'll be there in a minute."

I return Matt's call, my heart fluttering. The rational part of my brain knows they must be willing to take me back, but its connection to the fears-and-irrational-thoughts part of my brain seems to be broken.

"Emma, thanks for returning my call," Matt says in a cheery tone.

"Of course."

"I've spoken to the Management Committee, and every-thing's all set."

"That's great, Matt. Thank you."

Did I just thank him for giving me an opportunity to make

them hundreds of thousands of dollars every year? My pleaser complex must be in overdrive.

"We thought with it being Christmas, it would be best if you started in January."

"Sure, I understand."

"And we'd appreciate it if you'd do a bit of press in the interim."

"Press?"

"We've had a request for you to appear on Cathy Keeler's show."

"You want me to go on *In Progress*?"

"That's right."

"But millions of people watch that show. Why does she want to interview me?"

"It's a great story, isn't it? Everyone thinking you were dead, you being on the ground during the earthquake, your triumphant return to work."

I can hear the deep baritone voice-over already. *When Emma Tupper set out on her fateful journey, burdened by grief, she hoped Africa's beauty would heal her heart. She wasn't expecting to fall afoul of illness and destruction . . .*

I hate those goddamn shows.

"You really want me to do this?"

"It would be great publicity for you."

Great publicity for TPC, more like it.

"Yeah, I guess."

"Trust me, Emma, the benefits could be enormous."

Which means, of course, that I don't really have any choice in the matter. Not if I want to start things off on the right foot.

"Right, I understand. I'll do it."

"Excellent. Her people will be calling you to set up the details for tomorrow."

My stomach flips. "Tomorrow? Isn't that a little soon?"

"There's no time like the present."

Sure there is. There's the future, when I've had time to get some decent clothes and my hair cut, and I'm not quite so fragile.

I try to inject some confidence into my voice. "Sounds good."

"Good luck. I know you'll be great."

We hang up, and I take a long look at myself in the mirror. My wheat-colored hair is six months past a haircut. My eyes have always been a little too round and far apart for my liking, and my face is thinner than it should be. My ordinary lips are still cracked from the sun, and the bridge of my nose is peeling. I look older than the last time I saw myself this clearly. As I stare and stare, I don't know what I'm looking for exactly. My mother? Myself? The self before I became introspective and brittle? Well, she may have looked a lot like the girl in the mirror, but the person inside? The woman I was?

She's missing, presumed dead.

I walk to the kitchen, needing caffeine but no longer hungry. I sip my coffee as I watch Dominic make scrambled eggs with chopped-up bacon and cheese mixed in like a professional. I can tell by the blue patch of sky out the window that it's freezing outside.

He serves me a large helping along with the newspaper. "Look who made the front page."

I look at it with trepidation. The headline reads MISSING LAWYER RETURNS UNSCATHED. There's a TPC publicity shot of me staring at the camera with my arms crossed over my chest, a small smile playing on my lips. I look . . . ferocious.

"You're famous," Dominic says.

"I see that."

I put the newspaper down and start eating my eggs. They taste great, but my mind is preoccupied with the lingering disorientation the Dream always leaves, and seeing my life become front-page news.

"What's on the agenda today?" Dominic asks as he uses a piece of toast to shovel eggs into his mouth. "Christmas shopping? Skating on the canal? Making snow angels?"

I nearly choke on a piece of bacon. "Making snow angels? Do I look like I'm seven?"

He looks me up and down.

"What are you doing?"

"Trying to guess your age."

"This should be interesting."

He squints at me. "Thirty-four and three-quarters."

"What? That's impossible."

"I'm right, aren't I?"

"How did you know?"

"I'm psychic."

"No way I'm falling for that."

He taps the paper. "It says how old you are in the article."

I glance down at my serious face. It really wouldn't hurt me to smile once in a while. Show a little teeth. "It says I'm thirty-four and three-quarters?"

"I just added the three-quarters part for kicks."

"You get your kicks in some strange places."

"Sue me."

"Seriously? You know I'm a lawyer, right?"

"I've been trying to block that out."

"Ha, ha. Anyway, you asked about my agenda?"

"Did I?"

"Yes. A few minutes ago, yes."

"Well, then, I must've wanted to know."

"You ready for this? My office just signed me up for a session with Cathy Keeler."

His eyebrows rise toward his hairline. "You're going to be on TV with *her*?"

"Tomorrow, apparently."

"Jesus."

"You think He can help me find the right outfit?"

He points his fork at me. "See, I knew shopping was in there somewhere."

"Really, Dominic, you don't have to come with me," I say as we walk down the frosty street toward my bank. I'm wearing Dominic's old fisherman's sweater and his ski jacket. It's keeping out most of the wind that's swirling a fine mist of snow around us, glinting in the sun. The sun seems to have seeped into Dominic too. He almost has a spring in his step.

"I don't mind."

"You must have something else to do. Photographs to take? Stew to make? Other damsels in distress to save?"

"No, no, and . . . no."

"It's becoming clear to me that you really had no life before I came along."

He wags his index finger at me. "Watch it, honey. Watch it."

We walk past a familiar store. That last time I shopped there, it was with Steph. We tried on every dress in the store, from too expensive to too-ugly-to-imagine-what-anyone-was-thinking. We mocked and exclaimed, and I bought three of them. I wore one to my mother's funeral, a plain-black number that I'm actually glad I'll never see again.

What the hell has happened to my life? One minute Steph is teasing me about not having enough room in my closet, and the next I can't even reach her and I'm wearing a strange man's clothing. I start to shiver, my teeth clacking loudly as tears spring from my eyes. They feel cold against my cheeks.

"What's the matter?" Dominic asks.

What's the matter seems so obvious to me, like I'm carrying it around outside my body, visible to everyone, that I almost laugh.

"It's everything. Steph being where she is, and my career in the toilet, and not even having a picture of my mother, and . . . I have nothing. Nothing."

Dominic reaches into his pocket and pulls out a Kleenex. I take it from him gratefully and wipe my eyes and nose. Given the amount of crying I'm doing lately, I really should start carrying a handkerchief, but that feels like admitting something about myself that I don't want to. Weakness, maybe.

I bunch up the Kleenex and shove it angrily into my pocket. "Goddamnit! I wasn't going to cry today."

Dominic gives me a kind smile. "I think it's a normal reaction, Emma."

"Not for me. You don't really know me, but this is not how I normally react to things."

"How do you normally react?"

"I don't know. *Fiercely*, I guess."

"Well, you were pretty fierce with Pedro."

"I was, wasn't I?"

"I would've been scared if I were him."

"Thanks."

We walk in silence for a few moments. The snow crunches beneath our feet.

"You know," Dominic says, "if everything in your life is fucked up, you can change whatever you want."

"I guess."

He shoves his hands into his pockets. "I've been thinking about it a lot lately, ever since, well, you know. And the thing that keeps occurring to me, the *only* positive thing, is that I can start over. How many people have a chance to change something major in their lives without having to suffer the consequences?"

I give him a look. "You think I'm not suffering the consequences?"

"I didn't mean it that way. I meant, and maybe this sounds silly, but, I don't know, just imagine the possibilities."

"Like what?"

He thinks about it. "You could change your job."

"But I love my job."

He smiles ruefully. "Will you work with me here?"

"Okay, okay. I get it. I don't have to be me anymore, if I don't want to be."

"Exactly."

"I guess that could be a good thing."

"Trust me, it will be. Now . . ." He rubs his hands together. "You need some of that over-the-hip grandma underwear, right?"

A laugh bubbles out of me. "How'd you guess?"

Dominic sees me through the Catch-22 ordeal I have to go through at the bank to get access to my life savings, despite the papers Detective Nield gave me. (Sample exchange: "We need proof that you're alive in order to reactivate your account." "What are you talking about? I'm standing right in front of you." "Our files indicate that you're likely deceased." "You've got to be kidding me.") I consider going postal, but instead I go to my Zen place and explain my situation to the floor manager, branch manager, and finally regional manager, who, thankfully, read that morning's paper. After several apologies, I'm issued brand-spanking-new credit and bank cards, and I feel oddly rich. Maybe it's because I haven't spent any money in over six months, but the comfortable number of zeros in my bank account puts me in the mood to shop.

I get rid of Dominic 1.5 stores later, partly because it feels weird to be picking outfits with a man I hardly know, but mostly because he has some pretty definitive opinions on fashion.

"Leggings are for schoolgirls," he says as I eye a pair from Lindsay Lohan's collection.

"Who made you the boss of my wardrobe?"

"Just looking out for you, honey."

"I thought guys didn't care what girls wore, unless it involved schoolgirl uniforms."

"Mmm."

"What?"

"Now I'm imagining you in a schoolgirl uniform."

I take a whack at his arm. "Quit it."

Dominic laughs and directs me toward Banana Republic, telling me that it seems more like my kind of store. He's right, of course (my pre-Africa wardrobe was 85 percent Banana), but I act affronted. Didn't he just tell me I could change anything about myself I didn't like?

"But you like this store."

"Did it say that about me in the paper too?"

"Nah, I can just tell."

"You know what? I think I can take it from here."

"You want me to go?"

"I think it would be best."

"All right, but don't come crying to me if you buy a bunch of things you're never going to wear. And stay away from scoop necks. They make you look like a soccer mom."

"Out," I order.

I get home after dinnertime, full of food-court burrito and poorer, but with a good start on rebuilding my wardrobe. And not a scoop neck in sight.

Dominic's slouched on the couch in the living room with his feet propped up on the coffee table. He has a pair of over-sized headphones covering his ears, and his iPod rests on the couch next to him. I dump my packages in the hall and join him, taking a seat in the armchair that sits kitty-corner to the couch.

He slings his headphones around his neck. "Successful trip?"

"I bought five pairs of leggings."

"A bold choice."

"Whatcha listening to?"

"*Mermaid Avenue.*"

"What's that?"

"Billy Bragg and Wilco singing Woody Guthrie songs. They took these old, unrecorded lyrics and added music."

"Huh."

"It's really good. You should listen to it."

I shrug. "I'm not a big fan of country music."

He brings his feet to the floor and leans forward in a pose I recognize. He's about to try to convince me of the error of my ways.

"It's not country, it's folk."

"Mmm. Tell me. If I said that it's all the same to me, would you freak out?"

"You're not into music?"

"No, I like music. But not in that obsessive way most guys do. Like, I bet you know all the track names of the songs on this *Mermaid Sessions* thing."

He grits his teeth. "It's *Mermaid Avenue.*"

"You see what I mean? A woman would never get upset if you got something like that wrong."

"Some women might."

"Sure, right. If they were interested in you."

"You're saying women just pretend to be interested in things men are interested in?"

"This is news to you?"

"Kind of."

I lean back on the soft cushions. "You like that famous photographer, right? What's his name? You know, the black-and-white photos you have in your room?"

"You mean . . . Ansel Adams?"

"Yeah, him. Anyway, I'll bet the women you've brought home have all told you how much they like those prints, right?"

He gets a funny expression on his face. "You don't like them?"

"I find him a bit boring, to be honest."

"Okay."

"Sorry, is he a big influence?"

"You could say that."

"What kind of photographs do you take?"

He fiddles with the headphones in his lap. "Whatever catches my attention."

"Give me an example."

"Well, recently, I've been in Dublin photographing the countryside being gobbled up by housing developments."

"That sounds interesting."

He perks up a bit. "Yeah, it's actually turned out pretty well. I even found this family that's still traveling around by horse and buggy. I got a great shot of them with the IBM campus in the background, just visible through the mist."

"It's pretty cool that you can make a living doing that."

"I've been really lucky."

"I'd like to see some of your stuff sometime."

His mouth twists. "You already have."

"No, I don't think so. Oh. The boring Ansel Adams pictures?"

He winces. "So glad you repeated the 'boring' part. It didn't quite kill me the first time."

"I'm sorry."

"Don't worry about it."

"No, I do this. I try to make some stupid point and I end up being a jerk."

"Don't be hard on yourself, Emma. It's been a rough couple of days."

"True."

His eyes wander to a stack of boxes in the corner. "Speaking of which, I've got a surprise for you."

"You do? Really?"

"I need a few minutes to set it up."

"What is it?"

He smiles. "If I told you what it was, it wouldn't be a surprise. Why don't you go try on your new clothes, and come back in twenty minutes."

I try to protest, but he shoos me out. I unpack my bags in my room. I bought mostly suits, but I managed to find a couple of pairs of jeans I liked too. I slip on a roomy, boyfriend-cut pair and top it with a light-blue turtleneck. As I gather Dominic's clothes into a pile, I hear a loud *thunk!* in the living room. Dominic seems to be moving heavy things around. Like the couch, and possibly a lamp.

"What the hell are you doing in there?" I yell.

"You'll see," he calls back.

"You've got five minutes."

"Nice try! I have at least eight."

I brush my hair with my new hairbrush and check my cell phone for what feels like the millionth time. Still no callback from Stephanie. If I don't hear from her soon, I'm going to file a missing-person report. The irony of this is not lost on me.

I slip the phone into my pocket and go to Dominic's room to take a better look at the framed pictures sitting on the floor. They're black-and-white shots of a sharp mountain range in a desert. The frame is made of dense wood that's so dark it's almost black. When I look more closely at the base of the mountains, I realize there's a cityscape full of familiar skylines hidden in the shadows. Paris, and possibly Seattle. *Mahoney, 2010, Las Vegas* is scratched into the lower right-hand corner.

"You can come in!"

I walk into the living room filled with curiosity. Dominic's standing proudly in front of a tall Christmas tree strewn with small twinkling white lights and sparkly ornaments.

"How did you do this?"

"It's pretty good, isn't it?"

"It's amazing."

I walk closer, and now I can see that it's not a real tree, just a really good fake. I reach out and rub a few needles between my fingers. "How come I'm smelling pine?"

He grins. "I wondered if you'd notice. A couple of the ornaments are actually those car air fresheners."

"I don't know what to say. Thank you, Dominic."

"You think I put this up for you? Nah. This is what I was supposed to be doing the night you fell at my feet."

"Thank you anyway."

I step toward him and kiss him on the cheek. Dominic starts as my lips touch his skin, and we step away from each other.

I open my mouth to say something—I'm not sure what—when my phone starts to ring, its sound muffled by the fabric of my brand-new jeans.

"You should get that," he says.

"It might be Stephanie," I say at the same time.

I pull out my phone. "Hello?"

"Is this Emma Tupper?"

Disappointed again.

"Yes?"

"This is Carrie. From Cathy Keeler's show?"

I walk into the hall. "Oh, hi. How did you get this number?"

"Mr. Stuart gave it to us."

"Right. Of course."

"I just wanted to tell you that we are *so excited* you'll be doing the show tomorrow."

That makes one of us.

"Stories like yours are *so inspiring*, especially this close to Christmas. Our audience *just loves* happy endings."

Somebody thinks my story has a happy ending?

"Uh-huh."

She tells me where they're located. "We'll need you to be at the studio by three for hair and makeup. And, of course, we'll be doing a preinterview and a walk-through. Is that good for you?"

"I guess."

"Great! See you then. And call me if you have *any questions.*"

I close the phone and through a supreme act of will avoid throwing it at the wall. Of all the things I've let Matt talk me into over the years, this has to be the worst.

I walk back to the living room. Dominic's started the gas fire and is sitting on the couch, watching the hockey game with the volume turned low.

His eyes leave the screen. They're dark, troubled. "Was it Stephanie?"

"No."

We stare at each other awkwardly, an odd current in the air.

I break the silence. "Anyway, I'm feeling pretty tired. I think I'm going to turn in early."

"All right."

"Thanks for the tree."

"Anytime."

Chapter 8
Meet the Press

I wake up the next morning with a restless feeling in my heart. It's still pitch-dark outside, a blackness that doesn't reveal whether it's closer to midnight or dawn. I toss and turn, but I can't fall back asleep. I'm going to be interviewed today by a woman who relishes confrontation. Another me, only with better hair and makeup, and a much larger audience.

Matt is going to owe me big-time.

When I realize sleep isn't coming back, I go to the kitchen to start the coffee brewing. A half-empty bottle of my favorite wine is sitting on the counter, a reminder of better times. Craig and I bought it on a trip we took a year and a half ago to Sonoma. We spent our days wine tasting and our nights eating enormous meals in cozy restaurants with candles on the table.

Nothing felt like it was missing that week.

I called Craig last night after I left Dominic to his hockey game. He was in a meeting, and I knew thirty seconds in that the call was a mistake. I didn't know what I wanted to say to him, and I think he could sense my ambivalence. Which led him back to questioning why I'd been out of touch for so long, whether it had really been impossible to call or email him for all those months. How I must've known he'd be out of his mind with worry. All I could do was apologize and apologize, but he'd already heard that and it didn't seem to be enough. Like the night before I left, it wasn't the time for a serious conversation, but we could both sense it coming.

Thoughts like these don't quell my restlessness, and a few moments later, I find myself prying open the door to the dank basement. A bare lightbulb illuminates a set of furnaces and hot-water heaters for my apartment and the one above. Two little rooms have been built at the back to serve as storage lockers. Mine is on the right, locked tight with a lock I don't recognize. Dominic must have the combination, that twice-to-the-right-once-to-the-left-and-back-to-the-last-number pattern that might unlock a part of my past. But he told me it was empty except for the wine and the posters I don't need to see. Why am I down here?

I walk over to the long workbench that never used to hold any tools. Some of Dominic's photography equipment is stacked on it, along with a black portfolio case. I unzip it and flip slowly through the pages. It contains eight-by-ten versions of the photographs in his room and others from the same series. One page must've been shot in Ireland. It's of a rolling field filled with flowers—heather, maybe—and even though it's in black and white, it's so vivid it feels like the green grass of Ireland is just beneath the surface. It would only take a scratch to reveal it.

The talent on the page blows me away, and I stare at it for a few minutes before I hear the beep of the coffee machine above my head. I realize I'm shivering in the cold, damp room, and I trip up the stairs, shutting the door firmly behind me.

A cup of coffee later brings a sleepy-headed Dominic to the kitchen. His mood is the same as it was yesterday morning, and he happily serves eggs sunny-side up with large glasses of orange juice. While he's cooking, he tells me funny stories about when he worked as a line cook to pay his way through art school.

"Did you think about staying on, becoming a chef?"

"I did. But I had all these massive student loans, and a chef's life is pretty brutal."

"And you had landscapes to shoot," I say, smiling.

"I did."

After breakfast, I wash the pans while Dominic loads the dishwasher. And then I make a beeline for the one man I've never had complicated feelings about—my hairdresser, Antoine.

Forty, French, and fabulous, Antoine greats me with genuine happiness. His skin is milk chocolate, and his black hair is cropped so short it looks like a five o'clock shadow. He's wearing low-slung jeans that look like they were painted on and a black T-shirt with a decal of a spangly Christmas tree on it. A Lady Gaga song blares from the sound system. The air smells like a mixture of raspberry and hair spray.

When Antoine releases me from a tight hug, I give him the CliffsNotes version of the last six months, filling in the gaps from what he read in the newspaper as he leads me through the busy salon toward his station.

"You know, *chérie,* you look fabulous. Thin, tanned. This *aventure* you had, it agreed with you."

"Antoine, you can't be serious."

"But I am. Here, look." He sits me down in his barber's chair and spins me toward the large mirror that's framed by bright round lights. "You see. *La dernière fois* I saw you, your skin it was so pale, and *les cercles,* you know, the circles under your eyes, they were black."

I peer into the mirror, trying to see what he sees. While I still see all the defects I noticed yesterday, he is right about one thing: The semipermanent dark circles under my eyes are gone.

What does it say about my job that six months in an earthquake-ravaged country was what I needed to look rested?

"Well, maybe. But you can't think my hair is fabulous."

He makes a face. "*Non,* that is true. Your hairs, they are terrible."

"Can you do something for me?"

He picks up a chunk of my too-long, split-ended hair, folding it through his tapered, manicured fingers. He gets a faraway look in his eyes. "Oh, yes. I can see it now. We will cut it short, yes, with layers, and perhaps a spiky *toupette*."

I scan through my high school French. "A *toupette*, you mean bangs?"

"*Oui.*"

"*Non.* No big changes, Antoine. I'm going on television and I want to look like me, only better."

"*Mais pourquoi?*"

"Apparently Cathy Keeler thinks my story makes a good Christmas fable."

His brown eyes widen. "Cathy Keeler? *Mon dieu*, she's a . . . a cat, a tiger."

"Antoine, that is not helping my confidence."

He picks up his sharp stainless steel scissors, *snip, snipping* next to my ear. "Don't worry, *chérie*, I will give you all the confidence you will need."

I arrive at the TV studio at 3 P.M. with a garment bag containing several potential outfits and my hair looking, well, fabulous. Antoine cut off just enough to showcase my cheekbones, and talked me into a compromise on the bangs that I'm happy with. My hair feels silky and touchable. Now, if only Antoine could've done something about my booming heart.

The lobby of the ultramodern building looks like it was inspired by the starship *Enterprise*, with walls of white, glossy Formica and lighting so bright I wish I had shades. I give my name to the squat, overweight receptionist sitting behind a command-central desk made out of the same material. She calls Carrie to tell her I'm here, then leads me to my dressing room. As we walk down the brightly lit hall, I can't help but notice the familiar names on the closed dressing room doors. Big names. Famous names.

Why, oh why, did I let Matt talk me into this?

We stop at a door marked GUEST inside a yellow star. The room looks like a small hotel suite, with rich cream fabric on the walls and a squashy white couch. There's a frosted-glass coffee table in front of it holding a fruit plate covered in clingy plastic film.

"Carrie will be with you shortly," the receptionist says, already halfway down the hall.

I set my garment bag down on the couch and mentally scroll through the outfits I brought. I eventually decide on a pair of gray wool pants with a subtle check and a cobalt-blue cashmere sweater.

There's a gentle knock on the door and a tiny woman with black hair cut like a pixie pokes her head into the room. She's wearing cuffed tweed trousers and a crisp white business shirt. Several coats of mascara frame her caramel eyes. Her eyebrows are plucked into a thin, dark line.

"Hi, Emma. Is it okay if I come in?"

"Of course."

She extends her hand. "I'm Carrie. I'm *so pleased* to meet you."

We shake. Her fingers feel delicate, breakable.

"Such a *good choice* on your outfit," she says.

"Oh, uh, thanks."

"Rich colors look much better on-screen. Are you feeling nervous?"

Nervous? No. Like I might throw up? Yes.

"A little."

She shows me her tiny teeth. "That's *totally normal*. But don't worry, we'll go through everything when you're in makeup."

"Sounds good."

I follow her to the makeup room. She runs through the topics Cathy Keeler will be covering. No surprise, it's all about how I got lost and found. I test out my answers as I give myself over to the makeup lady. When she's done, the angles in my face have been augmented and defined in a way that makes me almost unrecognizable.

I peel off the white paper towel around my neck, and Carrie leads me toward the studio. The room seems smaller than it does on television. Most of it is taken up by the stadium seating that climbs toward the back of the room. The chairs are filled with fifty chattering audience members. I scan the crowd quickly. It looks like the usual mix of housewives and students.

"Who's that girl?" I hear one of the women say loudly to the woman next to her.

"I think it's the one who got lost in Africa. That lawyer girl, you know."

"Dang. I was sure today was going to be Christmas give-aways. I never have any luck."

Join the club, lady.

I turn away from the audience. There are two small orange armchairs facing each other on a raised dais under a circle of bright lights. The last time I watched this show, a former presidential candidate was admitting he'd fathered an illegitimate child. Freaky.

Carrie speaks behind me. "Emma, this is Cathy."

I turn and come face-to-face with Cathy Keeler. Her hair is bright-red-from-a-bottle, and it falls straight to her chin from a sharp center part. Her skin is ghostly white, and the dark frames of her glasses focus the intelligent look in her pale blue eyes. She's wearing a black pin-striped suit that looks hand-made and large square diamonds in her ears.

"Hi, Emma, thanks for agreeing to do the show," she says in her modulated broadcaster voice. Her cadence is perfectly timed for reading a script off a teleprompter. "Carrie filled you in on the subjects we'll be covering?"

"I think so."

"Good. Take a seat and make yourself comfortable. We'll begin in about five minutes."

Making myself comfortable seems out of the question, but I sit down in the armchair she points to anyway. I smooth out the wrinkles in my pants while a guy in his early twenties with a mod haircut slips a tiny microphone under my sweater. It happens so quickly I barely have time to be embarrassed, though I'm pretty sure he caught an eyeful of . . . well, not much, really.

Cathy Keeler sits across from me with a nonchalance born of years of experience. She flips through a set of index cards, muttering to herself. I take several sips from the water glass sitting on a small table next to me, surveying the sea of faces watching us. The most common expression is one of disappointment. I guess a lot of people thought they were getting Christmas giveaways today.

The cameramen turn on their lights. I blink slowly in their glare as another guy in a headset darts toward Cathy and takes her notes. She squares her shoulders as a voice yells, "Quiet on set," and the familiar, slightly bombastic theme music for *In Progress* fills the room. When it stops, Cathy looks into the camera over my left shoulder.

"Good evening. Tonight I'll be talking to Emma Tupper. For those of you not yet familiar with her story . . ."

She continues for several minutes, outlining the facts. When she's done, she asks me some easy questions about how it feels to be home, and what I'm going to do now. I stick to the script I worked on earlier: It's amazing to be home; I'm going back to work in the new year, can't wait. I feel like Nuke LaLoosh in *Bull Durham* following Crash Davis's instructions when he gets to the Show. I'm lucky to be here; it's such an amazing opportunity.

Cathy smiles and nods, and leads me along smoothly until I've just about relaxed.

My mistake.

"Ms. Tupper, I have to say, your story doesn't really add up."

"What do you mean?"

"Well, for instance, why would the tour company leave you in the middle of nowhere?"

"I was sick."

"Shouldn't they have taken you to a hospital?"

"We were days away from one."

She raises her right eyebrow. "So they left you in a remote village instead?"

Why is that tone familiar? Oh, right. She sounds like me when I'm in the middle of cross-examining someone.

My throat goes dry. I take a sip of water as she waits for my answer. I put the glass down and measure out my words carefully. "When I got sick, we were in the middle of a wildlife preserve. It took us two days to drive there, and the 'road' was just a dirt track full of bumps and ruts and mud. Every second on it was excruciating, like someone was trying to jackhammer my body into a thousand pieces. I was kind of out of it, but I'm pretty sure I begged them to leave me by the side of the road. Instead, they took me to a village where they knew there were NGO workers who had good medical supplies. And that's where they left me."

"Why didn't the tour company come back to get you?"

"You'd have to ask them that."

Great. Now I sound like someone I've been cross-examining. Defensive. Like I have something to hide. Like I might start to cry any second.

"And you really couldn't get a message home for six whole months?"

"No."

"I see."

"I . . . I'm confused, Ms. Keeler. You seem to be implying that I'm making this whole thing up. Why would I do that?"

She makes a dismissive sound in her throat loud enough for only me to hear. "I'm not here to answer your questions, Ms. Tupper, but perhaps you're seeking attention? Your fifteen minutes of fame?"

"You think I *want* everyone to know what happened to me?"

She motions to the room. "You're here, aren't you?"

I lean away from her, aware again of the glare of the lights and the room full of women watching me expectantly, wondering, Will she break down? Is she telling the truth?

I knew this was a bad idea.

"I'm here because *you* invited *me,* Ms. Keeler. I didn't go looking for this. It wasn't even my idea to go on the trip, as you very well know, and I gave up a lot to go there."

"I assume you're referring to your boyfriend, Craig. You still haven't seen him, I believe?"

A nervous flutter twinges in my gut. "Yes, that's right."

She gives a gurgling laugh that must sound delightful on TV. "Well, when we heard about that, I have to say, we couldn't resist organizing a little reunion."

Organizing a little *what?*

She looks over my shoulder again, only this time, I know she's not looking into the camera. I turn my head, and there he is: Craig Talbot, living and breathing and walking toward me looking tired, and cuter than I remember in his favorite light gray suit. There are laugh lines around his pale blue eyes. His sandy hair is cut short and parted on the left.

Our eyes meet, and I feel like the whole room, the whole world, is watching, waiting for me to react like someone should when she sees her boyfriend for the first time in six months.

"Emma? Don't you want to say hi to Craig?"

I stand up and walk toward him, forcing myself to smile

like a happy, normal person who's just been given a great surprise. When I get near enough, I reach out and hug him. After a moment's hesitation, his arms slip around me, holding me tight. I breathe in his familiar, spicy spell. My legs feel weak.

"Emma," he says into my ear. "Welcome home."

We break apart and stare at each other as the room watches. In the complete silence I can hear a camera shutter opening and closing.

"Aren't you going to kiss her?" someone in the audience shouts.

And suddenly I know why Matt and the Management Committee wanted me to come here. They're looking for exposure, all right, they just think bigger than I do—they always have. Because this has all been about manufacturing the perfect happy ending to my freak-show tale to ensure that it gets maximum publicity and spreads TPC's name far and wide.

"Kiss, kiss, kiss," the audience chants like it's an episode of *Jerry Springer.*

Craig looks uncomfortable and embarrassed, but what can we do?

We kiss. The cameras whir.

Chapter 9

Where Everybody Knows Your Name

Craig and I are riding the elevator to his condo, standing shoulder to shoulder.

When we broke apart from our made-for-the-media kiss, Cathy Keeler went to commercial. Without quite looking me directly in the eye, Craig suggested we go to his apartment to "talk" once the show was over.

It's always such a good sign when a guy wants to talk.

I must've been in a state of shock during the final segment of the show, because I don't remember a word of what Cathy Keeler asked me, or what I answered. When the studio lights dimmed, Cathy thanked me as a man with a sign that said CLAP! encouraged the audience to put their hands together. They complied perfunctorily. Still pissed about the lack of giveaways, I guess.

"I'm sorry about that," Craig says. "Matt—"

"Said that the Management Committee would greatly appreciate it?"

He smiles. "Yes."

"I got the same speech."

We reach his floor and the elevator doors ding open. I follow Craig down the hall. His front door is an impressive piece of solid mahogany with a shiny set of chrome numbers at eye level. Inside, his apartment looks just as it always has, like a single, well-to-do man lives here. The walls are a dark gray-blue, and the furniture is all the same heavy mahogany as the front door. A rain forest had to die to make this apartment.

It's a place I've never felt quite comfortable in, no matter how much time I've spent here. Maybe that's why I didn't take him up on his offer to stay here while he was away?

"So," I say when we've taken off our coats and hung them on the chrome coatrack by the door, "you wanted to talk?"

Craig runs a hand through his hair, smoothing it down. He looks a little heavier than the last time I saw him, like he hasn't been eating well or working out. Craig's a one-thing-at-a-time kind of guy, and whenever things get crazy at work, he eats like crap and stops going to the gym.

"Emma, this might seem like I'm putting you off, but I had a long flight. I'd love to take a shower and get changed before . . . well, you know. Do you mind?"

"No, that's all right." And maybe by the time you get out, I'll know what to say.

"I won't be long. There should be some food in the fridge. I asked Juliana to stock it."

"Is she still cooking for you?"

"Of course. Why wouldn't she be?"

"I don't know, I keep expecting things to be the same, but then they're different—"

Craig shakes his head. "Shower, then talk, okay?"

"Yeah, sorry. Go, go."

I watch him walk toward his bedroom, then I pull out my cell phone to check if there's a message from Stephanie. No new messages. I dial her number, now memorized. It goes right to voice mail like it always does, and I leave her another message (this is not a test, this is my life) and close the phone.

Surprisingly hungry, I go to the kitchen to see what Juliana left. She's an amazing cook and totally devoted to Craig, an only child whose jet-setting parents didn't have much time for him when he was growing up. Instead, he had Juliana.

I find some chicken and saffron rice in a Tupperware container and put it in the microwave. When the dinger sounds, I plate it up and bring it to the dining room table. My eyes wander to the glass cabinet in the corner, which is filled with odds and ends from Craig's life (books he's never read, the paperweights his parents brought back from around the world, a few formal shots of him growing up). I check the top shelf, and there it is: the trophy we won at a litigation workshop we attended together four years ago.

Litigation boot camp, as we called it, was mandatory for all of TPC's litigators after a couple of years of practice. It was led by a group of sadistic men who took great pleasure in breaking lawyers down before building them back up.

Craig and I were paired for the week, which culminated in a daylong mock trial. I knew Craig before boot camp, but we'd never spent much time together. Up until then, I'd kind of written him off as one of those private-school, uptight assholes you meet a lot of in my profession.

As we worked around the clock preparing, I learned that I was both right and wrong about him. He could be one of those private-school, uptight assholes (it was kind of his default setting), but he was also really smart and thoughtful. We were too busy for romance that week, but he did all these little things that caught my attention. Like he let me do the closing argument, though I could tell he wanted to, and he had this sixth sense about when I needed more coffee, or snacks, or even, briefly, a back rub. It felt like we spent the whole week moving toward each other. And when we held the Best Team trophy between us and smiled for the photographer, I knew it was only a matter of time before we slept together.

I thought that might be all it was at first. But we had fun together, and we understood each other's crazy, unpredictable schedules, even when Craig's got worse once he left litigation and joined the Corporate department. Sometimes, when we were stuck at work after hours, we'd steal forty-five minutes together for dinner in an unused conference room. A few times we even snuck into the back reaches of the library and made love.

It was like that for years. We had good conversations, went on nice vacations, and rarely fought. If you'd seen us together, and you were with someone who wasn't quite right, you would've felt jealous. Sometimes *I* even felt jealous when I thought of us abstractly. Why couldn't *I* be in that picture-perfect relationship? Oh, right. I was.

I finish my chicken and stand to look at the trophy more closely. Propped in front of it is a picture of us taken the day we won it. We both look slightly disheveled and exhausted from the all-nighter we'd pulled. I've never understood why he keeps it on display.

"I always thought you looked great in that picture," Craig says, coming up behind me.

I turn to face him. He's changed into jeans and a black sweatshirt. His hair is still damp.

"Funny, I was just thinking the opposite."

"You never think you look good in pictures."

"Because I don't."

He smiles ruefully. "Some things never change."

"True."

Our eyes meet briefly before Craig looks away.

"Should we sit?" he asks.

I follow him to the living room, and we sit on his mascu-line, dark brown couch. It's an L shape, and as if by agreement, we each take a different part of the L.

He stares at his hands, silent, thoughtful.

I feel compelled to break the silence. After all, I'm the party at fault here, right? "I'm sorry I wasn't able to call you, Craig."

"I know. You said."

"There really just wasn't any way . . ."

I stop myself because what I'm saying feels like a lie, even though it's mostly the truth. After the earthquake, there wasn't any way to call outside the country unless you had a satel-lite phone. Which our village didn't. But a few weeks after the earthquake, a rumor started among the villagers that the next village over had one, and maybe a working Internet connec-tion too. The rumor circled and circled, and in a day or two, the phone's existence, and its maybe working connection to the outside world, took on a mythic quality.

I admit I was taken up with the myth. How could I not be? A possible connection to home *had* to be investigated. And while the villagers seemed content to simply discuss the pos-sibility, I was not. I pleaded with Karen and Peter to show me the way, and they eventually agreed. They didn't believe the rumor, I could tell, but they wanted it to be true for me.

After they relented, Peter told me to put some things together discreetly—water, food, the sturdiest shoes I had—

and went off to haggle with Nyako, the village's procurer. If you needed something (and it was available somewhere), Nyako had it—and sure enough, an hour or so later, Peter walked toward me, navigating a bike with each arm.

"We're *biking* there?"

"No way else to get there, I'm afraid. I've got to keep the truck fueled for emergencies. No telling when I'll be able to get more gas."

I wanted to say that this was an emergency for me, but I knew it wasn't really. I took the smaller of the two bikes—a faded red Schwinn—and adjusted the seat to fit my proportions. Peter did the same with the rusty hybrid he was going to ride, and we slung our packs over our backs and set out.

It was ten miles to our destination, but it felt like twenty. The bike's seat dug into my behind, and my back started to ache from being crouched over the handlebars. Even if I'd had the energy, we couldn't bike very fast; the road was pitted and bumpy, and I was almost thrown from my perch more than once. The sun beat down on my neck, seeking out the band beneath my hair where I hadn't applied enough sunscreen.

When we finally got there, we were greeted by a group of teenage boys sitting on a large pile of rocks, holding guns lazily across their laps. My heart leaped to my throat, and I thought of Ishmael Beah and his book, *A Long Way Gone*—a Christmas gift from my mother because she loved even the bad parts of this place. Were these boy soldiers? Were they out of their minds on drugs and fear? Was I about to get us both killed just because I wanted to make a phone call?

Peter put up his hand in this self-assured way he has, and I stopped pedaling.

"Stay here," he said.

"Are you sure? We can go back."

"I think they're just protecting the village against looters. I'll talk to them first."

"Please, Peter. Don't go if it's dangerous. It's not that important."

"Sure it is. And don't worry, I'll be fine."

He dismounted and wheeled his bike slowly toward the boys, smiling, friendly, nothing to fear here, even though he seemed twice the size of even the largest of them.

As I watched him talking to them, I felt an odd urge to cough—just as I did before the earthquake, when I watched the snake—to draw attention to myself in some way. Like the urge to jump some people feel when they stand on the edge of Niagara Falls, to be swallowed up by the massive river. Even though I knew it could be bad—dangerous, even—it felt like a better alternative in the moment.

And then Peter beckoned to me, a smile on his face. I climbed down from my bike and walked toward the boys.

"Hello," said the tallest one. Sitting highest on the rocks, he was their leader, I assumed. "I am Tabansi."

"Hello, Tabansi," I said back. "My name is Emma."

"You are looking for satellite phone, yeah?"

Hope sprang through me. "Yes, do you have one?"

"Yes."

"And may I . . . can I use it?"

One of the smaller boys snickered. The boy sitting next to him shushed him.

"You cannot."

"Oh, I—"

"It is my father's, but it is broken. It fell to the floor when the earth shook."

"Oh no. I mean, I'm sorry."

He shrugged the shrug of a much older child, a man. "It is the way things are. We are trying to fix it. You may come back in two weeks."

I glanced at Peter and he nodded his head. There was nothing to be done here today.

"Thank you."

He flashed me a smile. "You are welcome. You should go now. It is a long way back."

"I tried to call you when I got back," I say now to Craig. "Did you change your number?"

He looks up. "I had to. I kept getting these crank calls from people about you."

"I'm really sorry, Craig."

"It's not your fault."

"Still, if I hadn't gone—"

"Don't beat yourself up, Emma. That's not what I want."

"But I feel selfish. This whole time I've only been thinking about me. I never thought about what you were going through."

"You didn't know."

"I didn't know you thought I was dead, but what I did think was enough."

He moves toward me on the couch. "Please, Emma. Don't."

His tone is so warm and familiar, it bring tears to my eyes. But despite my new weepy persona, I've never cried in front of Craig, not in sorrow or happiness or even anger, not even when my mother died. And somehow, crying in front of him now seems melodramatic and predictable. Like our kiss earlier.

I take a deep breath. "What do you want to do, Craig?"

"About us?"

"Yeah."

He hesitates. "Do you want me to be honest?"

"Always."

"Then, I guess . . . I don't know."

Somehow, in spite of all the signs, this wasn't the answer I was expecting. Not after the coded "I love you." But maybe I misread that? Maybe he wasn't speaking in code at all, just in trivialities?

"Oh."

"Are you mad?"

"No."

"What, then?"

"I don't know, either. Why don't *you* know?"

He shifts away. "I offered to go with you, remember? But you didn't want me to. You just left. We spoke that one time, and the next thing I knew there was all this horrible footage on the news. It was like you'd disappeared off the face of the earth.

"Then the government released these lists of names of people who were missing. When I saw your name on it, I didn't know what to do. No one would say it to me directly, but I knew everyone thought you were dead. And then . . . this is hard to admit, Emma, believe me, but someone had the courage to say it to me, that you might be dead, and I felt . . . I felt this . . . I wouldn't say weight, exactly, but something lifted, and I knew they were right. I knew you were dead."

The world seems to slow down, and it's like I can see the words *I knew you were dead* leave Craig's mouth and travel to me, but they don't quite make it. What does sink in is this:

132

Craig not only felt like I was dead but was in some measure *relieved* by it.

What am I supposed to do with that?

"Who said it?" I ask eventually.

He looks up from his twisting hands. "What?"

"Who said I was dead? Who did you believe?"

"What does that matter?"

"I just want to know."

"Emma."

Some instinct propels me to persist. "Just tell me."

"It was Sophie."

"Well, that figures."

"That's not fair."

"Whatever."

He shakes his head. "She was just being a friend."

But Craig and Sophie were never friends.

"Why are you defending her?"

"I'm not."

"No, you are."

I look at him closely. He won't look me in the eye, and he's clenching and unclenching his hands, a gesture I've always associated with him feeling guilty.

Why is Craig defending Sophie? Why would he believe her, of all people? Why was he even *talking* to her?

And suddenly, I know. This is what Jenny stopped herself from telling me in the food court, and why Matt seemed uncomfortable when I told him I hadn't spoken to Craig.

"You're sleeping with her, aren't you?"

"What?" he says, shocked, but not, you know, *denying* it.

"Sophie. You're sleeping with her."

"Why would you say that?"

"Am I wrong?"

"Emma."

"God, Craig."

Guilt floods his face. "I don't know what to say."

"Are you still together?" *Do you love her?* I can't quite manage to ask.

"Yes."

"Well, okay, then."

I stand and walk toward the front door.

"Where are you going?"

"Somewhere that's not here."

Craig follows me. "That's it? You're just leaving?"

I pick up my coat off the rack and slip it on. I clench my shaking hands. "Yes."

"I think we should talk about this."

"What's there left to say, Craig? You thought I was dead and you're sleeping with someone else." I can feel my throat start to close, my voice getting raspy.

Keep it together, Emma, you're almost out of here.

"We can't end things like this."

"Yes, we can."

I push past him. He reaches out to stop me, but I'm moving too fast.

"Please don't go."

I hesitate briefly, but it's only a hesitation. I'm out the door before the tears start to fall.

By the time I get down to the street, I'm crying in earnest and cursing myself for putting any faith in Craig. Because that's what I realize I've been doing—keeping him as a possibility. Feeling like if we were together again, everything would return to normal.

But now that's all out the window. I was prepared to settle for Craig, but he didn't keep up his end of the bargain. His end of the bargain being pining for me forever, of course. Or at least, for more time than he gave it. In fact, I'm pretty sure the appropriate lag time between hooking up with a new girl when your old girl is missing, presumed dead, is more than he gave it.

And how much time *did* he give it, anyway? A week, a month? Two? When did Sophie appear with her magical words of wisdom, and just how long did it take him to believe them?

I kick a ball of snow in front of me. Well, screw him! That's right! Did you hear me, Craig? I don't need you and your back massages! I'm okay on my own. I can survive with no mom or dad or friends or career or things. Just make me a big ole pity party, and I'll be there with bells on!

I catch sight of myself in the window of the pub on the corner. My face is a mess: red nose, red eyes, red cheeks. I look ridiculous and pathetic.

And wasn't I just saying to Dominic that this isn't me? I don't want to be a wallower, sitting in a pool of self-pity. I don't want to be giving myself this pep talk *again*. Once should've been enough. It should've been more than enough.

No, I want to be like those people I can see through the glass, sitting at bar stools surrounded by bags full of Christmas presents for their loved ones. They look warm and happy and . . .

I brush the tears off my face with one gloved hand and wipe my nose with the other. I straighten my shoulders and grasp the oblong door handle leading into the bar. In a moment, I'm seated between two smiling, happy, bepresented patrons. Moments after that, my hands are cupped around an Irish coffee and I'm well on my way to being smiling and happy too.

The next several hours pass blithely.

There's a TV high on the wall behind the bar, see, and halfway through my drink, the anchor begins to talk about me. There I am, sitting in front of Cathy Keeler, answering her questions. My face is flushed, but I appear to be handling myself.

At least, that's what it looks like with the sound off.

I look away and hope no one makes the connection, but the footage goes on and on, and eventually I can feel the curious gaze of the older man sitting next to me.

"That's you up there, ain't it? On the TV?"

I turn as far away from him as I can without being totally rude. "No."

"Course it is. You're even wearing the same outfit."

Damn. I left my garment bag at the TV station. One more thing I can blame Craig for.

I turn toward him. He's in his early sixties. The end of his bulbous nose is lined with small veins, and his brown eyes are a little bleary.

"I don't mean to be rude, but I just want to have my drink in peace."

"Sure enough."

I turn away and start mentally kicking myself. Didn't I come in here for exactly this reason? To have some human contact, some lighthearted interactions with people who don't know me or anything about me? And although this man knows I'm some sort of news, it's not the same kind of knowledge someone who's really in my life would have.

I touch his shoulder. "That *was* me."

He shifts his gaze from the TV and gives me a broad smile. "I knew it."

"Sorry about before."

"'S all right. You must've been through a lot."

"I don't want to talk about that."

"Nah, I can see you wouldn't."

"Thanks."

"First time here?"

The bar at the end of Craig's street? Not by a long shot. Maybe this wasn't such a good idea after all.

"No."

"Another bad subject?"

"Yeah. Look, can I buy you a drink?"

His eyes light up. "That'd be real nice of you."

So I do. I buy him a drink, and we talk about inconsequential things like the presents he bought his grandkids for Christmas and how he's waiting for his wife to finish up her shopping. When his wife arrives, we move to a table and I buy her a drink too. They tell me about their youngest son, who's graduating high school, and what do I think about military college? Johnny-boy can be a bit of a handful, and maybe the structure would help?

It isn't exactly an episode of *Cheers,* but it's pretty nice. And then it's time to go. Frank and Joanie have to get back to their grandkids, their lives. We say our goodbyes and pretend we might do this again sometime. We all know it won't happen (we don't even exchange phone numbers, so how could it?), but it's nice to pretend. I leave the bar in a happy glow.

Which lasts about thirty seconds into the cab ride home before the reality of my conversation with Craig comes rushing back. Craig and Sophie. Craig and *Sophie*. *Craig* and Sophie. However I say it, I can't make it come out right. And the more I try, the angrier I feel. Angry and stupid. That I care. That I didn't see it coming. That I care.

When I get home, the apartment is dark and has that empty-building feeling. I call Dominic's name anyway, but don't get an answer.

I flip on some lights and dump my coat on the corner of the couch. I feel restless and go searching for the box that the Scotch bottle came from the other night. I don't usually drink hard alcohol, but I feel like I need to come up against something hard right now.

In the third box I find a bottle of something called Laphroaig, which looks expensive and like it's spent many years in an oak cask. I check the faded price tag. Yikes. Maybe I should take up photography.

I pull out a cut-glass tumbler and pour a measure. It burns the back of my throat, but the warm feeling follows quickly. I've never appreciated Scotch before, but I seem to be getting a taste for it. I turn on the gas fire and settle into the couch, the bottle tucked under my arm. Craig and Sophie. *Craig* and Sophie. Craig and *Sophie.* Any way I emphasize it, it just comes out craziness.

I'm still mulling it over when Dominic comes home. He stops briefly in the doorway, giving me a vague "Hey," then walks down the hall. He doesn't even make eye contact.

What the hell? What did I do to deserve that?

I walk through the apartment, clutching my glass in one hand and the bottle in the other. I find him in the kitchen, pulling vegetables from the fridge and piling them on the counter.

"What's with the no hello?"

Dominic puts an onion on the counter and turns toward me. He has a sour look on his face. "I see you found the Laphroaig."

"Is that a problem?"

"I just would've thought someone who had all her stuff thrown out would be a little more respectful of other people's things."

"Excuse me?"

"Forget it." He pulls a knife from the knife block and starts chopping the onion aggressively.

"I'll buy you a new bottle, okay? Dominic? Hello? Earth to Dominic?"

He doesn't react, pretending, maybe, that I'm not here.

"Will you put the knife down and look at me?"

He puts the knife down slowly and raises his eyes to meet mine. "That make you happy?"

"I'm over the moon."

"Well, bully for you. Can I go back to my chopping now?"

"No, I want to know why you're being such a jerk."

He scoffs. "*I'm* being a jerk? That's rich."

What did I ever do to . . . oh. Is this . . . because he saw me on TV kissing Craig? No . . . that can't be right.

"Is this because of Cathy Keeler?"

"If you're implying that I'm in a bad mood because of your little kiss and tell, then no, it's not because of Cathy Keeler."

I feel another crest of anger, but it dissipates. Dominic's not the problem here. He's never been the problem.

"I'm sorry I didn't tell you about Craig, Dominic."

"It doesn't matter."

"No, I should've told you."

"Forget it."

"But I don't want to forget it. I'm trying to apologize. Why won't you let me?"

"Look, Emma, you don't owe me any explanations, okay? You have a boyfriend. And somehow, you never mentioned him. But hey, I don't know you very well. Maybe keeping secrets is just how you roll."

So much for letting go of my anger.

"Did you just call me a liar?"

His shoulders rise toward his ears. "I don't know, did I?"

"Fuck you."

"Excuse me?"

"I *said*, fuck you."

I know I'm totally overreacting, but it feels good to let it out, even if it's at the wrong person.

He puts down his knife and walks past me toward the door. I watch his retreating back and I want to make him stop. I want to make him come back and talk to me. So I do the only thing I can think of. I raise my arm and throw my glass with all my might.

Smack! It hits the door frame above him and shatters into a thousand pieces, flinging sixteen dollars of Scotch on the walls and Dominic's head.

He freezes. My heart starts pounding in my chest as Dominic turns around slowly.

"What the hell is wrong with you?"

"Oh God, I'm so sorry."

I pick up a tea towel off the counter and try to wipe some of the liquid from his forehead, but he pulls away.

"Are you hurt?"

He takes the towel from my hand and wipes his head and shoulders. "I'm fine."

"Be careful of the glass."

"Emma, will you just stop?"

I slump into one of the kitchen chairs. I cross my arms on the table and rest my chin on my wrists. The kitchen tap is dripping, the metal ping of the water amplified by our silence. After a moment, Dominic sits across from me, shaking his head in confusion. There are little bits of glass glinting in his hair.

"What the hell is going on?" he asks.

"We just broke up."

"You and Craig?"

"Yeah."

"What happened?"

"He thought I was dead and got over me by sleeping with my mortal enemy."

"You have a mortal enemy?"

"Her name is Sophie Vaughn, and I'm pretty sure she's half devil spawn."

The sides of his mouth twitch. "Only half?"

"You'd be surprised how far a little devil spawn goes."

"I guess. So, you just found out that Craig was sleeping with the devil?"

"Yeah. I'm really sorry, Dominic. About everything."

"It's fine."

"When you walked past me like that, I guess I thought you were mad at me, and—"

"Not everything is about you, Emma."

"I know that."

He runs his hand through his sticky hair.

"Careful of the glass."

"I should take a shower."

"Will you tell me why you were upset first?"

"It's no big deal."

"Sure seems that way."

"You're kind of pushy, you know that?"

"So they tell me."

He sighs. "I got an email that put me in a bad mood. That's all."

"I threw a glass at your head because of an email?"

"You were aiming for my head?"

"Nnnoooo."

"Oh, that's convincing."

"What was in the email?"

He stands and crosses to the sink, turning off the tap. "It doesn't matter."

"Tell me."

"You're relentless."

"It's part of my charm."

He pulls out his iPhone, opens an email, and hands it to me. It's from Expedia, transmitting him an itinerary for a trip somewhere.

"Getting a trip itinerary put you in a bad mood . . ." I trail off as I look at the email more closely. It's a trip for Dominic and Emily Mahoney. That's her name. Emily. "It was for your honeymoon?"

He nods.

"When were you supposed to get married?"

"On Christmas Eve."

"I'm really sorry, Dominic."

"Thanks. Now, why don't you clean up while I take a shower?"

I turn and hang over the edge of the chair, taking in the mess I have wrought. There are streaks of Scotch on the wall and shattered glass on the floor. The kitchen smells like a bar.

"I have a better idea."

"What's that?"

"Let's get drunk."

"I'm not sure that's the best idea."

"So? Are you with me or against me?"

He pauses, but not for long. "Oh, I'm with you."

Chapter 10
Silent Night

I wake up with a start, clutching the Laphroaig bottle to my chest like it's my childhood dolly. There's a trail of spittle leading from my mouth to my pillow, and my eyes are so sensitive to light that the small streak of sun that's seeping through the blind feels like a laser beam.

I feel like hell. But was it worth it?

It's all relative. Dominic and I shared a few laughs when we got to the silly drunk stage, but we were both too caught up in our own dramas to really let go. On the other hand, I now have an excuse to hide under the covers all day.

Sounds good to me.

When I wake up again, I still feel disgusting, but other feelings are there too. Hunger mostly, but also sadness. At least, I think that's why there's this tight hand around my heart.

Thanks for that, Craig. I owe you one. And it's nice to know, in a perverse kind of way, that I can still have my heart broken.

The first boy to do it was Graham Thorpe. He sat in front of me in math class. I thought he was cute, but I was fifteen and I thought a lot of boys were cute. Then one day, he turned around and asked to borrow my ruler. The way his black hair flopped across his forehead reminded me of Tom Cruise in *Top Gun,* and he had a crooked smile, which he flashed at me when I handed the ruler over.

The next day he asked to borrow my eraser. The day after that, a piece of paper. These pretenses to talk to me, to touch my hand as I gave him what he asked for, continued for weeks. I knew he wanted to ask me out, and I couldn't understand what he was waiting for. Or was I just imagining his interest?

He finally did it one day after basketball practice. He caught me between the gym and the locker rooms, sweaty, disheveled, embarrassed.

Did I want to go to the movies with him this weekend? he asked, in the blasé way of teenagers. *Yes!* I answered back, not quite as I-don't-give-a-shit as he was.

We went to the movie—I can't remember what it was— and as the lights dimmed, he gave me my first real kiss. I still remember the shock of his lips against mine. This was kissing. How had I gone this long without kissing?

We kissed a lot in the next three months. At recess, at lunch, after school. I don't remember talking, only kissing. Kissing so much that my mouth took on his taste and my lips felt half bruised. Kissing the way only teenagers can.

Then he began pulling away, not returning my calls, passing fewer notes. When he finally said the words I'd been dreading, I felt like I was falling. That wretched, pit-of-the-stomach, dream-falling feeling, my body tense, bracing for impact. But I never hit the ground, I just kept falling for what felt like forever. I walked around like that for weeks, feeling like gravity didn't apply to me anymore.

And then, one day, it was over. I was okay. I could breathe. I could laugh, even fall in love again. And I did, more than once, and more deeply than I had at fifteen. I've even had my heart broken again, but nothing ever hurt that badly.

Nothing ever does, right?

I stumble upright and shuffle to the kitchen. After a quick survey of the fridge, I make myself a grilled cheese sandwich and take it, and a large glass of orange juice, back to bed.

Dominic's nowhere in sight, though that sound might be him snoring. Or maybe it's a jackhammer outside?

I check my phone. Twelve missed calls, all from numbers I don't recognize. I call into my voice mail with my heart in my throat, but the messages are from journalists looking to do an in-depth interview about my "heartwarming story," and how I made it "home for the holidays." I erase them in disgust, mentally cursing Matt for giving them my phone number.

I pull the covers over my head and hide there for the rest of the day.

* * *

The next morning, Christmas Eve, I find myself at the kitchen table making a list of the things I need to do to start getting my life in order. I've spent too much time wallowing and hiding in liquor bottles; it's time to get some things taken care of.

My pen scratches against the paper.

1. Find a new apartment.
2. Track Sunshine down.
3. Sue Pedro.
4. Get in shape. Be strong enough to pin Sophie to the ground if opportunity arises.
5. Look for my car.

"Nice list," Dominic says, reading over my shoulder.

I turn it over and place my pen on top of it. "You're a very nosy person, you know that?"

"Which is why I'm not getting married. Thanks for the reminder."

6. Start thinking before speaking.

"I'm going to let that one lie there."

"That's probably best. Breakfast?"

"Do you need to ask?"

Dominic makes us French toast that's as good as any I've

ever had. He whistles happily when he's cooking, but as we trade sections of the paper back and forth, I can tell he's feeling unsettled. I can't blame him, really. How else are you supposed to feel on the day you were going to get married? I rack my brain for something to say, something that might make today easier, but nothing comes to mind. Maybe silence is best.

After breakfast, Dominic tells me that he's going to take some shots around town. I bundle myself into my new winter coat, don my new hat and boots, and set out on my mission.

Since most of the tasks on my list seem too big for the day before Christmas, I decide to tackle the one I should've done days ago—retrieve my car from the impound lot where it was sent after spending too many weeks at the airport.

I've always had a soft spot for my car, the one my mother gave me for my high school graduation. It's not the car itself—a white convertible Rabbit that screams 1982—but what it represented. My mother didn't want me to leave our safe suburb for the wilds of the big city. When I was applying to universities, she always put the brochures for those located in small towns on the top of the pile.

I didn't apply to any of those safe-seeming places. The brochures looked pretty, but I wanted a city, the bigger the better. And that's what I got. My mom hid her disappointment well, but I still knew. It was hard disappointing her on purpose for the first time, but not so hard that I didn't do it.

She gave me the car right before we left for my high school graduation ceremony. It was a bright June day, and she handed me the keys and suggested we drive with the top down. I didn't know what she meant until I noticed the Rabbit sitting in the driveway.

"Whose car is that?" I asked, my toes tingling with excitement.

She linked her arm through mine. "It's yours, my darling."

"But, Mom, you can't afford to give me a car."

"Don't you worry about that."

"Are you sure?"

Her face crinkled under the weight of her smile. "Of course I am. I'm extremely proud of you, Emma. And this way, you can come home on the weekends."

I enveloped her in black polyester fabric. "Thank you, Mom. I'll never forget this."

I've never replaced it. At first because I couldn't afford to, and later because it felt like a part of me, a part of us, the unit my mother and I made. So many drives home to see her on weekends. The road trip we took once with no specific destination in mind. Even the last drive home before she died felt less horrible somehow because I was driving in something that came from her love and support for me.

According to the airport security website, my car was taken to the central impound lot near the river. And that's where I direct the cab I hail at the bottom of my street. I watch the neighborhoods flash by through the windows. My own is full of neat brown brick buildings and well-manicured trees. Next comes a poorer area, where the brick is darkened by years of grime and there's not enough space between the houses and sidewalks for trees. Shoes hang from the power lines, and house after house is decked out with Christmas lights. It must be beautiful at night.

The cab stops at the corner of a street that runs parallel to the river. The bright winter sun glints off the gray water. Clouds of misty vapor hover above the choppy waves. Between the road and the river is a huge lot full of cars, surrounded by a rusty chain-link fence. A long line of people huddled in their winter coats meanders away from the entrance.

I wrap my scarf around my face. As I walk along the row of dispirited-looking people, I become concerned about the length of the line. It goes on and on; there must be three hundred people waiting to retrieve their cars instead of shopping for last-minute gifts.

I take my place behind a gruff-looking man in his late forties who's wearing a black leather coat that's not warm enough for this weather. He has a red-and-green snake tattoo on the back of his neck. Its menacing face snarls at me with yellow eyes.

Two more people join the line behind me, jostling for position. One of them bumps into me; I lose my footing and tip toward the snake.

Its owner turns toward me with anger in his round, ruddy face. "Watch it, lady, will ya?"

"Sorry."

"Pushing won't getcha there faster."

I glare at the young people behind me. "I know. It won't happen again."

"You see, that's what's wrong with society today. No patience. You think the Russians waiting in line for toilet paper were using their elbows to get a better place in line?"

"I have no idea."

"Well, they weren't, I can tell ya. Good people, the Russians. Patient." He grins, and I notice that he's missing a couple of teeth. "You ever been to Russia?"

"No."

"Me neither. But I will. I'm saving up, you see."

The wistful glint in his eye reminds me of my mother whenever she talked about Africa.

"That's great."

"Think you're too good to talk to me, do ya?"

"What? No. Of course not. I just don't normally talk to strangers."

"Sure enough. No one does these days. That's another problem with society."

I have a feeling I'm going to get the complete list of society's problems by the time I see the inside of this fence.

"Do you know why this line's so long?"

He leans toward me conspiratorially. "'Twas the night before Christmas."

Is this guy completely cracked?

"Right."

"The lot's closed tomorrow."

"I'd imagine."

He gives me a look like he's talking to an idiot. "This is the last day the lot is open this year. And on January second, they auction off the unclaimed cars."

"You mean, if you don't get your car today, then—"

"You have to buy it if you want it back."

"But that's ridiculous."

"I don't make the rules, lady."

"No wonder about the line."

He shrugs his broad shoulders. "That's what I was saying. Took me three hours to get through last year."

"Last year?"

"I get a little careless with my car sometimes." He extends his hand. "My name's Bill, by the way."

I shake his hand. It feels rough, even through my glove. "Emma."

He squints at me. "You sure look familiar."

"I have one of those faces."

"No, that's not it. You been on TV recently or something?"

Oh God. Not again. How do celebrities stand it?

"Um, well . . ."

He snaps his fingers. "Got it! You're that Africa girl, ain't you?"

"I guess."

"Imagine that. Right here in the line like an ordinary person and everything. That gives me faith, that does."

"Why wouldn't I be in line like everyone else?"

"Well, after all you've been through and everything. Now that I think on it . . ." He gets a determined look on his face and grabs my hand. "Come on."

I try to pull my hand away. "What are you doing?"

"Just trust me."

That feels like the last thing I should be doing, but at the same time, I don't feel scared. Maybe it's because we're surrounded by hundreds of people, but all I am is mildly curious as I slip along in Bill's wake.

We get to the head of the line and he drops my hand. "Wait here."

I catch an angry stare from the woman who's next in line. Her eyes are red and phlegmy. I turn away and watch Bill as he talks emphatically to the large, muscled man guarding the entrance. The swirling wind keeps me from hearing anything but a few snippets of their conversation. "Africa . . . wrong with society ... you *owe* me ..." These last words are open sesame. The guard grits his teeth and nods slowly, once. Bill lets out a whoop and barrels his way toward me.

"You're in."

"What do you mean?"

"You don't have to wait. They'll let you take your car now."

"What? No, Bill, thank you very much for trying to help me, but ... I can't, I really can't."

"Sure you can."

"No, it wouldn't be right."

"Of course it ain't right, but a lot of things ain't been right for you lately, seems to me. You should take this."

"Why do you care? You don't even know me."

The muscled man crosses his arms. "Offer expires in ten seconds, Bill, owe or no owe."

"What's it going to be?" Bill asks me.

I can feel the hard stare of some very cold people boring into the back of my head, but what the hell. I *do* deserve a break.

I mouth "Sorry" to the line and give Bill a quick peck on the cheek.

"Geez, lady, what was that for?"

"Merry Christmas."

Turns out that getting in the front door was only the half of it, and it's another hour of lines and paperwork before I'm sitting behind the wheel. And then, of course, my car won't start because the battery's dead, and the tires are flat. But they have the apparatus to deal with this! I am not the first person to have this problem! Many of the people waiting outside, braving the cold, cursing me for jumping the line (though they do not know my name, I hope) will face this too! For once, my problems aren't unusual. They don't make me stand out.

After yet another hour, I'm putting the car in gear and driving through the open chain-link gates. The line seems no smaller than when I left it hours ago. I slow as I pass Bill and give him a friendly wave. He nods, barely pausing in his conversation with the jostling couple who were standing behind me.

The roads are full of Christmas traffic. A city full of last-minute shoppers. I skip through the stations on the radio. I didn't know there were that many different recorded versions of "All I Want for Christmas Is You." Seems like just the one would do.

I get back to the apartment as the sun is setting. A quiet sunset, one of inches, forgoing spectacle. It doesn't feel like Christmas Eve, but it is. My first Christmas without my mother. Will I be visited by the Ghost of Christmas Past, or will I have to lump it on my own?

I'm guessing the safe bet is on the latter.

I hear sounds coming from the kitchen, and I feel a moment

of fright. Then I realize it must be Dominic. At least I hope it is. But why is he here on Christmas Eve?

"Dominic?"

"I'm in the kitchen."

The kitchen smells wonderfully of browning pork and onions and . . .

"Do I smell thyme?"

Dominic's pushing dough into a bright-red pie plate. His jeans and black sweater are covered with flour fingerprints. "No, it's sage."

"Whatcha making?"

"*Tourtière.*"

"Did you say *torture*?"

"No, *tourtière*. It's a French word for meat pie."

"I thought you were Irish, Irish, Irish."

He smiles. "My grandmother was French Canadian."

"Well, whatever it is, it smells wonderful."

"It'll taste better with a nice salad."

"Okay, okay, I can take a hint."

I get the salad stuff out of the fridge and start putting together a mixed green salad with cut-up cherry tomatoes.

"How come you're here? I mean, it's Christmas Eve, right? You didn't want to be with your family?" I ask.

Dominic shoots me a look but answers me anyway.

"I'll be going to Mahoney Central tomorrow."

"But how come you're not there tonight?" I persist, kind of annoying myself really, but old habits die hard.

He hesitates. "I thought . . . well, with everything that's going on, I didn't think I could take more than one night there, to be honest."

"Big family?"

"You could say that. I'm the youngest of twelve."

"You're making that up, right?"

"Nope."

"Your parents really had twelve children?"

"The Catholic Church has a lot to answer for."

"I'll say."

Dominic slips the pie into the oven, and I make a vinaigrette out of oil, balsamic vinegar, grain mustard, shredded basil, and lots of freshly ground salt and pepper.

"Hold off dressing that," Dominic says. "The pie will take about forty-five minutes."

He picks up the bottle of wine breathing on the counter and pours me a glass. "Why don't you go relax in the living room?"

I take the glass suspiciously. "Why are you being so nice to me?"

"Are you saying I haven't been nice to you up to now?"

"You know what I mean."

"It's Christmas."

"It's the night before Christmas."

"Goddamn lawyers."

"Hey!"

He points toward the door. "Out of my kitchen, woman."

I smile at him and take my wine to the living room. I don't know what I would have done, really, without Dominic these last couple of days. And not just because I wouldn't have a place to stay. I slip into the armchair, tucking my feet underneath me. The lights dance on the Christmas tree, the way Christmas lights are supposed to, the way they always have. It's amazing, isn't it, how some things can be so different while others remain the same?

I chase my morbid thoughts down with a large gulp of wine. It's then that I notice a rather large box wrapped in green shiny paper sitting under the tree.

Oops! I almost forgot.

I scurry to the bedroom and dig out the present I bought for Dominic on my shopping spree. When I return to place it under the tree, Dominic's adjusting the flame of the fire.

"I thought we'd eat in here," he says as he replaces the fireplace screen.

"Sounds good."

His eyes travel to the box in my hands. "What you got there?"

"Your Christmas present."

He reaches out his hand. "Thanks."

"What? No way. Not till tomorrow."

"In my family we always open gifts on Christmas Eve."

"That sounds like a convenient tradition."

I walk past him and put his present under the tree. I can't help but notice that the large green box has my name on it.

"Bet you're wishing you had a Christmas Eve tradition now, aren't you?" Dominic says, catching me looking at the tag.

I stand up quickly. "I don't know what you're talking about."

"Help me bring the table in here, and we'll discuss it over dinner."

"What's to discuss? We both know we're opening those presents tonight."

He smirks, and we carry the table from the kitchen to the living room, returning for the chairs. While I set it, Dominic serves us and brings the plates to the table. I sit across from him and put my napkin on my lap. "This looks great. I always seem to be thanking you, but again, thank you."

"It's just a meat pie."

"Seriously, Dominic."

"You're welcome." He raises his glass and holds it toward me. "Merry Christmas, Emma."

"Merry Christmas Eve."

Our glasses clink, and we dig in. The pie is as wonderful as it smells, tender, moist pork in a flaky, crisp crust, but as we eat, an uncomfortable silence closes around us.

"We're two sorry bastards, aren't we?" I say eventually.

"Seems like."

"Maybe presents will help?"

He smiles. "Go for it."

I start toward the tree, then think better of it. "You have to open yours first."

"You don't have to ask *me* twice."

He goes to the tree and picks up the smaller box. He holds it next to his ear and shakes it. "Mmm. It sounds like something soft, maybe a sweater."

"Ah, but what color?"

He gives it another shake. "I'm guessing gray or blue."

"You're crazy."

"I'm so right."

"Just open it already."

He starts to carefully peel off the wrapper one corner at a time.

"You're not one of those people, are you?"

"If by that you mean people who take their time taking wrapping paper off packages, normally no."

"So you're just doing it to drive me nuts?"

"Pretty much."

"Cut it out."

He rips off the paper in one long strip. When he removes the gray cashmere sweater inside, he starts to laugh. He slips it over his head. It fits perfectly, emphasizing his broad shoulders.

"You like it?"

"It's great, thanks. Your turn."

I try to pick up the box. "What's in this thing, anyway?"

"Open it and see."

I sit on the floor, tucking my legs underneath me. I tear the first strip of paper off, hearing the click of a shutter as I do. I look up. Dominic's hidden behind his camera.

"Hey! What are you doing?"

"Capturing the moment."

"I don't really like having my picture taken."

He tilts his head to the side. "Indulge me."

"Fine. But only if I get final say on what you do with it."

"Deal."

I bend my head over the box and rip off the rest of the paper. Underneath is a dark brown banker's box. On the lid, in my own handwriting, is written, *Memories 0–18*. With my heart in my throat I lift off the lid. Inside, organized into vertical file folders, are pictures, report cards, school art projects and essays. Inside the box is my life from zero to eighteen.

I touch one of the labels, not completely believing it's real. "Where did you find this?"

"It was tucked behind the wine boxes in the storage locker."

Of course. I moved it there when I bought the wine. The other boxes, *19–28* and *Current,* were on the shelf above it, and were, presumably, trashed by Pedro you-will-be-served-with-papers-just-as-soon-as-I-get-back-to-work Alvarez.

"Thank you for giving this to me, Dominic."

He puts the camera down on the coffee table. "Of course. Now, why I don't I clean up and leave you alone with that?"

"No, don't go."

"Are you sure?"

"If I go through that box right now, I'm going to be a freaking mess. And I know I might've seemed like a mess these past few days, but trust me, it could get much worse."

"Maybe I shouldn't have given it to you."

"No, I feel better knowing it's around."

"I can tell."

"Really, it's perfect."

He gives me a slow smile, and I feel suddenly nervous, like I've been caught doing something I shouldn't. Being happy, maybe.

"Where did you come from, anyway?" I ask.

Whatever Dominic was going to say in response is interrupted by the loud *ding-dong* of the doorbell.

"Midnight carolers," he says, glancing at his watch, "at eight thirty?"

"You never know."

He shrugs and goes to answer the door. I follow behind him out of curiosity. A rush of cold air chases past the door and swirls my hair around my face. I hesitate for a moment, then fly toward the entrance. Standing there, huddled inside a white puffy coat two sizes too big for her, is Stephanie.

"Stephanie!"

"Emma!"

Her arms are around me, holding me close.

Finally.

Chapter 11

Heart on a String

When I eventually let Stephanie go, I introduce her to Dominic and usher her inside. As she takes off her coat, boots, and hat, I fill her in briefly on how we met. She's shivering from the cold, and I take her into the living room, placing her as close to the roaring gas fire as she can stand. When her teeth stop clacking, I start my cross-examination.

"When did you get back? Why didn't you call me? Didn't you get any of my messages? And how come you went to Africa in the first place?"

Okay, maybe *barrage* is a better word.

"I should be asking you the same questions."

"I know, I know, but answer me first, okay? I'll tell you everything after, I promise."

"Is she always this annoying now?" Stephanie asks Dominic, her bright green eyes laughing at me from her gamine face. She's wearing the twin of the outfit I was wearing the night I came back from Africa—linen pants and a matching shirt.

"Pretty much."

"How have you put up with it?"

Dominic leans forward in his chair. "Well—"

"Hey! I'm sitting right here."

Stephanie grins. Her small, slightly crooked teeth are bright white in her tanned face. "I know. Finally."

"Will you just answer my questions before I go bonkers?"

She tucks her chin-length hair around her ears. It's a gesture that's so familiar it brings tears to my eyes. "You know all about you disappearing, and everything?"

"You can't imagine how bad I feel about that, Steph. I would've called you again if I could have."

She pats my hand. "Don't be silly. It's not like you *wanted* to disappear."

I feel a spasm of guilt. "No, of course not."

"Nice TV coverage, by the way."

"Ugh, you watched that? It was awful."

"What are you talking about? You were awesome. But I do have a bone to pick with that Cathy Keeler woman. She was way out of line."

"I thought Emma handled herself pretty well," Dominic says.

Stephanie nods proudly. "Of course she did. Emma's always known how to handle herself, ever since she was a little kid."

"You don't say."

"Yeah, like this one time in high school—"

I cut her off. "Aren't you supposed to be answering my questions?"

"Right. Sorry. But, Em, you know where I've been. I've been looking for you."

My throat feels tight. "I don't know what to say."

"It's not a big deal."

"It's a very big deal."

"Nah. I wish I could've gone earlier, but what with the earthquake and all, it was impossible to get a flight until two weeks ago."

"But it was still too dangerous, Steph."

"Don't be ridiculous. You think I wasn't going to go looking for you because something might happen to me?"

Dominic looks impressed. "You're pretty brave for someone that small."

She wrinkles her button nose. "Five foot one isn't small, it's petite."

I smile at her fondly. Stephanie's always been a little sensitive about her height.

"But how did you know there was someone to go looking for? I mean, why didn't you think—"

Her eyes brim with tears. "You know I could never think that. Not unless it was certain."

I know exactly what she means. A life without Stephanie is one I'd never willingly accept either.

I squeeze her hand. "Thanks for that."

"Anytime."

"But how did you see Emma on *In Progress*?" Dominic asks. "Were you watching it in Tswanaland?"

"Oh, I only saw that today. On the airplane. You know those systems they have now, where you can watch all these programs? Well, they had these episodes of *In Progress,* and none of the movies appealed. Anyway, my plane landed a couple of hours ago."

"Is that how you found out I was . . . ?"

"No, no. Karen and Peter told me."

"How did you find them?"

"I found that guy, Barono, Basono—"

"Banga?"

"Yeah, that guy. Anyway, he told me where he'd left you. I paid him some money, and he took me out there."

"Not too much money, I hope."

She shakes her head. "Emma, you know I don't care about money."

I smile inwardly. "Is terrible with money" might be a better description, which is all the more reason that I need to find a way to pay her back.

"Did you enjoy the ride out to the reserve?"

She laughs. "Oh yeah, my coccyx is still bruised. But it was worth it, if just to meet Karen and Peter."

"Ah, the famous Karen and Peter," Dominic says.

I shoot him a silencing look. "Are they well?"

"They seemed very well. Missing you, though."

"I miss them too. Are they still coming back next week?"

"They said so."

"How's the school? Have classes started?"

"They were just about to. They wanted me to stay for the opening, but I needed to get home for Christmas."

Stephanie loves Christmas. Every year she takes on some huge project, like building a gingerbread house or stringing the outside of her apartment building with lights and electric reindeer that bop along to Christmas tunes.

"Karen told me to go home for Christmas, too."

"Smart lady."

"She is. I can't believe we only missed each other by a couple of days."

"I know. Ridiculous, right? If I'd been a little more patient, I could've met you at the airport," Stephanie says.

"Patience isn't really your strong suit."

"True. But I'm glad I got to see what you did there."

I look down at the floor. "I didn't do anything."

"I know twenty kids who would strongly disagree." She turns toward Dominic. "She built a whole schoolhouse, you know."

"Not a whole schoolhouse. I just helped."

"Don't be fooled, Dominic. She's not really modest."

He smiles. "You mentioned something about a story from high school?"

Her eyes light up. "Well, Emma was on the debate team, right?"

I hold up my hand. "Oh no, not that story."

Dominic looks disappointed. "Now you've made me *very* curious."

"You'll survive. How long did you stay with Karen and Peter?"

"Five days," she says wistfully.

"You sound sad."

She sighs. "I *was* kind of sad to leave. It was beautiful there." A memory of something unpleasant flits across her face. "I still can't believe Cathy Keeler was questioning your integrity like that. And that stunt she pulled with Craig—" She stops herself, looking guilty.

"Don't worry. I know all about Craig and Sophie."

"Did you find out before or after the kiss?"

Dominic stands abruptly. "I think that's my cue to leave. Nice to have met you finally, Stephanie."

She gives him an appraising look. "Yeah, you too. And thanks for taking care of Emma."

"My pleasure."

"Hello. Again—sitting right here."

Dominic places his hand on my shoulder gently, patting me twice. "I know. Good night."

"Night. Thanks again for my present."

"It belonged to you already."

He leaves, and before he's out of earshot, Stephanie leans toward me excitedly. "So tell me all about him."

"Craig?"

"No, not that idiot, and by the way, I can't believe he hooked up with *Sophie*. I mean Dominic."

"Um, well, there's nothing much to tell, really."

"Bullshit."

"I swear. We're just friends."

"But you're living together."

"That's a long story."

"We have all night."

I wake up the next morning to Stephanie's smiling face. We stayed up talking until two in the morning, finally drifting off to sleep when we couldn't stay awake any longer. It reminded me of a hundred similar scenes from childhood, when Stephanie would stay over and sleep seemed like an interruption to our endless conversation.

"What are you smiling at?" I ask. With messy hair and a makeupless face, she doesn't look much older than she did the last time we had a sleepover.

"You, silly."

"No, you're the silly."

She laughs. "That was pretty much our first conversation, wasn't it?"

"I don't remember. Was it?"

"Yeah. Remember, that kid was teasing me, that Roger kid, and you told him to get lost or he'd have you to deal with."

I think back but I don't even remember Roger. "Did I really say that?"

"Or some five-year-old equivalent. I was impressed, but I was also kind of scared of you."

"The story of my life. When did I call you silly?"

"Come on, you really don't remember?"

"Maybe. Tell me again."

She bends her pillow in half and adjusts it under her head. "Well, as I recall, I told you that now that you'd saved my hiney, we had to be friends for life, and then you crushed my little heart by telling me that I was silly. 'People aren't friends for life.'"

"I'm glad I was wrong about that."

"Me too. Hey, it's Christmas!"

"It is."

"I didn't get you anything."

"Sure you did."

"Oh, Em. I'm really glad you're okay." She raises her hand

to wipe away her sudden tears, and I'm fighting back my own.

"That makes two of us."

There's a loud sound in the hall, like someone tripped over something. "God fucking shit!" Dominic swears.

Stephanie smiles. "Your new roomie uses some colorful language."

"He's a great cook, though."

She sits up. "I should get back to my place. Come pick me up around noon?"

"Pick you up? For what?"

"We need to be at my folks' place by two."

"Steph . . ."

"You think I'm leaving you alone on Christmas? No way. You're coming to the annual Granger Liquor Fest whether you want to or not."

"Can I pick not?"

"No."

"Okay, then."

"Good. Now, get up and get ready. That's an order."

"When did you become so bossy?"

"Someone had to fill the gap while you were away."

I grab my pillow and whack her with it.

"That's the way it's going to be, huh?" She positions herself on the bed and takes a mighty swing at me with her own pillow.

A moment later we're involved in a full-fledged pillow

fight. Several rounds in, Stephanie lands a particularly good shot that catches me off balance and I tumble to the floor. The thud sounds bad, but I'm unhurt. I roll onto my side, laughing and clutching my pillow to my stomach. Dominic's bare feet are in the doorway. I look up into his amused face.

"A girl-on-girl pillow fight. It really *is* Christmas."

"Get him, Steph."

Chapter 12
Let the Sunshine In

Two weeks to the day after my first trip to the village-that-might-have-a-working-satellite-phone, I slung my pack over my back and mounted the old red Schwinn. Everything about the day seemed the same—a dry blue sky, a breeze that twined through the faded grasses, the nervous anticipation in the pit of my stomach—only this time Karen was coming with me. We started out with plenty of time to avoid the hottest part of the day, falling into an easy rhythm of squeaking wheels and weaving to avoid the pits in the road.

"Do you think they'll have fixed the phone by now?" I asked Karen.

"We'll see," she answered in a practical tone.

"They should've had enough time. I mean, if they know how to fix it, two weeks seems like enough time."

She glanced at me as I swerved to avoid a hole that could've had my bike for breakfast. "I don't think you should get your hopes up."

"Don't you want it to be fixed? You must have people you want to call."

"Of course I do. I just . . . I've learned not to put a time frame on things that I can't control. Who are you so eager to call, anyway?" she teased. "The boy?"

"I should call him. And my best friend. And the office, of course."

"Of course."

"What? It's important. People are relying on me."

"I'm sure the legal world will spin on without you."

"I know, but . . . I miss it."

"You miss *it*? Or *them*?"

I bent a little lower over the handlebars. "I meant them, of course. Plus, it's what I do for a living, right, so . . ."

Karen nodded, and we pedaled in silence until we turned the bend that brought us to the village. The same group of boys sat on the same collection of rocks, like they hadn't moved. Karen and I slowed to a stop at a safe distance, dismounting from our bikes, unsure of our welcome. But Tabansi stood up and shaded his eyes. Then his face broke into a grin and he flicked his wrist—*come, come*.

We wheeled our bikes up to him, and he bounded down from the rocks.

"You have come back," he stated in a way that should've been a question but wasn't. His jeans were held tight against his stomach with a piece of rope, and there were sweat stains around the neck of his T-shirt.

"Yes."

"You still want to use the satellite telephone."

"Yes," I said enthusiastically.

"It is still broken."

My heart fell. "Oh."

"You are disappointed."

"Yes."

"We are fixing it. You come back in—"

"Two weeks?" I said.

He grinned. "Yes," he said. "Yes."

Stephanie comes by her love of Christmas honestly, a gene she must've inherited from her mother. When people say "That family went all out at Christmas," I know they haven't met the Grangers, or seen the sight that is their house at Christmas.

The outside is restrained—in context, of course, with what's inside. The eaves and edges of the house are rimmed with white blinking lights. Next comes the enormous crystal wreath on the front door, and more lights wound around the wrought-iron baluster. Mechanical animals form a menagerie on the front lawn.

But Lucy Granger saves her real enthusiasm for inside. Each room on the ground floor gets its own tree, one white, one red, one green, and all strewn with reflective tinsel. The mantelpiece above the fireplace in the living room is crowded with a gingerbread village, lit with real lights and inhabited by dollhouse furniture. Below hang the stockings, all matching, and each embroidered with a family member's name. The air smells of cinnamon and chestnuts, with an undercurrent of rum.

The source of the rum smell is Brian's large glass of eggnog, sitting on a small table by his favorite armchair. From experience, I know this glass always looks full—barely touched—but can't be, because Brian becomes jollier by the hour and is usually nodding off by dinner.

We arrive in the early afternoon. Brian rises unsteadily to greet us. He's wearing a bright-red velour vest, in contrast with his conservative pants and shirt. His tie sports a Rudolph the Red-Nosed Reindeer motif. He envelops Stephanie and me in a joint hug, calling us his "girls," telling us not to give him a scare like that again.

When he releases us, Lucy swoops in. Her velour tracksuit matches Brian's vest, only it has a pair of reindeer antlers sprouting off the back. Her silvery hair is cut like Stephanie's; Stephanie inherited her hair-tucking motion from her mom too.

She kisses and hugs us both, smelling of turkey and cranberry sauce, and we're ushered to the comfy couch that sits under the bay window because it's present-opening time and we're behind schedule. We're just waiting on Kevin, perpetually late, at least when his parents want him to be somewhere at a particular hour.

"I didn't bring any presents," I murmur to Stephanie through the side of my mouth.

"Don't worry about it. You know Mom likes giving the most."

I nod at the truth of that, but I feel bad anyway. And then I notice something that makes my heart skip a beat: the row of bulging stockings contains one with my name on it, and also one with my mother's. If I weren't already sitting, I'd need to sit down.

These stockings are not new. They date from my childhood, when Stephanie and I treated each other's houses as extensions of our own. Somewhere along the line, we started getting invited to Christmas, and for Lucy that meant including us completely, right down to having our own stockings and innumerable presents under the tree. We didn't have the money to reciprocate fully, and I know my mother sometimes felt awkward and embarrassed, but Lucy and Brian never mentioned it. Maybe it was because of this, or maybe that's just the way of things established in childhood, but the tradition waned as we grew older, my mother and I (and sometimes Sunshine) forming our own, quieter unit.

But we were here last year, something I've been blocking out since Stephanie insisted I join her. Lucy knew my mother was sick and wanted to spare her the effort of cooking a Christmas meal. I wasn't sure whether she really wanted to come because she greeted the invitation with less than her usual enthusiasm, but when I asked her, she brushed the idea of not going aside. It would be fun, she said, to get the old gang back together. Neither of us said that it might be the last time.

My mother was frail and thin, and her hair was starting to become wispy, like a baby's, but we were still hopeful then that the chemo would work. At least I was. Maybe she'd already accepted that it wasn't going to, but she kept that to herself. Everyone at the Grangers' acted normally, like it was just another Christmas, just another gift exchange. I gave my mother an African tribal mask to add to her collection. She was delighted and I shared in her enthusiasm. And maybe this planted the seed that led to my trip. Or maybe she'd been planning it for a while; she left it so I couldn't ask.

Lucy catches me staring at the stocking. "I hope you don't mind, dear, but I thought it would be nice to put Elizabeth's stocking out too. So she's here with us, in a way."

I feel like I might burst into tears, but I force myself to say, "Of course. Thank you."

Stephanie squeezes my arm and hands me a Kleenex. I blow my nose, muttering something about allergies, but nobody's fooled. Sadness seems to radiate from me, dampening the *Perry Como Christmas* tracks, forcing down the level in Brian's eggnog glass. I feel like the antithesis of Christmas and am about to suggest leaving when Stephanie's brother, Kevin, shows up.

Two years older than me, Kevin was my first hopeless crush. Quietly gay—he came out the summer after graduation, to the surprise of many—he always seemed to me to be the perfect older brother. Tolerant when Stephanie and I hung around him, dryly funny and helpful in obtaining party supplies if we asked him nicely and promised to call him if the party got too wild.

No one in the Granger family is tall, and Kevin's no exception. About my height, with dark blond hair, his best feature is his dark blue eyes.

He kisses his mother perfunctorily on the cheek, shakes hands with his father, and ruffles the top of Stephanie's head, chiding her for not calling him the minute she got back. And then he lifts me up from the couch into a tight hug and says, loud enough for everyone to hear, "Well, this must fucking suck."

"You have no idea," I murmur into his chest.

"We all wish Elizabeth was here, you know. It's not the same without her."

"No." It isn't. It isn't the same without her at all.

"At least there's plenty of alcohol," he says.

I smile through my tears as Kevin releases me and heads to the bar stand in the corner of the room. He mixes three strong vodka tonics and hands them to Stephanie and me like he's a doctor dispensing medicine.

"Drink up, girls. It's Christmas, after all."

I wake up early the next morning in Stephanie's room nursing a turkey hangover. Steph is wheezing gently across the room in her childhood bed, the twin of mine. The beds are still covered in the matching pink flowered covers she chose when she was twelve. I hear her early-rising parents shuffling around downstairs, shushing each other and talking about letting "the kids" sleep in. I'd like that, but all I can think about is my own childhood house, a block away, sitting cold and abandoned, the furniture covered in dust sheets.

I rise as quietly as I can and take my clothes to the bathroom to dress. Then I creep down the stairs, bypassing the kitchen for the front entrance. I suit up and slip out into a gentle snow. The streets are muffled quiet, the light gray and still.

In a few minutes I'm standing at the edge of my old front porch. It looks the same as ever, maybe a little neglected. A simple white clapboard house, much smaller than the Grangers'. Black shutters. A bay window. The curtains shut against the world. A sagging porch holding a swing, dead leaves scattered between the railings. The swing has a dusting of snow on it, and the metal chain holding it up is starting to rust.

I wipe the snow away with my mitten and lift the seat's lid, and there it is: the heavy wool Hudson's Bay blanket we always kept there so we could swing in all but the coldest of weather.

I sit on the seat, tucking the blanket around my legs. I push at the floor absentmindedly while I gaze across the street. The swing rocks and creaks.

My mother grew up in this house. We moved here after my father left us, mostly for financial reasons. I don't think my mother had a very happy childhood, being the only child of an insular couple who'd found themselves expecting in their late thirties, but "they did their best," as my mother was fond of saying. They certainly took us in willingly, but it was a hushed-down childhood, noise and toys kept to a minimum. I knew they loved me more than I felt it.

They passed away ten years ago, within weeks of each other, leaving the house to my mother and, now, to me. Deciding what to do with it is one of the many things I tried not to think about while I was away. And the memories inside have kept me from coming here since I've been back.

Directly across the street is Sunshine's house. Or where she grew up, anyway.

Sunshine's parents still live there, as far as I know. It's how she and my mother met, growing up together like Stephanie and me. I know her number is inside, on the wall, next to the phone I spent too many hours on as a teenager.

And any minute now, any second now, I'll find the strength to go inside and make the call I should have made a week ago.

In the end, I don't need to. I don't know how many minutes go by, but I hear a scraping noise on the stairs, and when I look up, there's Sunshine.

"Emmaline?" she says tentatively, like she might be speaking to an apparition.

I stand up quickly, tripping over the blanket as it falls to my feet. She opens her arms and I collapse onto her broad chest. As she wraps her arms around me, holding me close, I smell her familiar smell—a mix of patchouli and earth—and for the first time in a long time, I feel safe. I feel home.

Inside the cold house, Sunshine holds me away from her and studies me from the top of my messy ponytail to my booted feet. Her grizzled gray hair is cut boy short, and there's a single red streak that flops across her forehead. Her face is round and lined, and her brown eyes are watery and kind.

"What are you doing here?" I ask her when speech returns.

"I was packing up to leave when I saw you out the window, sitting on the porch swing just like you always used to do."

"You came home for Christmas," I say, as much to myself as to her. Sunshine lives in Costa Rica, running an ecotourist supply shop on the edge of a jungle. She makes the trek home to visit her still-hale but disapproving parents infrequently. My mother's funeral was the first time she'd been home in years.

"I did. When did you get here?"

"You mean you don't know?"

"Don't know what, dear?"

I guess I've gotten so used to the idea of everyone thinking I was dead, it never occurred to me that Sunshine might not have even known I was missing. She left town a few days after I did, and she's never kept track of world events at the best of times. She shuts out the worst of times completely, refusing to read anything that involves destruction or human suffering.

We sit on the couch and I tell her my story, from Africa to finding Dominic moving into my apartment. I save Craig for last, and when I get to him, I'm emotionally spent enough that I only feel like crying but don't actually do so.

Progress, progress.

"I'm sorry, Emma. You didn't deserve that."

"No, but he thought I was dead. I should've known he'd move on."

"If he really loved you, he would've known you were still alive."

"I don't know. Maybe."

"No, you have a strong presence. I would've felt it if it had gone away. That's why it never occurred to me ... I heard about the earthquake, of course, but I knew you were fine."

"How?"

"Oh, honey, you know I can't explain my gifts. They just *are.*"

I hide my smile. I remember Sunshine telling me when I was seven that a fairy died every time someone said, "I don't believe in fairies." When I told her I knew that came from *Peter Pan* (I was that kind of seven-year-old), she just smiled and said, "Of course it does. Mr. Barrie's an expert on fairies."

"Lots of people thought I was dead," I say.

She appraises me again. "Yes, I can see that. There's death hanging around you."

"Do you mean my mother?"

"No, she's not a bad presence. She's the good you're feeling."

"Then who is it?"

"Who thought you were dead?"

"I don't know. Everyone."

She shakes her head. "Not Stephanie. She never gave up."

My heart constricts. "No, that's true."

I stand up and take a slow lap around the living room. The dark bookshelves on either side of the fireplace are filled not with books but with African artifacts, filmy now with dust. My mother's lifelong obsession, one I fed on countless birthdays and Christmases, saving up my allowance just to see the joy on her face when she'd unwrap the latest mask, or spear point, or beaded necklace. It didn't matter that what I bought her— particularly when I was younger—was mostly fake. It was the thought that counted, and what she thought and dreamt about was Africa. The place she most wanted to go and never made it to. In my book of regrets, number one is never asking her *why* she was so intrigued by the place. Perhaps because it was just one of those immutable things, like cotton candy at a fair.

But on the mantel, above the fireplace we never used because we couldn't afford to have it fixed, is the reason I should've come here much sooner: pictures, pictures, pictures. Of my mother, of us together, of all the important moments.

I pick up the shot taken on the day I graduated from law school and hold it close to my chest. Sunshine puts her hands on my shoulders. "If you're going to move on, we have to clear the death away."

"What do you mean?"

"Here, come with me."

She leads me back to the faded chintz couch. When my grandparents were alive, the furniture was covered in plastic, making it slippery, the perfect place for me and Stephanie to play our favorite game—living room slip and slide—until discovered and punished by my frightened-looking mother. She peeled off those covers the day after her mother's funeral with a determined look on her face. When I asked what she was doing, she only said, "Did you want another sliding session?" and then started laughing semihysterically. I hugged her, and we laughed and cried, missing Grandma even if we didn't want to live by her rules anymore.

Sunshine closes her eyes and places her hands on my shoulders. As she concentrates, the smell of patchouli seems to grow stronger. My mind starts to wander, flitting from my mom to work to Craig. God, Craig. He's the one I should be throwing glasses at. Only next time, I won't miss.

Sunshine's eyes open. "Stop thinking about him."

"Okay, Patrick Jane, now you're kind of freaking me out."

"Who's Patrick Jane?"

"It's the name of a character on a television show. He can kind of read people's minds, only not really . . ." I trail off lamely.

"Well, maybe I'll watch it sometime. Now, I think I know something that might work." She reaches into the large leather satchel she uses as a purse and takes out a pink crystal that's the size of my thumb. "Give me your hands."

"What for?"

"Just trust me."

I hold my hands in front of me and she places the crystal in them. "What's the crystal for?"

"I'm going to use it to draw out all the negative energy and localize it."

I think briefly of protesting, but what can it hurt? It's only a rock.

She holds one hand to her heart and the other on the crystal. She closes her eyes and hums a low, indistinct tune.

"Instead of death, life. Instead of pain, happiness. Instead of brain, heart," Sunshine murmurs over and over, almost singing the words.

It's strangely soothing. I close my eyes and feel myself drifting.

Life, happiness, heart. If only saying it over and over would make it so.

"You can open your eyes now," Sunshine says.

"Is that it?"

"No, I want you to keep this with you until you find a place where you feel safe and secure and ready to let go of all the death, pain, and unhappiness. When you do, I want you to bury it in the ground and leave it all behind you."

The crystal feels warm in my hand, and lighter somehow. Maybe I do too. "Thanks, Sunshine."

"You're welcome." She kisses the top of my head. "Your mother loved you very much, you know."

"I know."

Chapter 13
When the Ball Drops

The weather warms right after Christmas, as it often does. I remember more than one ski trip with Stephanie's family where we ended up in the lodge watching the rain wash the snow away. And so it is this year. One day of steady rain and above-freezing temperatures is all it takes to scrub Christmas off the sidewalks and leave brown strips of lawn. The lingering, twinkling lights look out of place.

I spend much of the week hibernating. As much as Stephanie lets me, at least. When she's not dragging me out for walks, or on a quest to find the perfect throw for her couch, or any of countless other manufactured errands to keep me from disappearing into the box Dominic gave me for Christmas, I immerse myself in books I've always meant to read. *The Time Traveler's Wife*, *A Million Little Pieces*, the collected works of Malcolm Gladwell.

Dominic returns from his parents', black mood back and firmly in place. He spends most of his time away from the apartment. He tells me he's at his studio, working on the photographs for his next show. I don't know him well enough to call him a liar, but judging from the smells he brings home with him, my bet is that he's spending more time on a bar stool than in the darkroom. Not that I can blame him. He was supposed to be on his honeymoon, sipping frothy drinks in a deck chair under a hot sun. And who am I to call him out? If I thought hiding in a bottle would fix things, I'd be right there with him.

"All right, Gloomy Head, enough of this shit."

I look up from *What the Dog Saw*. Stephanie's standing at the end of my bed in jeans and a ski sweater with a disapproving look on her face.

"How did you get in here?"

"Dominic let me in." Her eyes travel from the stack of books by my bedside to the dishes on the floor. "I leave you alone for one day and look what happens."

"I'm catching up on my reading."

"Uh-huh."

"I'm even reading books that are making me smarter. What's wrong with that?"

"Nothing, if you're sick. Are you sick?"

I give a halfhearted cough. "I do feel a cold coming on, yeah."

"Uh-huh."

"Will you stop saying that?"

"Only when you admit that you're hiding."

"From what?"

She stands and walks to the window, pulling back the filmy curtains. Cold sunlight streams through the dirt-spattered panes, falling across the bed. "From life."

"Ha! What life?"

"From the life that's passing you by."

"You mean my once brilliant career? Or were you referring to my ex-boyfriend?"

She raises her right hand. "Enough. I don't want to hear it. We're late."

"Late for what?"

"For finding the perfect outfit."

"I don't like the sound of this."

"It's New Year's Eve, and you're coming to Drop the Ball with me. Whether you like it or not."

"I don't."

"Too bad."

"I don't have a dress."

"I mentioned shopping, didn't I?"

"I don't have a date."

"I'll get Kevin to come. We'll make it a threesome."

"You did not just refer to me, you, and your gay brother as a threesome."

"Ask someone, then."

"Like who? Sunshine?"

"What about Dominic?"

I throw back the covers and stand up. "I doubt he'd want to come."

"You doubt I'd want to come to what?" Dominic asks, popping his head around the door.

"Nothing," I say at the same time as Stephanie says, "Drop the Ball."

His brow furrows. "You mean that thing at the convention center? Aren't we a bit old for that?"

"Yes, exactly. We *are* too old for that."

"Nonsense," Stephanie says. "I've been going for years."

"Tell him how old you were the first time you went."

She colors, remembering, perhaps, who she went home with that night. "I don't see what that has to do with anything. Besides, it's fun."

Dominic's eyes meet mine. "I'm in if you are."

I hesitate as my mind strays to the things I planned on doing tonight. Eating an entire can of Pringles. Watching *Bull Durham* for the zillionth time. Falling asleep at 10 P.M. feeling sick to my stomach.

"I guess we're going to a party."

Stephanie raises her hands toward the roof. "Woop, woop!"

* * *

We arrive at the convention center six hours later. It's all lit up, and there's a line of cabs and Lincoln Town Cars disgorging some suspiciously young-looking people dressed in pastels and tuxedos.

"Maybe this wasn't such a good idea," Dominic mutters to me, eyeing a couple who look about fourteen.

"What's that?" Stephanie says. She looks fresh and pretty in a ballet-slipper-pink satin gown that resembles Marilyn Monroe's dress in *Some Like It Hot*.

"I was just wondering if we were going to get carded," Dominic says. He's looking . . . well . . . dashing, really, in a black suit with a light-blue tie and a matching pocket square.

I shake out the black cocktail dress I bought this afternoon. It cost way too much money, but the shop was about to close and I was desperate. It's sleeveless with a high neck, a green sash around the waist, and a pleated bell skirt with pockets sewn into the seams. I twisted my hair up and made my eyes smoky to complete the look.

"Let's get inside before we freeze," Dominic says.

We walk through the crowd. The air is thick with aftershave and the kind of perfume teenage girls think makes them appealing.

"Is there anyone over thirty here?" I ask.

"Yes, *us*," Stephanie replies.

"Right, of course."

"You could at least *try* to have a good time, you know."

"You're right. Engaging good-time programming now."

Dominic's eyebrows rise. "Oh God, you're not a Trekkie, are you?"

"I don't know what you're talking about."

Stephanie walks up to a pretty teenage girl sitting at a card table outside the main ballroom. She pays the entrance fee and returns with a string of bright yellow raffle tickets.

"What are these for?" I ask.

"Drinks, of course."

Dominic shudders next to me. "I just had the worst case of déjà vu."

"Oh yeah?"

"Yeah. It involved waiting in line for more raffle tickets while my buzz died."

"Okay, that's it!" Stephanie says loudly enough to catch the attention of several other partygoers. "I've about had it with the both of you. Nobody else came up with any better ideas for tonight, and it's not like I forced you to come here."

"Well . . . ," I say.

"What?"

"I *was* forced to come here."

Dominic shoves his fist into his mouth.

"Shit. What's wrong with you guys?"

Dominic coughs.

"What now?" Stephanie asks.

"My fiancée cheated on me."

Stephanie looks annoyed. "Why did you say that?"

"You asked what was wrong. That's what's wrong."

"My boyfriend cheated on me," I say.

"But not with your best friend."

"Yeah, just while I was *missing*."

"Four weeks before my *wedding*."

"With my mortal enemy."

"In our bed."

I pause. "Okay, you win."

"Enough!" Stephanie shouts. She points at Dominic with a stabbing gesture. "You, go use those drink tickets." She points at me. "You, go find us a table."

"What are *you* going to do?" I ask.

"I. Am. Going. To. The. Bathroom," she says with as much dignity as she can muster. *"Capisce?"*

"Yes," we say in unison.

"Good."

We disperse on our separate missions. In the ballroom, there are thousands of little white lights on the ceiling and soft panels of pastel fabric covering the walls. Baskets of flowers hang from hooks all around the room, emitting a perennial-garden scent. There's a series of moving strobe lights at the edge of the stage. Behind them, a thirty-something cover band is doing a great rendition of Kanye West's "Gold Digger." Large round tables covered in white tablecloths and candles fill the area between the walls and the dance floor. It's full of pretty young things busting a move.

I walk along the edge of the room, searching for an empty table. A group of awkward boys are leaning against the wall, gazing at three maybe-eighteen-year-old girls. The girls have that queen-bee confidence, all blond highlights, flipping hair and dresses that are a little too short. These geeky boys don't stand a chance (even they know that), but they can't help harboring some small, *Sixteen Candles* hope that one of the girls will have a soft spot for a boy who might invent the next iPod.

I move a little closer so I can hear their loud whispers.

"She's looked at you twice, Ethan," says a tall, thin boy-man. His tuxedo hangs loosely on his lanky frame, and his white shirt gapes away from his pencil neck.

"Are you sure?" Ethan answers. He's rounder than he should be and in the throes of a bad case of acne.

"Totally. Look, she just did it again."

"Doesn't she look kind of old?"

"Haven't you ever heard of cougars? Don't be such a 404. Just ask her already."

Ethan peels himself off the wall and walks toward me with

a shy smile on his face. He's about my height, and his thick glasses magnify a pair of watery blue eyes.

Oh shit, they were talking about *me*. I'm the potential cougar.

"Hi, my name's Ethan. Would you like to dance?"

"Um . . . my, um . . . date was just getting me a drink."

A blush creeps up his face. "Oh, sorry."

"No, that's okay."

I try to give him a never-stop-going-for-it smile, but that's a lot to convey in a look. As is maybe-you-should-wait-until-college-before-you-ask-another-girl-out.

"Sorry to bother you, ma'am."

He shuffles back to his wall and his friends.

Dominic joins me with a drink in each hand, something bubbly and pink. "Did you just crush that poor kid?"

"Me crush *him*? He called me ma'am. And his friend referred to me as a cougar!"

"Ouch."

"I know. Can you beat him up for me or something?"

"You want me to beat up a member of the nerd herd?"

I consider him. "It wouldn't be your first time, would it?"

"Now who's being mean?"

"I didn't want to hurt his feelings."

"Why didn't you dance with him?"

"Seriously, Dominic? I could be his mom."

"I was going to say . . ."

I whack him on the arm.

"Hey! Don't spill the drinks."

I take one of the glasses from him and taste it. It's one part fruity punch and two parts Firewhiskey. It scorches the back of my throat and leaves me feeling short of breath.

"You want to dance?" Dominic asks.

"I don't know."

"Stephanie's orders."

"Well, in that case."

We leave our glasses on a table and push our way into the dancing throng. The band finishes a loud guitar song by Nickelback. Then the drummer kicks it up a notch and they launch into a pitch-perfect version of "Sunday Bloody Sunday."

"Where is Steph, anyway?" I yell over the music.

"No idea. You going to dance or what?"

"Just as soon as you do."

"Watch out, honey." Dominic raises his hand above his head, pushing it toward the ceiling, and bites his lower lip with his upper teeth. He swivels his hips in a way that is both geeky and sexy.

I start laughing. He lowers his hand and beckons me with his index finger. I sashay toward him, letting the music and the drink work their magic. Around us, the kids are jumping in unison and asking how long they have to sing this song. The floor is vibrating beneath our feet.

Their energy is infectious. We jump and sing, just as I used to do when I was the right age to be at this kind of event. And like then, I feel happy and young and free. Maybe Stephanie knows what she's doing, after all.

The song ends, and the band transitions into Sam Phillips's "Reflecting Light." The crowd around us melds seamlessly into couples. Dominic pulls me toward him and slips his hands around my waist. They feel warm through the thin fabric of my dress.

As I put my arms around his neck, it's my turn for a case of déjà vu. It's my senior prom, and I'm wearing a black dress and spinning slowly on the dance floor. Only then it was Bobby Jordan holding me close, and the alcohol on my breath was the Southern Comfort I stole from my mother's liquor cabinet. Bobby and I had sex in his parents' basement much later that night (such a cliché, right?), and broke up three weeks after that.

I lean away from Dominic. "Do you think Stephanie's trying to teach us a lesson?"

"What's that?"

"I don't know yet, but it feels like something."

He leans toward my ear. "Maybe she brought us here to forget. Isn't that what New Year's is all about?"

"I thought it was about remembering. Isn't that what 'Auld Lang Syne' means? All that stuff about old acquaintances."

"Maybe, but it shouldn't be. It should be about starting fresh. Starting over."

"Are you going to tell me to 'imagine the possibilities' again?"

"Hey, that was some good advice."

We twirl in silence for a moment, my chin resting on his shoulder. The band starts to play a song by Taylor Swift that I never caught the name of.

"This really is kind of like high school, isn't it?" Dominic says.

"Only with alcohol."

"Thank God. That really was the only thing missing."

I start to laugh. "You must've been really popular in high school."

"Why do you say that?"

"Because only someone who was popular in high school could think the only thing missing was alcohol."

"Are you saying you weren't popular in high school?"

"Are you kidding me? Between the braces and the loud opinions, I was one step above those boys on the wall."

He looks down at me. "I can't imagine it."

"Good."

He tightens his arms and pulls me close enough to smell

his aftershave. Warmth flows through me—a mix of the alcohol, the pretty song, and the solidity of Dominic.

When I look up again, he's looking at me with a focused expression. Everything seems to slow down as Dominic lifts his hand and brushes my hair away from my eyes. We pause for a moment, and then we move toward each other. He stops right before his lips touch mine, when they're close enough for me to feel his breath against my mouth. "You're vibrating."

My mind feels unfocused. "What?"

"I think your phone is ringing."

I reach into the pocket of my dress. My cell phone is jittering about. I take it out and hold it close to my ear.

"Hello?"

"Emma?"

"Craig?"

Dominic frowns and drops his arms. A chill spreads through me.

"Emma, where are you? I can barely hear you."

"I'm . . . it's a long story. Hold on a sec."

I raise a finger to let Dominic know I'll be back in a minute and walk toward one of the side exits. In the quieter corridor, my ears have that loud-music ringing feeling they always have after a concert. My heart's pounding and yet I feel oddly numb.

"Emma, are you still there?"

"I'm here. What do you want, Craig?"

"It's New Year's."

"What does that have to do with anything?"

"I know. It's just . . ."

He goes silent. I can hear a loud jumble of voices, chamber music, and popping champagne corks through the phone. I have that sense of déjà vu again, only this time it's Craig I'm dancing with and champagne I've been drinking.

Oh no, he isn't . . . he couldn't . . .

"Where are you, Craig?"

He sighs heavily. "Damn, Emma."

And now I know for sure. He's at our party. The party we always go to on New Year's at the Turner Hotel, a black-tie event where we eat extravagant food and drink champagne until the world is all bubbly. And at midnight, we watch the ball drop and count down to our first kiss of the year.

Ten, nine, eight . . .

"Who are you at the party with?"

"Emma."

"Goodbye, Craig."

"Please don't hang up."

"What is it? What do you want to say?"

"I just . . . I miss you."

I can't believe he has the nerve to call me from *our* party, with Sophie probably waiting for him in the next room, her lips all moist and kissable. I can almost smell her perfume through the phone.

"Emma? Are you still there?"

"No." I click off my phone, my hand shaking.

Goddamnit!

I kick my foot against the wall, then instantly regret it. High-heeled pointy shoes are not the right footwear for kicking concrete.

The exit door clanks open behind me. It's Dominic, his face full of an expression I can't read. Resigned, maybe.

"I'm sorry about that. I don't know why he called."

"That guy sure has some sense of timing."

"I'm sorry."

"It doesn't matter." He stuffs his hands into his pockets. "Stephanie's looking for you."

I scan his face, trying to figure out what he wants me to say, what I want to say. All I come up with is that neither of us is ready for whatever it was we were about to do out there on the dance floor.

And it's this uncertainty that makes me reply, "We'd better get back in there, then."

Chapter 14
Back in the Saddle

The Monday morning after New Year's has me questioning why I ever wanted any part of my old life back.

I arrive at the office at eight o'clock on the dot. Under my new knee-length, black wool coat, I'm wearing a crisp white blouse, a navy suit with a flirty pleated skirt, and a pair of knee-high boots made of soft black leather.

The elevator doors ding open and I walk into the lobby. The quasi-twin receptionists have turned the page on Christmas—there's not a trace of the tree, lights, or tinsel. It's January 3 and back to business.

I ask them if they know where my new office is. They don't, but apparently Matt wants to see me. With a fluttery stomach, I hang my coat on one of the wood hangers in the visitors' closet. The last time I hung a coat in here, I was a second-year law student looking for a summer job. I felt nervous and out of place that day too.

I give the receptionists a bright (fake) smile and walk to

Matt's office. Almost no one is in yet. The air smells faintly of cleaning products, and I can hear the dim hum of the air-filtration system, a white noise that's strangely calming. The air turns off at 8 P.M., its absence always a sign I'm working too late.

I pass my old office. Sophie's in already, sitting with her shoulders square to the corridor as she types away at something with meticulous precision. The perfect fit of her black blazer leaves me feeling dumpy, like I'm wearing last year's suit. She reaches a manicured hand toward her coffee cup. I jump away from the glass wall and out of view. The longer I avoid her, the better.

Matt's sitting at his desk, his sleeves already rolled up to his elbows, deep into a pile of boring-looking documents. The sun rises across the wintry city behind him, reflecting off the tall, shiny buildings.

I knock gently on his door. He looks up and gives me a welcoming smile. "There you are, Emma."

"Here I am."

"Come in, come in."

I take a seat in the black leather visitor's chair that's too low to the ground. Sitting in it always makes me feel ten years old.

"All rested and settled and ready to get back to work?"

"Absolutely."

"Great. I put some files in your office, simple stuff really, but everyone has to start somewhere." Matt's face twists into an ironic expression. "Sorry, I didn't mean . . ."

I almost start to laugh. I've never seen Matt tongue-tied before.

"Forget it. I *am* starting over. No need to pretend otherwise."

"That's my girl."

"Where have you parked me?"

"Yes, um, well, you know we couldn't ask Sophie to move."

"Don't worry, Matt. I get it. Anywhere will be fine."

And maybe, just maybe, I'll figure out a way to make Sophie pay for all of it. The office, my files, Craig.

"I thought you'd be best off in the office next to me."

My heart skips a beat. "I'm being put in the Ejector?"

No one who's ever worked in the office next to Matt has lasted at the firm for more than three months. It's like being perched on a shiny red Eject button, hence the name.

He smiles. "Are they still calling it that?"

I try not to sound panicked. "When I last checked."

"You'll have to give it a new name, then."

"Sure. The Phoenix, maybe." Matt's phone rings and I stand to leave. "Anyway, I should get to it."

He reaches for his phone. "I'll come check on you later."

That sounds nice, right? Only I never needed checking on before.

I leave Matt's office, turn left, and walk into the Ejector.

My old desk, made of teak and nicked in the left corner (I slammed my stapler against it after getting a particularly bad judgment a few years ago), is nestled against the window. My chocolate leather desk chair is tucked under it. Along the wall to the right of the door is my chaise longue, covered in a taupe chenille fabric that's just right for a catnap. My law degree and a picture taken with Matt on the day I became a member of the bar are hanging on the wall above it. There's a shiny new BlackBerry in a box in the middle of my desk. There's even a tall ficus plant in the corner.

So, unlike Pedro, TPC didn't throw my stuff away when they learned I was missing. Someone—Matt, probably, via Nathalie—had it packed away, waiting. And it's likely that same combo that's taken the time to make me feel welcome. But even an Extreme Makeover can't change the fact that I'm starting my career over at thirty-four and three quarters in a . career-ending eighty square feet of space.

Well, I'd better get to it.

There's a neat stack of buff-colored case files sitting on my desk in front of an oversized silver Mac desktop computer. I open the first one. It's an insurance defense file. This one is typical. Mr. Smith bought a washing machine two years ago. He left it running when he went out to dinner and returned to find his condo flooded. The insurance company paid out tens of thousands of dollars to repair the damage, and now it wants to sue the washing machine's manufacturer to recoup its payout. Yawn.

I sift through the pile. All of the cases follow this fact pattern. Apparently there's an epidemic of badly manufactured washing machines out there. Fantastic.

"E.W. Great to see you back!"

I swivel my chair toward the door. The Initial Brigade is standing there with bright grins on their preppy faces. I. William Stone, J. Perry Irving, and K. R. Monty, three associates in their early thirties who always seem to travel in a pack. Somehow, one of them found out my middle name is Wendy, and I've been "E.W." ever since. They must get their suits in three-for-one specials, or maybe it's just that all navy pin-striped suits look the same.

"How you doing, boys?"

"Same old, same old," I. William drawls in his coastal accent. He has light-brown hair cut in a right-of-center part. He looks like an advertising salesman from the early sixties.

"I see they put you in the Ejector," Monty says. He has washed-out blue eyes and medium-brown hair.

"Still pointing out the obvious, Monty?"

J.P. guffaws and slaps Monty hard on the back. He's a head taller than the other two, and he doesn't always know his own strength. He likes to assert his individuality by wearing suspenders. Today's are bright red.

"Of course he is. Nothing around here ever changes."

I try not to sigh. "Seems like some things do."

I. William looks sympathetic. "I told Craig to stay away from that grasping bitch."

"Careful, dude, Matt might hear you." Monty's eyes shift nervously.

J.P. lowers his voice. "If you need our help with anything in *that department,* you just let us know."

"Thanks, J.P. I'm touched."

"No worries. We're tom-tomming for cocktails. You'll get an email with the details later."

"Sounds great."

I. William glances at the files behind me. "Have fun slogging through the shit pile."

I give them a little wave as they push off, on to the next stop on their morning tour. I know they'll be back after lunch. I'm already kind of looking forward to it. None of their billable hours are what they should be, but they make up for it in entertainment value.

I begin dictating a model action for the stack of files so my assistant can plug in the details. The sooner I get through these, the sooner I can do more important things, like filing my too-long-delayed action against Pedro.

Speaking of which, where *is* my assistant? Or better question, who?

I walk tentatively toward the cream fabric divider that forms the walls of the Ejector's secretarial station. All I can see are two long, spray-tanned legs that end in a pair of very high strappy sandals. The owner's toenails are painted bright red.

I feel a little bubble of thankfulness as I peek around the divider, because it's Jenny, chewing gum and squinting at her computer screen. She's messaging with someone called PLAYR. I've never quite figured out how she manages to be as competent as she is while simultaneously carrying on at least three social-networking conversations at all times. Must be a generational thing.

"Hi, Jenny."

Her baby-blue eyes drift up toward mine. "Hi, Emma!"

"What are you doing here?"

She pops up and gives me a quick hug. "We're going to work together again! I *insisted.*"

"Hey, that's great." I pat her on the back a few times, and she lets me go.

"Is there anything you need me to do?"

"I'm dictating some proceedings. I'll need you to issue them later today."

She cracks her gum. "Of course." Her computer emits a pinging sound. PLAYR wants to know if she wants to *hook up 2nite?* Her eyes trail toward the computer screen. She's clearly itching to give PLAYR a meeting time. "But don't you want to take it easy on your first day back?"

"I'm not sure that's an option."

"Gotcha."

I close my door and sit down at my desk. I stare out the window at the urban landscape, feeling sorry for myself.

Shit files. The Ejector. Matt's pitying looks. All I need to complete this crap fest is an altercation with Sophie, and Craig telling me he misses me again. Of course, now that I've put that out there, it's probably what's coming next.

Needing to hear a friendly voice, I call Stephanie. She agrees to meet me at the apartment after work. Feeling reassured by the normalcy of our conversation, I return to my files. At noon, I send Jenny out for a sandwich rather than face the curious stares in the cafeteria. True to his word, Matt checks in/up on me several times, always arriving with his arms full of files, saying something like, "I thought you could help me with this [fill in really boring task, like organizing exhibits or summarizing depositions]," or "You don't mind doing some research on [fill in really basic research mandate that would normally have been given to a first-year]." By the late afternoon, my office is full of boxes, and I've got enough work to keep me occupied for months.

This is why no one survives the Ejector. They crumble

under the stress of unreasonable expectations. The thought of having to spend a whole year, maybe longer, dealing with this kind of shit has me surfing the Internet for graduate school programs.

Just when I'm thinking of packing it in, there's a soft rap on the door. I turn my chair with trepidation. Craig is standing in the doorway in a three-piece suit with a sheepish look on his face.

"Hi. Can I come in?"

Every bone in my body is screaming *no, no, no!* But a little part of my brain (probably the same part that agreed to come back to work under these ridiculous conditions) is curious about what he has to say.

"Yeah, all right."

He closes the door behind him and takes a seat on the chaise longue, placing a thick file next to him.

"How's your day going?"

"Fine."

He eyes the overflowing boxes on the floor. "Matt give you something to work on?"

"A few things. Insurance files."

"I guess that's to be expected." He looks around. "You know, they did a good job in here."

"Sure. I guess."

"It doesn't seem right, though, putting you in the Ejector."

"I can handle it."

He meets my gaze. "I know you can, but still, it's not right."

I look away. "It's no big deal."

"You going to that drinks thing the Initial Brigade is organizing?"

"I'm not sure. I thought I might head out early."

"Really? You?"

"It's this thing I'm trying."

He smiles. "Let me know how that works out."

"Sure."

He leans forward, his hands on his thighs. "Emma . . ."

Oh no, you don't, buddy. You lost the right to "Emma" me in that tone when you started believing I was dead because Sophie told you so.

"Seriously, Craig? Is this what we're doing now?"

"What do you mean?"

"Making idle chitchat like we're colleagues who haven't seen each other in a while? Like I've only been away on a long vacation?"

"I'm sorry. I thought it might be easier if . . . I mean, bringing up all that stuff, I don't see where it would get us."

It might get us closure. Or then again, it might get me arrested for attempted murder. At this point, it could go either way.

"No, you wouldn't."

"Don't you think it would be better if we started over? As friends?"

Someday, someone will explain to men that this is *always* the wrong thing to say.

"Imagine the possibilities," I mutter.

"What's that?"

"Nothing. Just something Dominic said."

"Who's Dominic?"

"A friend. No one."

His face clouds. "Is he that guy living in your apartment?"

"What does it matter?"

"Don't say that. I still care about you. Very much."

"Yeah, well, don't, okay?"

"Emma, please—"

"No, I mean it, Craig. I really can't handle this today."

He sighs. "All right, if that's what you want."

He stands but makes no move to leave. Instead, he stares at me like too many people have in the last few weeks. Like I need saving.

And I'm so sick of that look, that pitying, "poor Emma" look.

I march to my door and wrench it open, possibly dislocating my shoulder. Two female students are standing outside, whispering. They look fresh-faced and curious.

"If you don't want to end up in here next, I suggest you beat it."

Their eyes turn panicked and they can't get away fast enough.

I turn back to Craig. "You can follow them anytime you like."

Craig puts his hand on my shoulder. "I'm glad you're back."

"What's going on here?" Sophie says.

Craig drops his hand as we both turn toward her. She's standing in front of my door, looking pissed. And strangely, seeing her there makes the day feel complete somehow.

Completely fucked up, but complete nonetheless.

"It's nothing," Craig says in a conciliatory tone.

Her thin lips get thinner. "Having a little reunion, are we?"

"Sophie, we talked about this."

Her eyes narrow and release. I can almost hear her mentally counting to ten.

"I just wanted to welcome Emma back," she says through tightly clenched teeth.

Interesting. Sophie's jealous. Of *me*. That's almost funny.

"Thanks, Sophie," I say as neutrally as I can. No need to fuel her jealousy other than petty satisfaction. Besides, it's not like I have the upper hand here in the Ejector and all.

"Craig, can I talk to you in my office?" Sophie says.

The tips of his ears go pink like they always do when he's embarrassed. Craig doesn't like scenes, especially not public ones. But he's made his choice. Good luck to him.

"Sure. See you later, Emma."

They leave. I sit in my chair and twist it slowly toward the window. The sun has set and the city's lights twinkle past the reflection of my desk lamp. It's pretty, but my brain is whirring too quickly to appreciate it.

I'm back in the saddle, all right.

Chapter 15
That's the Idea

I don't know what it is that propels me to the Initial Brigade's drinks-I'd-normally-skip. All I know is that when I leave the office, fully intending to head straight home, I end up in the trendy bar two blocks away where half the associates have gathered to wage a campaign on several bottles of vodka.

Craig arrives solo about fifteen minutes later. He keeps his distance, mixing with lawyers from the corporate department while I try to concentrate on the I'm-sure-they're-hilarious stories being told by I. William in a loud voice. When I glance toward his side of the room, I catch Craig watching me. He looks away before I can be sure, but he seems sad, wistful.

Part of me wants to march the drink I'm nursing across the room and throw it in his face, but all that would do is waste a good drink. Besides, I've never been about big, dramatic gestures in my personal life. I leave those for the courtroom.

When the I.B. start talking about moving to a different venue, I decide to head home, thoughts of slumping into bed and pulling the covers over my head forefront in my mind. As

I take off my coat in the entryway, I hear the sound of voices in the distance.

"Hello?"

"We're in here," Dominic answers from the kitchen.

We? Oh, right. I invited Stephanie over for dinner. At eight. I check my watch. It's eight thirty. Damn.

"Be there in a sec."

I go to my room and change into comfy clothes (black leggings and a bright green hoodie that called to me from the teen section despite Dominic's warnings), the next best thing to hiding in bed. I pull my hair back into a ponytail, apply some Chap Stick, and go to the kitchen.

Stephanie's perched on the counter next to the stove wearing a black one-piece flight suit that has a silver zipper running up the middle. She's wearing sparkly silver eye shadow and her cheeks are flushed like they get when she's speaking passionately about something. Dominic's leaning against the fridge wearing jeans and the old fisherman's sweater I wore for a couple of days. There's a pizza crust full of tomato sauce and chopped-up sausage on the counter.

"Yeah, totally," Stephanie says, her legs dangling off the counter. "She always does that."

"Any idea why?" Dominic says.

"I always do what?"

Stephanie turns toward me with a wide grin. "You always

sneak up on people when they're dissecting your personality."

"I was hardly sneaking. I called out 'Hello' and everything."

Dominic bends his head toward the pizza, applying pieces of fresh mozzarella. "We weren't really talking about you."

"Nice try, Dominic, but Stephanie always tells the absolute truth."

"It's true. I cannot tell a lie."

"How . . . unfortunate."

"How annoying is more like it. What aspect of my scintillating personality were you guys dissecting, anyway?"

"How you're generally always on time," Stephanie says. "Where were you, anyway?"

"The Initial Brigade organized some drinks after work. I lost track of time. Sorry."

"What's the Initial Brigade?" Dominic asks.

"These guys at work."

"I see." He adds circles of green pepper on top of the cheese.

"Those guys are a bunch of tools," Stephanie says.

"They're not that bad."

"They're personality-defective. Which gives me an idea."

I shake my head. "Here we go."

Dominic looks up. "Here we go what?"

"Stephanie makes a living coming up with ideas."

"That doesn't sound like a real job."

"It's not," Stephanie replies. "But the pay is *fabulous*."

We laugh, but she's telling the truth. Stephanie's made a small fortune coming up with ideas for a technology company with a fruity logo, a television studio, and more than one bestselling, but writer's-blocked, author. Of course, not all her ideas have panned out, particularly when she keeps them for herself. She's great with ideas but terrible at business, and the last time I checked she'd lost all the fruit money on an ill-advised investment in a microbrewery.

"What's your idea?"

"Book dating."

"What's that?"

She tucks her hands under her thighs. "I'm thinking about adapting the software I wrote for that arranged-marriage service to books. You know, you take the personality test, and instead of matching you to a man, it matches you to books."

Dominic gives her a sharp look. "An arranged-*what* service?"

"Arranged marriage."

"That exists? For normal people?"

"Yup."

"That's crazy." He slips the pizza into the oven and sets the timer for thirty minutes.

"But what does that have to do with the Initial Brigade?" I ask.

"Oh, I was just thinking that those guys are like the guy the heroine starts out with in a romantic comedy, but he isn't the real guy, you know?"

"The way your brain works sometimes freaks me out." A thought pops into my own brain. "Hey, we should give Dominic that personality test."

"Yeah, that'd be fun."

Dominic's whole aspect says no fucking way. "Forget it."

I lay my hand on his shoulder. "Oh, come on. Don't you want to know what kind of woman you should be looking for?"

"Or book?" Stephanie adds.

Dominic's cell phone starts to vibrate insistently on the counter.

"Saved by the bell." He picks it up and holds it to his ear.

"Momentary reprieve," I warn him.

"Hello?"

An indistinct, high voice says something in reply to his greeting, and Dominic's face contorts in pain, like he's been punched in the stomach.

"No." Pause. "I said no." Pause. "Because I don't want to hear it."

He clicks the phone off and slams it onto the counter. His left hand is shaking and there's a vein pulsing in his temple.

"What was that all about?"

Instead of answering me, he raises his right hand and punches it hard into the kitchen cabinets. *Wham!*

He winces in pain as blood appears on his knuckles. "Motherfucker!"

He goes to the sink and turns on the cold water, placing his hand underneath it. I follow him to inspect the damage. The blood is flowing freely from his knuckles. The water in the sink is turning pink.

"Do you want me to take a look at that?"

"No," Stephanie says. "He wants to feel every second of it."

Dominic's mouth twists. "Truth telling *and* perceptive. Quite the combo."

"You have no idea." I grab a tea towel and turn off the water. "Here, give me your hand." I wrap his dripping hand in the towel. "Sit down and hold it tight. I'll be right back."

"Hurry back, Nurse Emma," Stephanie calls after me. "I think the patient might faint."

I start to giggle at the thought as I sprint toward my room. I duck under the bed and pull out my suitcase. In one of the zippered pockets my hand grazes against what I'm looking for—a travel first-aid kit I bought to take with me to Africa. It's full of alcohol swabs and bandages—the only first aid I *didn't* need.

When I get back to the kitchen, Dominic's sitting at the kitchen table looking pale. Stephanie is pouring him a drink from a fresh bottle of Scotch.

I pull up a chair and sit down in front of him. "You're not going to pass out, are you?"

He grimaces. "No."

Stephanie sets a tumbler on the table. "Here's your medicine."

"Thanks." Dominic drains it in one large gulp. He shivers and places the glass down. "Get on with it, woman."

"You might want to be a little nicer to me, given what I'm about to do."

"Maybe."

He extends his hand. The ends of the tea towel are loose. His cuts have stopped bleeding, but his knuckles look red and ugly. I unzip the first-aid kit and pull out a couple of packages of antiseptic wipes. I rip them open and take his hand in mine. It feels cold and damp, the skin wrinkled from the water. His green eyes watch me steadily.

"This might sting a little."

I swab the top of his knuckles. His hand twitches and he sucks in his breath. He picks up his glass with his free hand and waves it back and forth. "More medicine, please."

Stephanie laughs. "Coming right up."

She pours him several generous fingers, which he drains in two swallows.

"That's the ticket."

"Ready?"

Our eyes meet. His look a little soft around the edges. "Ready."

I wipe the rest of the blood off his knuckles. When I'm done, he stares at his angry, red hand with disgust.

"How the hell am I going to hold my camera?"

"I'm sure it'll be better in a couple of days."

"That doesn't help me much."

"What do you mean?"

"I'm going to Ireland tomorrow to finish the shoot for my show."

"You are?"

"I didn't tell you?"

I pick up the roll of white bandage, untucking the end with the carefulness of a drunk. "No, you didn't."

"Sorry."

"No big deal." I take his hand in mine and start to wind the bandage around it. "Was it Emily who called?"

He nods.

"What did she want?"

"To dig the knife in a little deeper."

The tone of his voice drives my eyes down. I concentrate on wrapping his hand, trying to be as gentle as possible. As his hand warms in mine, I can feel the tension slowly seeping out of him, his fingers growing supple. When I run out of bandage, I secure the end with the clear tacky tape from the kit.

The whole thing is strangely intimate. When I glance up at Dominic, he has a different look in his eyes, one that reminds me of those moments when we were dancing at New Year's before Craig-of-the-perfect-timing called.

I can feel the heat rise in my face. "All better?"

He flexes his fingers but lets his hand rest in mine. "Right as rain."

I give his hand a gentle pat and let go. "You should keep that elevated for a bit, in case it starts bleeding again."

"Thanks."

"Sure."

I stand up and catch Stephanie watching me thoughtfully. I have to admit, I kind of forgot she was here.

"I should be going," she says.

"What? No. We were going to have dinner."

"We can do that anytime. You have a patient to take care of. Night, Dominic."

"Night," he replies, still looking at me with that same heat.

I tear my eyes away and walk with Stephanie to the front door.

"Just friends, huh?" she mutters.

"Shut it."

Stephanie slips into her oversized puffy coat. "How did the rest of your day go?"

"Craig came to see me."

"And what did *he* want?"

"Who cares? Sophie can have him."

"Seriously. I'll call you tomorrow."

"You don't have to go."

"Whatever." She plops her fuzzy hat onto her head. "Call me with the details."

Before I can ask her what she means, she turns the lock and darts out into the black night. Cold air floods through the door. My teeth chatter as I watch her walk down the front steps. When she reaches the street safely, I close the door, locking it tight.

I sense Dominic's presence behind me an instant before he rests his hands on my shoulders. They feel heavier than Craig's. More substantial, somehow.

"Emma," he says, his voice a request.

I know what he's asking, and despite the chill of the entranceway, I can feel my body respond, the warmth spreading from where his thumb is brushing the edge of my neck.

Dominic takes a step closer, placing his hands on my waist. The bandage catches on the edge of skin between the top of my leggings and my sweatshirt. I close my eyes and lean against him. His arms slip around me as he rests his head on my shoulder. He turns his mouth toward my neck, his breath replacing his thumb's caress.

And God, it feels *good* to lean on a man, to feel wanted, present, the focus of his thoughts. Even if it's because of loneliness or loss or a smashed hand against a hard surface. I don't care, I don't care, I don't care.

His lips touch my neck, his tongue probing lightly. I pivot and Dominic's mouth is there to meet mine. It feels softer than I would have thought, and his kisses are soft too. His mouth tastes like Scotch, and feels familiar, like somewhere I've been before. I twine my arms around his neck and press myself to him. I can smell the aloe and spice of his shampoo, mixed in with the Bactine. He smells clean and dangerous.

We kiss and kiss, and I revel in the feel of his mouth, his tongue, his teeth. My mouth is absorbed, my lips are molded, my breath is stolen.

Dominic pulls me closer. His mouth travels along my jaw to my neck. I want his lips, his tongue, his teeth on every part of my skin. I want to feel every inch of his skin against mine. I'm one big pulse, my heart one big thud.

He moves his mouth to my ear, his breath hot against its edge. And now I'm gripped with fear that he's going to say something that will break this ridiculous spell we've placed ourselves under.

"Shh," I whisper against his neck, bringing my finger to his mouth to smother his potential words before they ruin everything.

And because this moment is perfect, because he is perfect

in this moment, instead of speaking, he takes my fingers into his mouth, and a groan of pleasure escapes me. He swallows my moan with his mouth. We kiss and kiss and kiss until my legs are shaking. His hands roam under my shirt, sliding up my back and down, applying gentle pressure.

Dominic scoops me up like I'm weightless. I open my eyes and look at him. His eyes are dark, his skin is flushed. I place my hands on the side of his face and lean into his mouth as he carries me to the bedroom.

We don't say a word.

Chapter 16
That Was an Invalid Response

I awake at seven, naked and alone, to the sound of a truck backing up.

My first thought is, I must be dreaming. But the space next to me feels empty and cold, and even my fuzzy morning brain knows that if this were a dream, there'd be a man lying next to me.

I concentrate, listening for the sounds of teeth brushing or coffee making, but there's nothing. Dominic's gone and I'm alone.

Even though I shouldn't be surprised—he told me yesterday he was leaving for Ireland in the morning, right?—this has never happened to me before. I've never slept with a man and woken up to find him gone the morning after our first time together. And let me tell you, if you've never experienced this particular situation, it feels about as shitty as you'd expect it to feel.

And it doesn't help that last night was amazing in a way

first-time-together sex usually isn't. There wasn't any of that usual awkwardness of sweaters getting stuck on heads or elbows or hair getting pulled. It was all a seamless flow of hands and skin and lips and tongues.

The things Dominic did to me with his tongue . . .

I turn toward his pillow, half expecting to find a note, or at least a depression that confirms I wasn't dreaming, but it's empty. The taut pillowcase stretches across it without betraying any evidence he was ever here.

My body bears the evidence, though.

Maybe I should think about something else.

I wrap the sheet around me and put a tentative foot on the floor. It creaks under my weight, and I stop, frozen, as the report echoes around the room.

Why am I being cautious in my own apartment, like there's someone sick who's sleeping in the room, a light sleeper? There's no one here, Emma. He's gone.

I stand up properly and walk to the door, the sheet trailing behind me like a train. Dominic's door is ajar across the hall. Small particles of dust float in a sunbeam, like it's been days, weeks, since he was here, instead of hours, maybe only minutes.

I cross the hall. His bed is made with square hospital corners, and there's a navy blanket folded at the end of it. The clutter is missing from the dresser, like it was from mine the night I came home. His boxes are lined up neatly under the window. Again, there's no note.

I finally find it in the kitchen, sitting propped against the salt and pepper shakers. I pick it up as I sit down, tucking the sheet under me. I stare at my name on the folded piece of paper, trying to decipher whether this note will make me more or less angry. But the neat block letters written in a blue ballpoint pen don't contain a clue.

I unfold it.

Emma, I'm sorry for leaving like this, but I have an early flight. I'll call you when I get in. Dominic.

I don't know what I was expecting, but these simple words don't relieve the achy feeling in my chest.

I let the note fall to the table and head to the coffee machine. There's a half-eaten pizza sitting next to it, its cheese congealed into an off-white mass. I pick up the pizza and put it in the trash. The swinging lid rocks back and forth, squeaking, then settles into place.

Last night, after, as we lay breathing into the silence, Dominic remembered the pizza in the oven and skittered naked across the floor to rescue it. I followed him with his T-shirt and boxers. We ate the slightly burned pie with silly grins on our faces, letting the cheese burn our tongues. After a couple of slices, we ended up back in each other's arms, our stomachs forgotten.

I *really* should think about something else.

If only my brain came with an off switch.

When I get in, the office is full of the usual hustle and bustle of phones ringing, emails pinging, and the clatter of fingers on keyboards. I walk toward the Ejector with the loose-limbed feeling I always associate with great sex, only this time, instead of having a happy glow on my face, I feel furtive and slightly guilty.

But why? I didn't do anything wrong. I'm single and so is he. And the fact that it's probably way too soon for me—or him, for that matter—to get involved with someone only makes me stupid, not a criminal.

I push my guilt aside, along with the recurring flashes from last night. When I get to the Ejector, I work my way through the night's accumulation of email, then plan my attack on the ten new files that have appeared on my desk. More boring insurance files from Matt, I assume.

My phone rings. "Emma Tupper speaking."

There's a click and a mechanized female voice says, "I'm sorry, that was an invalid response. Please press one—"

I hang up and start working my way through the files. Washer breaks causing flood, blah, blah, blah. I'm having trouble concentrating on the details. I stare out the window at the gray winter sky. The clouds are almost indistinguishable from the air and the earth below. More flashes from last night assault me. The way his skin tasted, a mixture of salt and soap. The way his fingers felt on the depression at the base of my spine. The rough caress of his teeth on my clavicle.

Why didn't Dominic wake me up before he left? Better question: Why did he sleep with me in the first place? Was it all just a reaction to the call from Emily? And what about me? What do I want? Was sleeping with him only a way to get back at Craig?

My phone rings again. "Emma Tupper speaking."

"I'm sorry, that was an invalid response. Please press one—"

You've got to be kidding me.

"Jenny!"

She arrives in my doorway looking panicky. She's wearing a military-inspired suit with a super-short skirt. Her hair is piled on top of her head in a messy tumble.

"Yeah?"

"I'm getting some kind of automated phone calls. I need you to call Tech Support and have them block the number."

"No problem."

She turns on her very high heels with a determined look on her face. I watch her through the glass wall, twirling the phone cord around her finger as she flirts with the tech guy. Not that I condone flirting as a technique for getting things, but life would be simpler if a hair twirl could get me what I wanted.

Maybe that's why Dominic left? Because I never twirled my hair around my finger?

What the hell is wrong with me? Seriously. I'm acting the victim with everyone. I should probably be in that group, that victims' group Detective Nield suggested. What did he say again? That people found it harder getting back into their lives than they expected? Well, he was right about that.

My distracted gaze wanders around the office. I notice something resting on the chaise longue. It's the thick file Craig was carrying yesterday. I flip through it; it's the Mutual Assurance file about the stolen Manet painting, the one Sophie's working on with Matt. I wonder what Craig was doing with it.

My phone rings. I consider not answering it, but Jenny's still on the line with the tech guy. I grab the phone. "Emma Tupper speaking."

"It's me."

A knot forms in the pit of my stomach. "What do you want, Craig?"

He sucks in his breath. "Is this the way it's going to be now?"

"Looks like."

"That's not what I want."

"Is that why you called?"

"No. I left a file in your office yesterday."

"I have it. I'll get Jenny to bring it to you."

"No, I meant to leave it. Matt and I talked about it, and we'd like you to handle it."

"But wasn't Sophie—"

"It's your file if you want it, Emma."

Do I want to work on something more interesting than the ABC insurance files littering my office? Hell, yes. Even if it is some guilt-driven act of charity from Craig.

"Okay, thanks."

"No problem. Call me if you have any questions."

We hang up and almost immediately my phone rings again.

"Emma Tupper speaking."

"I'm sorry, that was an invalid response. Please press one—"

Arg! If Jenny's flirting can't get this fixed, I'm going to have to get my number changed. This must've been how Craig felt when he was getting all those crank calls. No. Fuck that. I will not feel sorry for Craig.

I put my phone on Do Not Disturb and start googling Victor Bushnell. If I'm going to take over this file, I need to devote 110 percent of my attention to it. Sophie might be the devil, but I've never discounted her legal skills.

Victor Bushnell is a self-made billionaire who got his start by developing an online payment system that made access to pay-per-view porn sites easier. Once he sold that business, he moved into more legitimate online payment services, investing heavily in some of the Internet's biggest successes. Last year he made a large donation to the Concord Museum so they'd name a gallery after him. Construction was completed in November, and he held an opening gala the night I came home for five hundred of his close personal friends. Bushnell got several of them to loan their paintings for the event. The centerpiece of the collection was his own prized possession—a Manet he'd paid seven million dollars for several years ago. Security discovered the painting missing the next morning. So far, the police haven't even figured out how the painting was taken, let alone who took it.

The painting is insured for twenty million dollars, and Mutual is—no surprise—being shirty about paying out. I can see from the file memos that Sophie has spent a lot of time trying to figure out a way for Mutual to void the policy, without success.

I pull out a picture of the stolen article. It's a self-portrait of Manet sitting in a boat. He's painting while a white-robed lady watches him. The water around the boat shimmers like glass. It looks cool and inviting. It's beautiful and striking, and if I had a spare twenty million, I might just spend it on this painting. Or not.

I hear the phone on Jenny's desk ring. She answers it distractedly. "Ms. Tupper's office. Yeah, she's here. Hold on a sec."

The phone next to me buzzes. "Yes?"

"It's for you."

"Jenny, when I put my phone on Do Not Disturb, it's because I don't want to talk to anyone," I say a little more testily than I mean to.

"But he sounds really cute. I'm transferring the call."

I make a sound of protest, but before I can stop her, the line clicks over. It has that fuzzy quality overseas calls sometimes have.

"Emma Tupper speaking."

"Hey, Emma Tupper," Dominic says.

My tongue feels thick. "Hello, you. How was your flight?"

"Bumpy." Dominic's voice sounds low and serious.

"I hate that."

"Yeah. Look, Emma, about last night."

I glance up. Jenny's watching me.

"Hold that thought." I motion for her to close my door, which she does with a knowing smile. "You were saying?"

He clears his throat. "I was saying . . . I'm sorry I left like that. I had an early flight."

"So your note said."

"I should've woken you."

"That would've been nice."

"I'm sorry."

"No, it's okay."

239

"I feel like, like . . . I've fucked everything up."

Not yet, but I have a feeling you just might.

I stay silent.

He lets out a slow breath. "This is hard for me to say, but I thought a lot about this on the plane, and I think we made a . . . a mistake."

My throat constricts. "You do?"

"Yeah, not that it wasn't great."

"Right."

"I'm not happy about doing this on the phone, okay? It's just, I'm not there, and, you know, I'm all fucked up right now. About Emily, and . . . everything. And after everything you've been through, I don't want to—"

"Lead me on?"

"No."

"I understand."

"I'm sorry, Emma."

I look down at my hands. They're gripping the phone cord so tightly my knuckles are white. "It doesn't matter."

"No, it *does* matter. That's not what I want you to think."

"Okay, I won't think that." I pause, trying to steady my voice. And breathe. Breathing is important too. "Anyway, I'm kind of busy here. I'll see you when you get back."

"Emma, I—"

"Have a good trip, Dominic."

I hang up with a shaking hand and turn my chair until I'm shielded from the people passing my fishbowl office, living their ordinary lives. A few hot tears slide down my face. I let them fall.

He thinks it was a mistake. One of the better nights of my life is something that he wishes had never happened, that he wants to forget. Well, that probably won't be too difficult. I'm pretty forgettable these days.

Did I really misjudge Dominic by this wide a margin? I thought I was smarter than that.

But that's always been my problem, hasn't it? Thinking that because I'm smart, I should see things coming. Like being smart gives you precognition, or defensive skills that other people don't have. When all it really does is makes you blind, and stupid about the things that come easily to others.

My phone rings and I answer it automatically. "Emma Tupper speaking."

"I'm sorry, that was an invalid response. Please press one—"

"Will you think less of me if I collapse in a heap on the floor?" I ask Stephanie.

We're sitting on the squashy white couch in her beach house–themed living room. The cool-blue walls usually make me feel peaceful, but it's going to take more than a jar full of beach glass and an ocean-sounds CD to heal what ails me.

"Of course not," Stephanie says. She's sitting in the matching armchair wearing jeans and a white T-shirt. She looks about twelve years old, haircut and all. I think she may have been cutting her own bangs again. They have that ragged off-cut look I used to give to my Barbies.

"Good."

I lay my head down on the couch and pull my knees up into the fetal position. If only I had a nice, warm womb to hide in.

"That's all he said? That he didn't want to lead you on?"

"Yeah. Or maybe I said that, and he agreed? The details are a little fuzzy."

She looks thoughtful. "And he seemed nice too."

"Not at the beginning. That first night, when he was moving into my apartment, he didn't believe me. He thought I was a crazy person. I should've remembered that."

"I don't think that qualifies as a warning sign that he'd regret sleeping with you."

"No? I'm not so sure." I stare off into space for a minute. "I just wish my life would go back to the way it was."

"Why?"

"Because I was happy then. Things weren't perfect, but still. I knew where I fit. I knew where I was going."

"And you don't feel that way anymore?"

"No. I feel kind of . . . lost in the middle of my own life, if that makes any sense."

"I think it's normal to feel that way after everything you've been through."

"Then how do I make it go away?"

"Not by expecting everything to go back to the way it was, I don't think. Your life has changed, whether you wanted it to or not. You have to adapt."

"How do I do that?"

She leaves her seat and sits next to my head. She rubs her hand gently over my hair, smoothing it away from my face. "This really isn't like you, you know."

"I know, right?"

"What are you going to do about it, then?"

"What do you mean?"

"Are you going to lie here while your life passes you by, or are you going to fight for what you want?"

I sit up. "Hey! You said you wouldn't think less of me if I collapsed in a heap."

She smiles. "I don't, but I do expect more of you."

"Why?"

"Because you do great things. And you've done them all by yourself."

"Such as?"

She ticks a list off on her fingers. "Graduating near the top of your class. Getting that scholarship. Making partner two years before you're supposed to."

"No, I haven't done that," I say petulantly.

"Well, you did those other things." Her eyes turn thought-ful. "Where's that Emma?"

"I think I lost her in Africa."

"She's not lost. She's right here if you want her to be."

"You sound like Dominic. He told me I should treat what happened to me like an opportunity to change the things in my life I didn't like."

"That sounds like good advice."

I pick up a pillow and whack her with it. "I'm sorry, that was an invalid response."

Chapter 17
Groundwork

When I get to the office the next day, Sophie is sitting in my chair, waiting for me. She's wearing another one of her immaculate black suits, and a pair of shiny red heels that remind me of the ruby slippers the Wicked Witch of the West wanted to steal from Dorothy.

"Keeping bankers' hours, I see," she says in her tight, precise diction.

I glance at my watch. It's 8:13. I'd bet good money that she, Matt, and I are the only three people on the whole floor.

I will not let her bait me, I will not let her bait me, I will not . . .

"Gee, Sophie, are you thinking about taking over another one of my offices? I would've thought I'd be safe from that in the Ejector."

Her eyes narrow. "I came to retrieve something that belongs to me."

"Oh? And what would that be?"

"You know exactly what I mean. Where's my file?"

The file is in the briefcase swinging in my hand, where I put it last night in case I got inspired to work at home. I ended up moping at Stephanie's instead, but Sophie doesn't have to know that.

I put my briefcase on the floor. "Are you talking about *my* file?"

"*Your* file. Please. That file was mine, as you very well know. I want it back."

"I don't know what to tell you, Sophie. You know how Matt is when he makes a decision."

"Ha! I know what really happened."

"What's that?"

"You obviously cried victim to Craig, and he convinced Matt to give you the file."

I laugh. "You really think I'd ask Craig for anything right now?"

"Of course you would. You want him back."

"You're delusional."

"Then why'd you kiss him on Cathy Keeler?"

"Because I didn't know you'd stolen him yet."

She falters. "You were dead."

"No, I *wasn't*."

"You can't have him back."

"Sophie, let's get one thing straight: I don't want Craig back. But if I did, that would be for him to decide, not you.

He's not a piece of property, and this isn't the school yard. Grow up and leave me alone."

She stands aggressively, anger crinkling her face into a snarl. "I want that file."

"Take it up with Matt. Get out of my office."

"This isn't over."

She marches past me. I watch her red heels *click, click, click* down the hall toward my old office. I can almost hear the cackle of her voice muttering, *I'll get you, my pretty.*

"It's bad enough that we all have to work in the same firm," I say to Craig. "But to find her lying in wait for me, and to have you directing pity files my way. It's too much, Craig. I can't take it."

We're in the break room, where I went in search of a full-fat croissant after my exchange with Sophie. When I found Craig there, standing at the cappuccino machine, it took me about three seconds to lose it.

"It wasn't pity, Emma," he says, his frothing milk abandoned on the counter.

"Don't bullshit me, Craig. Please."

"Why'd you take the file, then?"

"Because the files Matt's been giving me are boring as hell. I'd be crazy to turn something like this down. And you knew that. You're manipulating me."

He raises his palms in protest. "When have I ever been able to do that?"

He has a point, but I can't let him know that. Especially not when too large a part of me wants to let him comfort me. Craig's always great in a crisis. It's one of his best qualities.

"Just keep Sophie away from me, all right?"

"I'll do my best."

I turn to leave.

"Emma?"

"What?"

He gives me a knowing smile. "Don't forget your croissant."

When my phone finally stopped ringing yesterday, I called the president of the museum and asked him if he could arrange a meeting with the detective in charge of the theft investigation. He was a little reluctant at first, but since it's in the museum's interest to cooperate with us for now, I eventually got my meeting. So here I am, back at the police station, walking through the rows of cubicles full of outdated computers and stained coffee mugs.

I shoot a look at the large case board as I pass it. I scroll through the names, but as predicted, mine is gone. A new year means the black standouts among all the sad red stories get erased, filed away. It's hard to believe I was standing here less than a month ago, sure I'd gotten the hard part over with.

Detective Nield walks toward me with a welcoming smile on his round face, his Newman-blue eyes glinting. He's accompanied by a tall, plain woman in her midthirties with strawberry-colored hair that's parted in the middle and falls stick straight to her shoulders. She's wearing gray slacks, a white dress shirt, and simple black pumps. She has an olive-green folder tucked under her arm.

Detective Nield takes my hand, pressing it firmly. "Ms. Tupper, good to see you again."

"You too."

"This is Detective Kendle. She's in charge of the investigation."

We shake hands. Hers is rigid and strong. "Thanks for meeting with me."

Her green eyes appraise me steadily, reminding me of Dominic. I've tried hard not to think about him since I left Stephanie's last night, and it's worked, mostly. I can't be responsible for my dreams.

"Of course." She has a flat accent that sounds like it's masking something broader, coastal. "Shall we go somewhere more private?"

She leads me toward a metal door that has a cutout made of that meshed safety glass you see on cop shows. She inserts a key into the lock and opens it. Inside, there's a simple metal table with a chair on either side. The walls are painted that builder's white that new homes come in. The air smells like fear.

"Is this the Box?" I ask.

The left corner of her mouth rises slightly. "We call it Interrogation Two, but yes, this is the Box."

I wonder how long it would take for her to get me to confess to a crime I didn't commit. Judging by the hard glint in Detective Kendle's eyes, I'm guessing not long.

"I know this might sound kind of juvenile, but . . . cool."

She gives me a trace of a smile. We sit across from each other, and she opens her file. It's thick with official-looking forms and witness statements. A photograph of the painting is stapled onto the left side of the folder.

"Why are you here exactly?" she asks.

"I'm investigating the claim before we pay out. It's standard procedure with claims of this size."

"Why don't you just invoke one of those loopholes you lawyers always put in the contracts?"

"We haven't been able to find one that applies," I say dryly. "What have you found out?"

Her eyes are full of displeasure. "We don't usually share the details of our investigation with civilians, but the museum authorized us to disclose whatever we could."

"They have a lot of money on the line."

"Naturally. I imagine your client's going to have to pay, though."

"Not if the museum is at fault."

"I don't know about that. Seems to me they had all the usual measures in place."

"Such as?"

"Well, for one, all the staff hired for the event were checked by a private security company."

"So no one with a criminal record, et cetera?"

"Exactly."

"What about the catering company?"

"They've been in business for over twenty years and have done a lot of high-profile events, several of them for Mr. Bushnell."

"Where did the party take place exactly?"

She flips through the file and pulls out a folded piece of paper. It's a floor plan of the museum, which is a large, circular building. A series of five interlocking circles make up the separate galleries inside.

"The party was here," she says, pointing to the innermost circle, which looks small on paper but is actually a space the size of a gymnasium.

"What time did it start?"

"Seven. They closed the museum at five. Security swept the building and set the alarms in all the galleries except the center one. The catering staff arrived at three and were confined to the main gallery, the kitchen, and prep rooms that are located here and here." She indicates a series of square spaces tucked between the right side of the inner gallery and the next circle out.

"Where was the painting?"

"In this gallery here." She taps the left side of the third circle.

"Not where the party was?"

"No. The Bushnell Gallery isn't big enough to hold that many guests, and there are no kitchen services."

"But wasn't the whole point of the party to celebrate the gallery opening?"

She shrugs. "Mr. Bushnell wanted to invite five hundred people and serve canapés. This was the only space large enough to accommodate them."

"The guests didn't see the paintings at all?"

"No, they did. Two security guards escorted groups to the gallery for viewings throughout the night."

"Were the guests vetted?"

"As much as they could be. Bushnell's people provided a final list forty-eight hours before the event, and Security ran basic checks. Of course, there were at least thirty people at the party who weren't on the list."

"Are any of them suspects?"

"No."

"Why not?"

She locates a list of names in the file and hands it to me. "These are the uninvited guests."

I read it. My eyebrows are raised by the third name. Most of them could afford to buy a Manet if they wanted one. All of them are names I recognize. It's highly unlikely any of them would be involved in art theft.

"I can see why they were let in."

She blinks slowly, her voice devoid of expression. "Yes. That kind of person will not be denied."

I smile. "How do you know all these people were there if they weren't on the list?"

"There are security cameras located at the entrance." Her index finger trails along the floor plan to the front doors. Her nails are blunt, unvarnished. "We've been going through the tapes, matching them up to the guest list."

"Who did it, then?"

"We have no idea."

"Do you at least know how they did it?"

She frowns. "We haven't figured that out either."

"But you must have a theory?"

"Sure. I've got lots of theories. Some of them even involve magic tricks."

I smile again.

"You think I'm joking?" She leans toward me. "The recordings from the security cameras for the Bushnell Gallery show nothing except for guests being led in and out all night. We don't know what time the painting was stolen, except that it must've been after the last group was taken through at about nine thirty. The problem with that, though, is that the alarms were put back on once the gallery was empty. The painting was discovered missing when the guards did their first sweep the next morning. The frame was on the wall; the canvas had been cut out of it." She leans back in her chair, placing her hands flat on the table. "Whoever did this knew what they were doing."

"Where are the cameras positioned?"

"Outside the gallery entrance."

"There aren't any cameras *in* the gallery?"

"They hadn't been installed yet. Construction only just got done in time."

"Who knew about that?"

"Way too many people for that information to be useful."

"Well, what about the cameras outside the gallery? Nothing shows up there?"

She shakes her head. "No, those cameras aren't fixed. They rove between that entrance and the one for the next gallery over. If you were careful, you could avoid being seen."

Well, that might be something to work with.

"When did the guests leave?"

"They were coming and going all night, but the event ended at eleven."

"Were they checked as they left?"

A flash of annoyance crosses her face. "No. You have to go through a metal detector to get in, but not on the way out. Seems no one thought that anyone would want to steal something from a museum, what with the million-dollar paintings and sculptures and all."

"But each painting must have some kind of security system on it?"

"A few of them do, yes. But generally, they rely on the fact that you can't just take a painting off the wall in the middle of the day, and the place really is in lockdown overnight. Laser sensors, heat sensors—you name it, they've got it."

"How big was the painting, unframed?"

"About four feet by four."

I think about it. "It would be four feet long if it was rolled up?"

She nods. "We've thought about that. It could be hidden inside someone's clothing, if they were tall enough."

"Are there cameras at the museum entrance?"

"Yes."

"I don't suppose you've looked to see if anyone was walking funny when they left?"

She looks unamused. "Of course we have, but we didn't find anything."

"Sorry. It sounds like you've been very thorough."

"Thank you."

I look through my notes, making sure I haven't skipped anything. "What's the video quality like?"

"It's pretty good. They use HD recorders that tape twenty-four-hour loops."

"So every twenty-four hours it starts to tape over what happened twenty-four hours earlier?"

"That's right."

"Isn't that a bit risky? What if it takes them longer to discover a painting's missing?"

"That's nearly impossible. Each gallery is checked several times a day. The guards would notice if something was missing."

"Would it be possible to get a copy of that video and the guest list?"

"I'll have to ask."

I take a business card out of my purse and hand it to her. "If you can, just call that number and I'll have someone come pick it up."

"Is that it?"

"For now. May I call you if I have more questions?"

"Yes, I suppose."

She gathers her file together and we leave the room. The air in the bullpen is full of the smell of too many bodies, but after being in the Box, it still smells like freedom.

I turn toward Detective Kendle to say goodbye. She's staring at my business card with a thoughtful expression on her face. "You're the one who was in Africa."

"Detective Nield didn't tell you?"

"No."

"Oh. Well, yes. That's me. Thanks again for your help."

"Good luck finding a loophole."

I nod. "There's usually one somewhere."

Chapter 18
Oh, the Memories

Two weeks after my last visit to the village-that-might-have-a-working-satellite-phone, I was back on my Schwinn, waiting for Karen to join me. It was early, and the day's noise hadn't yet drowned out the egrets' calls. The sun was still low on the horizon, a round orb that lit the path I was waiting to take to the satellite phone that surely must be fixed by now.

I heard footfalls behind me and turned to see Karen, her hair hidden by a blue baseball cap, walking toward me with her hands in her pockets.

"Here you are," she said as she stopped at my side.

"Of course. Aren't you coming?"

"Not today."

I tried to hide my disappointment. "Oh. Well, we can go tomorrow, though it's my turn to cook. Maybe the next day would be better?"

"No, I don't think so."

"Should I just go on my own, then?" I didn't relish this possibility, but I was willing to do it. "Tabansi's probably waiting for me . . ."

"The phone's not going to be fixed, Emma."

"What? You don't know that."

"Actually, I do."

"How?"

"Because if it were fixed, everyone here would be *there* waiting to use it."

"But just yesterday Nyako was saying that once I confirmed it was fixed, he'd arrange to take a group over."

She smiled. "If it were fixed, Nyako would be the first to know."

"How?"

"That's why he is who he is."

"Then how come he didn't tell me?"

"He probably didn't want to disappoint you."

Clearly, Karen didn't suffer from that impediment.

"It's really not fixed?"

"No."

I climbed off my bike, letting its weight rest against my side. One of the pedals fell, squeaking loudly. "Will it ever be fixed?"

Will any of this ever be fixed?

"Of course it will, Emma. You just need to be patient."

"I'm not very good at that."

"I had a feeling."

"So I'm just going to be stuck here . . . indefinitely?"

"It won't be that long, I'm sure. But in the meantime, the waiting might be easier if you . . . did a bit more around here."

My heart filled with guilt. While I'd been helping Karen with some of the small tasks—working in the kitchen they'd set up, making sure they didn't run out of supplies—I knew I'd been staying on the periphery of village life. I was leaving soon; what was the point of getting invested? But I *wasn't* leaving, and Karen clearly thought it was time to stop pretending I was.

"You mean, help you build the schoolhouse?"

"We could use an extra hand."

"I have no idea what to do."

She put a hand on my shoulder. "Don't worry, you'll figure it out."

I walk home after my meeting with Detective Kendle, tired and pensive. I can't help but think back to that first night home, when I skidded toward Stephanie's in a blind panic. I may be wearing thick boots and a warm coat tonight, but the ground doesn't feel any more solid, and my heart is cold.

I let myself into the apartment, momentarily overwhelmed by the loneliness it seems to emit. It's pathetic, really, how quickly I became used to Dominic being here, cooking things for me and making me laugh. Even when his moods were as black as mine, there was a certain camaraderie in that blackness.

I hang up my coat, walk to the living room, and sit on the couch. I lean back and stare at the twinkling lights on the Christmas tree I haven't bothered to dismantle. My eyes travel toward the banker's box that still sits under it. Me from zero to eighteen, the box Dominic found in the storage locker. I haven't had the courage to look through it yet.

I don't know what I'm scared of, really. I've already lived through everything in the box. It's what's outside the box that I'm having trouble with.

I turn on the fire and sit on the floor next to the tree. The heat plays against my face. A faint smell of pine lingers in the air. I pry off the dusty cover and lay it next to me. Inside is a row of multicolored hanging file folders. Their white, stiff labels have yellowed over time, and they emit a musty smell. PHOTOS, PERSONAL, ELEMENTARY, IMP. PAPERS, and MISCELLANEOUS, implying more order than I remember imposing when I made this box in the short weeks between college and law school.

I reach first for PHOTOS, and there my mother is, young and smiling at me like I was the most wonderful surprise. The date on the back, written in my father's spiked handwriting, identifies me as six weeks old.

The photos underneath, small, washed out, framed with a

white border, fall backward from then. Me at five weeks, four, two, newborn, hidden in my mother's distended belly beneath her soft hands and an acre of fabric that looks like the drapes Maria makes clothes out of in *The Sound of Music.* The only evidence of my father is in the precise dates on the back, and the consistency of the point of view. It feels like there's love in these photos, but I can't measure its quantity or gauge its direction.

The one photograph I do remember is here too—a shot of me on my third birthday sitting on my father's knee, soon before he left us for good. My father's wearing a business suit, his brown hair cut short. His hand is patting the top of my head like he doesn't know what to do with it, and he has a hesitant smile on his face. I'm wearing a white party dress, and my hair falls in Shirley Temple ringlets. This is the most perfect picture of me as a child. After, my dresses were never as nice, and my curls gave way to frizz, then disappeared altogether.

I have only one memory of my father living with us. It's a bad one, and I'm not even sure it's real. In my mind, it's right before he left, maybe even the day he did, and he was angry. "I don't want this," he kept saying to my mother, loud enough for me to hear upstairs in my crib. I couldn't make out her replies, but her devastated tone of voice scared me. I called for her, and when she didn't come, I climbed over the bars and thumped to the floor. My wail brought her to me, my father a shadow behind her in the doorway. "It'll be okay, baby," my mom said, holding me to her and stroking my hair, but somehow I knew it wouldn't be.

I put the pictures back into the folder and close the box. I don't know what I was looking for exactly, but I didn't find it.

A loud *slam!* from above breaks me out of my revelry. Tara must be back from L.A., and it sounds like she's brought an entourage home with her.

Clomp, clomp, clomp, ha, ha, ha!

They must be having a great time up there. A loud time, but great nonetheless. Maybe I should go up and welcome her home? Join the festivities?

Before I talk myself out of it, I put on some shoes, throw my coat over my shoulders, and slip out the front door. I follow two sets of snowy footsteps up the windy staircase, carefully holding on to the cold metal railing so I don't slip and fall at some other man's feet.

I give a tentative push on her doorbell. It rings loudly. I can see Tara approaching through the glass cutout of the front door. She's wearing a pair of black stiletto heels and tight black jeans that emphasize her emaciated frame. Her long blond hair is carefully waved, and her skin has that same fake golden tone as Jenny's. The hair and the tan are new, but her face remains the same—brown eyes a little too close together, a small bump at the top of her nose.

She opens the door. "Oh my God. Hi!" She leans in to kiss me on the cheek. She smells more expensive than I remember. "How *are* you?"

I return her kiss, just missing her skin. "I'm good. You know, back."

"Wow. I mean, wow. This is crazy."

"It was pretty crazy, yeah."

"Hey, do you want to come in?"

"Are you sure? It sounds like you have guests . . ."

"Of course! You have to tell me all about this amazing adventure of yours!"

I'm sick of talking about it, but the alternative is more time in the box and my head, so I say, "That'd be great."

"Hey, can you close that door?" a melodious voice calls from the living room. "It's freezing out there."

"Hold on!" She tugs me into the apartment by my arm. I close the door behind me and pull my coat from my shoulders.

"We were just about to have a drink," Tara says.

"That sounds perfect."

We walk into the living room. Her apartment is a mimic of mine, only instead of the muted creams and yellows I used, Tara has painted each room a shade from the fiery side of the color wheel. The living room is burnt orange, with a contrasting accent wall of lemon yellow. The couch and matching chair are turquoise, and there's a multicolored rug on the floor. The whole room shouts Portuguese restaurant. Only the plates on the walls are missing.

There's a very pretty woman sitting on the couch. She's about my age and has curly auburn hair that falls past her shoulders and a round, china-doll face, set off by eyes that match the color of the couch. She's wearing broken-in blue jeans and a faded blue argyle sweater. Her feet are bare and her toenails are painted bright red. She looks vaguely familiar.

"You wanted white wine, right?" Tara says to the woman.

"Please."

"That okay for you, Emma?"

"Sure."

Tara leaves without making introductions.

"Hi, I'm Emma," I say, giving a little wave.

"Emily."

I sit on the armchair. "I hope I wasn't interrupting anything."

"Nah. Tara was just telling me about her adventures in Tinseltown."

"Did it go well? She looks . . . great."

Her face scrunches up, revealing laugh lines around her eyes. "She's way too thin, but I think it went well."

"I'm glad to hear it."

"How do you guys know each other?"

"I live downstairs."

She frowns. "But doesn't . . . Dominic live downstairs?"

How does she . . . ? Oh no. This is *Emily*. Dominic's Emily. Emily who's obviously Tara's friend, which explains how Dominic knows her. Emily who called the night we slept together, who wanted to tell him something that he wouldn't listen to.

Shit.

"Are you . . . living with Dominic?" she asks.

Shit, shit, *shit*.

"No. I mean, yes, but not in the way you think."

Why am I sounding defensive? I'm not the one who cheated on him. I'm just the one he slept with and regretted.

I try again. "It was my apartment. I went on a trip and was away for longer than I was supposed to be, and my automatic rent payments got cut off, so my landlord thought I'd abandoned it and rented it to Dominic. But then I came back, and I had nowhere to stay, so Dominic let me stay there. I mean, he did after he checked with Tara that I was who I said I was, and . . ."

Ugh. I'm babbling like a complete idiot. And she'd have to be a complete idiot not to figure out that she's making me very nervous.

"Maybe you saw me on TV?"

Her forehead wrinkles. "I don't follow."

"Oh, there was some press about what happened to me. No

big deal. I'm not surprised you didn't see it. Anyway, I'm going to be moving out soon, so . . ."

"Did Dominic tell you about me?"

Why did I come up here again?

"Well . . . a little."

"A little what?" Tara asks, appearing in the doorway with a tray between her hands that's holding three oversized glasses of wine and some mixed nuts in a bowl.

"Did you know she's living with Dominic?" Emily asks, her eyes accusing.

"Oh crap. I forgot all about that."

"Forgot all about what?"

"Dominic called me a few weeks ago. The night Emma came back . . ." Her eyes turn toward mine, pleading.

"He wanted to make sure I wasn't some crazy person," I add. "It's kind of a funny story, really."

Emily looks like she doesn't quite believe me.

"He's not even in town right now," I add.

Wow. I really need to shut up. Witness 101: Talking when no one's asked you a question is a sure sign you have something to hide.

"What did he tell you about me?"

I can feel both of their stares, waiting for my answer.

"Nothing, really. Only that you were supposed to get married, and you . . . didn't."

"Did he tell you about Chris?"

"Who's Chris?" I ask as innocently as I can.

Emily stands and pulls her sweater down over her slim hips. "I think I'm going to go."

Not innocently enough, I guess.

"No, Emily, stay," Tara says.

She shakes her head gently. "Let's do lunch tomorrow, all right?"

She walks out of the room. A moment later the front door clicks open and then shut. Tara's left standing there, holding the tray full of wine, looking pissed.

"So," I say, "how was L.A.?"

Chapter 19
Exhibit A

Over the next week, life begins to fall into a routine. Early to rise, early to work, slog away at the files Matt keeps sending my way, have dinner with Stephanie, cull the classifieds for potential new apartments, early to bed. I feel like I'm treading in place, but at least my head is above water.

And where is Dominic this whole time? A question I try not to ask myself. Still in Ireland, I assume, taking pictures of the old world being eaten up by the new. Still regretting our night together, obviously, since he's made no effort to call or email or carrier pigeon. But he'll have to come back eventually. Nobody abandons all their stuff willingly.

I ought to know.

In the middle of my second week back at work, I have Sunshine over for dinner. She's postponed her intended return to Costa Rica, though I protested when she told me. "Your mother would never forgive me," she said, and that was that.

Tonight she peers at me as she unfurls a long, multicolored scarf. "Emmaline, my darling, have you been peeking into the past, by any chance?"

"How did you know that?"

"Your eyes say it all."

I sigh. "I don't know how you know these things, but yes. Dominic found a box full of stuff from when I was a kid. I was going through it the other day." And the next and the next. I keep getting pulled back to it, though I never feel any better when I do.

"What's in this box?"

"Stupid stuff. Report cards, art projects. Pictures."

"Of your mom. Oh, and of John, yes?"

John is my father. "Yes."

"Lead me toward the alcohol."

"But you don't drink."

"I do tonight."

I take her to the kitchen, and over a bottle of red wine and a prepackaged lasagna from the store around the corner that has kept me from starving over the years, I fill her in on the pictures I found, and the long-buried questions they've raised. Why he left. Where he is now. How he never came back, not once. Cradling the glass of wine in her hands, she lets me talk until I run out of questions.

"Do you want to have a relationship with him?" she asks when I finish.

I stab my fork into the gooey noodles. "No!"

"Are you sure?"

"Of course I am. Why? Do you think I should try to track him down?"

"I don't know. It might help bring you some closure."

I break off a corner of the lasagna with my fork and bring it to my mouth. The cheese is fresh and stringy, the sauce full of bright tomato flavor. I love this dish usually, but tonight I'm having trouble swallowing it.

"What was he like?"

"John? He was handsome."

"Is that all?"

She gets a faraway look in her eyes. "No. He was smart. You get that from him. He could be very funny sometimes. He was . . . confident. Self-assured. He had a way of making you feel that he was in control of things. Like nothing could go wrong when he was around."

"A fatal vision," I murmur into my wineglass.

"What's that, dear?"

"It's what Macbeth says when he's psyching himself up to kill the king. 'Art thou not, fatal vision, sensible / To feeling as to sight? or art thou but / A dagger of the mind, a false creation / Proceeding from the heat-oppressed brain?'"

"I don't think such morose thoughts are helpful."

"I know. Tell me, what were they like together? Were they happy, at least at some point?"

She raises her glass to her lips, sipping slowly. "I wouldn't say they were very happy, no, particularly as the years went on. I don't think they were a great match, but he did love your mother, very much, I think. Maybe too much."

"What do you mean?"

"Well, sometimes, dear, loving too much can be a problem. It didn't matter when it was just the two of them. You see, your father was a needy man, or at least, he was with your mother. He needed her attention, and she was happy to give it to him. But then—"

A lump forms in my throat. "I came along?"

Sunshine gives me a sad smile. "Yes, dear. Your mother was devoted to you, and I think your father felt left out. He wanted to be the center of her attention, and he wasn't anymore. That's not to say he didn't love you, in his own way. And maybe I'm wrong. I wasn't around much."

"I don't think you're wrong. It makes sense. Sort of."

"Enough sense to forgive him?"

"You think I should?"

"Of course not, Emmaline. Not if you don't want to."

"Would you?"

She pats my hand again. "I forgave him a long time ago, dear. As did your mother."

I shy away from this. And yet, it doesn't really surprise me. Forgiveness was in her nature, and I never heard her speak badly about him except the one time I provoked her when I was fifteen. There was some father-daughter day at school I couldn't participate in, and I shouted and stomped, and eventually she admitted she hated him, just as I did. Hours later, she climbed into bed next to me and said she hadn't meant it. "I don't want you to hate him," she said. "Hate is so hard." I told her I'd try to do better, and she stroked my hair until I fell asleep.

But I kept on hating him. I just kept it to myself.

"I know she did," I say to Sunshine. "I never understood why."

"To put it behind her, I think. And because of you. She couldn't hate him without feeling like she was hating you."

"Why?"

Sunshine lifts her hand to the side of my face. "You look very much like him, you know."

I pull away. "I wish I didn't."

"I understand. But whatever you do, you can't change that."

I don't know about that. They can do some pretty impressive things with plastic surgery these days.

"What would you do if you were me?"

"I'd do what felt right. But then again, I wouldn't ask washed-up old hippies for advice."

"He sued," Matt says to me the next morning, appearing in my doorway without warning, holding a thick sheaf of paper in his hands.

Yet another reason why no one survives the Ejector: Matt's cat feet.

"I think you just gave me a heart attack."

"Nonsense. You're too young for that. Besides, no one's left here on a stretcher yet."

His eyes twinkle at me. An answering smile creeps onto my face. "There's a first time for everything."

"I'll try to make more noise in the future. Victor Bushnell's attorneys just served this."

He hands me the lawsuit. I flip to the conclusions. Victor Bushnell is demanding twenty million dollars plus punitive damages from Mutual Assurance and the Concord Museum.

"That was quick."

"Apparently they got wind that Mutual was considering denying coverage and decided to force our hand."

"What did the client say?"

"They're pissed, but they'll pay out if they have to. Craig's meeting with them and the museum's president later today. Any chance you've figured out a way to get them out of paying?"

"Not yet."

"What angle are you working?"

"Sophie covered off voiding the policy. I'm trying to see if we can blame the museum for having inadequate security."

"Do you think that's going to fly?"

"I doubt it. Whoever took the painting knew what they were doing. Even the police are stumped."

"That doesn't sound promising."

"Agreed. Our best bet is probably to negotiate a settlement."

He nods. "Probably, but I don't want to go there until we've exhausted every avenue, given how much money's on the line."

"I'll keep digging."

"Have you been to the museum yet? Something might occur to you."

"That's a good idea."

Matt gives me an expectant look. "No need to say that if you could get Mutual out of this somehow, it'd be a great coup for us."

"No need to say it."

"You're doing well, Emma. Keep it up."

"Thanks . . . and maybe you could hold off giving me any more work for a couple of days?"

His eyes twinkle again. "You're the first person who's ever had enough guts to ask me that."

"You mean, all these years, all I had to do was ask?"

"That's right."

Maybe this office will be the Phoenix, after all.

At lunchtime I take a break to go visit Peter and Karen. They're back from Tswanaland and already working on their next project—setting up a community center in a row of old red-brick houses by the river.

They talked about the project a lot when we were building the school. They're partnering with Habitat for Humanity, which did the major renovations while they were away.

The three old houses now have sparkling windows and gleaming sandblasted brick. The central house has a glossy black front door. There's a shiny plaque on the wall next to it that reads THE POINT YOUTH CENTER. The walkway is well shoveled. The three steps up to the front door are protected by a woven fiber mat.

I climb the stairs and turn the shiny nickel doorknob. In contrast to the neat, clean exterior, the inside is chaos. The drywall is up and the resanded floors are being protected by thick cardboard, but there's dust everywhere and no paint on the walls. A single bare lightbulb hanging from an ornate rosette on the ceiling casts a gloomy light in the lobby.

I ask a man in dusty coveralls where Karen and Peter are, and he points toward the archway leading to the house on the right.

I find them in the room that was the kitchen but is now a makeshift office. There are several large drafting tables pushed against the walls. Fax machines and printers sit on the old kitchen counter. Karen and Peter are standing over one of the drafting tables, flipping through a large set of blueprints.

"Hey, guys."

They look up. Matching smiles light up their faces.

"Emma! Glad you could make it," Karen says. Her curly black hair is woven into braids held back from her high forehead. She's wearing a pair of blue painter's coveralls, and there's a smudge of white paint across the bridge of her flared nose.

She places her strong, capable hands on my shoulders. "I would hug you, but I don't want to get paint on your gorgeous suit."

"Don't be silly. I don't care about the suit."

I give her a hug. Turpentine tingles my nostrils. "The place looks great."

"Thanks. It's mostly Peter's doing."

Peter laughs. "Get that on tape, will you?"

I look at Peter affectionately. Neat, small dreads cover his large, round head. His dark brown eyes brim with intelligence. He's wearing an identical pair of coveralls, with matching paint stains.

Karen flaps her hand at him. "Please. You'd just play it over and over until your head got big."

He gives me a devilish grin and pulls me into a bear hug. Peter is six foot two and muscular; a hug from him can have consequences.

"Will you give me a tour?" I ask when the breath has returned to my lungs.

"Of course."

He hands me a yellow hard hat, and they show me around the building. The top floor has been made into several large dormitories for teenagers who need temporary housing, while the second floor is divided between a day care and a few administrative offices. The first floor is for the after-school program and the legal clinic.

"Come check out the backyard," Karen says, leading me out a set of doors behind the central staircase. "You can't get the full effect right now, but when the snow clears, it'll be amazing."

I follow her outside, and I can see what she means. Beyond the small wooden porch, the three backyards have been combined and replaced by a concrete basketball court. There's a net at either end, and it's surrounded by a high chain-link fence. Two teenage boys are shoveling a thin layer of wet snow with large, curved shovels, their breath swirling around them.

"This *is* amazing."

Karen smiles broadly. "I know. I feel happy every time I come out here. Those public courts are just a recruiting ground for the slingers. But here, the kids will be able to play almost year-round without being bothered."

"How did you arrange all this?"

"We set most of it up before we left," Peter answers. "But— and despite Karen's praise back there—we have a great team, and the people from Habitat for Humanity are amazing."

"When are you going to open?"

"Probably in a month or so. We're having a fund-raising gala in a couple of weeks. Will you come?"

"Of course."

"And persuade your firm to sponsor a table?" Karen asks in her forthright manner.

"They owe me that much at least."

"What does that mean?"

"Oh, nothing. It's just been an . . . adjustment coming back."

She looks sympathetic. "Stephanie was telling us."

"She was here?"

"Yesterday."

"Right, I forgot. She told me she was going to come see you."

Peter picks up a basketball from the rack on the porch and passes it back and forth between his hands. "She's quite a girl, that Stephanie. She already has all these ideas about how we can get corporate sponsorships, and she wants us to host some kind of dating-service thing here at night."

"That's Stephanie, an idea a minute. But I'd listen to her; she'll put you on the map."

"We don't need to be on the map. Staying afloat will do."

"Nah, you've got to think big. Think world domination."

Peter laughs. "That's your department, isn't it?"

"Speaking of which," Karen says, "we could really use some help setting up the legal clinic."

"My pro bono hours are yours."

"We were kind of hoping you might do more than that."

"Oh?"

Peter bounces the ball onto the hard concrete. The *thwap! thwap!* echoes around the yard. "To be frank, Emma, we'd like it if you'd run the clinic. Be our corporate counsel, that sort of thing."

"But I have a job."

"I know," Karen says, an intense look in her eyes. "But this is an opportunity to do something more important. This is about helping real people, changing lives."

"Well, duh," I say in a joking tone.

"So you'll do it?"

"I don't know, Karen. I have to think about it."

"Are you working on anything right now that would be as meaningful as this?"

"I'm trying to figure out who stole a painting, actually."

Karen makes a dismissive gesture with her hands. "You see? I'm talking about making sure that people don't get evicted, or that they keep custody of their kids."

I look at Peter. He's watching us, bouncing the ball in a distracted way.

"What do you think?" I ask him.

"I think you could be a real asset here," he says mildly. "And that you'd find it fulfilling in a way your current job never was."

I know they mean well, but do they have to make me feel guilty? And since when did it become open season to psycho-analyze me? Why does everyone suddenly have an opinion about what will make me happy?

"What'll it be?" Karen asks.

"I don't know. I really would have to think about it."

"I thought you'd be excited. I didn't think I'd have to convince you."

"I know. I'm sorry. I'm flattered you asked me, and I will think it over, but . . . look, I know this is going to sound shallow, okay, but I like what I do."

At least I did before Africa, and the Ejector, and Craig.

Karen looks down at the porch. Peter bounces the ball rhythmically.

"Please don't be too disappointed in me, Karen. I can't take it."

"All right," she replies. But she won't look me in the eyes.

"And I'll make sure that TPC sponsors at least two tables for the gala," I add lamely.

"That'll be great, Emma," Peter says. He bounces the ball hard against the ground, pivots, and tosses it toward the basket. It catches the rim, jerks backward, and falls to the ground. "Not our lucky day, I guess."

Karen shrugs. "Maybe that dating thing will work out."

In the cab on the way back to the office, I keep the wave of disappointment emanating from Karen and Peter from enveloping me by cocooning myself in indignation.

I mean, it's not like I made them any promises. And just because they're perfect and selfless doesn't automatically make me a bad person if I don't make my whole life about charity, does it? Of course not.

Arg! Visiting Karen and Peter was supposed to make me feel better. I thought we'd hug, talk about old times, have a few laughs, and make plans to have dinner sometime soon. But like everything associated with Tswanaland, it didn't go according to plan.

My cab screeches to a stop at a red light and I fly toward the plastic separator, stopping myself with my hands just before my head hits the Plexiglas.

"Will you watch it?"

"Sorry, lady. I didn't want to hit the kids."

I look out the window. There's a line of small children wearing bright snowsuits crossing the road. They're holding on to plastic handles attached to a long rope. Their teacher is at the head of it, leading them toward the steps to the museum.

The light changes before the kids have finished crossing.

"We can go in a minute," the cabbie says.

"You know what, forget it. I'll get out here."

I toss the cabbie a twenty, climb out, and cross the street to the museum, following the children's trail. The wide stone steps end at a set of huge and intricately carved wooden doors. Two smaller doors have been set into them, modern slabs of thick glass that should be out of place but fit in an odd kind of way. The whole building is like this—a mix of the very modern and the very old. A new archway held up by an old pillar. An old master in a new frame. The museum's benefactor had posterity on the brain when he gave them a large part of his fortune, and it shows.

After I get through Security, which is definitely heightened since the last time I was here (a stern-faced security guard even wands the kids), I walk around the cavernous gallery where the reception was held. Winter sunlight streams through the glass ceiling. The room is mostly empty except for the boisterous kids, now free of their snowsuits and climbing onto the bases of the naked Greek statues.

"Emma?"

I turn around, a knot forming in my stomach. Craig is standing there in his camel winter coat, a red plaid scarf knotted at his neck.

"What are you doing here?"

"What's with the hostility?"

"Nothing in particular, I guess."

"Is this *your* default setting now?"

"Don't do that. Don't use things from our past against me."

"I was only making a joke."

"I'm not sure we're ready for jokes."

"I'm sorry."

"What are you doing here?" I ask again.

"I had a meeting with the museum's president and our client about Bushnell's lawsuit."

"Oh, right. Matt said."

"And you?"

"I thought I'd take a look at the gallery."

"Mind if I join you?"

"I can manage on my own."

"I *am* the client contact on this one. We're going to have to work together."

"Okay, fine. Whatever. Let's get this over with."

We walk through an archway. After several more lefts and

rights I'm thoroughly turned around and almost grateful that never-been-lost-in-his-life Craig is by my side.

"What did the museum brass say?" I ask.

"They don't understand why Mutual doesn't just pay up."

"What did you tell them?"

"The usual bullshit. We have to complete our investigation before we can pay out such a large sum of money, blah, blah, blah."

"Did they buy it?"

"They're talking about getting separate counsel."

"They're expecting us to blame them?"

"It's the obvious play."

We walk past a gallery full of paintings of the Crucifixion. The forlorn face of Jesus stares out from a wall of canvases heavy with varnish.

I shudder. "Ugh. I hate those paintings. Where is this gallery, anyway?"

"It's through there." He nods toward a set of glass doors on the left. The words VICTOR BUSHNELL GALLERY are set out in shiny chrome letters above it.

The gallery is a large room with curved white walls. Its shape seems to push the paintings toward the viewer. The effect is strangely intimate, like you could step into the paintings at any moment. Corinthian pillars are interspersed throughout the room, their pilasters holding up the ceiling. One wall is covered in Impressionist paintings. There's a large space in the middle where the Manet was. Another wall is a mélange of great art through the ages. The third appears to be dedicated to the history of photography. The back wall is bare.

I look around. Two white-haired women are resting on a rectangular bench made of marble. There's only one way out—the glass doors we came through. There's an electronic keypad on the wall to the left of the doors. I know from the notes in the file that once the room's locked, it requires a key card and a six-digit code to get in. The code is changed weekly. There are no windows, only narrow rectangular light shafts near the ceiling, which is made of smooth, hard plaster— not the removable ceiling panels that give access to so many thieves in the movies.

"How did they get the painting out of here?" I ask.

Craig looks mystified. "No idea. But thankfully, it's not our job to figure that out."

I think back to Detective Kendle's grim face. It might be irrational to hope I can solve a mystery that's baffling the police, but I can't help but think that if I *can* figure it out, order might be restored to my universe.

Craig stops in front of a painting of a traffic-filled street that looks like a photograph.

"How do you think he managed to make it look like that?"

"I have no idea. Should we go?"

"Sure."

We walk toward the exit, where a member of the museum staff is setting up an easel. Next to it on the floor is a poster of a familiar-looking black-and-white photograph. A disconcerting mixture of skylines that exists in only one place. My eyes travel over the poster with trepidation, seeking out the artist's name, knowing what I'll find.

"Emma, are you all right?" Craig asks. "You've gone awfully pale."

Chapter 20
Evidently You Don't, Evidently You Won't

"Do you think I should go?" I ask Stephanie.

We're sitting in a booth in a sushi restaurant a week later. It's one of those chain restaurants with orange walls, white Formica tables, and bright fluorescent lighting, but the sushi is generally pretty good.

Stephanie studies the stiff paper flyer for Dominic's show. "It's on Friday."

"I know what day it's on."

"Hey! Don't bite my head off because you're pissed at Dominic."

"You're in the line of fire, I guess."

"Maybe you should think of using plastic bullets."

The waitress brings our miso soups. I dip my spoon into the cloudy broth, scooping up a few chunks of tofu and seaweed.

"Sorry."

"It's okay. Do you think he wants you to come?"

288

"I'm not sure. He was pretty quick to suggest that he leave the apartment."

Dominic called the day after I scoped out the museum. I was sitting at my desk, staring at the map of the gallery like it could provide the answer to the mystery of how the painting had been stolen. I had this sudden urge to whisper the incantation Harry Potter uses to make the people appear on the Marauder's Map. It left my lips almost unconsciously as I tapped the map with the tip of my pen. But of course, because I am a lawyer and not a wizard, nothing appeared.

My phone rang. I reached to answer it. "Emma Tupper speaking."

There was a pause, and then, "Hi. It's Dominic."

My back stiffened. "Oh. Hi. Where are you?"

"I'm here. In the city."

"How was Ireland?"

"It was fine. Listen, Emma . . . could we meet later? Talk?"

Though my mind shied away from the idea—I couldn't help but think of Craig wanting to talk after Cathy Keeler's show—I said, "At the apartment?"

"Sure, that would be fine."

And maybe it was that word—*fine*—but something snapped inside me. "Actually, I have to work late and . . . and . . . I need to go check out some apartments afterward."

"That's one of the things I wanted to talk to you about."

"Oh?"

"I was thinking . . . I should be the one to leave. It's your apartment, after all."

He had a slight joking tone to his voice, but it wasn't really something I felt like joking about.

"Where are you going to go?"

"I can stay at a friend's."

"Oh," I said again, at a loss for anything else to say.

There was a long silence.

"I guess we don't need to meet, then?" Dominic said.

"I guess not."

He cleared his throat. "Fine. I'll pick up some of my stuff while you're still at work."

"Good," I said, feeling hollow inside.

We said goodbye, and I haven't heard from him since. He's removed a few things from the apartment, but the bulk of his possessions remain. I haven't yet worked up the energy to call and ask when they'll be gone too.

Stephanie picks up her bowl and drains her soup in a few large gulps. "That hits the spot."

"Seriously, Steph? Could I get a little help here?"

She pats her mouth with her napkin. "I don't know what you want me to tell you. You clearly want to go, so go."

"But do you think it's a good idea?"

"Who cares? You're going to go no matter what I say." She eyes my cooling soup. "You going to eat that?"

I push it toward her. "Why do you think I'd go if you said I shouldn't?"

"Because. If you want to confront Dominic, that feeling's not going to go away because I come up with more items for the con column than the pro."

"You have more items for the con column?"

She shakes her head. "You're relentless."

"Of course I am. Think about how hard I've worked to become that way."

"Maybe your energy could've been put to better use elsewhere?"

"Probably. But it's too late for that now."

The waitress clears away our bowls and lays a plate full of maki between us. I prepare a piece with ginger, soy sauce, and wasabi. I pop it into my mouth and immediately start choking.

"That's crazy spicy."

Stephanie hands me her water glass. "Here, drink this."

I gulp it down. The fire subsides slightly. "What are your cons?"

She looks resigned. "He's just coming out of a screwed-up relationship. He clearly still has issues with his ex. He slept with you, then called to tell you he thought it was a mistake. Then radio silence until he wanted to 'talk.' Happy?"

"Thrilled, thanks."

"You're still going to go, though, right?"

"Probably."

"Why?"

"I guess because this seems like the easiest puzzle to solve right now."

Her blue eyes regard me calmly. "Are you in love with him?"

"What? No. That's ridiculous."

"That sounded convincing."

"Ah, shut up."

"Now she doesn't want to hear what I have to say."

"Just eat your sushi."

She pops a piece of maki deftly into her mouth. "I know one thing, though," she says around her mouthful.

"What's that?"

"It must be some pro list."

Why *do* I want to see Dominic again? Is it because I can't stand the idea of him becoming some one-night stand, or because I want something more from him? I don't know. I only know that I do. And so, even though I spend all day Friday pretending I'm not sure if I'm going, I'm not really fooling myself.

Jenny walks into my office. She's wearing a dress that looks like a potato sack that's been cinched above her knees.

"A bunch of people called for you while you were out for lunch."

She holds out a sheaf of pink slips. I flip through them. Detective Kendle called, as did Carrie, Cathy Keeler's assistant from *In Progress,* twice.

"Did that *In Progress* woman say what she wanted?"

"Nope. But it'd be awesome if you went on there again."

"*Awesome* is not *quite* the word I'd use."

"What do you mean? You kicked *ass* on that show. And you looked fabulous."

"Thanks, Jenny."

"Do you mind if I leave early today?"

"Sure, I'll see you Monday."

"Thanks, Emma! You're the BBE."

It takes me a moment to decipher this. Best boss ever. How does someone so competent come in such a *The Hills* package? Must be a generational thing.

I call Detective Kendle back first. She tells me in a clipped tone that the approval came through for me to get a copy of the security footage, and gets all huffy when I ask if there are any developments in the investigation. After she ends the call with an abrupt "Goodbye," I email our messenger service with a request to pick up the DVDs. Then I reluctantly return the calls from *In Progress.*

Carrie answers the phone with an enthusiastic "Hello!"

"It's Emma Tupper."

"Ms. Tupper! I'm *so glad* you called. We've been on *tenterhooks* all day."

What kind of person uses a word like *tenterhooks*?

"Why?"

"Wweeellll, we were *so hoping,* Cathy in particular, that you'd agree to come back on the show. You know, to do an update, how you're making out now that you've had a chance to get back into your old life."

You must be kidding me.

"No, I don't think so."

"Oh no! That's really going to disappoint your fans."

"My fans?"

"Of course! We received more viewer mail on your segment than we have in a long time. Everyone is *so curious* about how you're doing. Especially you and your boyfriend—what was his name again?"

"Craig."

"That's right, *Craig.* He's *sssooo cute.* And that kiss. I think I actually swooned."

"We broke up."

"Pardon?"

"He's with someone else now."

A shadow crosses my floor. Sophie's standing in front of Nathalie's desk, waiting to see Matt.

"Ohmygod! Who?"

We make eye contact. Sophie shoots me a dirty look.

"Someone from my office," I say quietly.

"Wow, this is *so great!*"

"Excuse me?"

"Think about it. This way we can recast him as the Bad Guy." She lowers her voice. *"While she was lost in Africa, he was screwing her best friend."*

"What? That's not what happened. She's *not* my best friend."

"Sorry, did I take it too far? I do that sometimes when I'm in the moment, you know?"

"Uh-huh."

"Anyway, we'd love to have you on Monday's show."

"I'm not interested."

"This is *so disappointing.*"

"I'm sure."

"Can I at least leave you my cell number in case you change your mind?"

"I guess."

I write it down mechanically on the pink slip that contains her original message and hang up. A few minutes later, the Initial Brigade appears in my doorway, brimming with gossip.

"What up, E.W.?" I. William says in a tone of voice he reserves for especially juicy news.

"Not much. You guys?"

"Just spreading a little g-o-s-s-i-p."

"Yeah," J.P. says, tugging on his red suspenders. "We're your friendly neighborhood news service."

"You're going to like this one. Guaranteed," Monty adds.

"Will you put me out of my misery already?"

I. William pauses dramatically. "Craig and Sophie are Splitsville."

"What? Are you sure?"

"Yup. Fiona's assistant told my assistant this morning."

Fiona is Sophie's one and only friend in the office. She has a big mouth, but she doesn't tend to make things up. If she told her assistant they broke up, it's probably true.

"When did this happen?"

"Two nights ago."

"Any idea why?"

J.P. steps closer and lowers his voice. "We're hearing it's because of you."

"Me?"

"Apparently, things starting going south between them when you came back."

"They almost broke up after that kiss," J.P. adds. "And when you guys went to the museum together, that was the last straw."

"Well played, E.W."

"You're giving me too much credit."

I. William taps the side of his nose. "Sure, I get it. Say no more, say no more."

"Seriously, guys. I had nothing to do with it."

"Why'd they break up, then?" J.P. asks.

"Search me."

"You're not getting back together?"

"No. God, no."

"Interesting," I. William says.

"Sorry to put a damper on the headline."

"'S all right. We can roll for a couple of hours on the breakup alone."

"Watch your billables."

"Don't worry, we always get by."

"I'll bet you do."

"You going to make it to cocktails later?" J.P. asks.

"I've got a thing."

"Catch you next time."

They leave as quietly as they arrived, making sure not to catch Matt's attention. None of those guys is ever going to make partner, but making partner isn't the be-all and end-all, right?

This is the point when somebody laughs hysterically.

I wonder why they broke up? He can't really think there's

a chance we could get back together. No, I can't believe that. Craig may be a lot of things, but stupid isn't one of them.

I, on the other hand . . .

I pick up the flyer for Dominic's show and stare at the photograph of the photograph that was propped against the wall in Dominic's room. I turn it over, revealing a black-and-white version of his handsome face—a studio pose. His hair is freshly cut, and the white of his shirt makes him seem tanned. He looks happy, like he just told a good joke and is appreciating the reaction.

I flick the flyer toward my desk. It hits the surface and skips like a stone across a calm pond, coming to rest on the floor. Dominic's face stares up at me, his smile an invitation.

I accept.

I arrive at the museum looking like you'd hope you'd look if you were about to do what I'm about to do—perfect hair, perfect makeup, and, of course, the perfect dress. All the education and near-death experiences in the world can't kill *that* basic instinct.

I leave my wool wrap at the coat check and exchange my winter boots for a pair of black slingbacks. I put the little numbered ticket in my purse and stop in the bathroom for a final once-over. Satisfied, I follow the signs toward the Bushnell Gallery.

I pass on the offer of a glass of champagne from a white-shirted waiter in a bow tie and stroll through the surprisingly large crowd. The room is full of thirty- and fortysomethings in their Friday-night best, clutching champagne flutes and dropping hors d'oeuvres into their mouths. The air smells of expensive perfume and aftershave.

Dominic's photographs are hanging on the wall that was empty when I was last here. About half of them are from the same series as the Las Vegas print. The others are from his recent work in Ireland. The one I like the most is the piece Dominic told me about. It's of a wizened man and a young boy driving a horse and buggy through the mist. Behind them, a large crane reaches toward an improbable sun.

I move sideways, giving each photograph its due. And when I reach the last one, I almost stop breathing. It's of a woman sitting on the floor with her head bent intently over a half-unwrapped Christmas present. The lights on the Christmas tree behind her are slightly blurred, like there was a time lapse on the camera or the photographer didn't have a steady hand. The woman's features are blurred too, enough so that she's unrecognizable to everyone but me.

I don't know whether to feel touched or mad that this private moment is hanging on a wall for all to see, even though he protected my privacy. Feeling shaky, I scan the crowd, looking for Dominic, but the only face I recognize is Victor Bushnell's.

I'm surprised to see him for a moment, but given that this is his gallery, I guess I shouldn't be.

Over six feet tall, he has a head of nearly white, bushy hair that rises back from a high forehead. His light-blue eyes stand out above a hawkish nose in his tanned face. His black wool suit is handmade, and his white shirt is perfectly starched. He's wearing a conservative platinum wedding ring. The only evidence of his trademark maverick tendencies is a diamond stud in his left ear.

I inch closer to get a better look, stopping in front of the marble bench where the old women were sitting the other day. His deep voice reverberates above the crowd as he gestures enthusiastically toward a Degas canvas. Two society women are listening to him with rapt attention.

I turn away and take in some of the paintings on the wall where the Manet rested briefly.

"They're very beautiful, aren't they?" a man next to me says a few minutes later.

It's Victor Bushnell. Up close, his eyes shine with intelligence and interest.

"Yes, very. The owners of these paintings are very lucky."

He gives me a slow smile. "You're right." He shifts his body toward Dominic's wall. "Do you know the artist?"

"A little."

"He's going to do great things, I think."

"Yes."

"Victor?" an older man calls from across the room.

He raises his eyebrows. "Duty calls."

I feel tense and nervous as my eyes resume scanning the room. I walk to the bench and sit on the cold, hard surface. The din of the crowd gets louder by the minute. Dominic remains invisible.

One of the catering staff walks up to me. "Excuse me, ma'am. I need to get in there. Do you mind?"

"Of course." I stand and move out of the way while the white-coated waiter bends down and lifts the heavy seat. Inside the bench, there's a large metal cooler full of white-wine bottles.

"Supplies," he says unnecessarily.

I nod and turn away. As I do, I catch someone's elbow and stumble. Two strong hands steady me.

"Emma?"

I look up into Dominic's startled face. Hours of preparation all ruined by one sloppy elbow. Of course.

"Oh. Dominic. Hi."

Oh. Dominic. Hi? That's great, just great. Scintillating, even.

His face reddens. "What are you doing here?"

"I, um, came to see your exhibit. It's great."

And now I'm incoherent. This was the worst idea I've ever come up with.

"What's going on?"

"What do you mean?"

"Man. I can't deal with this right now."

The blood rushes to my head. "*You* can't deal with this right now? That's rich. We . . ." I realize a couple of the other guests are staring at us and lower my voice. "We slept together, and then you told me it was all a 'mistake.' One minute you're Superman in a bright red cape, and then, *poof,* you're just another man up to no good in a phone booth."

Dominic's mouth sets into a thin line. "I've been trying to apologize for that, but you wouldn't talk to me."

"What are you talking about?"

"I left you three messages."

"You what?"

He looks past me to where a Waspy-looking couple are watching us intently over their champagne flutes. "I can't do this here."

He takes me by the elbow.

"Hey, what the—"

"Hold that thought."

He leads me toward one of the Corinthian pillars in the corner. There's a space between it and the wall that's a little more private. We stand there facing each other. My brain is shouting out questions like, Why'd you blow me off? Why didn't you want to come back to the apartment? Why won't you look me in the eye?

He looks up from the spot on the floor he's been staring at like he heard me. "How come you didn't return my calls?"

"You really called me?"

"Your assistant said she'd given you the messages."

That doesn't sound like Jenny.

"What did your messages say?"

"What do you think? That I called."

"Oh."

He raises an eyebrow. "Was I supposed to pour my heart out to your assistant?"

"Only if you wanted to read about it on her blog the next day."

He laughs, letting it fade into a smile. "God, I've missed you."

"This is where you're hiding," Victor Bushnell says as he appears at Dominic's side. "There are some people I'd like to introduce you to."

A spasm of annoyance crosses Dominic's face, which Victor misses as he turns toward me. "I didn't catch your name earlier."

"I'm Emma Tupper."

"Emma Tupper. Now, why is that name familiar?"

My heart skips a beat. He knows my name. And any second now he's going to figure out who I am. Oh well, in for a penny . . .

"I'm an attorney," I say, feeling bold. "I represent Mutual Assurance."

"Ah, yes. I was reading all about you just yesterday."

Dominic looks confused. "What do you mean, 'reading all about' her?"

"He's suing my client for twenty million dollars," I say. "But we really shouldn't talk about it."

Victor Bushnell laughs. "I'm sure you're right, but what's the fun in that?"

"There you are, Emma," Craig says, peering around the pillar. "I've been looking for you everywhere."

Now my heart's keeping double time. What the hell is Craig doing here? Dominic's looking at him like Victor Bushnell was looking at me a few moments ago. I can almost see his thoughts, and they're all falling into place.

"Are you . . . Craig?" he asks.

"That's right. And you are?"

"He's the man of the hour," Bushnell says.

"Did you come with him?" Dominic asks.

Craig's face registers recognition. "You're Dominic."

"You got it."

"Remind me how you met Emma?"

"He lives in my apartment," I say way too loudly in a high-pitched voice.

The three men surrounding me like tall trees turn my way, a mixture of surprise on their faces.

This is so not working out the way I thought it would.

I modulate my tone. "He's the person who was living in my apartment when I got back from Africa, or moving in, and anyway . . . um, Craig, have you met Mr. Bushnell?"

Bushnell looks amused as he extends his hand toward Craig.

"Nice to meet you, Craig . . . ?"

"Talbot."

"Ah. Always nice to meet another one of Mutual Assurance's attack dogs."

"Well, now, I don't think that's fair."

"Dominic?"

Oh, you've got to be kidding me.

I turn around slowly, and there's Emily, standing tall and collected, wearing a silvery silk dress. Her perfect red hair caresses her creamy shoulders.

"What are you doing here?" Dominic says, his voice thick with emotion.

Her cheeks are tinged with pink. "I wanted to talk to you, and you won't return my calls, and . . . what are you all doing behind this pillar?" Her voice falters as her eyes travel to mine. "I didn't know *you'd* be here."

"I . . . came to see the exhibit."

Victor Bushnell guffaws loudly. "Ha! I think this is where I make my exit. Come see me when you're free, Mr. Mahoney. We should talk."

Dominic's eyes don't leave Emily's beautiful face. "Yeah, sure."

Bushnell extricates himself from our tight little corner.

"How do you two know each other?" Dominic asks me.

"We met the other night at Tara's."

"Dominic, please, will you just talk to me?"

Craig takes my hand. "Come on, Emma. We should give these two some privacy."

Emily looks grateful. "Oh, could you? I'd really appreciate it."

"Of course."

Craig tugs on my hand, but I'm frozen to the spot. I turn toward Dominic, willing him to look at me, but his eyes are still locked on Emily. From this angle, I can't tell what he's feeling. Whatever it is, it has nothing to do with me.

And so, when Craig says, "You coming, Emma?" I follow him without another word.

Chapter 21
You're Shaking My Confidence Daily

When I finally manage to unlock my hand from Craig's, we're three galleries past Dominic and Emily and Victor Bushnell. A gallery later I find my voice, and I let Craig have it. What is he doing here? Why's he following me? What is going on?

He starts to give me some stammering excuse about how he'd noticed the poster when we were at the museum and was curious.

I cut him off. "Try again, Craig."

He looks sheepish. "I wanted to see you outside of work."

"So you're stalking me?"

"I'm not stalking you."

"It kind of feels like you are."

"No. I wanted to talk to you, and I knew you wouldn't say yes if I asked. I took my chances that you'd be here."

I consider him. "And you wanted to check out Dominic."

He colors. "I admit I was curious. Especially after how you reacted when you saw that poster."

I consider denying it, but what's the point? I *had* reacted, and pretending I hadn't wasn't going to change anything. "We know each other too well."

"Yes."

I walk to the coat check and give the girl behind the counter my ticket. Craig does the same.

"I could use a drink," he says. "You?"

I ignore him, staring silently at the rows of coats. The coatcheck girl comes back with my wrap and boots and Craig's coat. He takes my wrap and drapes it across my shoulders.

"One drink, Emma. Then I'll leave you alone, I promise."

I nod and he leads me outside, flags a cab, and directs it to his street. Though his apartment is the last place I want to go back to, I don't have the energy to protest. Having won his point—for the moment, anyway—he wisely stays silent.

When we get to his place, Juliana's still there, finishing up the meals she makes for Craig to get him through the weekend. When we were together I often wondered, idly, if Craig and Juliana were a package deal. If we ever got married, would she continue to play such a considerable role in his life? And if she did, would I care?

Juliana's in the kitchen, wearing the light-blue smock uniform she insists on, though I know Craig's tried a hundred times to get her to wear something else. Her still mostly dark brown hair is cropped close to her head. Her round face is creased with laugh lines.

"Emma, good to see you again."

"You too, Juliana."

We hug briefly, then I retreat to one of the bar stools on the other side of the room.

"I made your favorite," Juliana says to Craig. "Would you like me to take it out of the oven?"

"I can get it."

"I'll be going, then."

"Thanks, Jules," Craig says, his eyes on me.

"Of course." She pats me on the arm. "Yes, it's good to have you back."

I return her smile, but I can't return the sentiment. I don't want to be back, and I have to find a way to tell Craig that. Soon.

The kitchen door swings closed behind her, creaking ominously on its hinges. Or that's probably me reading too much into things, right? A door only swings ominously in a horror film. And as nervous as I feel, Craig's not a bogeyman waiting to take my head off.

Craig opens a cupboard, taking out two glasses and a bottle of liquor. When he places one of the glasses in front of me, I realize it's Scotch. And it's funny, because when we were together, I never drank Scotch, and I can't understand how he knows this new thing about me, that I've developed a taste for it. I ask him why he picked it.

"You looked like you needed it."

I take a sip and shudder. From the alcohol, but also because it feels weird, being back here. With Craig.

"Good call."

Craig loosens his tie. He sits on a stool on the other side of the kitchen island. We're separated by several feet of black granite, like we used to be most mornings. Back then, it felt comfortable and safe, but now it's just another thing I have to fix.

We sip our drinks in silence for a while. Eventually, he starts to tell me about him and Sophie, all the details I don't want to know but can't stop listening to. They *have* broken up, and I was the reason. Craig wants me to know, because he still loves me. He wants to get back together.

"But we've barely spent any time together since I've been back," is all I can think to say as he looks up at me expectantly.

"What's that got to do with anything? We were together for three years. The last few weeks don't change that."

I feel an odd urge to laugh, but instead I say, "But you said that you'd moved on, that . . . you were *relieved* when I was dead."

"I never said that."

"Yes, you did. After Cathy Keeler."

"That's not what I meant. I meant that . . . waiting to find out what was going on, if you were alive, was this horrible torture. And accepting that you were dead, *that* was a kind of relief. I could never be relieved that you were dead. Did you really believe that?"

"I don't know. I guess part of me did. And you chose Sophie, so—"

"No, it wasn't like that at all. I was trying to explain, but you wouldn't let me. You left. I thought *you* wanted to end things. I was trying to respect your wishes."

"What made you change your mind?"

"I figured I owed it to us, to you, to let you know what I wanted."

I watch him across the granite slab. "And you were jealous."

"Of Dominic? Maybe."

"Mmm."

"So?"

"'So' what? Will I get back together with you?"

"Yes."

"No, Craig."

"Why not?"

"Because too much has happened. We can't go back. If I've learned one thing, it's that."

"I know that, Em. I'm not asking for things to be like they were, I'm just asking for another chance. To . . . go back to the beginning."

He sounds so much like me, I almost smile. "You want to go back to litigation boot camp?"

He smiles back. "If that's what it takes." His eyes look surprisingly gentle, a million miles away from his default setting.

God, I wish I loved this man. I wish he was the part of my life I needed to get back to feeling whole.

I take a deep breath. "Craig . . ."

His smile slips at my tone. "Emma, don't you think—"

"No, I don't. I don't . . . feel that way about you anymore. And to be honest, and I swear, I'm not saying this to be cruel, I don't think I ever felt as much as you did. I'm not saying I didn't love you. I did—I still do—but you're not my future."

He's sitting perfectly still with his hands flat against the granite.

"Say something."

"You're sure?"

"Yes."

"What's next, then?"

I brush my thumb under my eye, catching a tear. "I don't know."

"But you know it doesn't involve me?"

"I'm sorry, Craig, but yes."

I stand up and walk around the island toward him. He watches me warily.

"Thank you for saying what you did." I lean forward and kiss him gently on the cheek. "It means a lot. More than I can say."

"I wish you'd change your mind."

"I know," I say, and we stand there like that for a long time.

The next morning, I'm walking through a slightly sketchy area of town trying to find the address Stephanie left me on my voice mail with instructions to meet her there at ten. Something about a great "business opportunity" that made me nervous for her. I've heard that tone of heedless excitement before.

It's one of those flat-light days when it's hard to tell exactly what time of day it is, and there's a harsh wind whipping between the buildings. Stephanie's cell phone was cutting in and out as she left the message, so I'm not sure I got it all down correctly. Given the dinginess of the area, I'm becoming less sure by the minute.

I'm about to give up when I find the address. 4356 BOSTON AVENUE is written in peeling white letters above the entrance to a closed-up shop. The glass windows are papered over with stiff brown paper. A crack of light illuminates the nondescript black door.

I push the white doorbell recessed into the wall. It buzzes harshly. The door creaks open. Stephanie's gamine face peeps out.

"You made it!"

"No thanks to your cryptic message."

"I knew I should've called back."

"Are you going to tell me what you're up to?"

She takes a step back. "Come into my parlor and see."

I walk inside. The store is about fifteen hundred square feet of empty space. The walls are lined with floor-to-ceiling bookshelves. The air smells stale, and there are dust motes floating in the air, illuminated by the harsh fluorescent lighting.

"What's this all about?"

She walks to the middle of the room and flings her arms wide. "Welcome to the Book Connection. Do you love it?"

"Really? You're going to do that bookstore/love-connection thing?"

"That's right."

"Are you sure this is the right moment in time to be opening a bookstore?"

She shoots me a look.

"I just meant . . . I worry about you. Have you really thought this through?"

"Of course I have."

"But when did you have time to arrange all this?"

She cocks an eyebrow. "What? You're the only super-achiever allowed?"

"You know I didn't mean it that way."

"I know. Anyway, I decided a couple of days ago that I was going to go for it, you know, and I found this commercial real estate broker who showed me around a bunch of places yesterday."

"You saw this place for the first time yesterday?"

"Uh-huh. And I signed the lease last night. Isn't that great?"

"Don't you think it's a little fast?"

"You know I've wanted to do something more concrete for ages."

"I know, but—"

"No buts. Don't you want to bust out sometimes and do something totally spontaneous?"

I laugh. "You know I don't."

"Maybe that's your problem."

I feel a flutter of annoyance. "What do you mean?"

"Oh, I don't know. It's just . . . you could've *died*, Emma. Hasn't that changed anything for you?"

"You can't be serious."

"I know lots of bad things have happened to you, but what have *you* changed? You know, in your life?"

I walk toward the window. The brown paper blocks out the view of the street. I perch on the window ledge, pulling my knees up under my coat.

"Are you all right, Em?"

"Why does everyone expect me to change my whole life just because of what happened to me?"

"Who expects that?"

"You. Matt. Dominic."

"Dominic?"

"He had this whole thing, remember? 'Imagine the possibilities' or some such nonsense."

"And did you?"

"No. I don't want my life to change."

She starts to laugh. Hard.

"What's so funny?"

"Your life already has changed, Emma, whether you like it or not."

"Don't you think I know that?"

"No, I'm not sure you really do." She sits on the window ledge beside me. The dust motes rise in a swirl. "You're not the only one who lost things in all this, you know. Remember, everyone told me you were dead."

A lump forms in my throat. "I know."

"I mostly didn't believe it. But sometimes I couldn't keep my mind from thinking that it might be true."

"Steph—"

She stops me. "No, that's not why I'm telling you this. What I wanted you to know is that in some ways, especially because it all turned out all right, I'm grateful for the experience." She shakes her head. "That came out wrong. What I mean is, I was glad you knew how much I loved you and how important you were to me. I knew that if you really were dead, at least I wouldn't have any regrets about us."

"Everyone has regrets."

"I know, but I think maybe we should try to minimize them."

"What are you saying? That I should live each day like it's my last?"

"Maybe. Yeah."

"You can't live like that."

"Some people do."

"Maybe. But I don't want to."

"What do you want, then?"

"Can you answer that question?"

"We're not talking about me."

"I know, but why do I have to live up to some standard no one else does? Just because of what happened to me?"

She rubs my back as I struggle for control. A few fat tears fall to the dusty ground, flattening into small moist circles in the dirt.

"I just want you to be happy."

"I'm trying to be. Why is that so hard to believe?"

"I don't know, it just is."

"It's that stupid movie-plot thing, isn't it?"

"That what?"

"All those movies where someone has a near-death experience? And then she realizes she always wanted to be a concert pianist or go skydiving, and the guy who teaches her to jump from a plane is gorgeous and slightly lost, and they fall in love and live happily ever after."

"What movie was that?"

"You know what I mean. And I didn't even really *have* a near-death experience, unless people thinking you're dead counts as one."

"You'd just go back to where it all started?"

"Maybe I would. Except for Craig. I might leave him out."

She smiles. "I can think of at least one new thing you wouldn't want to erase. One person, anyway."

"Mmm, maybe not." I fill her in on Dominic, Emily, Craig, the Christmas Eve photograph.

"So I guess that's it," I say. "Two men down in one night. I impress myself."

She shakes her head. "You can be so dense sometimes."

"What are you talking about?"

"What you said to Craig, about not being able to go back, do you think it doesn't apply to you?"

"No, I know it applies to me. But I guess . . . I wish that it didn't."

"You can't undo what happened. Or turn back time."

"I know," I say, but in my mind I'm building my time machine.

Chapter 22
First Things First

The Dream again. Africa. The safari. The fire. Banga-just-Bob. The excitement of my fellow travelers, the exotic mix of meats. I wash my dinner down with large mouthfuls of the local brew, a brackish mixture of throat-stripping alcohol and something that smells like bark. It tastes awful, but the result isn't unpleasant. Plus it has the added benefit of dulling the effect of my mother's sudden ethereal appearance. Or maybe it's that I'm finally numbed to seeing her like this, alive, well, and warning me against danger.

Only this time she says, "Look in the box."

"Why, Mom? What's in there?"

She brushes her hand across my forehead, pushing my hair out of my eyes like she used to do when I was home sick from school. "The answers, of course."

The answers to what? I want to scream, but I can't. I can't scream at my mother. I don't have the energy, only the alcoholic bark flowing through my veins, evening me out, making me care less than I should.

She kisses my forehead and turns, floating away from me like she has too many times before. I feel sad like I always do, but also, for the first time, a little hopeful.

If I remember this right, I'll get the answers soon.

My mother said so.

Though it's impossibly early, I wake up feeling hopeful. It's strange because my head is throbbing with the beginning of a migraine and my mouth feels like I've been chewing on the inside of a twig, but I push that aside. Hope feels good. Hope feels right. Hope feels like just about all I've got.

I hold on to this feeling for as long as I can, lingering beneath the covers. But something gnaws away at it. Something feels . . . *off.* It takes a second to figure it out, but then I know.

I'm not in my own bed.

This bed is at the wrong end of the room. And these aren't my sheets. They're stiffer. Familiar, but distantly so, like they come from another lifetime. Like my apartment felt when I got home.

My eyes fly open.

I'm in Dominic's room.

I can't believe I did this.

Last night, when I got to the apartment, which is still full of Dominic's things, I undressed and stepped into the hot shower, hoping the water would revive me like it did that first night back, when I was overwhelmed by confusion and loss and the familiar sights and sounds of my bathroom. I toweled off and changed into the most comfortable pair of pajamas I own. And then, because I was still feeling weak and confused and lost, I went to Dominic's room and climbed into his bed, letting his smell lull me to sleep.

And so this is where I am. In Dominic's room, in Dominic's bed. Like an idiot.

Well, I can do something about that, anyway. I exit Dominic's bed and remake it, making sure not to leave any traces of my weak moment behind.

After confirming what I already know—that there's nothing in the fridge—I pull on some jeans and a fleece and suit up for the outdoors. I walk out into the dawn, heading for the local diner, which I know from experience is open at this hour. I'm the first customer, and I order the biggest, greasiest breakfast on the menu. It makes me full and sleepy, but instead of giving in to it, I order a second cup of coffee, forcing myself to wake up.

When I leave the diner, it's brighter out but not quite light. I feel as if there's somewhere I need to be, but I'm not exactly sure where. Unable to put my finger on it, I go to the office. That's usually where I need to be when I feel like this.

The lobby is echoey and empty. The night watchman looks

bored in his round guard station. I swipe my key card and pass through the turnstile, then ride the stainless steel elevator to my floor. I leave my coat and boots in the lobby and pad in my stocking feet down the corridor, creating a bluish static charge as I go.

It's oddly peaceful being in the office when no one's here. I used to come in on weekends all the time, looking forward, in a way, to working through my files with the sound off—no emails pinging, no phones ringing, no Matt. I could get lost in my own world and figure things out. An angle for a case I was working on, a line of questions that would elicit the admission that would eventually lead to a settlement or victory.

I stop at Jenny's desk. The pink message pad is sitting next to the phone, a bottle of sparkly nail polish holding it in place. I pick up the pad and flip through it. In between the carbon-paper messages Jenny gave me is the evidence I'm looking for. Dominic called, Dominic called, Dominic called.

I carry the message pad to my desk. I notice a matching flash of pink on the floor. It's the message from Carrie, Cathy Keeler's assistant. It has her cell-phone number written on it, in case I change my mind.

I smooth it out absentmindedly as I look out the window. I stare at the view for a long time, watching the sunrise, tracing the pattern of numbers in the messages I never received. When the sun gets too bright, I close my eyes and try to clear my mind, to focus on what it is that drove me here, the thing that seems just out of reach. I let every bad thought linger, but only for thirty seconds. Then I push it away and reach for the next one. One by one by one.

Time passes and I run out of problems. My mind feels clearer, and I finally feel connected to my brain in a way I haven't in a long time. Ideas start to take shape, a path to where I want to go, and maybe the destination too. I open my eyes, pick up a pen, and pull a pad of paper toward me, making a to-do list like the one I made before Christmas.

Maybe this time I'll get it right.

I spend the rest of the day working, formulating, happy.

Yes, *happy*. I'm in a groove. My neurons are firing. All systems are go. I feel like I used to feel, and it feels good. This is why I worked so hard. This is what I love. This is what I've been looking for since I got back. I owe it to Matt, but also to Craig, which makes me a little sad but mostly grateful. Love can bring unselfish happiness to others. I've always known this, but now I feel it.

When a good day's work is done, I head home. And of course, because my life is what it is these days, I find something I'm not expecting: Dominic's been here.

I don't notice it at first. There's no extra coat on the hooks, no boots that shouldn't be there. But there is *something* different, something about the air that tips me off. It feels less lonely than it usually does, even though I'm still alone.

I walk down the hall listening for him, but the apartment is silent. The door to his room is ajar. I push it open. The boxes that were lined up neatly against the wall are askew. OLD CLOTHES seems to have disappeared altogether.

I sit down on the edge of his bed, waiting for something, maybe for him to reappear, though I know deep down he won't. And then, telling myself it will be only one more time, I crawl into his bed, drinking in the mixture of our smells until it lulls me to sleep.

On Monday morning, I'm waiting for Matt in his office. The sky is dark. Small, hard pellets of ice are pinging against the window.

"This is a pleasant surprise," Matt says as he hangs his fawn-colored coat on the back of his door. "What's up?"

"I think I might've cracked something in the Mutual Assurance case, and I wanted to talk it through."

His face brightens. "That sounds promising. What is it?"

I tell him as he settles into the chair behind his desk, rolling up the sleeves on his banker's shirt into their customary union-negotiator position.

"So if you're right, we have a case for negligence against the museum?"

"I think so. It's kind of a big miss on their part."

"How can we prove that's the way the painting was stolen?"

"That's why I need some help." I tell him about the surveillance video.

"Who did you have in mind?"

"I thought I'd put the Initial Brigade to some good use."

He smiles. "Are you sure they're up to the task?"

"I can manage them."

"I'm sure you can." He drums his fingers on the corner of his desk. "You know, if you're right, more people than just our client are going to be interested."

"I know."

"Why not pass on your hunch to the police? Let them do the work?"

I shrug. "The detective in charge of the case thinks I'm tilting at windmills. It'd be nice to prove her wrong."

"And the Management Committee?"

I meet his intelligent gaze. "Them too."

"All right. Keep me in the loop."

"Will do."

Matt smiles at me proudly. "It's nice to have you back, Emma."

"I've been back for weeks."

"Have you, now?"

* * *

An hour later I've taken over one of the boardrooms and assembled my team. They sit scattered around the long cherry-wood table watching me with a look of trepidation. I explain what needs to be done: I want them to watch the museum video footage to see if everyone who went in also went out.

They gripe and grumble, but I can tell they're interested.

J. Perry puts up his hand.

"Come on, J.P., you don't have to put up your hand to talk."

He lowers it. "You really think the robber dude hung out in that box all night long?"

"Well, I'm not sure, but I think so. That's where you guys come in."

"So, essentially, you want us to watch hours of tape looking for something that's not there, based on a hunch?"

"That's right. You guys game?"

I. William shrugs. "Beats doing research for Sophie."

Amen.

"All right, then. Why don't you get started? Tell me if you find anything immediately. If you don't, let's meet here tomorrow at the same time for a status update." I turn toward Monty, who's doodling stars around the edge of his yellow legal pad. "Can you hang back a minute?"

I wait for the others to leave. "Did you get that research done?"

Monty shifts back and forth on his heels. "Yup. But it's not looking good. If a landlord gets an expulsion judgment and the tenant doesn't leave of their own volition, the landlord has the right to remove any property they find."

"They don't have to warehouse the property anywhere? They can just give it away?"

"Apparently."

"Damn."

"What's this got to do with the museum thing, anyway?"

I gather together my papers. "It's another matter a client needed looking into."

"Sure enough."

I walk away from his curious expression and head back to my office. Jenny follows me in, wearing a conservative (for her) navy suit. She tells me that Stephanie called, as did the I-won't-give-up-until-you-agree assistant from *In Progress*. "And Mr. Bushnell's lawyer called. He wants to schedule a date for the depositions."

"Anyone else?"

"Nuh-uh."

"Are you sure?"

She gives me her innocent face. "Of course."

"Listen, Jenny, I know you didn't give me those messages from Dominic."

She turns bright red. "I'm sorry."

"You know how important it is for me to get my messages,"

I say as gently as I can. "And it's not like you to forget. What's going on?"

"I didn't forget. I did it on purpose."

"Is that supposed to reassure me?"

"I was doing it for you."

"How so?"

"You were just so totally sad the last time he called. I didn't want you to go through that again. Not after everything that's happened."

My throat tightens. "I wasn't that sad, was I?"

"You didn't talk to me for two days."

I wonder, briefly, if that's true, but the days after Dominic called to tell me he was leaving the apartment are a little hazy.

"You have to give me all my messages, no matter who they're from, okay?"

"Does this mean I'm not fired?"

"Of course you're not fired. You're the only one keeping me sane around here."

She flashes me a bright white smile. "I do my best."

"Thanks."

"What for?"

"For . . . trying to protect me. I appreciate it."

"Anytime."

She bounces out of the office, and I take a seat at my desk. Almost instantly, my email pings. It's from Jenny telling me the dates and times that Dominic called. There's a PS at the bottom of the email that reads: *Are you going to call him?* ☺

I pick up the pink slip with Carrie's number on it and add Dominic's below, doodling a box around and around it until the ink makes a deep impression.

Are these numbers a path to peace or disaster?

If only I knew.

Chapter 23
As Per Usual

I'm at home working on the Mutual Assurance file, killing time until a late dinner with Stephanie. I'm going through the investigator's report Sophie ordered on Victor Bushnell. It's not generally something I enjoy doing, but since he took the time to learn all about me, I thought I'd repay the favor. It's fascinating stuff really, like seeing behind the curtain in the Land of Oz. Many of the details are in the public domain, of course, but others are not. Like the fact that Bushnell has a massive personal loan that's guaranteed by the painting, and that he doesn't have enough unencumbered assets to pay it back if the insurance money doesn't come through.

The doorbell rings. I get up to answer it, rubbing the crick in my neck along the way. Our insurance plan covers ten massages a year, but I never manage to take advantage of it. I should get Jenny to book me one tomorrow. I definitely deserve it.

I open the door as Stephanie presses the bell a second time.

"Are we late for something?"

She smiles at me from the middle of her fur-lined hood. "It's freezing out here."

The air swirling in *is* freezing, at least ten degrees colder than earlier. I step back to let her in, then close the door behind her quickly.

She looks me up and down. "How come you're not ready to go?"

I'm wearing a pair of sweatpants captured from Dominic's OLD CLOTHES and a cream V-neck wool sweater I've managed to get yellow highlighter all over.

"You think I should change?"

"If you still want to go to Studio."

"Right, I forgot. You wanted to go fancy tonight."

"What I want is to dig into their old-fashioned mac and cheese."

"Why don't I make us some Kraft Dinner and save you the thirty-six bucks?"

She shakes her furry head. "Uh-uh. You agreed to go out, and we're going out. You've been hiding in here for too long."

"I'm not hiding."

"Whatever. Go. Change."

I leave her in the entranceway and search through my closet for something that's chic/warm enough for this month's fancy restaurant on a freezing-cold night.

"What are you wearing under that coat?" I call to Stephanie.

"My wool sweater-dress."

That means *my* wool sweater-dress is out. I stare at my half-filled closet. I really need some more clothes. Fucking Pedro. I can't believe I can't sue him. Maybe I should have someone a little more thorough than Monty look into it? No, no, that's silly. I need to accept that I don't have a case against him. Though . . . he doesn't know that . . . I could take him to small-claims court. Maybe that'll make him think twice before he does what he did to me to someone else.

Man, will you listen to yourself? You sound like Sophie.

"Come on already, Em! Just put on a nice pair of jeans and one of your new sweaters and be done with it!"

I follow her instructions and run a brush through my hair, checking my reflection in the mirror. My tan is almost gone. Only the extra freckles across the bridge of my nose and the faint outline of my sunglasses around my eyes betray where I've been.

I walk into the hall. Stephanie's standing in front of Dominic's room. She turns toward me with a quizzical look on her face. "I thought you said Dominic wasn't staying here?"

"He isn't."

"Then how come his bed's unmade?"

I knew I forgot to do something this morning.

I shrug. "He's a guy. It's been like that since he left."

"His bed was made the last time I was here."

Ah, hell.

"Do you have to notice everything?"

"Will you spill already?"

Is there any way I can tell her what I've been doing that won't make me seem pathetic and weak?

"I've been having trouble sleeping."

"Don't tell me you've been sleeping in his room?"

I nod.

She starts to laugh. "Hoo boy, you've got it bad."

"Yes, yes, are we going to dinner or what?"

"Was it just once?"

I walk to the entranceway and lift my coat from the hook.

"Twice? Please tell me it wasn't more than twice."

I pull on my boots.

"Now I really need to see that pro list."

I open the door and gesture to the dark outside. "I'm hungry. Do you want to keep mocking me, or are you ready to go?"

"Oh, I'm ready." Her eyes twinkle as she pulls her hood around her face. She hops from the step onto the snowy walkway.

I start to follow her, then think better of it. "Hold on a sec, okay?"

"What the—?"

I sprint down the hall to Dominic's room. I pull up the sheets and fluff the pillows. I tug the comforter into place and smooth my hand over it, eliminating the creases. That's better. Now . . . a quick glance around reveals a half-drunk glass of water on the bedside table. I pick it up and put the glass on the table in the hall. I join Stephanie outside, locking the door behind me.

"What was that all about?"

"Covering my tracks."

"To think, people pay you hundreds of dollars an hour to solve their problems."

"Fuck off."

"And she has a mouth too."

I flash my teeth. "You'd better believe it."

I get home around ten, my stomach full and my ears ringing from the too-loud music. The restaurant was one of those half-club, half-restaurant places, and the DJ was spinning disks at club-level volume. It made conversation difficult, but the upside was that Stephanie gave up on quizzing me about my recent sleeping habits when I pretended I couldn't hear her.

As I hang up my coat and scarf, I can feel a bout of brain-won't-turn-off insomnia coming my way. After getting caught by Stephanie, I've promised myself that I'll stop sleeping where I shouldn't. I have a feeling I'll be up late watching infomercials.

I notice the hall light is on as I leave the entranceway. The door to Dominic's room is ajar, though I swear I closed it two hours ago.

My heart leaps. Dominic's been here. Maybe he's still here? But why? What does he want? Why did he call me all those times? And what did Emily want with him at the museum?

As per usual, I don't have any answers. Thank God I made the bed.

I hear the scrape of a chair across the kitchen floor. Either it's Dominic or I'm being robbed. I'll take option A, please.

I walk cautiously down the hall, my heart lifting. He's here. He must be waiting for me, right?

Dominic's sitting at the kitchen table wearing jeans and the sweater I gave him for Christmas. He's flipping through the file I left scattered across the table.

"What are you doing?"

He looks up. "That's some interesting reading you've got there."

I walk toward the table and start collecting the file together. "You shouldn't be reading that."

"It was sitting on the table."

"I shouldn't have left it out. I had no idea you were coming."

"I'm sorry," he says testily. "I didn't know I needed permission to come to my own apartment."

"You don't. You can come whenever you want. Only . . ."

"'Only' what?"

"I'm just a bit confused, I guess. I mean, you come back from Ireland and say you're going to stay somewhere else, but then you keep showing up here without even calling first . . ."

"I called a bunch of times. You never called me back, remember?"

"I told you at the gallery. I never received those messages."

He pushes his chair back and walks toward the sink, gripping the counter. On the cabinet above his left shoulder are the faint scratches he left when he punched it. The night Emily called. The night we slept together.

"What did Emily want the other night?"

He turns toward me, his eyes spreading a chill across the warm room. "Leave her out of this. And don't tell her anything more about us."

His words hit me like a slap. He doesn't want Emily to know we slept together. They're back together. He took her back after everything she did to him.

"I didn't tell her *anything* about us."

"Oh, really?"

"I don't have to defend myself to you, but yes, really."

"Right, whatever."

My hands start to tremble. I want to take the file folder and throw it across the room like I did with the Scotch glass, but the time for infantile gestures is over. Besides, it wouldn't make the same satisfying crash.

He starts to move past me and I grab onto his arm. "Wait, Dominic. Please don't go."

He shrugs me off. "I have to."

"Will you at least tell me why you came here tonight?"

He looks down at me, but I'm not sure he can see me, not really.

"I don't remember," he says, and walks away.

Chapter 24
Low-Percentage Shot

Stephanie was wrong about the pro/con list. As much as I like making lists, I never made one about Dominic. I didn't want to reduce whatever there is between us to two columns. But that was before tonight. Because tonight, I want to reduce him to something, all right. I believe it's called a pulp.

The upside to all this anger is that I have no trouble avoiding his bedroom, and in the end, no trouble sleeping either. In fact, I fall asleep to a count of the ways in which I can make Dominic's life miserable. It's stupid and immature, I know, but men behaving badly have a way of bringing that out in me.

My punishment for all this easy sleep is that I once again wake up early, early, early, with my brain whizzing a million miles a minute.

I slip into my bathrobe and go to the kitchen. I rinse out the coffeepot, start a fresh one brewing, and dive into the Mutual Assurance file. By the time I'm surrounded by coffee smells, I'm deep into it, trying to make a trail out of the scattered crumbs of information.

Two hours later I'm no further ahead, but I do have a splitting headache for my troubles.

I rest my head in the palm of my hand, rubbing my eyes with my fingers. I feel sick to my stomach, like I had too much to drink last night, though I hardly drank a drop.

Can't anything in my life be simple and straightforward? And wasn't I supposed to be getting a turning point in here somewhere? I must be in the third act of this farce by now, right? Which means there's just one twist left, and I can have my happy ending.

Better get on that, then.

When I get to the office, I find Jenny surrounded by several of the other secretaries. The object of their collective cooing delight is a simple vase of multicolored tulips.

"What's all this?"

Jenny's friends shoot me guilty looks and scurry back to their cubicles.

"They're for you!" Jenny says excitedly.

"Oh . . . um, well, I'll take them to my office."

I hold out my hands. She lifts the vase toward me. I catch a whiff of their subtle scent, the soft caress of spring.

"I think they're from *him*!" She raises her eyebrows suggestively.

"What makes you think that?"

"Because he delivered them himself."

"What? Dominic was here?"

"Does Dominic have dark hair, green eyes, and a really cute butt?"

"Um, maybe."

"I told him he could wait for you, but he just wanted to leave the flowers and go."

"Did he say anything else?"

"No, but he left a card, see?" She points to the flowers. There's a small white card tucked into the large, flat leaves. "What do you think it says?"

"I have no idea."

"Did you guys get in a fight or something?"

"Or something."

I close the door to my office and hit the switch to turn the clear glass opaque. I sit down on the chaise longue and place the flowers gently on the coffee table. I pluck the card from its perch. My name is written in the same block letters as Dominic's postcoital note. I fight off a flash of the feel of his lips as he kissed the inside of my thigh and open it.

I'M SORRY, it says. I'M SO SORRY. FORGIVE ME?

Without stopping to think, I dig my phone out of my purse and dial.

"This is Dominic. Leave a message."

"Hey, Dominic, it's me. Emma. I got your flowers. They're

beautiful. Thank you. And I wanted to say . . . you don't have to keep staying somewhere else. You can come . . . home. If you want." My voice catches in my throat. "I—"

Beep!

Goddamnit.

Well, maybe I said enough. I hope so, anyway.

I sit there for a while, waiting for the phone to ring, waiting, wishing, for Dominic to call me back. But wishing someone would call me hasn't worked before, and it doesn't work now. Of course it doesn't.

When I've arranged my flowers on the windowsill and composed myself, I go to the boardroom to check on the Initial Brigade.

One look inside convinces me that leaving them with instructions to use whatever resources they needed to evaluate the videotapes quickly was a bad idea.

The blinds are pulled down and someone's taped the edges so no light creeps in. At the front of the room are three flat-screen TVs on metal rolling stands, the kind I last saw a member of the AV club pushing into health class. The guys are each sitting in front of a screen, ensconced in a dark brown leather club chair. Their quasi-identical blazers are draped over the backs. Their eyes are trained on the flickering black-and-white images.

"E.W.!" I. William drawls as he hits Pause. "Pull up a chair and join the fray."

"The fray" is right. The room is littered with half-empty food cartons and soft-drink cans. I can see the green edge of a beer bottle poking out from behind the garbage. The air smells like the inside of a locker room.

"I asked you guys to work hard, but this . . . this is—"

"Surprising, ain't it?" Monty says, keeping his eyes on the moving images on his screen. "Who would've thought working would actually be kind of fun?"

"You call watching TV working? You guys ought to spend some time in the Ejector."

I. William looks indignant. "A little respect, please. We've been wearing out our eye sockets here."

"What have you been doing, precisely?"

"Let me show you," J.P. says, pausing his own screen.

He walks toward the enormous whiteboard at the front of the room. The louvered wood doors that normally cover it are folded back into the corners. On the board are two columns headed "Entered" and "Left." Below each heading is a list of names, some of which I recognize from the list Detective Kendle showed me.

"I. William's watching the entrance camera. When he identifies someone on the list, he writes their name here and notes the time they arrived."

I glance down the list. "Weren't there a lot more people than that at the party?"

"That's where Monty comes in. You see, the celebrities and socialites were the easy people to identify. That knocked off about fifty people. But the rest of the list, well, I don't know about you, but I wouldn't know Bill Gates if I bumped into him on the street, let alone tried to identify him from the distance those cameras are set up at."

"Do you have some massive knowledge of rich people's faces I don't know about?" I ask Monty.

"Nah, I looked up pictures of the guests on the Internet. When I find a good one, I print it up on the color printer and we all stare at it until we've memorized it. Then we search for that person until we find them. When we do, we add them to the list."

That would explain why the far wall is plastered with the (mostly) smiling faces of over a hundred men and women, some of whom are vaguely familiar. None of them looks like someone who steals paintings for a living. Then again, what does an art thief look like? Blending into a rich crowd is probably an essential skill.

"This is going to take longer than I thought."

"You're telling us," I. William says. He picks up a glass tumbler from the floor and shakes it. The ice rattles. "Looks like we're going to need some more supplies."

"I'll send Jenny out for some things. How can I help?"

Monty scratches his chin. "Well, it'd go faster if we had two people who could search for the 'unrecognizables.'"

"All right. Why don't I spend some time getting to know our party guests?"

They nod in agreement and turn back to their TVs. I use the conference room phone to call Jenny and let her know where I am. With a bubbly laugh, she agrees to get some non-regulation supplies.

I stare at the faces on the wall one by one, trying to associate the name with some defining characteristic. Pointy ears = MacAfee. Widow's peak = Grafton. Sharp nose = Hosseini. It's like that memory game I played when I was a kid, where the faces popped up on a yellow plastic flap. I can't remember the rules, but I'm pretty sure I kicked some kindergarten ass.

"Okay, I think I'm ready," I say about twenty minutes later.

I. William turns and hangs over the back of his club chair. "Such a sweet kid. There's no way you memorized enough faces in that amount of time."

"I think I did."

"All right, then. Pull up a chair."

I drag one of the conference room chairs across the room and sit next to him.

"You ready?"

"Hit it."

He points the remote at the screen, skipping backward through several hours of footage. He gets to the beginning and presses Play. The camera is pointed at the entranceway.

There are two rectangular metal detectors manned by a team of bored-looking guards. The time stamp in the right-hand corner of the screen reads 7:04. The black-and-white images make the building's features sharper but also somehow blur the guards' faces.

Maybe this is going to be harder than I thought.

"This is when the first guests started to arrive. And in case you were wondering, no one you'll recognize shows up for a long time."

"All fashionably late, huh?"

"Oh yeah."

An elderly couple comes into view. They're both wearing dark fur coats. He's thin and angular with pointy ears and a sharp nose. She's softer, a little frail, and might have a widow's peak.

I. William shoots me a look. "Any guesses?"

"Um . . . Mr. and Mrs. Jenkins?"

"Nope."

"The Cliftons?"

"Not even close."

"You know who it is, don't you?"

"Of course. They were the easy ones."

"How come?"

He nods toward the screen. "Watch."

The elderly couple passes through the metal detector. The

man sets it off and is directed to the side by a security guard in his late forties with a protruding belly. The elderly man's annoyance is apparent in the set of his shoulders, even in blurry black and white.

As he's being patted down, Victor Bushnell strides into view, looking immaculate in a well-fitting tux. He says something to the security guard. The big-bellied guard shakes his head. Bushnell stabs his finger into the security guard's lapel. The guard shifts nervously from foot to foot. A younger guard with stripes on his shoulders walks over and says something. Big Belly shrugs and returns to his post. The elderly man straightens his shoulders and collects his wife. Bushnell's super-white teeth flash at the couple. The older woman kisses him gently on the cheek.

I. William hits Pause. "Can you guess who they are?"

"Obviously someone important to him."

"Go on, you're getting there."

Why would Bushnell get angry because the security guard was doing his job? Who would he want to protect like that? And why would he get a kiss for his efforts?

"Are they his parents?"

"Correct!"

Monty gives me a weary smile. "That's two down and four hundred and ninety-seven to go."

* * *

Three hours later, I've identified a grand total of seven new faces. My vision is blurry, and I feel like I'd have trouble recognizing my own face on these tapes.

There's a knock at the door.

"What's the password?" J.P. bellows, his eyes never leaving the screen.

"The Daily Show," a muffled voice answers.

"You know, having her yell it through the door like that kind of defeats the whole purpose of a password." I walk to the door and let Jenny in. Her arms are loaded with bags of "supplies."

She dumps them on the conference table. The Initial Brigade hits Pause in unison and pushes past her to the goods.

"Where are my Nibs?" J.P. mutters. "I gotta have my Nibs."

"They're there already. Sheesh. What are you guys up to, anyway?"

"Sorry, Jenny, but it's top secret."

"Yeah, I know, but you can trust me. I swear."

I hesitate, then decide to give in a little. "We're working on something for the Mutual Assurance file. And that's all I can tell you."

"Okay, I get it. Say, did you call him yet?"

The tips of my ears feel pink. "Call who?"

"Oh, you know. *Him.*"

I. William's head rises. "There's a him?"

"It's no one."

"Oh, there's someone," Jenny says.

"That's enough. Back to work, Jenny."

I follow her to the door to lock it behind her. I'm not quite sure why I'm being so security-conscious, but I feel justified when I see Sophie lurking in the hallway. I walk into the hall and close the door behind me.

"What do you want?"

She flicks her stick-straight hair over her shoulder. "What's going on in there?"

"Nothing."

"You expect me to believe that?"

"I don't care what you believe."

"Everyone's talking about how you've commandeered the Initial Brigade and all the AV equipment. Do I smell alcohol?"

"Just give it up, Sophie."

She folds her arms across her chest. "I know it has something to do with the Mutual Assurance file."

"Brilliant deduction."

"I want to know what's going on."

"Well, you're going to have to learn to live with disappointment."

"This isn't over."

"Oh, but it is."

I slip through the door so she can't see inside, then I lock it behind me. The Initial Brigade are back in their seats, snacks at the ready in their laps, hands curved around their remotes.

"Should we go to orange alert?" I. William asks as I sit down next to him.

"If orange alert is the color for not telling Sophie anything, then yes."

"Orange it is."

I stare at the screen. I'm not sure I can take much more of this. "Maybe we're going about this all wrong."

"What's that?" Monty says.

"Pause for a second, will you guys?"

They hit their Pause buttons with practiced synchronicity. I walk to where I can face them. Behind me on the wall is a blowup of the museum.

"Follow me here. Our theory is that the thief found a way to hide himself in the bench in the Bushnell Gallery, probably while the security guards were getting the next group of guests."

"How come the security guards didn't notice that someone was left behind?" J.P. asks.

"I'm not sure, but he probably created a small diversion somehow to confuse them."

Monty lifts his hand.

"I told you, Monty, that's not necessary."

He grins. "Right. Well, what if he said he was sick? Then

he could pretend he was going to the bathroom but actually hide somewhere close to the gallery so he could slip back in between groups."

I turn and examine the map. "He could have hidden himself in this bathroom here." I point to the bathroom around the corner from the Bushnell Gallery. "I'll find out from Detective Kendle whether there are alarms on the bathrooms.

"So group leaves, thief slips back in, making sure to stay out of view of the cameras, and conceals himself in the bench. And there he waits overnight until the alarms are turned off in the morning. Then he gets out, removes the painting from its frame, conceals it inside whatever he's wearing, and leaves the museum once it reopens."

I. William's eyes light up. "Which means . . . we should be able to see him leaving on the video!"

"Precisely. If we can identify one of our guests on the video footage the next morning, then we have our man."

J.P. sighs. "So now we're going to have to try to identify people from the back?"

"Plus the guy has to be wearing something different from the night before, or he's a total idiot," Monty adds. "That could take days."

"Do we even have that footage?" I. William asks.

"The recordings are twenty-four hours long. What time do they start?"

"At noon."

"What time do they open in the morning?" J.P. asks.

I think back. "The party was on Saturday. I think they only open at eleven on Sunday."

J.P. goes to the computer and types for a few seconds. "Yup. She's right."

"Which reduces the window to one hour."

"That's pretty tight."

"But he must've been eager to get out of there. I can't believe he'd hang around for longer than he'd have to."

"Stands to reason," I. William agrees.

"Let's hope so," Monty says emphatically.

"All right, let's give it a go," I say.

I. William picks up his remote and starts to fast-forward toward the day after the party. The video blurs through endless hours of an empty lobby punctuated by the infrequent visits of the overnight security guards. When it gets toward 11 A.M. on the video, he slows it down to real time. We watch the screen intently. The time stamp says 10:52.

"That's the head security guy from the night before," I. William says, pointing to the man I recognize from the altercation with Bushnell's parents. "He left around eleven."

"How come they didn't find the painting missing overnight, by the way?" I ask.

"They don't patrol the whole museum," J.P. says. "There are

heat and motion sensors in all the galleries. The guards just patrol the halls."

"The day guards are coming on shift. Do they have to disable the alarm section by section, or is there a master switch somewhere?"

"There's a master switch," J.P. replies. "It was in that security manual the museum sent over."

Monty rolls his eyes. "Show-off."

The time stamp flips to 10:59. The head security guard comes into view, followed by three other guards. The head guard gesticulates as he gives them instructions. Two of them lumber off reluctantly, while one takes his station at the metal detector. The head guard nods to someone off-camera and makes a slashing motion at his throat. It's 11:02.

"He must be telling someone to turn off the alarm," I. William says.

"Right. Eyes front, boys."

We watch the silent movie unfold. The Sunday before Christmas is a slow day. The first visitor is an elderly man with a cane who arrives at 11:08. Over the next several minutes, there's a trickle of traffic. Harried-looking mothers with young children, a couple in their early twenties with their hands entwined.

"Oh shit," J.P. says.

I take the remote from I. William and hit Pause. "What?"

"I just remembered something." He stands abruptly and walks toward the conference table, riffling through the stacks of papers, candy wrappers, and bottle caps. He locates a crumpled piece of paper and scans it. "Yeah, that's what I thought. They're about to discover that the painting's missing."

"What happens then?"

"They shut the whole thing down. No one out or in."

"How long was the museum closed for?"

He checks his notes. "Two days. There's no way our guy could stay in there that long."

My mind crowds with doubt. This has to be the answer. Doesn't it?

"Let's keep watching. He still has time."

I hit Play.

11:12.

11:13.

I. William's face is so intense I almost believe that it's going to work. That the mystery man crouching hidden in a marble bench holding a painting worth millions of dollars is going to reveal himself. Instead, a family arrives, a little boy of about four years old darting in and out of the metal detector. The guard reaches out to snatch him by the collar, just missing him. His mother looks affronted. She speaks precisely enough that you can read her lips, demanding to see his supervisor. The head guard comes over to placate her.

A man comes into view behind the family. He's wearing a plain tan overcoat that reaches past his knees. One hand is holding a cell phone to his ear while the other is thrust in his pocket. His hair is hidden by a black ski cap, similar to the one Dominic was wearing when I first met him. As he passes the commotion caused by the four-year-old and his angry mother, he gives them a quick glance, revealing his profile. I feel a flash of recognition.

"No fucking way," J.P. breathes.

"It's Victor Bushnell," I. William and I say together.

Chapter 25
The Half-Life of Happiness

"Holy crap," Monty says.

"Dude," I. William says, "we just figured out that a *billion-aire* pulled off a massive art theft, and all you can say is 'holy crap'?"

Monty looks sheepish. "It seemed appropriate at the time."

"But hold on," J.P. says, staring perplexedly at the screen. "He's not coming *out* of the museum; he's going in. That doesn't make any sense."

The air seems to leave the room.

"You're totally right," I. William says. "What do we do now?"

I watch the silent movie playing out on the screen, my gut churning. Something offscreen draws the attention of the guard at the metal detector, as well as Victor Bushnell's. Clearly, someone's discovered that the painting's missing.

Bushnell turns abruptly on his heel and leaves the museum while the guard's focus is diverted. Moments later, several guards come into view, all talking and gesticulating excitedly.

"He left," I say quietly.

"What's that?" I. William asks.

"He left. Victor Bushnell. When he saw the guards coming. Why would he do that if he didn't know about the theft?"

"But he couldn't have stolen it, right? Not personally. Maybe he had an accomplice?"

Something niggles at the edge of my brain. "Wait a second. Oh, I know . . . wrong movie."

"What do you mean?"

"I mean . . . we've been assuming that the thief was hiding in the museum overnight so he could take the painting out of the museum. But what if that isn't it? What if he never took the painting out at all? What if it's still in there somewhere?"

"And that's why Bushnell was there?" J.P. asks. "To take it out?"

"Yeah."

"But he'd be running an awful risk. And it didn't work."

"No, I know. But it still could. Once all the chaos has died down, he could walk in and take it anytime."

"But why would he steal his own painting?"

"He has a large personal loan. The painting's collateral for it."

He shakes his head. "But why steal it? Why not just sell it?"

"But then he wouldn't have the painting. This way, he gets out of his financial pickle *and* either keeps the painting or sells it on the black market in a few years."

I. William pops a pretzel into his mouth. "We should tell Matt about this."

"No," I say. "Not yet."

"Why not?"

"I want to make sure first."

"Make sure of what?"

"That he did it."

I. William points over his shoulder. "Isn't that his face up there on the screen?"

"Yes, but we should make sure there isn't some other explanation for him being there. And that the painting's still in the museum."

Please, please, let the painting still be in the museum.

"Wouldn't they have searched for it already?"

"I'm not sure they did," I say, a flash of my mother's words in the night coming to me. "And I think I have an idea where it might be. Let me make sure before you say anything to Matt, okay?"

I. William shrugs and positions a can of spray cheese above his mouth.

"That's disgusting," J.P. says.

"How do you know unless you try it?"

"Trust me. I know."

I sigh. "Can we focus here for a second, guys?"

They grumble their assent.

"Thanks. I. William, maybe you can find a facial-recognition specialist who'll confirm that's really Bushnell."

"On it."

"And, J.P., if you could clean all the physical evidence up and collate it; we'll need that if there's ever a court case."

"No problem."

Monty puts up his hand.

"Seriously, Monty, still with the hand?"

"What should I do?"

"How about summarizing what we've found until now?"

"Should I leave out the snacks?"

"That would probably be a good idea. Email it to me when you're done so I can review it."

"When do we crack the champagne?" J.P. asks.

"Soon. I promise. Don't stay too late."

"There's no danger of that."

The next few hours pass in a blur as I persuade Detective Kendle to come with me to the museum and check on my hunch—that Victor Bushnell hid the painting in the base of the bench in his gallery, and that it's been sitting there ever since because he hasn't had the opportunity to remove it. If I'm right, it must've been killing him to know it was there the whole time during Dominic's show. Or maybe he doesn't care about the painting at all and it really is just about the insurance money?

Detective Kendle flashes her badge at Security, and I follow her through the metal detector. She says something to the head guard, and he swears loudly, the guttural sound echoing off the marble walls. He stabs his finger toward two guards standing on the other side of the room in a gesture reminiscent of World War II movies—eyes-on-me and follow. They comply, and when we get to the gallery it seems like we're all holding our breath as the youngest of the guards pries open the seat lid and looks down into the empty bench.

Detective Kendle takes over. She pulls on a pair of latex gloves with the expertise of a surgeon and moves her strong fingers around the base until they catch on something—an almost invisible latch to a hidden compartment. And there it is: a rolled-up piece of innocent-looking canvas that people are willing to pay millions for. The young guard reaches for it until Detective Kendle's bark stops his hand. She reminds him about fingerprints as she plucks her phone from her pocket. She glances at me, looking mildly surprised, as if she can't quite believe this is really happening.

I just shrug and look away, trying to figure out what I'm feeling. Shouldn't I be elated? Or at least relieved? Wasn't I happy today? For a moment? Right when we figured out the last piece of the puzzle, I felt elated. And now all I can feel is the echo of it, a small, uneven beat on the contour of my heart.

The half-life of happiness, I guess.

Chapter 26
A Piece of the Puzzle

"Let me get this straight," Sunshine says the next afternoon as I navigate through traffic in the fire-red MINI Cooper that she rented but feels too stressed out to drive. "Victor Bushnell stole his own painting?"

"Looks like it."

"But why?"

"It likely has something to do with the loan he took to finish building his corporate headquarters when his stock price sank in the market meltdown." It was right there in the investigator's report. The building was supposed to be the Trump Tower of his enterprise, but when the credit crunch arrived, the banks weren't willing to lend the company—already overextended—any additional money. They would, however, be all too happy to lend it to Bushnell, provided he could give them the right kind of collateral, of course.

"He went to all this trouble because of a building?"

I shift the car awkwardly, depressing the clutch at the wrong moment.

"It's not just the building. If he doesn't make his loan payments, the bank will call the loan, and that could trigger a cascade effect. His whole business could have gone up in smoke."

"But I thought he was a billionaire?"

"Just on paper. He pretty much leveraged everything he had."

"That's our exit coming up." She points to a green sign that hangs above the highway.

"Where are we going, anyway?"

"You'll see. Go on."

I accelerate to pass a van blocking my access to the off-ramp. "There's not much more to tell, really."

"How'd he hide the painting without the guards seeing?"

"He was in the last group of guests to go into the gallery. He told the guard that he'd forgotten something in the room right before the guard locked it. The guard let him go back in alone."

"Well, that wasn't too smart. Look lively."

I turn my attention back to the road. It curves sharply to the right.

"Easy on my gears!"

"This wasn't my idea, remember?"

"It wasn't an idea, honey, it was a vision."

That's what she'd said on the phone earlier. She'd had a "vision" about me and wanted to pick me up so she could take me somewhere. I asked her if we could do it another time.

"Do you think I get visions like this every day, Emmaline?"

"I'm kind of busy."

"The memo will wait. I'm picking you up in thirty minutes."

"How the hell did you know I was working on a memo?"

"I told you, I—"

"Had a vision. I heard you." I stared down at the blinking light on my Dictaphone. That had to be a lucky guess, didn't it? "I really need to work on this. Can it wait until tomorrow?"

"It can't. It's important. I promise."

I heard the seriousness in Sunshine's tone, a seriousness I wasn't sure I'd ever heard before. And it occurred to me that what I was doing could wait a few hours. That I owed Sunshine that, at least.

I agreed to go, spent the next twenty minutes dictating, then synched my Dictaphone with my computer, sending the file to Jenny.

"Can you have this finished by the time I get back?" I asked her as I buttoned up my coat. "And I need you to password the file."

Her eyes flitted briefly away from her Facebook page to meet mine. "Sure, no problem."

"I still don't get why he'd steal the painting himself," Sunshine says now.

"Maybe he couldn't find anyone he could trust. Or maybe it was the thrill of it."

"I guess . . . Stop the car!"

I brake, checking the rearview mirror to make sure no one's behind me a fraction too late. A man in a black Mercedes slams on his brakes and swerves to avoid me, applying his horn liberally. I catch a flash of his finger as he passes within inches of my bumper.

"Sorry about that. I wasn't paying attention."

"No problem. Why did you want me to stop?"

She straightens her wool hat. "Because we're here."

"We are?" I realize we're in front of the gates to a cemetery. My mother's buried within.

A chill runs down my spine. "What are we doing here?"

"We're going to visit your mother."

"What? Why?"

"She was part of my vision."

I feel queasy. "I'm not sure this is a good idea."

"I know, dear. Well, let's go, we don't want to be late."

"Late for what?"

"You'll see."

I sigh internally as I put the car in reverse with minimal fuss. I back up far enough to pull into the entrance. The front gates look imposing.

"Are you sure it's open?"

She nods. "I called ahead."

I put the car into first. The gates swing open like the automatic doors at the grocery store. I press the accelerator lightly, being cautious, since the road doesn't appear to have been plowed since the last snowstorm.

Maybe it's the change of season, but nothing looks familiar. I've only been here once, the day of my mother's funeral. It was warm then, and bright. And of course, I wasn't paying attention to where I was going as I followed the hearse through the groves of trees and rolling grass.

"I don't remember where to go."

"Just follow this road."

We drive in silence for a few moments, our location staying our tongues.

"Park at the top of the hill."

I give the car a bit of gas. The wheels begin spinning halfway up the hill, and we stop moving forward. The smell of burning rubber fills the car. I try the brake, but it has no effect. We come to rest at the base of the hill and skid off into the ditch. My hands are shaking.

"I guess I should've listened to the car-rental company and got the one with the four-wheel drive, eh?" Sunshine says with a wavering smile.

"Not part of your vision?"

"I don't get practical information like that, I'm afraid. Anyway, off we go."

"Shouldn't we do something about the car?"

She flings her scarf over her shoulder. "It'll keep. Come along, now."

I grit my teeth and follow her out of the car, leaving the hazard lights blinking. I climb up the bank of the slippery ditch, buttoning my coat against the cold. We trudge through the snow to an area that feels vaguely familiar. We get to a cleared path, and now I recognize where I'm going. My mother's grave is up ahead, past a large stand of trees. Their dark branches are highlighted by a dusting of snow.

"Sunshine, is this really necessary?"

"Shh. We're almost there."

My hands feel cold and stiff inside my gloves. I want to turn back, but something propels me ahead.

Sunshine disappears behind the black trees. I take a few last strides and catch up with her. She's standing at the foot of my mother's grave, looking down at a bunch of dried-out yellow roses half buried in the snow.

"We've missed him," Sunshine says with uncharacteristic bleakness.

"Who?"

"Your father."

"This is about my father?"

"I saw him so clearly."

"Sunshine, please tell me what's going on."

She grimaces guiltily. "I was meditating this morning, and I had a really clear vision of this place."

"And my father was here?"

"Yes. He was holding a bouquet of flowers."

I walk toward her. Even faded, the roses are oddly vivid in this black-and-white world.

"Are you playing some kind of trick on me?"

"Oh, Emmaline, how could you think such a thing?"

"I'm sorry. I just . . . I don't know why you brought me here."

"I thought it might bring you some peace, of course."

Of course. How could running into my father leaving flowers to the woman he abandoned years ago without a backward thought bring me anything but peace? Was he even really here?

I realize with a saddening certainty that I don't want to know. What I do know is enough, and it's time to let go of the hurt that I've been holding on to for so long. It's time to say goodbye, not just to my mother but to my absent father too.

"I wish you wouldn't," I say. "Try to bring us back together, I mean."

"Why not, dear?"

"Because I have to choose whether I want him in my life. You can't do the choosing for me."

She raises a hand to my cheek. Her fluffy mitten tickles my skin. "I wish I could."

"I know. Thank you for trying. But I think . . . I'm going to let him be where he is, wherever he is."

"Are you sure?"

"Yes. For now anyway, yes."

She sighs. "Well, should we head back to the car?"

I look at the curve of my mother's headstone. I remember picking it out a few days after she died, but I've never seen it in place.

"Will you give me a second?"

"Of course."

Sunshine crunches away, her boots squeaking through our footprints. When she's out of sight, I turn and crouch down. I take off my glove and trace my fingers along my mother's name, Elizabeth Kara Tupper. She kept my father's name to the end. BELOVED FRIEND AND MOTHER, it reads, WE WILL LOVE YOU FOREVER.

You hear that, Mom? I will love you forever. And I forgive you for making me leave. I'm still not sure I get why you did it, but I don't think that matters anymore. Not today, anyway.

I'm about to follow Sunshine when I remember. Something I've been carrying around, waiting for the right moment to let it go. I reach into the bottom of my purse. My fingers touch its cold, smooth surface. I pull out the rock crystal and repeat Sunshine's words under my breath. "Heart, head, life." I squeeze it tightly and place it gently on top of the headstone.

I stand up and brush my cold tears away. I join Sunshine where she's waiting for me beyond the trees. She smiles at me like I've just taken my first shaky steps.

"Ready?"

"Yes."

"Do you think Dominic might help us out of here?"

"Why don't we try AAA instead?"

Chapter 27
A Woman Scorned, a Woman Changed

Two hours later, Sunshine's car is sorted out and I'm heading back to the office, feeling like a weight has been lifted. It isn't until I swing open the heavy glass door to the lobby of my office building with a whistle on my lips that it hits me. This is how I used to feel all the time: competent, excited, ready to take on the day.

You'd think I'd know better by now.

"Jenny, is that memo ready?"

She looks up from one of her messaging conversations, confused. "Sophie's working on it."

"What did you say?"

"Sophie said you wanted her to look it over before you finalized it."

My heart starts to pound. "When was this?"

"About an hour ago. I'm sorry, she seemed so certain. I mean, you know how she can be—"

Her bottom lip starts to quiver, but I don't have any time to comfort her. I rush to my desk and bang my mouse against it to revive my computer. I can hear the murmur of voices from Matt's office through the wall. With barely working fingers, I type in my password and work through the network to the memo. I click on it and get prompted for a password. I type mine in. *Damn!* The password's been changed. That little bitch. Will she stop at nothing?

On the edge of hyperventilating, I leave my office and hurry down the hall. My old office is empty, but I can smell Sophie's perfume—that mix of Chanel and brimstone. She's got to be around here somewhere.

But where?

Oh fuck. She couldn't have. She wouldn't dare.

I turn on my heel and nearly sprint toward Matt's office. The door is closed, the glass wall fogged so I can't see what lies within. Something tells me that the voices I heard through the wall earlier hold the answer to where Sophie is and what she's doing.

A bad, bad answer.

As I near his door, I try to breathe normally, trying not to look like an escapee from a mental institution. Though I might be headed there after this.

Nathalie's sitting at her desk with her earphones on, typing away. I tap her on the shoulder to get her attention. She pulls the earphones from her ears.

"What's up?"

"Who's he in there with?"

"Sophie and Craig. They're on a conference call."

Thump, thump, thump.

"Who are they talking to?"

"Why are you asking?"

"Please, Nathalie, I don't have time to explain."

"I put him through to Connor Perry."

Connor Perry is the VP Legal at Mutual Assurance.

I walk toward Matt's door.

"You can't go in there!"

I put my hand on the knob and turn it. I fling open the door as dramatically as I can. It smacks into the wall loudly. If this is the end, I might as well go out with a bang.

My gesture doesn't go unnoticed. Craig and Sophie both jump in their seats, and I get a flash of Matt's angry eyes, a look I haven't seen in a while.

He raises his palm toward me, stopping me in my tracks.

"That's about the size of it, Connor."

An indistinct voice issues from the phone on Matt's desk. "Great work, guys. You really knocked it out of the park on this one."

Craig shoots me a guilty look, but Sophie's all business. "Thanks, Connor. Happy to do it."

They say goodbye and Matt ends the call.

"What's going on?" I ask, my voice trembling.

Matt leans back in his chair, folding his hands above his belt. "Sophie, Craig, can you give us a moment?"

"Of course, Matt," Sophie says in her cat-that's-got-the-cream purr.

"Maybe I should stay," Craig says.

"No, Craig, thank you. That will be all."

They leave the room—Craig a little reluctantly—closing the door behind them.

"Sit," Matt commands.

I perch on the edge of his low, low visitor's chair. "What was that call about?" I ask, though I have a pretty good idea.

Matt gives me that dark, baleful look again. "Why didn't you tell me Victor Bushnell stole the painting?"

I clear my sandy throat. "Because the police haven't confirmed my findings yet, and I wanted to be absolutely sure before we took this any further."

"That's not acceptable, Emma. I told you to keep me in the loop, and instead, I had to find out from Sophie what was going on in my own file."

"Only because she was snooping," I say before I can help myself.

"You know I don't have any patience for your petty little grievances with Sophie."

"I know, Matt. I'm sorry. And I'm sorry I didn't tell you as soon as I found out, but—"

"No buts. It seems I was mistaken to give you this much responsibility right away. It seems you're not the person I thought you were."

"Please don't say that. You can trust me. I'm the same Emma I've always been."

"The Emma I knew would have come into my office full of excitement, bursting to tell me what she'd found the minute she uncovered it."

That does sound like me. Why didn't I do that?

"Okay, maybe you're right, but think about what I've been through. Can you really blame me for being cautious?"

"I don't buy that. The cautious thing would've been to keep me apprised of what you'd discovered. Something else is going on. Would you like to tell me what it is?"

He watches me intently as my brain whirs. Can I tell him I was hoping that if I solved this case, I'd get on the express train to partnership? That I was also kind of hoping that when I got there, my old life, my old self, would be waiting for me? That I'd finally get that happy ending I've been expecting ever since my life turned to shit? No. I can't say that out loud.

If I say it out loud, it will never come true.

"I was only trying to make sure we really had the answer before I made a big fuss."

He purses his lips. "Still sticking to that story?"

"Yes."

"That's too bad."

My stomach falls. "What does that mean?"

"I'm not sure yet."

I leave Matt with my confidence shaken but with a firm purpose. If this is the end of my career, I'm not going down without a fight. Or at least a catfight.

I stop briefly in my office to grab my Dictaphone. Moments later, I slip into Sophie's office and close the door behind me. I flick the switch that turns the glass from see-all to hide-all. I may be spoiling for a fight, but that doesn't mean I want an audience.

Sophie turns away from her computer screen as the light in the room shifts. Her eyes shine with triumph. "What are you doing here?"

"You know what."

"If you're looking for an apology, you've come to the wrong place."

"Don't treat me like an idiot. I know you're never going to apologize."

"Then what do you want?"

Good question. Can I ask her to step outside without sounding like a character in a bad B movie?

"I think I'm entitled to an explanation."

"I thought you were the big brain around here. Can't you figure it out for yourself?"

"Do you think I'd be here asking you if I had any clue why you do the things you do?"

She lets out a sinister laugh. "Well, then, why should I tell you?"

I study her for a moment. I can tell a direct approach isn't going to get it done. So instead, I deliberately release all the tension from my body and sit in her visitor's chair. This chair is her all over. It looks sophisticated and welcoming, but it isn't. The rim hits my shoulder blades, and the seat doesn't give an inch.

"You should tell me because I give up."

"Excuse me?"

"I give up. You win. Whatever we're fighting over, you can have it."

She looks at me suspiciously. "I don't believe you."

"What's not to believe?"

"You know why we're fighting, and what we're fighting over."

"Craig?"

Her lips curl into a snarl. "Of course not."

"This office?"

"That was just the icing."

"Then what?"

She hesitates. "I would've been made partner a long time ago if it wasn't for you."

"How do you figure?"

"It should've happened two years ago, but no, the Management Committee wanted to wait until they could name you too because they saw us as equals."

"I didn't know that."

"Of course you did. You're always taking things from me. Steven. Craig. Matt."

Steven is the ex-boyfriend I hooked up with all those years ago at the firm's Christmas party. And she's got it backward about Craig, but . . . "Matt Stuart?"

"Do we know another Matt?"

"No, but I still don't get it. What does this have to do with him?"

"It's not just him, it's you and him."

"Me and him? There's no me and him."

"Oh yes, there is. There has been ever since you showed up, the little bright-eyed, bushy-tailed summer student." She raises her left hand, brushing away the tears that have suddenly appeared with her knuckles. "Ever since then it's been Emma this and Emma that, and why don't you get Emma to work on that with you, Sophie? It's not fair. I'm just as good a lawyer as you are, better even."

"But what did you expect me to do? Say, 'No, Matt, I'd really like to work on this case, but I think you should give it to Sophie'?"

"Of course I didn't expect that. But you didn't have to rub it in my face."

"When did I ever do that?"

She gives me a hard look, and I feel a twinge of guilt. She might be right. I knew I'd replaced her as Matt's favorite. And I took some pleasure in it, particularly as the years went by and her animosity grew. But still, is that any reason to actively seek to destroy my career? Especially when it's so precarious as it is?

"Okay, maybe what you're saying is true, but that doesn't justify pulling the stunt you just did."

"I don't have to justify myself to you."

"You don't honestly think you're going to get the credit for solving the Mutual Assurance case, do you?"

"Of course not. But with you out of the way, well, then there'll be nothing in *my* way."

"This was just a way to get Matt to stop trusting me so you could make partner?"

"Yes."

"Huh."

"That's all you have to say?"

"Yeah, I think so."

Her eyes narrow. "Then get out of my office."

"Fair enough."

I stand to leave, letting Sophie's malevolence bounce off me. There's nothing she can do to me anymore.

"Thanks for telling me, Sophie. Believe it or not, it helps."

I walk to the door, flicking the privacy switch as I go. The clear glass reveals the curious stare of her assistant, who turns away quickly, busying herself with a stack of filing.

I turn back. Sophie looks smaller somehow, like she's been shrunk down to size. There are tears running down her cheeks. And now, for the first time, I feel something close to sorry for her. Or maybe it's just empathy. No crying at the office. The professional woman's code.

"Get out," she says again, angrily brushing her tears away.

I nod and tuck my hand into my jacket pocket, placing my thumb over the warm, red recording light on the Dictaphone.

Chapter 28
Nothing but Net

I'm standing on the free-throw line of the basketball court at Karen and Peter's community center, lining up a basket. The court is lit up by two square spotlights attached to the exterior of the building. The cold day has given way to a milder evening, making the snow that soft sugar snow of spring. The *drip, drip* of melting ice muffles the city sounds.

I hold the basketball between my gloved hands. "What are we doing out here, again?"

Karen adjusts her hat as she blocks my way toward the basket. "You wanted to talk."

"I was thinking we'd sit in the living room and have some tea."

She shrugs. "Too busy. The gala's almost here. You get my exercise time."

I give the ball a few tentative bounces and lurch toward the basket. Karen blocks me and steals the ball. She pivots and launches it toward the net. It swooshes through easily.

"Nice."

"Thanks. What's on your mind?" She bounces the ball hard twice on the ground, then throws it to me. I catch it at the last moment, barely keeping it from barreling into my stomach.

I guess Karen isn't *quite* over her disappointment at me not taking the legal aid job.

"I was wondering . . . if that job might still be available?"

She wasn't expecting me to say this. I take advantage of her momentary inattention to dribble around her and try an ill-conceived jump shot. The ball grazes the bottom of the net and falls to the ground with a sad *thunk*.

Karen retrieves it. "I thought you were happy where you are?"

"Yeah, well, it isn't working out like I hoped."

"And we're the sloppy seconds?"

"No, of course not."

"Come on, Emma. I knew you were never going to take the job."

"How did you know that?"

"Because all you talked about when we were building the schoolhouse were your cases, and the office, and Matt this, Matt that. It was quite annoying, really."

My face flushes. "I don't remember talking about it so much."

"Relax, it wasn't that bad."

"Thanks very much." I grab the ball from her hands and bounce it on the cleared concrete. The hollow *thawp* echoes around us. "I'm curious, though. If you knew I wasn't going to take the job, why did you ask me to take it?"

"A girl can dream, can't she?"

I toss the ball at her as hard as I can. She catches it easily.

"Why do you want the job now?"

"I was working on this big case and I screwed up." I explain it to her briefly. "So now, not only am I not going to make partner, but I might be out of a job."

"You really think Matt's going to fire you?"

"No, no, he won't do anything that direct. He'll just stop giving me cases, and I'll have nothing to do and won't make my hours."

"Death by a thousand cuts?"

"Precisely."

She looks thoughtful. "But you solved the case, didn't you?"

"Yes, but the client doesn't know that. Or the Management Committee."

"Then figure out a way to tell them."

"I have. I just haven't decided if I want to go through with it."

"Seems like a no-brainer to me." Karen passes me the ball. "Your shot."

I catch it distractedly, wondering if Karen is right. I bring the ball above my head with both hands and hurl it toward the basket. It drops through, nothing but net.

* * *

I'm dragging my feet up my block after seeing Karen, dreading my empty apartment, wishing I'd made plans with Stephanie, Sunshine, anybody. The air feels wet, like it wants to rain. I see a shape huddled on my front step, and my spirits rise.

"Steph!"

Her head jerks up. A thick braid of red hair swings against her shoulder. I feel a moment of confusion before recognition clicks into place.

"Emily. What are you doing here?"

"I was waiting for Tara." She stands and brushes the snow off the back of her simple black coat. Her china-blue eyes look tentative and reddened. The porch light emphasizes the porcelain perfection of her skin.

"Did she stand you up?"

"I don't know. Maybe I got the day wrong."

She sounds lost, a feeling I'm all too familiar with.

And maybe that's why I say, "Why don't you come in for a moment? You must be chilled to the bone."

She stays silent for long enough that I almost repeat the question, but just as I'm about to, she nods her head and mutters, "Thank you."

"Of course."

I unlock the door. Neither of us says anything as we remove our outerwear and I flick on the lights. A glance down the hall tells me Dominic's door is thankfully still in the position I left it in—firmly shut against temptation.

Emily follows me into the living room. Her eyes flit around the room, coming to rest on the boxes in the corner where Dominic's handwriting announces their contents.

"He's not here," I say. My voice sounds loud in the silence.

"Yeah, I know."

Right. Of course.

"So—" I start to say, meaning to offer her a hot drink, I think, though my thoughts aren't fully formed.

"Why isn't he staying here anymore?" Emily asks.

I falter, remembering Dominic's admonishment not to tell her anything about us. I sit on the footstool, trying to buy time.

"Why are you asking?"

She shrugs and drops to the floor next to a box marked CAMERA EQUIPMENT. The tape seal is broken, and I know from looking in there myself the other day that it's empty. Dominic made sure to remove what's important to him. She reaches toward the flaps, pulling them apart.

"What are you doing?"

Her hands fall to her side, startled. "I don't know."

"What's going on, Emily?"

She tucks her knees up under her chin, wrapping her hands

around her shins. Her jeans are loose against her lean frame. "I think it's really over."

My heart skips a beat. "You mean you and Dominic?"

She nods.

"Why do you think that?"

"He made it pretty clear." She winces, pulling her knees more tightly. "He told you about Chris, didn't he?"

I think briefly about lying, but what's the point? "Yes."

"I don't know why I did it."

"I can't help you with that."

"No, I know. It's funny, though. I feel like you're affected by it too."

"Why?"

"Because you're with Dominic now."

"No, I'm not. I don't even know where he is."

She releases her knees and flexes her feet against the floor. "He'll be back."

"How do you know?"

"I saw that picture he took at the exhibit—that was you, right? The woman opening the Christmas present?"

"Yes."

"Dominic doesn't usually take pictures of people—not like that, not of people he knows." She looks down at her feet, and I can tell: Dominic never took any pictures like that of her.

So why hasn't he called me back?

"We've had a bit of a falling-out since then," I say.

She folds the box back together. "You'll work it out."

"Maybe."

"Do you want to?"

I meet her gaze. Her face is so different from mine, but her expression seems familiar. Uncertainty, doubt, a life full of unanswered questions.

"We probably shouldn't be discussing this."

She nods and stands, moving toward the hallway. I rise to follow her. She plucks her coat from the hook, slipping into the sleeves. Watching her lace up her boots, I feel bewildered by our entire exchange.

She straightens up. "If you want him back, you should tell him how you feel."

"Why are you telling me this?"

"Because I want Dominic to be happy. I owe him that, at least."

She turns the lock and opens the door. The wet night waits for her.

"Will you be all right?" I ask.

"I'll find my way."

Chapter 29
Lights, Camera, Action

After Emily leaves, I sit in the living room for a long time, my phone in my hand, wondering if I should call Dominic again or whether his radio silence is all the answer I need. Maybe all he wanted to do was apologize and he never meant anything more by it. It occurs to me at some point how absurd it is that all I have to do is push a few buttons and I could be talking to him, or hearing his voice on his voice mail at the very least. After so many months without that option, how can I be so uncertain now?

But I guess I was uncertain then too. Because after that day when I stood ready with my Schwinn but Karen wouldn't go with me, the thing I haven't told anyone—that only Karen and Peter know—is that I never made it back to the village-that-might-have-a-working-satellite-phone.

At first it was because I didn't want to get my hopes raised and dashed again; I'd been on enough ups and downs, and all I wanted was an even keel. And then, as I grew more skilled with the hammer, as I hoisted beams and laid in floorboards and took fewer and fewer walks away from the village, it all seemed to recede. To fall away. I may have spoken about home to Peter and Karen in the way you do when you're working together on a project—exchanging funny stories, keeping it light—but it seemed, it *was,* half a world away, a world I couldn't reach, a world I needed a break from.

I didn't think so at the time, but I can admit it now: I was being selfish. I was thinking of my own heart, my own head, and the break they needed from what I'd been through at home, the time they needed to heal. I knew that I could be doing more, that I could be trying harder to get in touch, that people must be worried. But Karen said to let it go, and I did. More completely than I thought possible. More completely than I should have.

And then one day the real world came rushing back, and I thought I was ready to return to it. In many ways, I was eager to. But I was still really only thinking of myself. Thinking that now that my heart and head were okay, or close enough anyway, I could just waltz back in and do whatever I wanted to do. That it was my decision, alone, to make.

These are not pretty thoughts, and they keep me frozen in place well into the night. And in the end I decide that there's something I *can* do about it, at least one little thing, and so I put my phone away and leave Dominic to himself.

* * *

A day later, I'm sitting in the *In Progress* audience watching as the touch-up girl applies loose powder to Detective Kendle's face. Cathy Keeler is sitting next to her, flipping through her notes, muttering to herself. The room is hot and the air is filled with the sweaty smell of the audience's excitement, thrilled to be this close to the queen bee of trashy journalism.

The arc lights are turned on, and the supporting players flit away from the stage. I feel a nervous pricking in my thumbs, like something wicked is about to happen.

Thankfully, Stephanie came along for the ride.

"How did you persuade Cathy Keeler to swap you for Ms. Hatchet-Face?" she asks, tucking the loose ends of her hair behind her ears. She's wearing tight jeans and a black sweater and has topped her outfit with a jaunty beret. Her *artiste* look, as she calls it.

"Once I told Carrie that the detective who cracked the Bushnell case was available, she forgot all about boring little me."

Victor Bushnell—whose fingerprints *were* found on the lid to the hidden compartment and on the back of the painting, the part obscured by the frame—was arrested yesterday, and the news broke late last night. It's all over the papers and the news channels today, but the public details are scanty. No surprise that Carrie had been *all too happy* to book Detective Kendle on the show, and even to keep my involvement from Cathy Keeler.

Stephanie looks impressed. "Who knew you were so devious?"

"I'm learning."

The assistant director puts up his hand, showing us three fingers. "Rolling in three . . . two . . . one." The bombastic theme music blasts through the studio. Cathy Keeler's face settles into its on-screen mix of deep intelligence and mild malevolence.

"Good evening, I'm Cathy Keeler. Most of you will have heard by now about Victor Bushnell's arrest for the theft of a valuable Monet painting. We'll be exploring why he did this daring but misguided act . . ."

"She sounds as if she admires him," Stephanie mutters.

"She probably does. He's her people after all."

While Cathy fills the audience in, I watch Detective Kendle sitting uncomfortably in the wide leather chair, her mannish hands clasped tightly between the knees of her black slacks. She's wearing a thick mask of makeup. Her pale hair shines under the bright lights.

"We have a very special guest with us tonight, the detective who solved the case. But first, let's learn a little more about Victor Bushnell."

The lights dim. The enormous flat screen behind Cathy Keeler is filled by Victor Bushnell's face—a studio pose that projects confidence, trust, competence.

"Victor Bushnell, president and CEO of Bushnell Enterprises, is a man of many talents. Inventive genius, maverick, daredevil, and patron of the arts, he first came to prominence in . . ."

"Speaking of patron of the arts," Stephanie says, "did you receive any more flowers from you know who?"

"No."

"Have you spoken to him?"

"No, but I did get a visit from his ex-girlfriend."

"*What?*"

Several people turn in their seats. Cathy Keeler's head snaps up, searching the crowd for the disturbance. I sink lower in my seat, willing the darkness to hide me.

"Keep it down, will you?" I hiss.

"When did this happen?"

"A couple of nights ago."

"What did she want?"

"She was looking for Tara, really, but she ended up telling me that she and Dominic were over, and that he'd be back."

She shoots me a look. "That's kind of odd."

"I know. I don't quite believe it myself."

"And he still hasn't called you?"

"No, but I think . . . I'm okay with that."

Stephanie gives me a look like she doesn't believe me, but she keeps silent.

The video ends and the lights come back up. Cathy Keeler stares into the camera. "With us tonight is Detective Kendle, the detective who broke this case wide open. How'd you do it?"

Detective Kendle shifts uncomfortably in her seat. "The break in the case came from an outside source, actually."

"An accomplice who helped him steal the Monet?"

"It was a Manet."

"Pardon?"

"It was an Édouard Manet painting, not a Claude Monet."

Cathy Keeler laughs fakely. "Oh well, we don't need to get caught up in minor details."

Detective Kendle gives her a contemptuous look. "There are no minor details in my profession, Ms. Keeler."

"Yes, of course not. You were saying something about an outside source?"

"That's right. We had covered the groundwork, but it was one of the lawyers for Bushnell's insurance company who cracked the case."

"Why did he do it?"

"We believe it was because he had a loan he couldn't repay that was guaranteed by the painting."

"Do you know why he stole it himself?"

"I could only speculate."

Cathy Keeler leans forward eagerly. "Please do."

Detective Kendle lifts her nose in the air. "I deal in facts, Ms. Keeler. Not speculation."

A crease forms between Cathy Keeler's eyebrows. Her dermatologist would be alarmed if he was watching.

"This must be satisfying," Stephanie says.

"You have no idea."

"Will you tell us how Mr. Bushnell went about the theft, at least? How did he manage to evade the museum's security?"

"We haven't worked out all the details yet."

Cathy Keeler gives her a treacly smile. "Yes, of course. Well, I'm sure you'll be receiving a commendation for your great work."

"It's Emma Tupper who deserves the credit, Ms. Keeler, not me."

"Emma Tupper? The lawyer who was missing in Africa?"

"Yes. She's the one who solved the case."

Cathy Keeler blinks rapidly a few times, putting the pieces together. "And, of course, she was a previous guest on our show. Perhaps you saw that episode?"

"Yes," Detective Kendle says huffily.

"Yes. Quite. Ms. Tupper *does* seem to have a way of keeping her name in the media."

"That's not what she's like at all."

"No?"

"No."

"Admire her, do you?"

"I do, actually."

Stephanie slips her hand into mine. "You've got someone in your corner, at least."

Tears spring to my eyes. "More than one person, I hope."

"The Management Committee wants to see you," Jenny says to me nervously the next day.

"Thank you, Jenny."

She twirls the end of her hair around her index finger. "You look nice."

I took extra care with my appearance this morning, putting on my most conservative suit and slicking my hair back into a sleek chignon.

"I was going for ferocious."

"What do you mean?"

"Nothing, it's an inside joke."

Feeling giddy, I straighten my blazer and slip the Dictaphone into my pocket. "If I'm not back in forty-five minutes, send the Initial Brigade after me, will you?"

"You're in a funny mood today."

I give her a smile instead of explaining and take the long way around so I don't have to walk by Matt. I haven't seen him since our altercation, though I've felt his disappointment seeping through our communal wall.

I walk through Reception and push the Up elevator button. The Management Committee meets five floors up, on the penthouse floor. I've only ever been there once, when I got hired on after I graduated from law school. TPC has a hiring ritual that dates back to when you had to belong to the right eating house to get a job here. If you were "in," you got called into the real boardroom, where you were slapped on the back and glad-handed by a room full of middle-aged men calling you "little lady." If you were "out," you ended up in a side room with the motherly woman from HR.

I wonder which room I'll end up in today?

The elevator arrives and I step into it. The doors start to close.

"Hold the door," a familiar voice rings out.

Before I can reach for the Close button, an expensive black shoe pokes through, stopping the doors in their tracks. They pull back to reveal Sophie, who's wearing a nearly identical suit to my own. Her straight blond hair is even molded into a similar hairstyle.

She meets my eyes, looking flustered. "I'll take the next one."

I grip the Dictaphone in my pocket. My hand feels slippery against the silvery metal. "No, that's all right."

She enters and stands next to me. I hesitate for a moment, then hit the Up button. The doors slide closed. She glances at the row of buttons, her finger moving toward the one I've already pushed. She pulls her hand away.

"I guess we're going to the same place," she says, forcing a smile.

"Looks like."

We watch the numbers silently light up one by one. What can it mean that we've been called to the Management Committee together? Maybe the *In Progress* ploy wasn't such a good idea after all? And am I really going to have to expose Sophie while she's sitting right next to me?

"Nice coverage on Cathy Keeler."

I turn toward her, checking for signs of sarcasm. All I see is a reflection of my own apprehensive face.

"Thanks."

"Your doing, I presume?"

I nod.

"Impressive."

"Thank you," I say, feeling a twinge of surprise, and maybe a little guilt too.

"What do you think they want with us?"

"Your guess is as good as mine."

The doors ding open. We exit and walk down the long corridor. Our whole office is plush, but the penthouse floor is out of this world. The carpet's so thick I can't hear my own footsteps, and the walls are covered with a richly colored hand-made wallpaper. Heavy oil paintings of former members of the firm look down at us with a disapproving air.

"Did Matt say anything?" she asks.

"I don't think he's talking to me at the moment."

She looks at the floor. "Mmm. Me either."

We arrive at the large black doors of the boardroom. Rumor has it the Management Committee meets here every morning to pore over receivables and plot how to steal clients from other big firms. My chest feels hollow, like my heart has been removed.

"Well, good luck," Sophie says.

I can't help but smile. "You too. Nice suit, by the way."

She gives me a quick once-over. "You wear it better."

Again, she actually seems sincere. The Dictaphone starts to feel like a weight in my pocket.

A woman in her midfifties is waiting for us at the door. I recognize her as the chairman's personal assistant, who has also been, if the same rumor mill is to be believed, his mistress for the last thirty years. Good thing her first name is the same as his wife's.

"Ms. Tupper, Ms. Vaughn, right on time."

"Yes," we say together.

"They're waiting for you."

She opens the door. I cast a nervous glance at Sophie. "After you."

"Oh no, I insist."

I square my shoulders and walk through the door. The boardroom is long, wide, and windowless. More dead partners' images line the wood-paneled walls. There's an enormous oak table in the middle of the room, surrounded by fifteen old men wearing dark suits. I can almost smell the fading testosterone.

I catch the eye of the lawyer who handled my mother's estate. The one who told me not to go to Africa, who said it would hurt my career. How angry I was that day, how indignant. I'm glad, now, that he told me no. I might not have gone otherwise. And that would've been a mistake, despite everything that's happened.

Matt speaks from the end of the table. "Emma, Sophie, welcome. Please have a seat."

I almost don't recognize him in this austere setting. His suit jacket is done up and he's exuding an air of authority I've only seen in the courtroom.

"Did you know Matt was on the Management Committee?" I whisper to Sophie.

She shakes her head as she sits in one of the red leather chairs at our end of the table. I take the seat next to her, my hands slippery on the hard leather.

Matt folds his hands in front of him. "We've asked you to come here today to discuss your work on the Mutual Assurance file."

I open my mouth to protest his inclusion of Sophie, but then, amazingly, Sophie does it for me.

"That was Emma's doing, not mine."

The chairman raises his hand to stop her. His fierce brown eyes stand out in the middle of his florid face. The spidery web across his nose is evidence of way too many cocktails.

"That's modest of you, Ms. Vaughn, but Connor Perry called me personally to express his gratitude."

She shoots me a glance. "Yes, I'm sure he did, but you see—"

"That's really *not* necessary, Sophie," Matt says, a warning in his tone.

I look from Matt to a struggling Sophie. She seems uncertain but doesn't say anything more.

"The coverage you got on *In Progress* yesterday was a great coup for our firm, Ms. Tupper," says an elderly man sitting to Matt's right. "As Price said, Mutual Assurance is extremely pleased with the outcome, and so are we."

"Thank you," I murmur, thinking briefly of the last time the firm engineered a similar publicity stunt. It's a little sad, really, how predictable some people can be.

"You've both done some excellent work for the firm over the years," says a man with thin black hair that flops across his forehead. It takes me a moment to place him as Kevin Wilson, the head of the Mergers and Acquisitions Department. "And we think it's time we recognized it by making both of you partners."

My heart is back and making its presence known.

"We usually wait for the end of the year to make these kinds of decisions," Matt says. "But given the circumstances, we thought it best to break with tradition and have you join the partnership immediately."

"What's he mean by 'given the circumstances'?" I ask Sophie through the side of my mouth.

"Mutual Assurance is looking for a new in-house counsel," she replies quietly. "They offered it to me. And after yesterday, you can write your ticket anywhere."

"Did you say something, Emma?" Matt asks.

"No."

"Good. Kevin will fill you in on the details later, but we thought we'd announce it in today's bulletin and have the usual cocktail party celebration on Friday. Does that suit you?"

"That would be great," Sophie says brightly. "Thank you."

"Emma?"

I know that this is the moment where I should whip out the Dictaphone and expose Sophie for the wrong that she has done, but somehow I can't form the words. I don't know if it's the stress or the unreality of this moment really happening, but I don't feel the joy I thought I'd feel, or the anger I need to expose her in this public forum.

"Is that it?" I hear myself say.

Matt frowns. "Is what it, Emma?"

Sophie kicks me hard under the table. I bite my lip to keep from calling out.

"What is it, young lady?" says the chairman.

"What are you doing?" Sophie hisses.

"I'm not sure," I whisper back.

"What's that, dearie? I can't hear you."

"Well, it's just . . . I'm really grateful for this vote of confidence, but . . . you didn't even ask us if we *want* to become partners."

"We're not in the habit of being turned down," the chairman says. "But if you'd rather *not* become a partner—"

"No!" Sophie blurts.

"What Sophie means is of course we want to be partners, but before we accept, we'd like a few changes around here."

The chairman looks like he wishes it was cocktail hour. "You mean a maternity leave policy, I suppose?"

"Of course, but that's not really what I was getting at."

"What are you looking for exactly?" Kevin asks.

I formulate my thoughts, and then I tell them what I want. I can see reluctance form on several of their lined faces, but the chairman looks intrigued and Matt has that hard, proud expression he used to get when I met his expectations.

"And if we agree to this, you'll accept our offer?" the chairman says.

I hesitate. "Can I ask for one more thing?"

Matt shakes his head. Sophie looks like she might pass out.

"What's that?" Kevin asks.

"We could do with some new art on the walls, don't you think?"

Chapter 30
Try and Try Again

My first week as a partner at TPC passes ... well, not gently, exactly, but with fewer bumps than the previous ones. The shit files disappear, the Ejector is history, and Sophie and I are almost talking to each other. The icing on the cake is the ball gown Jenny finds for me that I'm wearing tonight to Karen and Peter's black-and-white gala to raise money for the youth center. It's gorgeous. A white silk Regency-inspired gown that makes me feel like a character in a fairy tale. All I need is a handsome prince to find my missing shoe, and I'll be all set.

But that is not to be. Despite Emily's predictions, Dominic hasn't called or come to the apartment. But that's okay. You can't have everything in life. Besides, Stephanie's starting that book-lovers dating thing, so ...

The sun crosses the city, the shadows long, then short, then lengthening. I leave work early to pass by Antoine's. He works wonders with my hair, as always, and puts a smile on my face. A cab drops me off at the gala at ten after seven, just in time for cocktails.

The ball is being held in an old train station that's been converted into an exhibition space. Tonight, the stalls have been cleared out and replaced with fifty round tables covered in crisp white tablecloths. The flower centerpieces are tall stalks of sugarcane with fragrant climbing roses twined around them. Votive candles float in small bowls. Huge bolts of white fabric drape from the ceiling. The band on the raised dais at the front of the room is playing a Viennese waltz.

A random sampling of the city's glitterati are chatting between the tables and floating around the dance floor. Last year's mayor is talking to next year's congresswoman. The latest It Girl is flirting with the guy who reports the sports statistics on the nightly news. I spot Karen in a white lace dress with a bright red sash weaving her way through the crowd. She's talking to a woman with a headset on, looking stressed. I can't see Peter, but my bet is he's somewhere near the bar.

"E.W., looking fine," I. William says, giving me a once-over. We air-kiss with the best of them, and he plucks two flutes of champagne off a passing waiter's tray.

"Is one of those for me?"

"Nah. For your friend over there." He nods toward one of the tables I got TPC to sponsor as part of my partnership deal. Stephanie's sitting there looking shy and nervous in a clingy satin gown.

"You know that's my best friend, right?"

His eyes twinkle with mischief. "So she told me."

"Hurt her and you'll have me to answer to."

"Is that supposed to scare me?"

"Okay, Sophie, then."

"Consider me warned."

He ambles toward Stephanie, looking dashing in his tuxedo. She blushes as he hands her the glass and gives me a wave. I make a mental note to corner her later and warn her about I. William's commitment issues.

"Hey, Emma, you ready for your big speech?" Karen says, appearing out of the crowd.

"Absolutely."

"Did you remember your notes?"

"No notes required."

"Are you sure that's wise?"

"I do this for a living, remember? Don't worry about it."

"Well, if you're comfortable embarrassing yourself in front of a thousand people . . ."

"Thanks for the vote of confidence."

She throws me a smile. "No, thank *you*."

"It's nothing."

"It's more than you had to do."

One of the headphoned women appears at her elbow and murmurs in her ear. Karen's eyes widen and she shakes her head vigorously. The woman turns away and barks into her headphone.

"I've got to go take care of something," Karen says, looking stressed again.

"Trouble?"

"Maybe." She twirls away in a blur of white and red.

I spend the next half an hour having brief cocktail conversations with several lawyers from my firm whom I arm-twisted into coming. Craig and I wave to each other across the room, but we keep our distance. At one point I see Sophie approach him, her face a mixture of surety and contrition. Good luck to them, I think, with only a small twinge of regret. When my champagne glass has been empty for five minutes too long, the lights flicker in the universal symbol that means sit down, people, it's time for eats.

I wend my way back toward Stephanie, who's still blushing up at I. William, though it might now be a champagne blush— there are several empty glasses on the table. Steph looks happy to see me, but I don't get a chance to sit next to her. Instead, I get hauled off by the headphoned minion who scared Karen earlier. Apparently, I'm supposed to address the crowd before it gets completely liquored.

Peter is waiting for me. He gives my shoulder a squeeze and takes the stage to enthusiastic applause. He's looking dapper and relaxed in his tuxedo. He loosens up the crowd with some well-placed jokes about cocktails-circuit philanthropy and then goes on for far too long about, well, me. By the time I get to the microphone, my face is hot and I'm wishing I'd jotted down some notes after all.

"Thanks, Peter," I say too close to the mic. My voice echoes around the room. I stare out into the crowd, looking for inspiration. And that's when I see him: Dominic, leaning against the wall off to the left side of the stage, staring at me intently.

Our eyes lock and my heart starts to catch in that first-love way, that way you never think you'll feel again once it's been disappointed and you've learned better. I can't understand what he's doing here, but for some reason, the words I was planning on saying no longer seem good enough.

The room's silent expectation intrudes, and so I start to speak.

"Some of you might think I paid Peter to say those things about me. Well, you'd be right. Or to be more accurate, and you know lawyers like being accurate, I got all of you to pay Peter to say those things about me."

In the pause caused by the modest laughter sputtering around the room, I gulp in some air, lock eyes with Dominic again, feel my knees weaken, my courage faltering, but I have to say something, I have to say the right thing.

"I was asked to speak tonight about a very special contribution to the community center that was made by my law firm, Thompson, Price and Clearwater. But before I get to that, I want to take a minute to salute the two wonderful people behind tonight's event, Karen and Peter Alberts.

"As many of you probably know, we met under unusual circumstances; in fact, we were never supposed to have met at all." I clear my throat. "Have any of you ever played that desert island game? You know, that game where you say what thing you would miss the most, or what person you'd want to be with you?" I pause again, and a few people nod their heads. "Well, I was always terrible at that game. Mostly because I couldn't see myself in that situation. Maybe no one can, but I didn't even like thinking about it. Being stuck on a desert island seemed like a terrible thing, not like a cocktail-party joke.

"Then there I was, stuck in a desert island situation. I wasn't alone, but I didn't get to pick the people who were with me. And though these people were some of the best people I've ever met, all I wanted at first was to get home. I wanted to get back to my life. I thought, naïvely, that when the chaos cleared, it would be there, waiting for me. But I was wrong about that." I pause to take a sip from the glass of water next to me. My hand is shaking, but hopefully only I can see this. The room is ghostly silent. Dominic hasn't moved an inch. "Life doesn't wait. You have to make it happen. You have to live it while it's happening around you. Life moves on.

"Why am I saying these serious things on a night that's supposed to be about celebrating? I guess it's because while we're all dressed up and drinking and eating well, it's important to remember why we're here, why the community center exists. There are so many people less fortunate than us. I know we say that all the time, but when you've lived it, when you've seen and heard and breathed it, you don't have a choice but to realize how lucky we really are, and how much we ought to give.

"So, Karen, Peter, I want to say thank you. Thank you for my life, and thank you for what you do. As for all of you, well, I hope you give generously tonight and continue to do so long after your dresses are dry-cleaned and your next gala is just a date on a calendar. And finally, I want to salute Thompson, Price and Clearwater, which, I'm proud to say, has committed to providing thirty hours a year of free legal-clinic time from every lawyer in the firm." I raise my glass of water. "To Karen and Peter, and to the future of the Point Community Center."

I step away from the mic, coming back to myself as the room erupts in applause. After being enveloped in a bear hug from Peter, I allow myself to look at the honor table, where Matt is sitting with his wife and TPC's chairman. He looks happy and pleased with himself, like this is the culmination of some well-thought-out plan. And maybe it is. Didn't all of this start because he was looking for some publicity for the firm?

Or maybe that wasn't the start, but it was near enough to the beginning to feel that way.

Why not? He deserves applause. I put my hands together and clap in his direction. Kudos, Matt. Take a bow.

I step aside and am replaced by the emcee. His tux is a smidgen too tight, and his black hair is slicked back from his high forehead. He unhooks the microphone from its static stand.

"You ready for it to get loud in here?" he booms.

I walk to the safety of my table, searching the room for Dominic, who seems to have disappeared. Did I just imagine him? And if I didn't, what am I going to say to him?

Stephanie gives me a fierce hug, and I know she's saying she's proud of me, though I can't really hear her. I sit in my seat and half listen to the emcee as he tells bad bawdy jokes through the first course of mixed greens and berries. I block him out by listening to I. William attempting to impress Stephanie, while trying not to search out Dominic's face in every dark-haired dinner guest.

When the waiters clear away the plates, the emcee is thankfully replaced by the band, which starts an ABBA/Village People mash-up. It knows its audience—the dance floor fills up quickly.

I. William tugs on Stephanie's elbow. "Let's dance."

She shoots me a look. "Oh, I don't know."

"Don't be silly, Steph. Go ahead."

"Why don't you come too?"

"Yeah," I. William says. "Let's boogie."

We find a space on the dance floor between the old folks doing the Watusi and the few young 'uns who were dragged here by their parents and who've clearly been taking advantage of the open bar.

It's hard to move in this almost–wedding dress, but I manage. I. William acts the gentleman and splits his attention between the two of us, twirling Steph, then me, until we're both dizzy and smiling.

Then the band takes it down a notch and segues into that song from the movie *Once,* "Falling Slowly." The three of us stand there awkwardly as the guests couple up.

"I'm going to head back to the table," I say.

"I'll come with you," Stephanie replies.

"Don't be ridiculous."

I turn away, but not before I. William gives me a grateful look. I smile to myself as I weave around Matt and his wife. His hand is placed on the small of her back, holding her close.

Someone catches my hand on the edge of the dance floor. I turn. It's Dominic.

He's here. My great, big romantic ending is standing in front of me in a tux, for God's sake. And what the hell am I wearing?

Is there a panic button I can hit? Or better yet, a button

that will pause this whole scene while I figure out how I want to play it?

But no. That's not how it works in real life. How it works is I say, "Oh no."

His face falls. "What is it?"

"No, no, no, this *cannot* happen this way."

"What way?"

"Like this." I motion toward my dress. "Me here like this. You wearing that."

"What's wrong with the way you're dressed? You look amazing."

"It's too much, it's too . . ." *Perfect,* I want to say. "Contrived," I say instead.

"So you're saying you won't talk to me because of the way we're dressed?"

"It's bigger than that. It's . . . what are you doing here, anyway?"

"You invited me."

"No, I didn't."

He reaches into the interior breast pocket of his jacket and pulls out an invitation. "How did I get this, then?"

I think about it. "I'm guessing Stephanie had something to do with it."

He cocks an eyebrow. "You're not actually trying to blame your best friend, are you?"

"Well . . ."

"Will you just dance with me already?"

"No, Dominic. I can't."

I start to move around him, but he blocks me, taking hold of my arms above the elbows. "Emma, please."

Something in his tone stops me. He needs something from me, and I want to give it to him. Maybe I have to give it to him.

I nod, and he pulls me toward him, lacing his hands behind my back. I breathe in the scent of his freshly laundered shirt. It makes me feel safe and warm. But I'm not safe. Not safe at all.

He leans toward my ear. "Does all this protesting mean you're not happy to see me?"

"It's not that."

"So you *are* happy to see me?"

"Of course I am."

His arms tighten, pulling me closer. "I'm glad."

The fabric of his suit grazes my lips. "But, Dominic—"

He gives me an ironic smile. "What? The flowers didn't cut it?"

"Can't you take anything seriously?"

"A few things."

"But not this little scene?"

His mouth twists. "Honey, if I was taking this scene seriously, I might scare the shit out of both of us."

My heart is beating so loudly it's drowning out the music.

"I don't think I want to have the shit scared out of me," I say eventually.

"Me neither."

I tilt my head down. My ball gown blocks the view to my feet, a cocoon of fabric that isn't protecting me from the heat of his touch. "Is that why you never called me?"

"Mostly."

"Then why did you come tonight?"

"I thought it was time."

"Time for what?"

"For this." He brings his fingers to my chin and lifts my face up. His eyes are full of the night we spent together.

"Dominic, I—"

"Shh." He moves toward me. In the movies, this moment always happens slowly, but here, in real time, his lips are on mine in an instant.

An instant later, something is vibrating between us. We break apart.

"I feel like we've been here before," Dominic says, his lips inches from mine.

"I don't have my phone with me."

His jacket shakes and he reaches into his pocket with a sheepish expression. It's quickly replaced when we both see who's calling. Emily.

"This isn't what you think," he says quickly.

"You don't know what I'm thinking."

His phone buzzes again in his hand, insistent. Emily's calling. Pick up, pick up, pick up. So much for her "Because I want Dominic to be happy" speech. And she'd seemed so sincere.

"Answer your phone."

He gives me a desperate look and turns away, bringing the phone to his ear as he walks off the dance floor. I think I hear him say, "I can't hear you," but I can't be sure.

I feel a surge of immature rage. God, fucking, shit. Can't anything go right for me, for once? Can't anything be simple? Here I am, in the middle of this ridiculous romantic moment, and then, *poof,* it's gone. My leading man is off talking to his ex-fiancée, and I'm left in a white dress (okay, off-white, but still), surrounded by twirling couples while the band plays a pretty song. David Gray's "Ain't No Love," to be precise. I *love* that goddamn song. Or at least I did. Now it's just going to be the song where I realized things were never going to work out with Dominic, no matter how much I might want them to.

Well, at least I don't have to wait here for him like an idiot. In fact, I don't have to stay at all. My speech is over, TPC's commitment to staffing the legal clinic has been announced, and Stephanie and I. William are dancing closer every second.

I think my work here is done.

I leave the ballroom and walk toward the coat check, pulling off my shoe to retrieve the ticket hidden in the toe. There's no one on the other side of the counter. Instead, there's a small sign that reads: BACK IN 10 MINUTES. I have no idea if the sign was put up nine minutes ago or one. Ten minutes seems like an awfully long time to wait, and kind of antithetical to slinking out of here sight unseen.

I try the door next to the counter that leads into the cloak-room. It's locked. Of course. I knew I should've learned how to pick a lock at some point in my life. I've even got a few bobby pins in my hair, for all I know what to do with them.

Well, you know what? Fuck it. I give a quick glance over my shoulder and hoist myself onto the counter. My silk dress is slippery, and I suspect this is going to leave a mark. I bring my legs up and spin, intending to turn myself around so I can land on my feet. But instead, I misjudge the distance and the force of my spin, and slide. I land hard on my ass, my feet in the air above me.

"That looked like it hurt," Dominic says, leaning over the counter.

Why hasn't teleportation been invented yet? Society clearly needs to devote way more resources to figuring that out than it has up to now. Because if we had, I could press my handy little transporter button, which I'd wear around my neck at all times in case of emergencies like this one. One push and I'd be gone. Like magic.

I put my hands on the floor and prop myself up. The whole back of my body is throbbing. "I've got an alcohol cushion."

He smiles. "You want a hand up?"

"I got it." This time.

I climb gingerly to my feet and walk toward the rows of coats. If you were coat 8456, where would you be?

"Where are you going?" Dominic calls after me.

"To get my coat." My voice is muffled by the rows of furs and cashmere.

I think I spy my coat wedged into the corner. The first three numbers on the tag match the little yellow ticket in my hand, but the last number's been torn off. It looks like mine, but what the hell do I know? I've had too much to drink, my backside is throbbing, and this coat is black. It'll do.

I yank it off the hook and start to put it on.

"Let me help you with that," Dominic says behind me, holding it for me like my grandfather used to do.

I slip my arms into the holes. It feels alien and big. I turn to face him. "Thanks."

He looks amused. "Are you sure that's your coat?"

"Of course it is." I try to button it up, but my fingers aren't working very well. Dominic brushes my hands away and takes over. He buttons each button deliberately, working his way up to the button just below my chin. And of course, my stupid brain kicks out another memory of our night together, of me unbuttoning his shirt just as deliberately and kissing the flesh I exposed.

"There you go," Dominic says.

I look at him, and I have to ask. "What are you really doing here, Dominic? Why do you keep showing up?"

"I . . . I want to come back to the apartment."

"Is that what this is about? Someplace to live?"

"Come on, Emma, you know that's not what I mean."

"No, I don't. I don't know what you mean unless you say it. What do you want to say?"

His hand brushes my cheek. "I wanted to tell you I made a mistake."

I look away. "You already told me that."

"No, Emma. I mean it was a mistake for me to say what I did after we spent the night together. I was a jerk."

"And?"

He gives a small laugh. "You're going to make this as difficult as you can for me, huh?"

"Damn right."

"How come?"

"Because I don't understand why this is the first real conversation we've had since we slept together."

Now it's his turn to look away. "It's Emily."

My heart sinks. "You're back together."

"No!"

"Then what?"

"Don't you remember what I was doing when we met?"

"Moving into my apartment?"

"So you kept saying. But why, Emma?"

"Because you were moving out of your place with Emily."

"Right. My life was falling apart."

"So was mine."

"I know. I was right there as it was happening."

"You were."

"Everything was messed up, and I didn't know what I was feeling. I only knew that being around you made things . . . better. And then it didn't anymore."

"Oh, okay."

"No, Emma, no." He puts his hands on my shoulders, forcing me to stay, forcing me to stand and take it, whatever it is. "What I mean is that everything that happened to me, and to you, caught up with me after the night we spent together."

"I see."

"Is that what you felt?"

"No."

The left corner of his mouth twitches. "Want to enlighten me?"

Part of me does and part of me doesn't. But what the hell? I don't know how this is going to end. I only know what I felt. What I feel.

"I felt overwhelmed too, but mostly, I felt like . . . I finally had something that was mine. Something that didn't have anything to do with who I was before I went away, or what I was. And it didn't have anything to do with what I was going through either, though you were a big part of that. I was just . . . happy, and nervous, and hopeful. That's what I was feeling. And then—"

"I ruined it."

"Yes."

"I'm sorry. I suppose it's too much to ask . . ."

"To ask what?"

"For what I want."

"Do you know? Do you really know?"

He smiles down at me. "Yes."

I look at him shyly. "It's me, right?"

"Emma, do you seriously think I would've gone through all this to tell you I was picking someone else?"

"I was just checking."

He pulls me toward him. "I don't want you to doubt me." He starts to kiss me in that soft, slow way I remember from the night we spent together. My body remembers too, only it's covered by this enormous coat, a wall between us. I don't want any walls between us anymore.

We break apart. "Okay, I believe you," I say.

He pulls me toward him again, tightly, holding me close, swaying me to the music seeping in from far away. "Thank you for getting your firm to buy my photographs."

"You're welcome."

He smiles and we move toward each other again, kissing more urgently, kissing full of possibilities, kissing full of future. When we break apart my face is hot and the coat feels like a blanket.

"Maybe we should take this coat off, whoever's it is."

"But the sign says she'll be back in ten minutes."

He gives me a devilish look. "I'm willing to risk it if you are."

I lean toward him, an answer on my lips. Something starts to vibrate.

"Are you going to get that?" I ask.

"Not a chance."

Acknowledgments

As always I'd like to thank my earliest readers, especially Katie, Amy, and my mom, for important plot suggestions when I was straying off course.

My friends for their support and encouragement, especially Tasha, Phyllis, Janet, and Tanya. And for their advice, support, and inspiration, the members of the Fiction Writer's Co-Op, Nadia Lakdhari and Shawn Klomparens.

Agent extraordinaire Abigail Koons, and the whole team at Park Literary. I couldn't ask for better representation, or friends.

My editors at HarperCollins Canada, Jennifer Lambert and Jane Warren. My editors at HarperCollins U.S., Stephanie Meyers and Emily Krump. And all of those in production, design, and marketing who make sure my words are correct, nice to read, and well covered.

My family, Mom, Dad, Cam, Mike, and David, for bringing the love.

And to my readers, without whom I would have no reason to do this.

Read on for an excerpt from

SPIN

Catherine McKenzie

wm

WILLIAM MORROW

An Imprint of HarperCollins*Publishers*

Chapter 1
Must Love Music

This is how I lose my dream job.

It's the day before my thirtieth birthday when I get the call from *The Line,* only *the* most prestigious music magazine in the world, maybe the universe. OK, maybe *Rolling Stone* is number one, but *The Line* is definitely second.

I've wanted to write for *The Line* for as long as I can remember. It still blows me away that people get paid to work there since I'd pay good money just to be allowed to sit in on a story meeting. Hell, I'd sit in on a recycling committee meeting if it'd get me in the front door.

So, it's no surprise that I almost fall off my chair when I see their ad in the Help Wanted section one lazy Sunday morning. I sprint to my computer and wait impatiently for my dial-up to connect. (Yes, I still have dial-up. It's all this struggling writer can afford.) When the scratchy whine silences, I call up their webpage and click on the "Work for Us!" tab, as I have too many unsuccessful times before, and there it is. A job, a real job!

The Line *seeks self-motivated writer for staff position. Must*

love music more than money because this job pays jack, brother!
Send your CV and music lover credentials to kevin@theline.com.

I spend the next twenty-four hours agonizing over the "music lover credentials" portion of my application. How am I supposed to narrow down my musical influences to the three lines provided? Then again, how am I going to get a job writing about music if I can't even list my favorite bands?

In the end I let iTunes pick for me. If I've listened to a song 946 times (which, incidentally, is the number of times I've apparently played KT Tunstall's "Black Horse and the Cherry Tree"), I must really like it, right? Not a perfect system, but better than the over-thought-out lists sitting balled up in my wastepaper basket.

And it works. A few days later I receive an email with a written interview attached. I have forty-eight hours to complete the questionnaire and submit it. If I pass, I'll get a real, in-person interview on *The Line*'s premises! Just the thought of it has me doing a happy dance all over my living room.

Thankfully, the questionnaire is a breeze. *Pick five Dylan songs and explain why they're great. Pick five Oasis songs and explain why they suck. What do you think the defining sounds of this decade will be? Go see a band you've never seen before and write five hundred words about it. Buy a CD from the country section and listen to it five times. Write five hundred words on how it made you feel.*

I stay up all night chain-smoking cigarettes and working my way through two of my roommate Joanne's bottles of red wine. She's always buying wine (as an "investment," she says), but she never drinks any of it. What a waste!

When the sun comes up, I read through what I've written, and if I do say so myself, it's a thing of beauty. There isn't a question I stutter over, an opinion I don't have. I've even written it in *The Line*'s signature style.

I've been waiting for this opportunity forever, and I'm not going to fuck it up.

At least, not yet.

The next two weeks are agony. My brain is spinning with negative thoughts. Maybe I don't really know anything about music? Maybe they don't want someone who can merely parrot their signature style? Maybe they're looking for some new style, and I'm not it? Maybe they should call me before I lose my goddamn mind!

When the spinning becomes overwhelming, I try to distract myself. I clean our tiny apartment. I invent three new ramen noodle soup recipes. I see a few bands and write reviews for the local papers I freelance for. I clean out my closet, sort all my mail, and return phone calls I've been putting off for months. I even write a thank-you letter to my ninety-year-old grandmother for the birthday check she sent me on my sister's birthday.

I spend the rest of the time alternating between obsessively reading *The Line*'s website (including six years of back issues I've read countless times before) and watching a young star's life explode all over the tabloids.

Amber Sheppard, better known as "The Girl Next Door" (or "TGND" for short), after the character she played from ages fourteen to eighteen on the situation comedy called— wait for it—*The Girl Next Door,* is Hollywood's latest It Girl. When her show was canceled, she starred in two successful teen horror flicks, followed by a serious, Oscar-nominated performance for her turn as Catherine Morland in *Northanger Abbey.* She's been working nonstop since, and has four movies scheduled to premiere in the next five months.

When she wrapped the fourth film just after her twenty-third birthday, she announced she was taking a well-deserved, undisclosed period of time off to relax and regroup.

And that's when the shit hit the fan.

Anyone really seeking relaxation would rent a cabin in the woods and drop out of sight. But not TGND. She partied all night, slept all day, and dropped twenty pounds from one pho-tograph to the next. There were rumors appearing on such reliable sources as people.com, TMZ, and Perez Hilton that she's into some serious drugs. There were other rumors, of the Enquiring kind, that her family had staged an intervention and packed her off to rehab. It seems like there's a new story, a new outrageous photograph, a new website devoted to her every move every day, and I read them all.

Such is the fuel that keeps my idling brain from going crazy as I wait and wait.

The call from *The Line* finally comes the day before my birthday at 8:55 in the morning.

Mornings are never good for me, and this morning my fatigue is compounded by the combination of another bottle of Joanne's investment wine, and the riveting all-night television generated by TGND's escape from rehab (turns out *The Enquirer* was right). She lasted two days before peeling off in her white Ford hybrid SUV, and the paparazzi who follow her every move captured it from a hundred angles. It was O.J. all over again (sans, you know, the whole murdering your ex-wife thing), and the footage played in an endless loop on CNN, etc., for hours. I'd finally tired of it around three. The phone shatters my REM sleep what feels like seconds later.

"Mmmph?"

"Is this Kate Sandford?"

"Mmm."

"This is Elizabeth from *The Line* calling? We wanted to set up an interview?" Her voice rises at the end of each sentence, turning it into a question.

I sit bolt upright, my heart in my throat. "You do?"

"Are you available at nine tomorrow?"

Tomorrow. My birthday. Damn straight I'm available.

"Yes. Yes, I'm available."

"Great. So, come to our offices at nine and ask for me? Elizabeth?"

"That's great. Perfect. I'll see you then."

I throw back the covers, spring from bed, and break into my happy dance.

This is the best birthday present ever! I'm going to nail this! After years and years of writing for whoever would have me, I'm going to finally get to write for a real magazine! For *the* magazine. Yes, yes, yes!

"Katie, what the hell are you doing?" Joanne is standing in the doorway looking pissed. Her curly orange hair forms a halo around her pale face. She looks like Little Orphan Annie, all grown up. Her robe is even that red-trimmed-with-white combination that Annie always wears.

"Celebrating?"

"Do you know what time it is?"

I check the clock by my bedside. "Nine?"

"That's right. And what time do I start work today?"

I know this is a trick question.

"You don't?"

"That's right, it's my day off. So why, pray tell, are you dancing around and whooping like you're at a jamboree?"

Despite the inquisition, my heart gives a happy beat.

"Because I just got the most fabulous job interview in the world."

Joanne isn't diverted by my obvious happiness. "I think the answer you were looking for is, 'Because I'm an inconsiderate roommate who doesn't care about anyone but herself.'"

"Joanne . . ."

"Just keep it down." She turns on her heel and storms away.

As I watch her leave, I wonder for the hundredth time why I'm still living with her. (I answered her in-search-of-a-roommate ad on craigslist three years ago, and we've had a love-hate relationship ever since.) Of course, she's clean, pays her share of the rent on time, and never wakes me up when I'm trying to sleep in because she's yelping with joy.

Then again, I've never seen Joanne yelp with joy . . .

Ohmygod! I have an interview at *The Line*!

I resume my whooping dance with the sound off.

I spend the rest of the day vacillating between extreme nervousness and supreme confidence. In between emotional fluctuations, I agonize over what I should wear to the interview. I lay the options out on my bed:

1) Black standard business suit that my mother gave me for my university graduation. She thought I'd have all kinds of job interviews to wear it to. Sorry, Mom.

2) Skinny jeans, kick-ass boots, T-shirt from an edgy, obscure nineties band, black corduroy blazer.

3) Black clingy skirt and gray faux-cashmere sweater with funky jewelry.

I settle on option three, hoping it strikes the right balance between professional and what I think the atmosphere at *The Line* will be: hip, serious, but not too serious.

In the late afternoon, I receive a text from my second-best friend, Greer.

U free 2nite?

No. Very important blah, blah am.

Must celebrate bday.

Bday 2morrow.

Aware. Exam in 2 days. Party 2nite.

No.

Insisting.

Must sleep. Need beauty for blah, blah.

Never be pretty enough to rely on looks for blah, blah. Still insisting.

LOL. Need new friend. Still can't.

Expecting u @ F. @ 8. Won't take no for answer.

No.

LOL. 1 drink.

It never ends with 1.

Will 2nite, promise.
Can't.
I'm $$.
Well . . . maybe just 1.
Excellent. CU @ 8.

I throw down the phone with a smile, and try to decide whether any of my outfits will do for a night out with my university-aged friends.

I'm a nearly thirty-year-old with university-aged friends because the only way I've been able to survive since I graduated (and the bank stopped loaning me money) is to keep living like I did when I was a student, right down to scamming as much free food and alcohol as possible on the university wine-and-cheese circuit. I met Greer this way two groups of friends ago. She's the only one who stuck post-graduation. She thinks I'm a fellow graduate student who writes music articles on the side to pay for my education and that tomorrow's my twenty-fifth birthday.

My own-age friends have all moved to nicer parts of the city. They work in law firms and investment banks, have dark circles under their eyes and pale skin. Their annual salaries are twice what it cost me to educate myself, and the only wine and cheeses they go to are the cocktail parties given by their firms to woo new clients.

They mostly don't approve of the way I live—the part

they know about anyway—but I mostly don't care. Because I'm doing it. I'm living my childhood dream of being a music writer. It's not a well-paying life, but it's the life I've chosen. On most days, I'm happy.

If I get this job at *The Line*, I'll be over the freaking moon.

Shortly after eight, I meet Greer at our favorite pub in my number two outfit: skinny jeans tucked into burgundy boots, obscure-band T-shirt, and black corduroy blazer to keep the spring night at bay.

The pub has an Irish-bar-out-of-a-box feel to it (hunter green wallpaper, dark oak bar, mirrored Guinness signs behind it, a whiff of stale lager), but we like its laid-back atmosphere, cheap pints, and occasional Irish rugby team.

Greer is sitting on her usual stool flirting with the bartender. The Black Eyed Peas song "I Gotta Feeling" is playing on the sound system. She orders me a beer and a whiskey shot as I sit down next to her.

"Hey, you promised one drink."

"A shot's not a drink. It's just a wee introduction to drinking."

Greer is from Scotland. She has long auburn hair, green eyes, porcelain skin, and an accent that drives men wild. Sometimes I hate her.

Tonight she's wearing a soft sweater the color of new grass that exactly matches her eyes and a broken-in pair of jeans that fits her tall, slim frame perfectly. I'm glad I took the time to blow out my chestnut-colored hair and put on the one shade of mascara that makes my eyes look sky blue. Nobody wants to be outshone at their almost-thirtieth-birthday party.

She clinks her shot against mine. "Happy birthday, lass. Drink up."

I really shouldn't, but . . . what the hell? Tomorrow *is* my birthday.

I drink the shot, and take a few long gulps of my beer to chase it down.

"Thanks, Greer."

"Welcome. So, tell me about this very important interview. Is it for a post-doc position?"

A post-doc position? Oh, right, that bad job you get after your Ph.D. Biggest downside to the fake-student personality? Keeping track of my two lives.

"Nope . . . Actually, I'm thinking of going in another direction. It's a job writing for a music magazine."

"Well, well, the bairn's growing up."

Greer is always tossing out colloquial Scottish expressions like "bairn" (meaning child), "steamin'" (meaning drunk), and her ultimate insult, "don't be a scrounger" (meaning buy me a drink, you miserly bastard). Depending on the number of drinks she's consumed, it's sometimes impossible to understand her without translation.

"Had to happen sometime."

The bartender, Steve, brings us two more shots that Greer pays for with a smile. He only charges her for about a quarter of what she drinks, but since I'm often the beneficiary of his generosity, who's complaining?

She pushes one of the shots toward me.

"No, I can't."

"A wee dram won't hurt you."

"There's no way anyone actually says 'wee dram' anymore. That's just for the tourists, right?"

"I canna' break the code of honor of my country. Now drink up, lass, before I drink it for you."

I upend the shot and nearly choke on it when Scott claps me hard on the back. He's a history major I met about a year ago at, you guessed it, a wine and cheese. We bonded while arguing over who had deeper knowledge of U2 and the Counting Crows (me, and me). His athletic body, sandy hair, and frank face are easy on the eyes, and given our mutual single status, I'm not quite sure why we've never hooked up. Maybe it's the fact that he's twenty-two, which puts him on the outside edge of my half-plus-seven rule. ($30 \div 2 + 7 = 22$. A good rule to live by to avoid age-inappropriate romantic entanglements.)

Scott orders another round. When it comes, he slides shot

number three my way. I protest, but he flashes his blue eyes and wide smile, and talks me into it. Into that, and the next one. When Rob and Toni arrive a little while later, they buy the next two. And when those are gone, the room gets fuzzy and I lose count of the drinks that come next.

The rest of the night passes in a flash of images: Rob and Scott singing lewd rugby songs. Toni telling me she had a pregnancy scare the week before. Me blabbing on about how I'm going to nail my interview tomorrow, just nail it! Greer *Coyote Ugly*–ing it on the bar as Steve plies her with more shots. Someone dropping me off at my door, ringing the doorbell, and running away giggling. Joanne looking disappointed and resigned, then putting a blanket over me.

I lie on our living room couch with the room spinning around me, happy I have so many good friends, and an awesome job waiting for me to take it.

Tomorrow, tomorrow, tomorrow. I bring my watch to my face so I can see the glow-in-the-dark numbers. 3:40 a.m. I guess it's today. Hey, it's my birthday. *Happy birthday to me, happy birthday to me, happy birthday, happy birthday, happy birthday to me.*

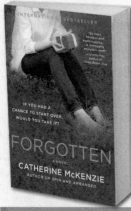